REVEALED SECRETS

MIKAEL CARLSON

WARRINGTON

Danbury, Connecticut

Printed in the United States of America
First Edition
ISBN: 978-1-944972-24-0 (paperback)
         978-1-944972-23-3 (ebook)
         978-1-944972-25-7 (hardcover)

Book cover designed by JD&J

Also by Mikael Carlson:

For Chief and Mara

PROLOGUE

IAN DRUCKER

Lehigh Valley Printers
Allentown, Pennsylvania

One Month Until the General Election

The rusted-out white Econostar van pulls up to the loading dock area to the rear of the building perched at the end of the industrial park. Unlike the trucks that can back right up to the raised platform and freely move their cargo to and from the building, the van isn't high enough to make that viable. Mike stops at the end of the concrete ramp, fifteen feet from the edge of the dock.

The five men in the van take off their ski masks. They're more of a precaution than meant to serve a practical purpose. It won't stop Ian's antsy cohorts from complaining about it.

"This is stupid. This van has been seen by a handful of traffic cameras on the way here," one of the men whines.

"So nervous," Ian sarcastically mocks. "That's the point. We want it to be noticed. Your face was obscured, so stop worrying."

"Whatever. It's still a dumb idea."

"He's right, Ian," Remy says. "The government is everywhere."

Ian looks up at the building, checking the corners and the space over the door. There's not a camera to be found. Not that he didn't already know that.

"They're not here. Let's go."

The five men climb the concrete ramp to Lehigh Valley Printers. This industrial area is crawling with workers during the day but is eerily quiet at night. LED streetlights flood the facility's front, but there isn't much lighting in the back. With a treeline obscuring a road a couple hundred feet away and no line of sight to the other businesses, this is the perfect place for illegal activity.

Ian raps on the roll-up door. It rises, and Danny Athersmith comes out of his office to greet them.

"Hello, Danny."

"Ah, Mr. White. Good to see you again. Your order is ready. I'll get the paperwork."

He barks some orders at his two men, who disappear into a cage as their boss retreats to his office.

"Mr. White?" Remy asks, leaning in. "That's a little racist, isn't it?"

"I thought you guys were white supremacists. What does it matter?"

"We're freedom fighters. There's a big difference."

Ian smirks. "Mr. White was my favorite character in *Reservoir Dogs*."

"In what?"

"*Reservoir*...don't you guys watch movies?"

"Does *Rambo* count?" Mike asks, causing Ian to shake his head.

Two carts are wheeled up, each containing three dozen cardboard boxes. Danny returns from the office with a clipboard and opens one of them.

"We worked three straight nights to get these right."

Ian is handed a sheet and inspects it. The Pennsylvania mail-in ballot was hard to reproduce. These came out perfect.

"How many on your crew?"

"My two guys there. I know what you're going to ask. Don't worry. They all know how to keep a secret."

"Do they?"

"There isn't much good work for ex-cons in this country. They served time, just like I did. This is their second chance, and they're happy to participate in society."

"Load them up," Ian commands two of the militia members.

"Money first," Danny demands.

"Okay. Twenty thousand, as agreed," Ian says, pulling a thick envelope out of his jacket pocket and handing it to Danny.

"I'm afraid that won't do," the print shop manager says, checking the envelope's contents. "We had cost overruns. I need another five grand."

Ian stifles a scowl. "You're changing the terms?"

"Our costs go up, so do yours."

"Not on a fixed price contract, they don't."

"Who ever said our contract was fixed?"

This development wasn't unexpected, but that doesn't mean Ian has to be happy about it. To the manager's delight, he reaches into his pocket and pulls out another five thousand.

"A pleasure doing business with you, Mr. White."

"Load up," Ian says over his shoulder to the men behind him. They take control of the carts and wheel them down the ramp.

"You understand that there are parts of this arrangement that can't be negotiated, correct?"

"Hey, you came to me," Danny argues, his hands outstretched. "You seem like a smart guy. You would've checked me out and know we can keep secrets."

"You don't want to find out what happens if you don't."

"Is that a threat?"

"No. I don't threaten. I deliver."

Ian eyes the other print shop workers, who look amused at the exchange. He turns and walks to the overhead door.

"I met a lot of guys in the joint who thought they were tough," Danny calls out after him. "You know what they all had in common?"

"No, tell me," Ian says, stopping on the other side of the roll-up door.

"They talked a good game but couldn't back it up when it mattered. Don't make the same mistake."

Ian presses his lips together and nods. "I understand, Danny. You know, I was in law enforcement for a hot second before becoming disgruntled. You know what I learned?"

The manager offers a smirk. "No, what?"

"Dead men tell no tales."

The two militiamen swing out from behind the exterior wall of the loading dock, with one of them sidestepping across the opening. They bring up their AR-15s and open fire. The three men don't have time to piss their pants. The rifles belch their .223 rounds and rip through the two print shop workers and the obnoxious shop owner with ruthless efficiency. Five seconds later, the weapons fall silent.

"Seriously, why the 'Mr. White' alias?" Remy asks, walking over to Danny's blood-soaked body. "You're at the top of the FBI's Ten Most Wanted List. How could they not know who you are?"

"Danny knew. He was playing us. Then they would have turned us in the moment we pulled out of the parking lot. That's why they're not breathing anymore."

Ian walks over and collects the envelope that Remy retrieved from Danny's pocket. It's only twenty-five thousand, but there's no point in wasting it.

"You know what to do."

Remy nods and heads to the van with Mike and their two men. Ian walks into the office and pulls the cables out of the laptop. He knows what the regional forensics labs of the FBI are capable of, so he doesn't want to tempt fate. Assumptions are how criminals get caught; he won't make the mistake of leaving this to chance. The laptop is coming with him. Plus, he could use a computer at the Forge.

A few minutes later, the floor and walls of the building have been doused with enough gasoline to make NASCAR blush. The van was a rolling gas tank on the way here. Nobody in the back dared spark a cigarette.

"Do you want the honors?" Remy asks.

"Revolutions start with a single flame that gets fanned into an inferno. History should remember you as the man who sparked it." Ian gestures to the shop.

Remy smiles, and Mike hands him a Zippo. He flips the cover, spins the wheel against the flint, and stares at the flame for a long moment. He lights the contract paperwork on fire before dropping it on the ground.

A sheet of fire races across the building's floor, with the heat forcing the men to retreat down the loading dock ramp to the van. Within moments, the entire print factory is ablaze, bathing the area in an orange glow. There is a mountain of paper stored in this place. It is a gigantic tinder box that will burn for hours.

Ian moves to the rear of the van and opens a box. He grabs a wad of papers on the top and throws them up in the air. They disperse over the ground, some blowing away in the light breeze. The treeline will catch many of them. Perfect.

"Fire companies and police will be responding within minutes. We should go," Ian says to the militia leader.

"I'm just admiring our handiwork."

"Watch it on the news. It won't do this country any good if our modern-day George Washington is behind bars."

Remy grins and climbs into the van. Mike steers them out of the parking lot and down the access road. Ian watches the blaze in the side mirror after donning his mask. The dash to the finish line has started.

SIX DAYS LATER

CHAPTER ONE

TIERRA CAMPOS

Front Burner Washington Office
Washington, D.C.

Three Weeks until the General Election

Until now, I never thought it was possible to be equally exhilarated and depressed coming into a meeting. That's the current situation at *Front Burner*. I join Austin, Logan, Olivia, Tyler, and Wilson Newman at the conference table. The investigative arm modeled after *The Boston Post's* Spotlight team is the new core of what's left of this media company.

Our managing editor has managed to find enough money to hire a few new people, but not many. The vibrant atmosphere I saw on my first day here is long gone. The office feels like a crypt.

To everyone's surprise, Jerome came back. We have him working in the field to find and enlist new contributors. The same could not be said for Janey or Madison. They've both moved on to new endeavors with our competitors. I liked Janey and miss her, but Madison is another story. I'm still bitter about what happened in New Hampshire.

Olivia has fully recovered from her New Hampshire crash, at least physically. The mental scars will take longer to heal. It's been tough for her to overcome the thought that she was specifically targeted and almost killed. I know the feeling, at least on some level. I once had a mob of Ethan Harrington's supporters bust into my apartment looking for me.

For all the reconciliation, we still have a long way to go. Trust is earned, and Austin still needs to earn mine. It's a work in progress, just like *Front Burner* itself. We are a hollow shell of the powerhouse we once were. My antics at the Republican National Convention breathed new life into our brand, but the vultures are circling. The news model we are pioneering is a threat, even if none of the major news outlets will ever admit it.

"What did I miss?" I ask, tuning into the tension around the table.

"It's just your run-of-the-mill philosophical disagreement," Wilson says, gesturing at Austin and Tyler.

"Let me guess. Tyler is complaining about our approach again."

"Some things never change, do they?" Olivia asks with a meek smile.

"It's not a complaint. There is a massive crisis of trust in journalism. Americans have no faith in the veracity of the news they're consuming. We can't fix that by crowdsourcing our reporting."

"And I disagree," Austin says. "The Founding Fathers solved the problem of unchecked government power by distributing it to the people. We can do the same thing for journalism."

"Yet we see government abuse every day," Tyler argues.

"He has a point, Austin," I say, sticking my head in the lion's mouth.

"What? You said you were on board with this!"

"I am, but we need to understand the problem to solve it. Partisan journalism didn't emerge in a vacuum. News organizations sacrificed quality for financial sustainability. They catered to a specific audience to ensure advertiser dollars would keep pouring in."

"I know that."

"Then you know that those quote-unquote journalists were weaponized to exert pressure on people, institutions, and corporations and for their own ends and not the greater good," Wilson adds. "For-profit journalism lost its integrity and compromised standards to preserve audiences and advertisers by acting as lobbyists to advance their interests to the public."

Austin leans back and folds his arms. "Whose point are you making, Wilson?"

"Both of yours," I say, leaning forward and resting my elbows on the table. "If trained journalists can be corrupted by the money in the system, then novice ad-hoc contributors are equally susceptible."

"That's why bloggers and at-home pundits on YouTube aren't going to get it done. We need to hire people with journalism experience."

"Who, Tyler? Tell me who! Everyone with experience has already taken sides!"

"We need money to hire anyone, with experience or otherwise," Naomi says, causing everyone to turn and see her leaning against the door jamb.

Naomi Merritt was a digital broadcast producer for a podcast that never got off the ground. When management fled the company, she and Austin remained. Naomi is now getting the trial by fire treatment. With no experience running a news outlet, she has one hell of a steep learning curve.

"We leave you to worry about that," Austin says, grinning.

"As managing editor, I pass that down to our employees…all twenty-five of them," she says, plopping a pile of folders on the table.

"It's more than we thought we'd have now," Logan says, sounding like the optimist in the group.

He's right. After I was drummed out of *Capitol Beat*, Austin confessed that their collapse left them with no reporters and only enough financial resources for a couple of weeks. It would have been easy just to close up the shop, but those who remained weren't about to give up on the promise of *Front Burner*.

"That's the good news. Wilson is keeping the lights on. He's now the fifth most watched podcast across major online distributors."

There is applause around the table as Wilson smiles and brushes some imaginary lint from his shoulder. I shake my head and smack him on the shoulder.

"You're only fifth. If you were any good, you'd be second or third by now," I say with a smile.

"If I had a lovely co-host who had agreed to join me, maybe we would be," he fires back.

"Someone who actually works here needs to write content."

"Tierra provides the perfect segue into the bad news. Our site is barely breaking even. Advertisers are still leery of us. The ones we have are covering our costs, but that's it. Our subscription model is growing, up ten percent from last month. That sounds like a big number until you look at the number of subscriptions we started with."

"The numbers will get better as our contributors become more recognizable," Austin says, trying to stay positive.

"Until someone makes them a better offer or they sell out," Tyler grumbles.

"That's a risk," Naomi admits. "We compensate them well, but that means there isn't much left over to grow."

"We should lower their share," Tyler offers.

"That would end the experiment. I understand your argument, Tyler, and you have valid concerns. Unfortunately, we can't afford to hire staff, even if we could find actual journalists without an ax to grind. We can't compete in the marketplace the traditional way. We're stuck with this, whether we like it or not. If it doesn't work, it'll end *Front Burner.*"

Tyler nods. He understands the predicament they find themselves in. I wish I could say something inspirational, but nothing comes to mind. Wilson is a draw with his podcast, and I have a couple of awards and decent name recognition. That's all we have going for us now.

"Keep doing what you guys are doing. I'm convinced this will work," Naomi says, jamming her index finger on the table. "We are giving the people what they want and what no other organization does."

"What's that?" Olivia asks.

"Facts."

CHAPTER TWO

BRIAN COOPER

The John F. Kennedy Center for the Performing Arts
Washington, D.C.

Brian straightens his tie. He may not be refined enough to enjoy the symphony, but that doesn't mean he shouldn't look the part. Next to the Watergate and a twenty-minute walk from the Lincoln Memorial, this center is a living memorial to one of his favorite presidents.

President Dwight D. Eisenhower signed bipartisan legislation creating a national cultural center, and Kennedy launched a fundraising campaign for a world-class performing arts venue. The center's mission is to present classical and contemporary music, opera, drama, dance, and other performing arts from the United States and worldwide.

Each season, the National Symphony Orchestra welcomes the world's greatest guest artists to the Kennedy Center Concert Hall. Tonight, it's Beethoven's Ninth Symphony with its emotional melodies and inspiring final "Ode to Joy." Brian isn't here to enjoy any of that. He heads to the bar on a mission to find an eccentric pollster.

"I thought you only liked numbers," Brian says to the head of ISO Media as he sidles up next to him.

Cubic Zirconium can't possibly be his real name, even if his parents were jewelers. Despite his social awkwardness and aloofness, he's a messiah in political circles. After calling the past five presidential races correctly, three of them with a perfect score in the electoral college, he's a sought-after source for election information. When considering the abomination that the polling industry has become, it means Cubic is a wealthy man.

"Music is numbers, you sophomoric cretin. It's the result of a numerical organization interpreted by our brains. When a string vibrates, what we hear isn't a single sound but a superposition of several. Those frequencies are called harmonics and are multiples of a fundamental frequency. The proportion that harmonics are added to a fundamental frequency contributes to the timbre of each instrument."

"Scotch, rocks," Brian orders the bartender. "Please, continue. You're on a roll."

"It's why a tuba sounds different than a flute. Harmonics adds richness to the sound, giving it body. The bottom line is that if you're a musician, you're a mathematician. The pleasure you feel when listening to music hides the subliminal calculations in the sound."

Cubic stares at Brian, who looks lost because he is. It may have helped had he paid any attention at all.

"When did I lose you?"

"Back at 'music is numbers,'" Brian says, sipping his drink. Cubic isn't amused about his lesson being ignored.

"What do you want, Brian?"

"An update. You aren't returning my calls."

"I was ignoring you," Cubic admits.

"We have a deal, Cubic. Fail to uphold your end, and I'll do the same."

The pollster may be good with numbers, but Brian is a master political strategist used to getting what he wants. Since Cubic would never willingly provide information campaigns pay millions for, he dug up dirt on an ISO Media board member with a long history of womanizing and a taste for underage girls. He was listed on flight manifests with a disgraced billionaire who owned an island for such rendezvous.

The deal they struck was simple: Cubic trades information and voter trends up to Election Day in return for that information not finding its way onto the front page of *The New York Times*. So far, both men have kept their end of the bargain.

"This is the last time."

"Unless there needs to be another," Brian warns. "This doesn't end until Election Day."

"You work for the Republican candidate for president. I'm sure the GOP can afford internal polling."

"They do daily push polls. Yours are better."

"Of course they are!" Cubic shrieks, causing heads around the bar to turn briefly before conversations resume. "Fine. It's all over in forty-nine states. It all comes down to Pennsylvania, just like I predicted."

Brian nods, having come to that conclusion himself. "Who's winning in Pennsylvania?"

"Nobody."

"What do you mean?"

Cubic smirks and adjusts his glasses. "Just what I said – it's a toss-up in the purest form of the term."

"Don't BS me. No state is fifty-fifty."

"That's true, but we're not talking about who registered voters think should win. It's about likely voters who will bother mailing a ballot or show up to vote. Any polls measuring anything except that is worthless, including yours."

Brian purses his lips. He explained to the campaign staff that their internal polls were garbage. They disagree because they paint a rosy picture of Bradford's chances, which is the message they want to deliver to the candidate. It doesn't matter to them that they only measure "adults," meaning people of voting age, without considering whether they will actually cast a ballot.

"And?"

"Blacks are lukewarm about Standish," Cubic continues. "If turnout in Philly or Pittsburgh is depressed, so long as Bradford turns out the rural areas, he wins. If minorities show up, Standish will eke out a victory and claim the presidency. Either way, the margin of victory will be a point or point-and-a-half at the most."

"What can be done to tip the scales?"

Cubic holds his hands up and shakes his head. "I'm a pollster, not a strategist."

"Humor me."

"You already know what to do. Bradford is making a swing through Pennsylvania, probably at your urging, but it's not enough. Standish has already made enough trips to the state to establish residency. You've done the math, so why did you *really* track me down at the Kennedy Center?"

"New Hampshire."

"I assume you don't mean the actual state."

Brian takes a long pull on his scotch. The "Sword of Freedom," or SOF for short, almost tilted a primary race that should have been an easy win for Standish to her socialist opponent, Luther Burgess. They likely would have succeeded if not for Victoria Larsen's investigative work and Tierra Campos's reporting.

"I mean what happened there in the Democratic Primary. If the margins in Pennsylvania are this razor-thin, any interference could spell trouble."

"Are you more worried about suppression or malfeasance?"

"Both, actually," Brian confesses.

"Then you're not the moron I thought you were. You should be worried because both are going to happen. Our two major political parties will do anything to obtain power. I don't expect either side to fight fair, and neither should you."

Cubic pats him on the shoulder as the flickering lights indicate that the show is about to begin. People begin filtering out to find their seats, and the pollster is about to join them.

"The Democrats are worse," Brian calls out, causing the man to stop.

"Maybe, or maybe not, but neither side likes to play by the rules. Both are going to cheat in this election, and the side that does it better wins the White House."

CHAPTER THREE

SPECIAL AGENT VICTORIA LARSEN

Meridian Hill Park
Washington, D.C.

Meridian Hill Park in Washington earned its name for lying on the exact longitude of the original District of Columbia milestone marker. It's home to a thirteen-basin cascading fountain that's one of the longest in North America. Victoria makes her way up the hill beside the fountain and stops at the Joan of Arc statue. There are dozens of monuments featuring men on horseback in the city, but this is the only depiction of a woman riding one.

Victoria has two connections to this place now. Joan of Arc was her favorite heroine growing up, and Victoria always felt a connection to her. It's also the spot where Rigo offered her an assignment that kept her in the FBI after she decided to leave the Bureau. After what happened with Vassyl and Ian at the abandoned mill in Massachusetts, she isn't sure she made the right decision.

"Fancy meeting you here," Rigo says, coming up alongside Victoria as she admires the statue.

"Your idea, not mine. I'd prefer not to travel across the city to see you."

"Would you rather meet under the prying eyes of our colleagues?"

Victoria frowns. She rendezvouses with Rigo in private because it's a place where they can keep in touch without making it obvious. Victoria and Rigo are the only survivors of the Loughborough debacle that left nine FBI agents dead in an ambush. He was shot, and Victoria was seriously injured in an explosion triggered by Vassyl Strachenko. The real damage was done in the aftermath. The Hoover Building dissolved Rigo's team and reassigned them after they recovered.

"No, I wouldn't. How's your shoulder?"

"Healing. What about you?"

"I'm serviceable, not that it matters. I used all my sick time and can't afford unpaid leave."

Rigo looks at her quizzically. "What about the agents association? Please tell me you were smart enough to buy in."

The FBI Agents Association was founded in 1981 to safeguard the careers and welfare of active and retired agents. One of their offerings is a program that pays for injuries, treatment, and follow-up from an accident or injury. Another is an additional benefit paid directly to the member to cover deductibles and other expenses.

"Yeah, I just didn't want to use it."

"That's what it's there for, Vic."

"What about you?" Victoria asks, not wanting to discuss taking more time off.

"I'm doing my penance, same as you."

"We did nothing wrong," Victoria says after a scoff.

Rigo stares at the ground and kicks at a stone. "That's the minority opinion. You were Black Widow up in Loughborough. Vassyl's death was our only win. Me, on the other hand...I got people killed."

"Stop it, Rigo! Neither of us could have known that was an ambush."

Rigo shakes his head. "I should have. Had I followed procedure, my team might still be alive."

Victoria crosses her arms. "And maybe the machine guns they were firing would have jammed. Maybe Vassyl wouldn't have had a Zippo to light gasoline that caused an explosion and blew me into a wall. Maybe a brick chimney would have fallen the other way instead of on me. We can play this game all day. We took them out. Well, most of them."

"Drucker," Rigo moans.

"He's still out there, so what's the plan? Because I need you to show me something."

Victoria's former superior tightens his jaw. "I have nothing. He escaped, and we got left holding the bag. There's nothing more I can do. Drucker—"

"That's crap! You can fight."

"What do you want me to do?" he almost shouts. "We've been demoted. I have no authority and am on the shortest possible leash. Given your history, you're probably lucky to have your badge. I would love to say I see a way out of this, but there isn't one."

Victoria exhales deeply. She's known as a maverick within the FBI. The events in Brockhampton, Manchester, and Loughborough have done nothing to tarnish that reputation. The Bureau sees this as an opportunity to get rid of her. There's no doubt that Conrad Williams is pushing that agenda, which is the only reason she's staying put.

"That's not good enough."

"It has to be," Rigo whispers, sounding defeated.

"Drucker is still out there! Machiavelli is *running* a presidential campaign. Williams could be behind the whole thing. Who knows what others could be involved."

Victoria has stopped short of calling this a cabal, despite it likely being one. They know who some of the players are, and it's terrifying. Andrew Li is the mastermind behind the SOF who killed a man during an arson spree, attacked Wilson Newman and Olivia, framed Brian Cooper, ambushed the New Hampshire State Police, and nearly changed the outcome of a presidential primary.

Conrad Williams is the deputy attorney general of the United States. He's in a position to exert enormous influence on policy in Washington and within the FBI. The Bureau reports to the Department of Justice. Victoria has no doubt that he's involved in this but doesn't have enough hard evidence to prove it.

"That's all someone else's problem now," Rigo concludes.

"What the hell happened to you?'

Victoria watches Rigo's face contort into confusion and then anger. He takes a step toward her.

"Men died, Victoria. On my watch! It was my mission! I was in charge!"

"Yeah, and it went badly," Victoria says, not retreating an inch. "Sometimes, good men die. It doesn't mean you stop fighting."

"You really don't get it, do you? The deputy attorney general has more power than his boss does. If he's calling the shots, the war's over. We lost. I'm surprised he's had the Bureau keep us this close to Washington."

"I don't care why we're here, just that we are. If we don't stop this, nobody else will. Andrew Li and Conrad Williams are complicit in Fuller's and Nashimoto's deaths. You're a fool if you think they'll stop there."

Victoria knows that this is somehow about the general election. She also knows that, outside of Tierra and what's left of *Front Burner*, Rigo is the only other person who can help her stop them. The FBI won't do anything, and the rest of the federal government will turn a blind eye. The media will politicize it. It amazes her that everyone is looking away from the greatest threat to our Republic in its history.

"We can't go up against the system and expect to win. It's over, Victoria. Everyone realizes it except you."

"You're a quitter," Victoria says, pushing her index finger into Rigo's face.

"Yeah, I guess I am. If you knew what was good for you, you'd quit, too. The FBI is all I have. Being a federal agent is all that I know how to be."

Victoria closes her eyes and shakes her head. "You lied to me. You stood in this park and promised me you'd be different."

"I am," Rigo says before biting his lip. "I was. Then I realized that I'm not as good at this as I thought. This is where our journey ends. Best of luck to you, Victoria."

There are no hugs or handshakes. Rigo doesn't even force a smile before turning and walking out of the park. Victoria watches him hit the sidewalk and disappear before she turns back to face the statue. She's running out of time. More importantly, she's short on allies.

"I'm starting to know how you felt, girl," she says to the woman mounted on the horse in front of her. "I'm getting tried for heresy, and they're ready to burn me at the stake, too."

CHAPTER FOUR

DEPUTY AG CONRAD WILLIAMS

Independence Mall
Philadelphia, Pennsylvania

When Conrad was told that the rally was being held at Independence Mall, his first thought was the shopping area in Wilmington, North Carolina. That would be unusual since a large political rally isn't something typically held at a massive retail outlet. It also would have been a bold move considering it's located in Alicia Standish's opponent's home state. He could almost imagine the look on Bradford's face after seeing that.

Instead, the Standish for America rally is being held in "America's Most Historic Square Mile." Independence Mall occupies three blocks directly north of Philadelphia's Independence Hall and south of the National Constitution Center. It is trumpeted by the parks department as a home for free speech, special events, and public programming.

"Senator Standish," Conrad says after being cleared through the convoy's perimeter as it waits to take her to the next stop on this barnstorming tour.

"Deputy Attorney General Williams," Alicia says, taking his outstretched hand and giving it a shake. "I'm surprised to see you in Philly."

"I was in the neighborhood. The hardest part was staying away from the press."

"I bet. It's been a while."

"It has," Conrad says with a smirk. "The last time we had a proper conversation, you were threatening me at The Wall."

Conrad met up with her on two occasions while partnering with Ethan Harrington on the Safe America Act legislation. The last, at the Vietnam Veterans Memorial, was when he first heard Victoria Larsen's name. The senator was convinced that the rogue agent's investigation into Ethan was politically motivated and wondered if it was sanctioned. It was the first indication that Larsen would be a thorn in their side. It's why Machiavelli was supposed to have her eliminated.

"A lot has happened since then," the senator offers.

"That's the truth. How's the campaign going?"

"Long days, but I think my message is getting to the people. I only hope it reaches enough of them."

"Bradford is doing better than I thought he would."

"Yes, he is," Alicia admits, pressing her lips together hard after the words slip from her mouth.

"How much of that has to do with Brian Cooper?"

Alicia cocks her head. "You like opening old wounds, don't you?"

"Apologies, Senator. That's not my intention."

"Yes, it is," she says, forcing a grin. "It's okay. Cooper joining Bradford's campaign was a personal and professional loss for me. I made a mistake in New Hampshire, but that doesn't mean I don't have every intention of beating him."

"No, Senator, I'm sure it doesn't."

"What brings you to the City of Brotherly Love?"

"I'm stretching my legs," Conrad explains. "I'm heading to Harrisburg to meet with the governor tomorrow."

"That sounds ominous. Anything I should know about?"

"No, just routine business," Conrad says, lying again.

"Somehow, I doubt that," Andrew Li says, walking up to them and causing Conrad to grin. "Nice job, Senator. I promised a reporter from *The Examiner* five minutes before we leave. He's waiting just outside the press area."

The senator excuses herself, leaving the two men to talk. Conrad doesn't know if Andrew arranged that for his benefit or if it was a happy coincidence. Campaigns are driven by harried, overcaffeinated staffers conditioned to spend every useful second promoting the cause. The timing is convenient, though.

"Take a walk with me, Andrew."

"We're leaving in a few minutes."

"You can catch up."

Andrew frowns and hustles to catch up to Conrad as he walks away from the convoy to find a quiet spot on the sidewalk.

"You are taking a risk coming here. We shouldn't be seen together. What do you want?"

"Isiah Burgess's lawyer is becoming a problem."

Andrew scoffs before checking to see if anyone is in earshot. "You should have killed him like I told you to."

"For such a brilliant political strategist, you don't pay too much attention to optics, do you?"

Andrew shrugs. "Accidents happen."

The deputy AG rolls his eyes. "Yeah, I'm sure that's how people will see it."

"You've been a bureaucrat for too long, Conrad. People see what the media shows them. Nietzsche has that covered. All you need to do is keep the lawyer bottled up until after the election. Or is that too much to ask?"

"The FBI is doing its part."

"And if that isn't enough, then handle it," Andrew decrees. "We all play our parts. Yours is to keep the government off our backs."

Each partner in this endeavor brings a unique skill set to the table and has a position to best exercise it. For Conrad, it's his influence within the Department of Justice, and by extension, the Federal Bureau of Investigation. Without him, the other members risk exposure. That doesn't mean that he's omnipotent.

"I don't have unilateral control. Lisa Ehler can easily step in."

"She won't be in the picture much longer if things go as planned."

Andrew stops and looks back at the campaign staff loading into their cars. He doesn't want to miss his ride. Hitchhiking isn't a thing in this part of the country.

"What's going as planned? Vassyl was supposed to neutralize Victoria Larsen, yet she's still alive. *Front Burner* is still in business. You said that we all have our parts to play. Step up and play yours."

This plan has been successful only because Lady Luck has stayed on their side. When that streak ends, and it will, they can only hope for the best. Rasputin, Machiavelli, and Nietzsche fail to realize hope is not a tactic.

"Vassyl's failure cost him his life. None of us expected Larsen to be this resilient, but she's been neutralized, as has her team."

"She's been sidelined, thanks to me. She's far from neutralized and is a threat as long as Ian Drucker is still breathing. Vassyl should have killed him. Instead, he's working for you."

"Vassyl wasn't as good as he thought. We need a capable man in Pennsylvania, and Ian fills the void. Using him to finish our plan has its advantages," Andrew argues.

"Name one. Vassyl failed every mission you've given him."

There is no arguing against that fact. The assassin was sent to Chicago to kill Isiah Burgess and failed. He was supposed to kill Victoria Larsen and failed. His final mission was to take care of Ian Drucker, and he couldn't even do that. All he accomplished was leaving a wake of collateral damage without making a meaningful contribution to the cause.

"We have nobody left that can complete this mission. I will take care of my business. You focus on yours. That's Rasputin's expectation."

"Your business has a bad habit of becoming mine, Andrew," Conrad says with a sneer. "That needs to end."

The political operative rolls his eyes. Conrad is fully aware that his colleague thinks his role is the most important. That's the problem with Andrew. He makes everything about him.

"Rasputin's expectation is success. That's it. It doesn't matter how we get there."

Conrad takes a deep breath of cool October air and stares at the buildings lining the street. Andrew is the optimist in their quartet. There is a point when optimism becomes naïveté.

"There are too many loose ends. I don't know if you see that. I know that Rasputin doesn't. Nietzsche sure as hell is clueless."

"Are you only here to complain?" Andrew moans. "Because I have another rally to get to."

Conrad folds his arms across his barrel chest. He knows Isiah Burgess met with Tierra Campos and claimed that he had information about an attempt to subvert the United States government. Vassyl couldn't find the information before killing the governor's son. He may have been bluffing, but every conspiracy leaves a trail. He can't know whether Isiah picked up theirs.

"You say that Drucker is still valuable? Fine, have him prove it. Instruct him to find out whether Isiah Burgess had intelligence on us, and if he did, where it is."

"He's a little busy right now," Andrew argues. "You have the FBI and NSA in your back pocket. You're in a better position to handle it than I am."

"We don't want the world's foremost investigative organization looking for evidence of treason. One leak, and it will end up on *FOX News*. Or worse, *Front Burner*. Burgess is your mess. Tell Drucker to make time."

Andrew grabs his arm as he starts to walk away. "You're a real bastard, Conrad."

The deputy AG stares at Andrew's hand before prying his fingers off his biceps. "I believe the senator is about to leave without you. Best hurry along."

Andrew glares at him before striding back in the direction of the convoy. Conrad is content that he got the message. His mission is accomplished, so he heads back to his car to continue the drive to Harrisburg. He has his own responsibilities to handle.

CHAPTER FIVE

IAN DRUCKER

"The Forge" Militia Compound
Liberty, Pennsylvania

Remy Mitchell and Mike Brescia are trying to hold back a tsunami of anger. The militia members gathered in this room are worked up tonight. Candidates from both major political parties are in the state, and neither is popular with this group. Standish is the hated standard bearer of the left. Bradford is the weak establishment candidate who's only interested in the status quo. Neither stands for the people or the freedoms the Constitution enshrines.

"We are on the verge of civil war!" a man named Stag shouts.

"That's right! Like in 1859," another adds. "That's where we are."

"We have zero trust or respect for either of these clowns. Standish is a fascist who wants our guns and won't stop until she trounces all our freedoms."

"Bradford is bought and paid for by the globalist new world order!"

"What are we gonna do, Remy? Sit on our hands?" Stag asks.

"Now's not the—"

"We've been training here at The Forge for years!" another militia member interrupts. "It's time to put that training to some damn use!"

Ian watches from the corner as the men applaud and shout with unmitigated enthusiasm at the call to arms. This is how riots start. These men have bloodlust and won't be pacified until it's satiated.

"The Forge" comprises a dozen buildings on the grounds of the Liberty Lumber Company. They have an armory, barracks, bunker, planning center, and rifle range dedicated to training these men for the coming revolution. The buildings are inconspicuously set among the lumber storage sheds, loading docks, an office, and an automated sawmill.

Whether their anger is over illegal immigration, concerns about a socialist takeover, gun regulations, or erosion of freedoms, militias have long pledged their willingness to fight. The members of the Keystone Minutemen militia are no different. In fact, their patience while waiting for their chance to rise up has worn thin.

"The time to act is now! Both candidates are here. We need to strike."

"And then what?" Remy asks. "We succeed, get annihilated as retribution, and the Republican and Democratic Parties find two new jokers to run?"

"But the first blow of the revolution would be dealt."

"This could be our Lexington and Concord!"

Ian watches from the corner of the room with his hands tucked between him and the wall. Remy and Mike have lost control of their people. Now isn't the time to move. As leaders, they can't allow the mob to compel them to action. They might command this militia, but their power isn't absolute. That means that their disciples need to be persuaded.

"Lead from the front, Remy! If you're not willing to, then get out of the way," Stag demands.

"And then what?" Ian barks, having heard enough. "You bound ahead leaderless and disorganized? That's the *Charge of the Light Brigade*, my friends."

"Who the hell are you to tell us what to do?" one of the militia members asks.

"Yeah, if you are not with us, then you're in our way," another adds.

"Get him out of here!"

Stag storms up to Ian and reaches out with both hands to grab him by his jacket. Ian pushes himself off the wall. When his hands emerge, one of them holds the Heckler & Koch HK45 that was holstered in the small of his back. He presses the muzzle to the man's forehead while everyone draws their weapons.

"Pull that trigger, and you're as good as dead," Stag warns.

"If I pull this trigger, you *are* dead. Walk backward."

The man slowly backpedals into the middle of the room. Ian stops and turns to address the militia while keeping the man in his peripheral vision. Every militiaman in this room has his gun pointed at him.

"You want vengeance. I know the feeling. I get why you're all angry."

"You know nothing about us!" another man in the militia shouts.

"The Keystone Minutemen mobilized in response to government overreach with the Brady Bill and Assault Weapons Ban. The founders of this group watched what happened at Ruby Ridge and Waco and wanted to protect American rights."

"And they didn't do anything," the man at gunpoint laments.

"You're right, and today, things are far worse because of that. The government is chipping away at every right we have. They allow hundreds of thousands of illegals to pour in every year and raise our taxes to pay for them. We're censored, burdened by ridiculous laws and regulations, and beholden to our overlords in Washington."

"Then let's do something about it!" another man in the back shouts to the approval of the rest of the militia.

"That's why I'm here. Here's the thing: If you attack the candidates now, you won't be dying for a cause. You'll be dying because you're stupid."

Ian withdraws his weapon from the man's forehead, keeping an eye on any telltale signals of a retaliatory attack. Stag doesn't flinch, let alone move. The gathered men lower their weapons.

Most militiamen envision themselves as heroes preparing for an existential threat that jeopardizes their families and communities. These men believe now is the time to fight because the country's fate rests on their shoulders. Some Americans agree with them. Others think they're delusional. In Ian's mind, the truth is somewhere in between, but that's not his concern.

"You all think you're alone in this fight. You're not. Millions of Americans are willing to fight for their beliefs. The media doesn't want you to realize that. Historians have rewritten the books to make people believe that only three percent of colonists supported the Revolution. It's a lie. There was overwhelming popular support for that war, and there will be for this one."

"What's the problem with hitting the candidates then?" Remy asks. Ian appreciates the setup.

"George Washington fought the war in a way British forces weren't used to. He avoided large-scale confrontations and ceded control of cities and the capital because it meant nothing. He needed to keep his army intact to win, so he used it in guerrilla-style attacks learned during conflicts with Native Americans.

"Then there were the British. They were overconfident and underestimated the patriots from the start. They didn't understand that this conflict was about freedom, and the men waging it were fighting for their homes and families, just like you. Unlike you, the colonials prosecuted the war in a way that gave them the highest chance of success."

There are murmurs among the men as they turn to each other. There is no doubt that they are all armchair students of the American Revolution, at a minimum. None of what Ian said was surprising, but they may have never contemplated how it relates to their cause.

"What do you suggest?"

"Remy, Mike, and I have a plan to bring the government to its knees."

"We know your plan. You want to disrupt the election."

"You only know a part of our plan. As you are soldiers, I don't need to explain operational security to you. Disruption is a means to an end. My question to you all is, are you willing to walk the walk, or are you just 'summer soldiers and sunshine patriots who will shrink from the service of their country in this crisis?'"

The Thomas Paine quote has the desired effect. Even the skeptics are bobbing their heads in agreement. Side discussions break out among the militia members. Unlike military units, there is no rank structure here. This is a democracy, maybe in its purest sense. Ian needs the buy-in from the most vocal among them to build the support he needs. If the majority agree, the rest will go along.

"Laying it on a little thick, aren't ya?" Remy leans in and asks as the conversations continue.

"I'm interested in results, nothing more."

"Well, it's working," Mike seconds.

Ian knew that this assignment would require some salesmanship. Militias are inherently deeply suspicious of outsiders. What he's advocating could land them in prison and be viewed as a possible entrapment. It's how the FBI brings cases against these groups, so their distrust is justified. The men at the Forge accepted him as a former agent because he's sitting atop their ten most wanted list. That provided a level of street cred.

"All right, Ian. We're with you," the man in front says.

"Good. Then let's begin. Come Election Day, we're going to 'cry havoc and let slip the dogs of war.' When the feds try to bring us to our knees for what we've done, we'll cry out in one united voice, 'we have not yet begun to fight!'"

Cheers go up in the room. Ian joins in, wondering if he missed his calling as a motivational speaker. Tony Robbins has nothing on him.

CHAPTER SIX

TIERRA CAMPOS

Front Burner Washington Office
Washington, D.C.

Despite taking on responsibilities at *Front Burner* that far exceed those of running his old team, Austin kept his office. It could be nostalgia, or he may be too busy to move. I think it's the former, but only he knows.

His door is open, and I give it a cursory knock before walking in. He removes his feet from the desk and fumbles for the television remote. I heard the voice of my nemesis as soon as I entered our area. His attempt to shield me from his rant is pointless.

"Don't bother. What vile things is the illustrious Oliver Jahn spewing now?"

Austin mutes the television. "The usual gaslighting nonsense while howling at the moon. He took a couple of shots at us in the monologue before moving on to juicier targets and cheerleading for Alicia Standish. Nothing about you."

"That's a refreshing change, although I'd hate to think I'm losing my status as 'Queen of the Pretenders.'"

That is Oliver Jahn's moniker for me. It began months ago after he embarked on his personal crusade to destroy me and my career. It's a classic case of deflection. Nobody is more fake than he is. His show is an act, and Oliver is more of a court jester than a journalist.

"TNT isn't the problem. They give other media outlets the permission and opportunity to pile on. A couple of columns and at least one cable news segment openly mocked us today."

I read one of the columns and saw the clip. They were hit pieces meant to kick us in the teeth. It's a strange tactic. The media would be better off ignoring us if their goal is to render *Front Burner* irrelevant. Instead, they're giving us visibility and free advertising. Even negative publicity has advantages.

"We're a threat. If we succeed, it'll change journalism in this country. That scares them."

Austin rubs his chin. "What if there's more to it? What if we're fooling ourselves?"

"Did Tyler get under your skin in the conference room?"

"No. This has been on my mind for…well, forever. Journalists have never been without bias. It's why we had newspapers called the whatever Democrat or so-and-so Republican."

I take a seat across from him. This is turning into one of those conversations.

"And those papers had op-ed pages. Articles that actively supported one party or ideology over another at the expense of facts were never featured on the front page above the fold."

"People like reinforcement of their beliefs," Austin argues. "That's how the country ended up in this mess. What if partisanship is so deeply integrated into our society that there's no appetite for fact-based reporting?"

"Naomi doesn't think so."

"I love Naomi, but she doesn't have a strong background in this. She could be wrong."

I can't argue with that, so I decide not to try. "We're going to find out one way or another. But if you ask a hundred people about the news, ninety will say they only want facts. Twenty of them actually mean it. I think a solid majority do want fairness. That's the point guys like Oliver Jahn miss completely. He preaches to the choir, nothing more."

"At least he has an audience. I'm not sure we can succeed in keeping analysis out of our reporting. People are conditioned to hear it now."

"Maybe or maybe not. But we can start with equal coverage. We need to encourage contributors to not just eviscerate someone they don't like and then bury their heads in the sand for someone they support. That's the path forward."

Austin sighs. "It was hard enough building *Front Burner* when nobody was paying attention. Now, everyone is trying to finish us before we can climb to our feet."

"Which means we're on the right track. The flak is heaviest over the target."

"I can't believe you just used a World War Two reference."

I smile. "Josh likes to watch the History Channel and bore me with the stories. Sometimes I remember them."

"Are you two an item yet?"

"No, and we never will be," I say, looking down at my hands as I feel my cheeks start to burn. "We're close friends. That's all."

Austin smirks. "Right."

I owe my life to Josh. He pulled me off the ground when a gunman was killing our classmates and dragged me into the storage closet. We have remained close friends since the day we escaped Summerville High School with our lives. I'm terrified that a romantic relationship could ruin that. It would complete the tragedy of that fateful day.

"I'm heading out," I say, standing and shaking off any thought of Josh.

"Me, too. I have plans."

I check the clock. "Wow, it's an early day for you. That's almost unprecedented."

"Yeah, I have a date with Victoria."

I can't stifle my surprise. I spoke to Vic yesterday, and she didn't mention it. Not that she's under any obligation to, but I'm surprised I didn't get a heads-up. It's a big deal. Not because she's going out with Austin, but because she's actually going on a date with anyone.

"She didn't tell you?" Austin asks.

"No."

Austin grimaces and then frowns. "Does she like me, or is this a pity date?"

"Austin, she's a friend. One of the few women I can call one. You're my boss. I'm not coming within miles of commenting about whatever's going on with you two."

"I understand," he says, disappointed. It sounds like he needs some encouragement.

"She likes you, Austin," I say, stopping when I reach the door. "Victoria is the strongest person I have ever met. She would never have agreed if she didn't."

"Thanks," he says, forcing a smile as he wrings his hands. "I can't believe I'm this nervous. Any advice?"

"She's a violently independent woman with confidence and smarts in spades. It's what makes her a great agent. Respect her and her space, and you'll be fine."

"Okay."

I start to leave, then stop. "One more thing. You get one shot with a woman like Victoria. Don't say something stupid and screw it up."

Austin lets out a laugh. "Good advice."

I wink at him and meander through the empty desks to the exit. Victoria and Austin being an item would be…weird. But I would be happy for both of them. At least someone around here has some semblance of a love life.

CHAPTER SEVEN

SPECIAL AGENT VICTORIA LARSEN

Victoria's Apartment
Pentagon City, Virginia

Victoria finishes sliding on her black heeled boots and rises to smooth out her dark blue jacket and matching pants. She moves to the mirror and checks her hair. It's pulled tight into a bun to keep it out of her face. This is her armor. Despite losing some power that comes with her feminine qualities, she feels more confident wearing this than a sundress and strappy high heels.

The doorbell rings. Victoria checks her watch and pulls her Glock off the table. She makes her way to the door of her apartment, sliding the gun into the holster as she walks.

"Oscar, I said I would pick up my packages—"

Victoria swings the door open to see Austin wearing a jacket and tie and holding a beautiful bouquet of red roses. A wave of intense guilt washes over her. Things were so hectic at the end of the day that she forgot to call him.

"Austin...I...uh...."

He takes in her attire. "I was thinking about a romantic dinner, but I'm down with wandering the streets like Batman."

Victoria offers a half smile. "That would make you Robin."

"Yeah, I didn't think that through."

"I'm sorry, Austin. I meant to call you. Something came up last minute."

"I gathered that," he says, disappointment dripping from his tone.

"Please, come in for a moment."

Austin looks at the flowers and then back at the elevators. "Maybe it's best that I leave."

"No, please! Come in. Let me explain."

He hesitates, and Victoria thinks about grabbing his coat and hauling him in. Under these circumstances, he won't find that amusing, so she stares at him with pleading eyes. He relents and enters as she exhales. She can't do anything right these days.

"I've been looking forward to tonight since you asked me. Please believe that."

Austin nods, but the look on his face says otherwise. He took a big chance when he asked her out. He was a complete mess hunkered in his office, fighting for *Front Burner's* survival. She was wearing the sundress and strappy heels, feeling vulnerable and out of her element. After recovering from her injuries in the Loughborough ambush, he tried again, and she eagerly accepted the invitation.

"Well, whatever you're doing must be important."

"It is. Let me show you why."

Victoria moves to the laptop computer on her small desk, flips it open, and logs into her email. Austin sets the flowers down on the kitchen counter and joins her.

"An agent from our Philadelphia Field Office sent me this."

"Should you be showing me this?" Austin asks.

"No, but I shouldn't even have this information. It's why it's encrypted and was sent to my personal email."

"What am I looking at?" he asks as she opens a .jpg file and stands back.

"An official election ballot of the State of Pennsylvania for November's election."

Austin leans in and studies the image. "It looks like it's seen better days. So what?"

"It was found at the scene of a fire in Allentown."

"At the industrial park?" Austin asks, perking up. "I heard about that blaze. Three people were killed due to smoke inhalation."

"Try multiple gunshot wounds," Victoria corrects, causing his eyes to widen. "They were murdered before the building was doused in gasoline and torched."

"Jesus. That's not what the media is reporting."

"Because the FBI and local authorities lied to them. Imagine that. This time they had a good reason. Firefighters found this ballot, and four dozen like it, in the parking area while dousing the inferno. It's a perfect duplicate, indistinguishable from actual official ballots."

"Forgeries," Austin mutters. "Do you know how many were printed?

She brings up a picture of the fire and another of the smoldering ruins. The building burned to its foundation.

"We may never know. I've never believed that this ended in New Hampshire or Massachusetts. The more I dig, the more I'm convinced that everything that's happened so far is the opening act. Machiavelli is going to seriously screw with the general election."

"The polls have Pennsylvania a toss-up. Standish and Bradford are neck and neck in the electoral math. Any number of fake ballots could skew the election result."

"Or cast enough doubt on it to throw the entire country into chaos. Half of the population would believe the election was stolen, and the other half would scream that they're sore losers."

"And the result is a president who can't get anything done."

"Or worse," Victoria whispers.

"So, you're heading up there tonight?"

Victoria's face softens. "I need to meet my contact tonight. The Bureau is watching me like I'm a kindergartener, so I must be back at my desk in the morning to avoid raising any suspicion."

Austin rubs his chin. "You know I could find a corroborating source and report this."

"Yes, it would be breaking news assuming you could prove it. A massive story like this would catapult *Front Burner* back into relevance. I also know that you won't."

At least, she hopes he won't. Desperate times call for desperate measures, but whatever is happening is much bigger than saving *Front Burner*. This is a conspiracy of epic proportions. The conspirators have already demonstrated that they are willing to kill to succeed. They need to be brought to justice, and a premature article could put Austin and his entire team in their crosshairs.

"We've come a long way," he says, smiling.

"Yes, we have, and I think we still have a long road ahead. There's one more thing you should know," Victoria says, picking an envelope up off the desk and handing it to him. "I got this before I left the office. The good news is that they ended my probation."

Austin opens it and reads. "You're reassigned to Africa? Are you kidding me?"

"That's the bad news. I wish this was a joke, but it's not funny."

"When?"

Victoria presses her lips together. "I need to report by the end of the month."

"That's two weeks from now. What are you going to do?"

"They've made it nearly impossible to say no. But a cabal is trying to rig a national election, and only a handful of people know about it, let alone are in a position to stop it. What do you think?"

"Okay. I'll let you get to it."

"Austin, I feel horrible about canceling tonight. Please believe me."

He takes her hands in his. They're warm, and she feels a tingle in her spine.

"Victoria, you're the most incredible woman I have ever met. You're also a federal agent. Rushing off to save the country comes with the territory. It's who you are, and I never want to see that change. I've waited this long for a date. What's a little longer?"

"Honestly, it's already been too long. I will make it up to you. I promise."

Austin grins and nods. "Be safe out there, Vic."

She watches him leave her apartment, and then closes her eyes. He said all the right things. But it's more than that. None of that explains what she's feeling.

Victoria bolts for the door and swings it open. She charges into the hallway.

"Austin?"

He stops short of the elevator and turns to face her. Victoria rushes up, wraps an arm around him, and presses against the back of his head. She kisses him, hoping that she hasn't forgotten how to. It's been so long. The kiss isn't sloppy or unnecessarily aggressive. Nor is it too soft or slow. It's...perfect. She stares into his surprised eyes when their lips finally part.

"What was that for?"

She holds his face in her hands. "Motivation. I don't want you to stop looking forward to our first date."

CHAPTER EIGHT

DEPUTY AG CONRAD WILLIAMS

Pennsylvania State Capitol Building
Harrisburg, Pennsylvania

The Pennsylvania State Capitol houses the state's general assembly, supreme and superior courts, and the offices of the governor and lieutenant governor. It's the third state capitol building constructed in Harrisburg, the first being destroyed in a fire and the second left unfinished when its funding evaporated. Politics in the 1800s weren't much different than today, apparently.

The building features decorative Pennsylvania-themed murals, sculptures, and stained-glass windows. Conrad got to appreciate some of the works before meeting the governor in his office and was disappointed when he learned the press briefing would be held outdoors so Pennsylvanians could watch from the perimeter.

There is nothing controversial about what Governor Fox will announce, so there's a diminished risk of hecklers and protesters. Who wouldn't want election security in this country? Conrad smiles. He can think of a few people.

"Thank you," Governor Fox says, taking his place at the podium. "There is nothing more sacred in the great American experiment than one voice, one vote. The act of voting is considered not only a civic duty but an expression of personal freedom. It is liberty in action, and it is being threatened.

"An increasing number of Americans are now questioning the integrity of our elections. The past few cycles have brought accusations, but nothing was more terrifying than what we witnessed in New Hampshire. As we begin the final stretch to choose the next president of the United States and elect representatives and senators to Congress, we focus on securing that process to ensure that what happened in the Granite State will not be repeated here.

"Our Department of State has developed a plan to increase monitoring and fortify our voting system defenses. The new voting system includes a risk-limiting audit designed to check the accuracy of election outcomes. This will increase voter confidence by using statistical verification to ensure our results are accurate."

Conrad patiently waits next to the governor for his turn to speak. Fox's precautions are prudent and reasonable. They're also going to be proven worthless.

"My team, along with our partners in the legislature, worked hard to fix past issues such as poor security controls for mail-in ballots, reconciliation, lack of chain of custody documentation, and unobserved ballot counting. We suffered from a lack of transparency in the past few election cycles. That is about to end. I can guarantee that this administration will conduct the smoothest election process in our fifty states.

"We will not allow anyone to deprive Pennsylvanians of their right to cast a ballot. Deputy Attorney General Conrad Williams is here to coordinate federal efforts. He can explain what measures Washington is taking to help secure the election."

There is light applause as Conrad takes the governor's place at the podium. "Our republic maintains a tradition of separation of powers. Local and state authorities are responsible for their elections, but no state can bring to bear the resources the federal government can muster. To that end, the FBI and other agencies stand ready to assist these authorities with whatever needs they may have.

"Unfortunately, election interference has entered the digital realm. Foreign governments use social media disinformation to attack democracies. Bad actors spread false information to confuse people and obfuscate issues. With a relatively small investment of manpower and financial resources, anyone can use social media and other online tools to sow disenfranchisement in our electoral process.

"As the governor articulated, free, fair, and regular elections are the cornerstone of democracy. This administration will not tolerate election interference or fraud. The FBI is tirelessly working to identify groups or individuals attempting to suppress or alter the vote. Anyone caught trying to manipulate this election will be prosecuted to the fullest extent of the law."

Conrad nods at the governor and steps back so that he can continue his remarks. This is nothing more than a dog and pony show. It's a hollow reassurance to a jittery electorate that everything is okay. Everything most decidedly isn't okay. Governor Fox is about to learn that the hard way.

CHAPTER NINE

BRIAN COOPER

Lake City Hotel & Suites
Erie, Pennsylvania

The Pennsylvania governor's press conference isn't as enlightening for Brian as it is for the candidate's staff gathered in this suite. He expects elected officials from around the country to reassure their constituents about the integrity of the coming election. What happened in New Hampshire rattled everyone, and with good reason.

"I've heard enough," Governor Bradford says, prompting a communications staff member to mute the television. "They're going to cheat."

"Of course they are," Joel Graham confirms, "and they'll do it while accusing you of doing the same."

That may be the smartest thing that has ever come out of his mouth. Joel was hired by Governor Bradford after Brian assumed the campaign manager position. He's a devout Republican, Brevin Hawkins disciple, and argumentative pain in the ass. The governor wanted a set of eyes to ensure that Brian wasn't driving the campaign off a cliff.

"How do we stop it?"

"We can't," the press liaison states. "The media is firmly on Team Standish. It doesn't matter how ridiculous any accusations are. They'll repeat them until they're a universal truth. Evidence be damned."

"Then we should do the same thing. Hit Standish now and hit her hard."

There is near universal agreement in the room. Brian watches from a spot along the wall and says nothing. The team discusses the details for a few moments before the candidate realizes that his campaign manager is silent.

"Brian? Your thoughts?"

"Sir, I would normally agree with that tactic, but not this time."

The room falls immediately silent. Brian was on Alicia Standish's staff and hasn't completely earned their trust. Now he's running the campaign of her opponent for the presidency. It's a safe bet that many Republicans think he's a plant scheming to undermine them. If Colin Bradford loses, that will be the first excuse.

"Why not?" the governor asks.

"Because that's what they are expecting us to do."

"So?"

Brian walks over to the whiteboard showing their polling today from just before the convention. Bradford has gained ground and is within the margin of error in the popular vote. That doesn't mean much in electoral politics for the presidency, but it illustrates a point.

He taps on the number. "We got to this point by doing the unexpected, not springing the traps Andrew Li sets for us."

"We have to fight back."

"I agree completely, Governor. I'm not saying we should stand and watch them connive their way to an inauguration. We have to pick a tactic they aren't expecting."

Bradford nods.

"Okay, what do you suggest?" the consultant asks.

"Pennsylvania isn't just a battleground state. It's *the* battleground state. This election is going to be won or lost here."

"We know that."

"Do you, Joel? Because you have the governor making a swing through the deep red parts of this state in the hope that it will help turn out the vote. That's fine, but it won't solve the real problem."

"The cities," Bradford mumbles.

Brian points at him. "Specifically, the minority voters in those cities."

Colin Bradford doesn't have a reputation for lifting a finger for minority communities. His governorship of North Carolina saw the state enact policies his political enemies characterized as racist. It was an albatross around his neck in a presidential campaign, especially if Alicia Standish had successfully exploited the Tyrell Grant story.

"I addressed my race issues like you told me to."

"You did, and getting ahead of those attacks with faithful responses to the American people is why you aren't staring at an electoral landslide right now."

"The governor will never earn the black vote," Joel states with a dismissive wave.

"Thank you, Captain Obvious. Most Republicans don't earn more than ten percent of it in a good year, and the governor isn't in a position to change that trend. I'm not talking about earning the black vote. I'm talking about making sure that Standish doesn't either."

"Voter suppression?" Joel asks.

"That's illegal, and I have no interest in depriving any citizen of their constitutional rights. If that's what you're suggesting—"

"I'm not asking you to have goons block people of color from standing in a line at a polling location. I'm talking about giving them reasons not to want to."

The staff erupts. Brian returns to his spot along the wall while everyone in the room screams at him. They likely misinterpreted what he's suggesting, and that's okay. These people aren't technically his enemies, but they aren't friends, either. When adversaries are making a mistake, you don't stop them.

"What are you suggesting, Brian?" the governor asks after getting everyone in the room to simmer down.

"We cancel the Southwest trip and focus our efforts here. We're going to win Arizona and lose Nevada. Even if Arizona somehow slides into her column, it won't matter in the electoral math. We cannot lose Pennsylvania, period."

"Cancel the trip and campaign—"

"Where?" the governor asks, cutting Joel off.

Brian moves to the state map taped to the wall. "Pittsburgh, Philly, Scranton, Harrisburg, and Allentown."

"Those are all solid blue areas!" Joel screeches.

"Precisely. We take the fight to Standish by going after her base."

"It's pointless. There is zero chance of us flipping any of them."

Brian shakes his head. For a high-paid consultant, Joel is slow on the uptake.

"We don't need to. The tactic is to get minorities to sour on Standish. In a race between 'no way' and 'who cares,' Americans stay home and watch Netflix."

"Interesting proposition," Governor Bradford says, "but I don't know what I can say that would make a difference."

"I do, Brian says. "Be honest. Appear in front of those crowds and rehash all your sins. Admit your mistakes. And then point to hers. Stand and bear your soul while challenging Alicia Standish to answer for a half-century of misguided policies that only succeeded in holding them back. Explain that you don't expect their vote and can't guarantee immediate results but promise you'll work harder to earn it during your four years at the White House than she will."

Grumbling echoes through the room. Brian tries to get a read on the side conversations. A third of the staff thinks he may be on to something, while the remainder thinks it's the dumbest idea they've ever heard. He would have preferred a fifty-fifty split, but at least he isn't being laughed out of here.

The governor looks at Joel, who shrugs. "It will make you look weak."

His gaze shifts to his communication director. "It's bold, honest, and will help you everywhere if you do it right. Americans are tired of politicians saying whatever it takes to get elected and forgetting their promises once they recite the oath of office."

"Standish *is* that politician," Brian says. "It's time to make people understand that."

"You'll get blasted by the media and pundits as desperate for campaigning in those cities," Joel argues. "They'll eviscerate you weeks before the polls open."

"And the people who agree won't vote for the governor anyway," Brian says. "Undecideds will interpret his message differently. Minorities may rethink whether voting in this cycle even matters."

"Okay. I have some things to think about. Thank you, everyone. Let's get some rest before tomorrow."

The campaign staff files out and begins heading to their rooms. Joel hangs back, hoping for a word with Bradford until the governor thanks him for his input and gestures toward the door. Brian is about to follow him until a hand touches his upper arm.

"Brian, hold up. How sure are you about this?"

Brian presses his lips together. "Eighty percent."

"That's not good enough."

"This is a national campaign for the presidency of the United States, not for town clerk in a backwater village. Anybody who tells you they're sure about anything is lying, just like Brevin was. That's why you replaced him."

Brevin Hawkins was the governor's campaign manager until the days after the convention. He was also a moron willing to accept losing this race. He despised Brian and resented that the governor hired him as a consultant. Their antagonistic relationship became untenable after Brian disobeyed him by allowing Tierra Campos to speak to the delegates and a national prime-time television audience.

The tactic saved a disastrous convention and changed the governor's fortunes in the race. Brevin gave the candidate the cliché "him or me" ultimatum. He was gone five minutes later, and Brian was named the new campaign manager. Considering Cooper's resume, it was a bold move that the press had a field day with.

"Putting Campos on that stage during the convention was a huge risk that could have backfired spectacularly."

"That's true of all bold plans. D-Day could have been a disaster for the allies. The Afghanistan withdrawal was. All we can do is understand the situation and make the best possible move. Standish is convinced she can turn out more supporters here than you. She expects you to go crazy trying to energize the base in Pennsylvania. You can play the game that she wants, or you can start your own. The choice is yours, Governor."

CHAPTER TEN

SPECIAL AGENT VICTORIA LARSEN

Lehigh Valley Printers
Allentown, Pennsylvania

Victoria pulls her sedan to the yellow police tape strung across the road at the print shop's parking lot entrance and turns off the engine. The entire corporate park is illuminated, including what's left of the hulking structure that burned down to its foundation. A woman climbs out of her vehicle and greets Victoria.

The petite woman looks like she could still be in college or even high school. With flawless mocha skin, pretty eyes, and a lean build, she likely has no problem getting a date. Of course, the same is said about Victoria, who didn't manage to keep the one offer she accepted.

"Glad you could make it, Agent Larsen."

"And I'm glad you were willing to meet me here in the middle of the night."

"Don't mention it. There's nothing good on television anyway. I'm Imani Bangura."

"It's nice to meet you. This must have been one hell of a fire."

"Five alarms. It burned for hours. The heat was so intense that it melted the printing presses. There was nothing left by the time they knocked the flames down."

Victoria suppresses the urge to walk around. There isn't much to see. The building was reduced to its concrete slab, and the grounds were already thoroughly searched.

"I didn't know they made print shops so big. I always think of them as mom-and-pop shops."

"This place did high-volume printing of everything from corporate brochures to junk mail."

"Nobody is going to miss that. Did they identify the bodies?"

"You mean ash piles? Forensics is still working on it. Police suspect they were the manager and two of his men. All three were shady ex-cons."

That sounds about right. Individuals with previous convictions and incarcerations are more likely to engage in other criminal behavior. The owner of this facility likely had no idea what was happening after hours. This was a side hustle that cost these men their lives.

"How many people know about the ballots?"

"Hard to say. Some firemen and local police, for sure. Agents in the Philly Field Office who were sent here with me to investigate. It's being kept under wraps, but people talk. You know how it is."

"And you called me. Why?"

Imani looks up and takes a deep breath of crisp October air. "I know what you did in the Ethan Harrington case. I know about the SOF and what happened at that mill in Massachusetts. The SAC should have requested that you be brought in immediately."

Victoria almost laughs. "That might have gotten him reassigned. I'm the renegade who flaunts procedures and disobeys orders. Apparently, I also get the people around me killed. That's my reputation around the Bureau, isn't it?"

Imani nods. "That's what people say, yes."

"So, why?"

"Because we're a lot alike."

"That's a career-limiting move, Imani."

The FBI isn't an organization that rewards outside-the-box thinking. It comes in handy during investigations, as Victoria adeptly demonstrated with the apprehension of a sordid character known as "The Devil Rancher," who earned his name by branding his enemies. Most of the time, it's viewed as disloyalty and insubordination. Neither of those traits is a career bell ringer.

"Do you want to know why I went to Quantico?" Imani asks, eliciting a nod from Victoria. "I'm West Philadelphia born and raised, just like in the Will Smith song. My grandpa was a cop in the 18th Patrol District."

"Please don't tell me he was killed in action."

"Thankfully, no. While most of my friends would hang out and get high, he would take me to see all the blue markers in the city."

Victoria cocks her head. "Blue markers?

"The Pennsylvania Historical Marker Program installed metal plaques onto large boulders starting in 1914 to commemorate individuals, events, and landmarks throughout the state. They've been redesigned and mounted on poles and such since then. There are over two thousand, and my grandfather took me to all the ones in Philadelphia. We even traveled to some outside the city when I was older.

"He loved his country and was incredibly proud of this state and its heritage. He passed away right after I graduated college. I wanted to follow in his footsteps, but he told me to be more than he was. So, I joined the FBI."

"He sounds like he was quite a man."

Imani nods. "He was. I have grown to love this state and country as much as he did. I don't like the idea of someone messing with an election. I hate the idea of them doing it here. I don't know if the Sword of Freedom is behind this or not, but it feels like they are."

"And that's why you called me."

The Sword of Freedom were four former soldiers who Machiavelli employed to sabotage the New Hampshire Democratic Primary. Marx, Engels, Trotsky, and Sartre were killers, arsonists, hackers, and manipulators. Their plan almost succeeded until the attack on Wilson Newman at a shopping mall allowed the group to be traced. Marx,

Sartre, and Trotsky were subsequently killed. Only Engels, identified as former FBI Special Agent Ian Drucker, is still at large. Victoria is responsible for their downfall…and Drucker's escape.

"I don't know what I can do, Imani. The Bureau watches me like a hawk and is reassigning me to Africa at the end of the month."

"That's bullshit. Are you taking the position?"

"Not if I can avoid it. I'll help under one condition."

"Whoa, I'm not good with conditions," Imani says, holding her hands up to chest level and causing Victoria to smile.

"Me neither, but this one is non-negotiable. You need to understand what you're getting yourself into. You could find yourself in Africa for even meeting me here."

"Back to the Motherland," she quips.

"I'm serious. I believe some powerful people are caught up in this – people who could end your career with the snap of their fingers. They thought nothing of killing Fuller and Nishimoto in Boston. This is dangerous and deadly."

"That's a warning, not a condition."

Victoria really likes this woman. "True. Here's the condition: There is no stopping this train once it pulls out of the station. There is no getting off because you suddenly don't like the view. And there's a good chance of it derailing and crashing before it reaches the next station."

"Great metaphor. Luckily for you, I like trains. Thank you for warning me about the risks, but there's a fate worse than career suicide or death."

"What's that?"

"My grandfather haunting me for not doing something about this. Where do you want to start?"

There is nothing stronger than the heart of a volunteer. Imani has a sense of duty, connection to her state, and apparent fear of her grandfather's ghost. She's making this decision for herself, not because she is compelled by any outside force. That makes her an ally Victoria can count on.

"I need you to tell me every detail about this fire."

CHAPTER ELEVEN

TIERRA CAMPOS

Front Burner Washington Office
Washington, D.C.

It's been a while since I've been down here. Austin had a board in his room where he tracked all the information we had gathered about the SOF, Machiavelli, and the other players in this apparent conspiracy. As the *Front Burner* rebuild began in earnest, he moved it to this unused conference room.

This "war room" hasn't gotten much use lately. We've all been too exhausted and stressed to spend any energy on it. The leads have dried up. The only man who made any progress on pulling back the curtain was Isiah Burgess, and he was found dead shortly after I met with him in Illinois. We're nowhere, so why bother digging further?

"There you are," I say, spotting Austin staring blankly at the massive whiteboard. "I've been looking all over for you."

"Hey," he says without looking at me.

"What's wrong?"

"Nothing."

"Yeah, it sounds like nothing."

He points at the information laid out in front of us as I take a seat. "Have you ever stopped to think that we dropped the ball?"

"What do you mean?"

"This. We've been so busy rebuilding *Front Burner* that we haven't looked at it in a month."

"There aren't many of us here, Austin. Calling us a 'skeleton staff' is an insult to skeletons. It isn't practical to rebuild a news organization and chase ghosts."

"Yeah, and that's the problem. What if that was Machiavelli's plan all along?"

"It'd be a tad egocentric to think we're that important. We're not the only ones who could investigate the cabal. Every other major media outlet has the financial resources of a massive corporation behind it."

"That's the problem, isn't it? Information is corporate now, and they only care about bottom lines and reputations. It makes them easy to influence and control. That's why we're the only ones who were even looking."

"You think we were targeted?"

The corner of his mouth curls up. "Don't you?"

I think about it for a moment before shrugging. "Maybe. I'm conspiracy theoried out."

He doesn't say anything, and the room gets uncomfortable. I have five articles I'm working on that need to get posted on the site. I don't have time to deal with this and make my deadlines.

"I'll leave you alone to ponder," I say, standing.

"Victoria canceled our date last night."

I slowly sit back down. That explains his foul mood.

"She did?"

"Yeah. When I got there."

"I'm sorry, Austin. I know you were looking forward to it."

He looks at me for the first time. "I was, but I understand why. Victoria got a tip from an agent in Pennsylvania that she needed to explore. Machiavelli may have been behind the inferno at that industrial print shop."

"Really?"

That explains why Austin parked himself in here and why he thinks we may be asleep at the wheel. He tells me what happened at Victoria's apartment and what she showed him on the computer. My mouth hangs open by the time he finishes.

"That's a huge story, Austin."

He nods. "One told in confidence."

"Ah." It's all I can utter.

"I know. I'm singing a different tune now, aren't I?"

He sure is. When Tyler, Olivia, and I were sent to New Hampshire after the arsons against Luther Burgess's campaign offices, we ran into Victoria, and she provided off-the-record insights. Austin was keen on publishing the news anyway. It would have burned Vic as a source and destroyed a friendship. It ultimately created a rift between me and Austin that is only now closing.

"No, it's more of an oldie but goodie. It's what you would have done when we first met."

"Victoria is risking more than her career. Her life is on the line with Ian Drucker still out there. The deputy attorney general may be involved, Andrew Li certainly is, and who knows who else? This is a massive story about a conspiracy that could undermine our whole Republic. It could spell the end of democratic principles, yet here it sits, untouched."

I stare at the board. I used to know the content, position, and color of every Post-it note. When someone made a change or addition, I would recognize it in less than five seconds. That was then. This is now.

"We don't have anyone to chase this, Austin."

"I disagree. We have the one person that matters."

I suddenly don't like where this conversation is heading. "What are you saying?"

"You've done a remarkable job helping *Front Burner* get back on its feet. Now I need you to get back to work on this."

That's not what I expected when I walked in here. Part of me feels like the collapse was my fault. I have a sense of duty to raise it from the ashes.

"Austin, I need to—"

"You're not a beat reporter, Tierra. You're one of the best investigative journalists I've ever seen. You have a Peabody and Pulitzer because you have great instincts, are fearless in finding answers, and then report them without prejudice. Very few journalists do that today. I need you to get back to work to identify and expose this cabal before polls open in November."

"Without Isiah's information, what is there for me to do?"

When I met with Isiah, he tantalized me by giving up the codenames of Machiavelli's co-conspirators. He claimed to know the identities of Robespierre and Nietzsche but had yet to identify the kingpin. I have only managed to uncover who the former is.

The slip of paper he handed me at the end of the meeting was the key to a lock that could be opened if anything ever happened to him. Then something did. Only the treasure chest with the Holy Grail that would expose this conspiracy has never been uncovered.

Austin shrugs. "Maybe it got intercepted."

"And maybe he was full of crap, and it never existed in the first place. Austin, mail-in balloting has started in some states. We're already too late."

He shakes his head. "I don't think so. Whatever is going to happen will happen in Pennsylvania. Those ballots weren't printed by accident. The fire wasn't an accident. It's all a means to an end, and I need you to figure out what that is. Talk to Victoria and see what threads you can pull without exposing her as the source."

"Okay," I say, relenting. He's the boss. "It's been almost a month, so I can look at this with fresh eyes, but I need coffee first. Do you want to join me for a walk across the street?"

"Thanks, but no. I'm going to stay here for a bit."

The words were mundane, but Austin's tone speaks volumes. It's the same malaise he had when I walked in.

"For the record, I'm sure Victoria looked forward to the date as much as you did."

He smiles as broadly as anyone I have ever seen. "I know. Thanks."

CHAPTER TWELVE

IAN DRUCKER

"The Forge" Militia Compound
Liberty, Pennsylvania

There are plenty of nooks and crannies at the mill. During the workday, it's a regular business with workers going about their tasks. Since he arrived, Ian began hiding out in a bunker on the edge of the east tree line. It gives him privacy and allows him to stay out of sight. Only Remy and Mike spend any time here, so he's not taking anyone's space.

He boots his laptop and launches his VPN. The Keystone Militia controls the wi-fi network, and it won't do for anyone to know anything about his online activity. Especially when it comes to this game.

Knights of the Crusade is an old-school, first-person "adventure" saga with terrible graphics and a meaningless plot. Most of the time, characters just walk around talking to each other and looking for trinkets, new armor, or better weapons. Once in a while, they fight, if that's what the game's players can call it.

It's also one of the most politically incorrect games he's ever seen. That's what makes it a relic. No modern game maker would ever release a product where Christian knights run around slaughtering Muslims. It's something he could see members of this militia playing, though.

The minimap in the corner guides him to the tavern he's looking for. His female avatar struts into the nearly empty bar. It's always that way. It feels like nobody plays this multiplayer game anymore except Ian and the two knights seated at the bar.

One of them is admiring his sword. That's fitting. Ian didn't put much thought into his name or character. He typed the first handle that popped into his head and chose the opposite gender for fun.

The chat on the side of the screen opens, and the character names and text pops up in obnoxious calligraphy:

Machiavelli>>> You're late.
TavernWench>>> I don't get great internet here. Deal with it.
Machiavelli>>> Of the three of us, you have the lightest schedule.
TavernWench>>> And the most risk. This game is dumb.
Robespierre>>> But effective. Some conversations shouldn't be had over a cell phone, encrypted or not. This game doesn't store its chat.

That's because developers wrote this game when the average hard drive offered only five hundred megabytes of space. Of all the communication methods in the modern age, it's ridiculous that the two men picked this archaic one.

Ian starts to type a snarky response and thinks twice about it. There is no use poking the bear. It won't change anything. He rests his chin on his hands and waits for one of them to type something.

Machiabelli>>> Are things on schedule?
TabernWench>>> Yes.
Machiabelli>>> You have the militia in line?
TabernWench>>> For now. They want details.
Robespierre>>> I don't care what those useful idiots want. You have your instructions.

He should care. Conrad Williams is a big cog in the very system that they despise. He is as much in their crosshairs as the candidates running for president.

TabernWench>>> It will be taken care of. Everything will be in place for the election.
Machiabelli>>> Good. We expect nothing less.

"Yeah, yeah, yeah," Ian mumbles.

He has no interest in addressing the obvious. They expect results, and he promised to deliver them. There is more pressing business to get to. Ian types a question and hovers his finger over the enter key. Yes, he needs to know. He smashes it and leans back in his folding chair.

TabernWench>>> What about Victoria Larsen?
Robespierre>>> What about her? She's being taken care of.

"Oh, hell no. You're not stealing my glory, buddy," Ian grumbles.

The deal was always that he would get the chance to finish Larsen. For these men, her death is just business. For Ian, it's far more personal. She killed his friends and almost ended him in Loughborough. That's a score that must be settled.

TabernWench>>> That's my job.
Machiabelli>>> No, your job is to carry out missions we assign you. Nothing more.
TabernWench>>> We have an arrangement.
Machiabelli>>> You had an arrangement with Vassyl, the poor dead bastard. You had your chance and blew it.

Ian inhales sharply and exhales slowly. Keyboard warriors act like fools online because they're anonymous and don't face immediate consequences. They say things to people that they wouldn't utter in the real world because you can't get punched through a computer screen. Ian knows that saying the wrong thing to these men could mean his untimely demise, despite wanting to put the arrogant bastards in their place. He's not anonymous.

TavernWench>>> She needs to die. I could kill her and be back before the next day.

Robespierre>>> You will have all the time and money you need after the election.

TavernWench>>> That's not good enough.

Robespierre>>> Are you under the mistaken impression that you're calling the shots here? Because, I assure you, you're not.

Ian stares at the screen. He's feeling a little underappreciated. Neither of these men could do what he's done. This plan of theirs will spectacularly fail without him. They could at least acknowledge that and hear him out.

TavernWench>>> Your plans rely on my efforts. I think I have a say.

Machiavelli>>> You have a mission that you are being handsomely compensated for. It's what you agreed to. That is all the say you get.

TavernWench>>> Or else what?

Nothing happens for a few tense moments before Robespierre's knight rises from the table and hefts his sword. Ian knows what's coming next but doesn't have any weapons to stop him. He doesn't play this game and hasn't found one.

The knight arcs the sword and swings it hard, lopping his avatar's head off. He doesn't get to see the gore, which is a shame. A black message box in the center of his screen informs him that his character has died.

Getting killed in this game means that you start all over. There is no character respawn at your level or with the items you collected in your travels. It raises the stakes and is an interesting way to force players to behave like they would in real life. Luckily, he doesn't care. "Tavern Wench" is a level-one assassin who doesn't have so much as a butter knife to lose.

Ian closes the lid on the laptop. Conrad's message was loud and clear. He's disposable, or at least they are treating him that way. Victoria Larsen can wait. The money he's receiving will allow for early retirement, but it's only good if he lives long enough to enjoy it. Marx, Sartre, and Trotsky would agree. His Army buddies in the SOF learned that lesson the hard way.

CHAPTER THIRTEEN

DEPUTY AG CONRAD WILLIAMS

U.S. Department of Justice
Washington, D.C.

Just to the north of the National Mall and Smithsonian Museum of Natural History is the building Conrad Williams calls home. He's here far more than at the house he owns. The Department of Justice Building's limestone façade and red-tile roof shrouds distinctive interior spaces, including the Great Hall and the Law Library.

The Office of the Attorney General was created by the Judiciary Act of 1789 as a part-time position for one person. How times have changed. The act specifies that the attorney general is charged with the prosecutorial duties in suits concerning the United States and with providing the president and department heads advice in matters of law.

Conrad serves as Lisa Ehler's right-hand man. She leads over one hundred thousand Justice Department employees working in all fifty states and dozens of countries worldwide. She's close to the president and his family and has a good working relationship with Senator Alicia Standish. That's why he was sent to meet with Pennsylvania's governor. Ehler's relationship with Standish could be scrutinized, so she wanted to avoid the appearance of impropriety.

"How was your trip?" the AG asks from her desk without looking up.

"It was fine," Conrad says, sitting across the desk from his boss. "The governor was committed."

"I'm sure he was. He doesn't want election trouble when the polls are within the margin of error."

"You should expect trouble there," Conrad says, prompting her to look up.

"What do you mean?"

Conrad grimaces. "Because there already is some."

"I haven't been briefed on anything."

"No, ma'am, you haven't. I purposely had it withheld from you."

Lisa places her pen down and leans back in her chair. "Conrad, it's no secret that you want my job, but you aren't the attorney general. I am. As deputy, you work for me. If you have information about possible election interference, you had better tell me *right* now."

"I'm not deliberately holding out on you. Please understand that. I'm protecting you and the president."

"We don't need your protection."

"Lisa, anything I tell you will be briefed in the Oval Office. Right now, it's a state problem. If the president gets involved, it becomes a national problem, meaning it's his problem."

"You, of all people, know that's not how this president likes to do things."

"I understand completely. The decision is yours. I've been working with Director Krekstein. The FBI is fully engaged with the governor and state authorities."

"Are you offering to run point on this?"

"If you want me to. It shields you from responsibility and frees you from devoting the time this requires."

Conrad watches his boss contort her face in thought. He isn't stupid. He knows the value of the deal he offered her and how badly things could go for him. Machiavelli, Rasputin, and even Ian have taken risks. Now, it's his turn.

It shouldn't take her this long to decide. If everything goes right, Ehler takes credit. If Conrad fails, she has a built-in scapegoat. It's simple political math, and he's counting on her reaching that conclusion without him having to spell it out.

"All right. I'm counting on you to come through on this. There's one condition, though. You need to inform me immediately if you uncover actionable evidence of fraud or interference."

"Yes, ma'am."

"I'm not kidding, Conrad. Don't try to be a hero and keep me in the dark. This election is important."

"I won't let you down."

She nods. "Very well. I have another meeting."

Conrad rises and leaves her office. He can't suppress the smile when he reaches the corridor. That was easier than he thought it would be.

CHAPTER FOURTEEN

BRIAN COOPER

Bradford Campaign Office
Hanover, Pennsylvania

Campaigns move around the country at blazing speeds. It's not unheard of to hold rallies in three states in the closing weeks of a race. It's a logistical nightmare, beyond stressful, and incredibly exhausting. It's not much better moving around within a state. Just substitute long plane rides for long car rides.

Colin Bradford hasn't said anything in two days about Brian's strategy. He's been content to execute their plan of rallying support in rural areas while mulling it over. The decision needs to be made now with them set to pack up and fly across the country tomorrow.

"We're staying in Pennsylvania," he announces to the staff assembled in their Hanover campaign office. "We'll start with a rally in Philadelphia, then go to Scranton, Allentown, Harrisburg, back to Erie, and ending in Pittsburgh. We can evaluate where we need to go from there. We'll return here before the election, and I'll return to North Carolina on Election Day."

A mix of grumbles and enthusiasm ripples around the room. Some of Bradford's advisors are disappointed, and others are optimistic. One of them is angry.

"That's a mistake, sir," Joel warns.

"You don't agree with the strategy?" Bradford asks.

"With all due respect, Governor, I think it's the dumbest thing I've ever heard. Your campaign manager is throwing the fight in the final round."

All heads turn to Brian for a reaction. They don't get one.

"We wouldn't be here without him."

Joel bites his lower lip and nods. "That may be true, but politics is a 'what have you done for me lately' game. He's fumbling on the one-yard line. You will be jeered and shouted off stages in those cities, and the media will play that on an endless loop. Americans will have those images in their heads as they fill out their ballots two weeks from now."

"That might not work against us if it happens," the communications director argues.

"I disagree."

"You don't agree with much, do you, Joel?" Aimee asks.

Brian smiles at the speechwriter. He plugged her for information at the convention after Bradford and Brevin Hawkins froze him out. Her job was on the line, but what she said helped set him on the path to inviting Tierra Campos to speak from the stage. He screamed at her to provide plausible deniability. It wasn't even three months ago, but it feels like a lifetime.

"She has a point," the governor says.

Joel adjusts his position in the chair. "I believe in you, sir. I want you to win because I know the dangers of a Standish administration. This country can't endure four years of her reckless policies. It's my duty to object to this course of action."

"If you can't get on board, maybe you don't belong here," the communications director says, earning a glare from the consultant.

"He does," Brian interjects, surprising every staffer in the room. "Groupthink is dangerous, and he is making an argument against our approach because that's what he's paid to do. I appreciate his opinion and agree that it's risky, but the reward is the White House."

"I don't need you defending me, Brian," Joel says with a sneer.

"I'm not defending you. I'm defending your argument. So, let's take a look at that. I'm assuming you saw the two recent polls that suddenly have Arizona as a toss-up and us within the margin of error in Nevada."

"Yes, I did. That's why we need to go to the Southwest."

"Hispanics are the key demographic in both states. Agreed? What policy measure have we released that would cause such a dramatic swing with them? What has the governor said or done that would lead to a two-point erosion in one state and an almost five-point gain in its neighbor?"

Joel smirks. "I know what you're going to say. The polls are biased, and we shouldn't pay any attention to them."

"No, I wasn't. I was going to say that the polls are rigged, and we shouldn't pay any attention to them."

Joel throws his hands up and stands in frustration. "They're both reputable pollsters!"

"Who consistently oversample Democrats and have missed the last three presidential races by an average of six and a half points. And before you say that our internal polls mirror that, which they don't, you yourself said our internals are garbage."

The political consultant scowls. He's losing the fact-based fight because he's better at making emotional arguments. There is a place in politics for that, but more on the messaging side than the strategy one. Joel is out of his depth.

"This is crazy."

"Joel, why were those two polls released today?" Brian asks, not getting a response. "Anyone?"

Heads shake. Even the governor remains quiet.

"You all watch the news. The Standish camp announced that she was adding dates to a Western campaign swing. Only she isn't going."

"How could you know that?"

"I know a head fake when I see one. She makes an announcement, and two polls show the race tightening there. We're forced to respond by pulling up stakes and heading west."

"Leaving Standish in Pennsylvania by herself," the speechwriter says. "That's smart."

"Andrew Li is no dummy. It's a trap."

"You're accusing pollsters of working for the Democrats," Joel moans.

"With them, not for them. The Democrats send their talking points to every major news outlet in the country. Most eagerly cover them. It's an accusation that we've made a thousand times. What makes you think they don't do the same with their favorite pollsters?"

Joel looks around the room and begins to see what Cooper did five minutes ago. The staff has abandoned his line of thinking. They think the governor should stay here.

"You'd be putting all your chips in Pennsylvania. The governor can't claim to want to be president for all Americans and spend the last two weeks in one state."

"He can if he wants to be president. I didn't set up the Electoral College. The math is the math. This election will be settled here, so here is where we need to be. It's that simple."

The governor has heard enough. He stands and moves to the center of the room. Every set of eyes watches him for the final decision.

"We're staying in PA and holding the rallies. Start setting them up. If things get nasty, so be it. We'll deal with it," he says before turning to Brian. "How do we get them to sour on Standish?"

"By telling them a truth about her that nobody knows yet."

CHAPTER FIFTEEN

IAN DRUCKER

"The Forge" Militia Compound
Liberty, Pennsylvania

Ian spots the truck's headlights and checks his watch. It's already after ten. Their task was as simple as it gets, and he would have expected the vehicle to return on time. Militias. They may fancy themselves soldiers, but they don't act like them. He's willing to bet they stopped at a bar or restaurant before returning.

The box truck finally arrives and stops when it reaches him. Ian toys with the notion of ripping them a new one. He decides against it and opens the back. Salvage yards have a great many things of use. He inspects the cargo of about four dozen rusted propane cylinders that would never again be trusted to hold a flammable gas. Fortunately, Ian doesn't need them to.

"Nice work," Remy says to the driver as he comes alongside Ian. "Get these off-loaded into the storage shed and then call it a night."

"You got it."

Ian walks away as the truck fires up and drives the short distance to the shed. A half-dozen men join in forming a chain to quicken the work. He returns to the bunker and stares at a map of Pennsylvania spread across the table. Critical points are marked with chess pieces using a system none of the militia members can decipher.

He knows how they feel about being kept in the dark. He was a small part of Machiavelli's master plan with the rest of the Sword of Freedom up in New Hampshire. That scheme was conceived at least a couple of years ago. Long enough for them to recruit Ian and get him into the FBI. Given his colorful history serving with the Army in Europe, he still can't figure out how he became a federal agent, much less how he graduated from Quantico.

That was then, and this is now. Ian has a broader understanding of the goal, and it's the militia's turn to be in the dark. Operational security is everything. Federal agents have a long history of infiltrating groups like this. He can't afford to fail this close to success and refuses to expose himself despite Robespierre's assurances.

"You can be accused of many things, Ian, but laziness isn't one of them," Remy says, entering the bunker and handing him a beer.

"Thanks."

"Is it all coming together?"

Ian nods and takes a swig. "We're getting there."

Remy joins him in studying the map. He sees the pieces but has no idea what they mean outside of the obvious grandness of this operation's scale.

"Are you ever going to share what this is about?"

"Liberty. And payback."

"I don't mean the strategic goals. I mean the tactical ones."

Ian continues to stare at the map. "It's better that you don't know."

"You need to tell one of us," Remy says, jerking Ian's shoulder around and causing the former agent to slap his arm away. "Those men out there are following your lead for now, but that won't last. They are coming to me with questions I don't have answers to. You want to keep them in the dark? Fine. If you keep me in the dark, there will be a point where I stop defending you."

Threats are verbal indications of a crossroads. They are issued either by the weak trying to look strong or the strong warning of the consequences of challenging their power. In either instance, the one being threatened needs to choose how to respond: Cave in or call the bluff. There is a third option that is the path less followed: Ignore it.

"Remember when we first met, Remy?" He nods. "We talked over a beer about changing the country, just like we are now. You went on about wanting to return to the roots that made this a great Republic."

"And you said you could make it happen. So what?"

"I also told you we would have to do it my way to get results."

"I accepted the terms, despite having no reason to trust you. Those men haven't."

"They work for you."

"No. They work with me," Remy says, setting his beer down. "We're not a military outfit. There's no rank structure, code of conduct, or enlistment contract. Each man is free to leave as he pleases. Your speech was inspiring. None of these men would ever consider themselves summer soldiers. But they don't have absolute allegiance to a cause based on flowery words alone. That has to be earned."

"It will be."

"I believe you. But you haven't earned it yet, and Election Day is right around the corner. Look at things from their perspective. They know about the SOF and what happened in New Hampshire. To them, you're a socialist representing an ideology they despise. You could be infiltrating us as part of a plea bargain with the feds. I'm surprised they trust you as much as they do."

"Then why am I here?"

Remy picks up one of the chess pieces and inspects the bottom. There's nothing there except green felt meant to protect the board. He clenches his fist around it.

"Massachusetts. You killed those two agents and ambushed that tactical team. There is no plea bargaining your way out of a life sentence for those murders."

"No, there isn't. Everything I've done is preparing for an event that will fundamentally change the fabric of this country for the better. Not just for a year or an election cycle...forever. The government will do everything it can to stop us and preserve its power over the people. If even one of those men is a mole—"

"No way."

"Is a mole or gets cold feet, everything we are working for will end. The government will make examples of us in show trials or declare us domestic terrorists to deprive us of any due process. That's how it works."

Remy holds his hands up in surrender. "You don't need to convince me. Just understand that a point will come when you will need to convince Stag and the rest of them."

Remy places the chess piece back on the map and nods at Ian before exiting the command bunker. Ian returns to checking the map. Machiavelli and Robespierre's previous plans were far too complex for his tastes. This has many moving parts but doesn't rely on many exterior influences. He knows they can pull this off. That's assuming that the cabal doesn't decide to make things harder than they need to be.

CHAPTER SIXTEEN

TIERRA CAMPOS

Josh's Apartment
Georgetown, Washington, D.C.

Josh welcomed me with open arms into his tiny Georgetown basement apartment after I broke my lease. It's a one-bedroom, but he has a sleeper sofa that works just fine for my needs. The absence of windows is oddly comforting, considering what I have been through in this city.

It's early, and I didn't switch on the light to avoid waking him. The brightness from my laptop's LED screen is more than enough illumination. That's what I'm focused on when an amber glow bathes the room. I look up to see Josh standing in the doorway to his bedroom.

"Were you up all night?"

"No," I say, leaning back into the sofa. "I got a couple of hours of sleep."

Josh moves to the kitchen to pour the coffee I brewed an hour ago. "You were job hunting the last time I saw you on a laptop."

"I'm sorry, Josh. I'll be out of your hair as soon as possible. I promise."

"You mean as soon as *Front Burner* starts paying you?" he asks with a smile. "I didn't mean that as a complaint or an eviction notice. Stay as long as you like. I wish my sofa was more comfortable."

"It's better than a cardboard box and cold sidewalk."

That's what I would be staring at without his generosity. My apartment in Navy Yard was affordable on the generous salary I earned on *Capitol Beat*. Once DeAnna Van Herten sent me packing, I had to dump the place before I blew through my savings. Since *Front Burner* can barely afford paper clips, I'm working without a salary until it gets re-established. I don't know where I would be if Josh didn't insist I crash with him.

"Do you miss your old place?"

"It was nice, but it was never home."

"Well, for what it's worth, I like having you here," he says, plopping down next to me and almost spilling the coffee in his lap. "My place is a lot cleaner."

"Jerk," I say, smacking his chest lightly. "I'm sure you can develop the required motor skills for dusting and vacuuming."

"I know how to do both. I just choose not to."

"You are such a guy," I say, shaking my head.

"Yup! Right down to the three laundry piles."

"Whites, lights, and darks?"

"Clean, dirty but wearable, and hazardous waste."

Josh always seems to make me smile. I haven't done much of that recently. With the stress of rebuilding *Front Burner*, the election, and attacks from the likes of Oliver Jahn, I don't expect to for the foreseeable future.

"You have issues."

"What are you working on at this ungodly hour?"

"Austin has me looking into Drucker, Machiavelli, and Robespierre again."

"I expected you to pick that up a while ago. Why didn't you?"

"Honestly? I don't know where to start."

Josh sips his coffee. "You're a great journalist and investigator, Tierra. You'll figure it out."

I shake my head. "I'm not, Josh."

"What do you mean?"

"Think back to Brockhampton. Ethan Harrington wasn't exposed because of my brilliant investigative work. He stumbled on a question. I didn't intend to take him down. I stepped on a LEGO in the middle of the night and hopped around, bouncing off walls."

He smirks at the mental image. "You're being a little hard on yourself, aren't you?"

"Josh, I'm not an investigative reporter. I don't know what I'm doing. Everything I've accomplished is because of the help I received."

"Yes, and Woodward and Bernstein never would have cracked the Watergate scandal open without Deep Throat's help. Are you saying they aren't good?"

I frown at his ridiculous analogy. "It's not the same."

"It is the same. Austin saw your talent. Wilson saw it. Austin saw it…again. You have incredible instincts. You've always had them, so what are they telling you now?"

"Nothing," I say with a shrug and heavy sigh. "I don't know whether Isiah had information or was bluffing. He could have been Machiavelli, and the link to Conrad Williams is coincidental. We could be wrong about all of this."

"You're overthinking it."

"I know. I'm sorry."

"You're a woman. It's expected."

He gets another slap to the chest, this one a little harder. The coffee he's holding spills on his shirt, and he looks down at it before taking another sip.

"I need to start a fourth pile for 'clean but marinated.' What do your instincts say about Isiah?"

I start to apologize for the shirt and don't bother. "That he was telling the truth."

"So, go with that. Suspend disbelief and assume everything Isiah told you was true. Where do you go from there?"

I push my hair back. "I don't know. Isiah would have found a way to get us his information by now. It could have been intercepted by the FBI or NSA, but that means this cabal is bigger than we thought. We're getting into coup territory."

"At the risk of sounding paranoid, I think you have to assume that anyone could be involved if Conrad Williams is. Why don't you find out? There has to be a way to get this cabal's attention without getting yourself killed. Or me, since you live here now."

I smile at the revelation that gives me, and I press a key to wake my laptop out of sleep mode. This man is a genius.

"I guess this means that you have an idea."

I hear him but am focused and don't respond. He tries to get my attention, but I'm locked in a train of thought.

"I love you and want to have your baby," he whispers to get some reaction out of me.

I hear the words crystal clear but continue ignoring him. Josh laughs and retreats from the sofa to the bathroom to shower and dress for work. All I can do is smile as I complete a quick search, navigate to a site, and find exactly what I need to get the ball rolling.

"I love you, too," I whisper.

CHAPTER SEVENTEEN

SPECIAL AGENT VICTORIA LARSEN

FBI Field Office – 4th Street Northwest
Washington, D.C.

The Hoover Building ranks among the most prominent federal buildings in Washington, D.C. It's part office, part tourist attraction. Most people don't know that the FBI has several buildings in the district. Victoria is sitting outside her boss's office in the least popular of the three field offices located across the street from the Building Museum and near the Law Enforcement Memorial. Rigo is posted at the second worst.

"You can go in now, Agent Larsen."

This is a familiar feeling for Victoria. She lost track of how often she waited outside Lance Fuller's office in Boston. Sometimes, she didn't wait and barged right in. Fuller was political, and Victoria wanted to get results. They found themselves at odds on countless occasions. Now is another one of those times.

"Have a seat. I suppose you know why you're here," Special Agent in Charge Dyson Pritchard says from behind his desk.

"I actually don't."

The man is a caricature. His head looks oversized compared to the rest of his body, which could be generously described as puffy, and he sits like he's constipated on the toilet. Those are among the nicer descriptions that Victoria can conjure. He's also by the book and a Bureau cheerleader. If the FBI was accused of selling children to recreate ancient pagan rituals, he would explain to the world that it was a necessary sacrifice and that the FBI acted in the country's best interest.

"How are you feeling?"

"Fine."

"No adverse effects from what happened in Massachusetts?"

There is not an ounce of concern in his voice. He's fishing for information.

"No. Should there be?"

"You were blown into a brick wall and had a five-story chimney fall on you. I would expect a long recovery from something like that," Pritchard says in a voice that could best be described as clinical.

"Maybe I'm tougher than you think."

"Right. You look like crap, and your job performance is abysmal. I'm happy to be rid of you. I called you in to wish you luck in Nairobi."

"Thank you," Victoria says, matching his sterile tone. "Only I'm not going."

"Are you kidding me?" he asks, showing the first hint of emotion. "You should be honored to get such a prestigious posting. The per diem alone makes it worthwhile. Do you have any idea how many agents would kill for this assignment?"

"They don't need to kill for it. They can have mine."

Pritchard starts moving files around his desk. "It's a done deal, Agent Larsen. It's what you signed up for when you became an agent. Needs of the Bureau, and all."

"Needs of the Bureau," Victoria mumbles. "I'm sure there's a dire need, considering Africa is such a 'sought after' assignment."

The SAC bristles. "You'll be working with—"

"I said I'm not going." The declaration was as adamant as Victoria could get.

Pritchard leans back in his chair and stares at her. "Fuller was right about you. His reports state that you're a great investigator and skilled agent who believes you're above the rules. Look, you've been demoted and placed on probation. Kenya is the last chance to salvage the dumpster fire your career has become. Make the most of it."

"And if I don't?"

"The OPM is itching to put you out on the street. You were dumped on me, just like you're getting dumped in Kenya. Take the assignment or resign. Either way, you're off my task force."

"Gee, what will I do without all the excitement? How exactly did you come to run this task force? Screw the director's daughter? Grope his wife?"

This task force does nothing but scrub documents and report irregularities. It strikes Victoria as a place where agents are put out to pasture. Pritchard may eventually get a promotion because of the asses he kisses, but the other agents here are ready either for retirement or to start a new career doing something else. It makes sense that she was deposited here.

"Nice try, Larsen. I'm not going to initiate an insubordination case against you. The paperwork will take months to process, and I'll be stuck with you. Get on a plane or hand me your badge. Either way, I get to wave goodbye."

Pritchard opens a file and begins studying its contents. After a moment, he looks over his reading glasses as if he forgot that Victoria is still seated across from him. It's a childish thing to do, not that she expected anything resembling professionalism.

"You're dismissed."

Victoria rises and strides out of his office, slamming his door on the way out. It sounds like he's laughing on the other side. She turns into the corridor and leans up against a wall.

Despite her successes in Brockhampton with Ethan Harrington and New Hampshire with the SOF, she's a pariah. Mavericks cannot and will not be tolerated in the ranks of the FBI. An agent is expected to toe the line or be an example. With her notoriety in the Bureau, they are making it clear that nobody is untouchable.

That bothers her, but not as much as what she just realized. The system is powerful and changes the game's rules when it suits them. Right now, they're winning.

CHAPTER EIGHTEEN

DEPUTY AG CONRAD WILLIAMS

Il Diplomatico Infuriata Ristorante
Washington, D.C.

The Furious Diplomat, or just the Diplomat as it's colloquially known, is a popular destination for the who's who in Washington. Politicians, lobbyists, and celebrities frequently dine here, causing the tourists willing to cough up eighty dollars for a steak to have their heads on a swivel.

Conrad loves the food, but that's not the point of this visit. He knows who else is in town and won't pass up the opportunity to be spotted sitting at a table. He takes a position at the crowded bar as her bill is paid and ambushes her as she reaches the coat check.

"DeAnna, what brings you from the safety of Wolfwood Estate to the big, bad city?"

"You make it sound like I live in a bunker or something," DeAnna Van Herten says, handing over a stub to retrieve what is likely the fur of some poor dead animal.

"More like a bubble, I think."

"You're beginning to sound like my many detractors. How are you, Conrad?"

"Busy. Justice never sleeps," he says, edging her away from the crowd after she retrieves her coat. "I got a strange request this morning from *Front Burner*."

"Ah, my old nemesis. How are the vanquished faring these days?"

"Better than either of us thought," Conrad admits. "My office received a truckload of FOIA requests from them."

The Freedom of Information Act provides the right to request federal agency records. It's used extensively by the media and interest groups to petition for information unprotected from disclosure. There are nine exemptions for classified information and three to protect law enforcement sources, criminal investigations, and counterintelligence. Otherwise, people are entitled to almost everything else.

There is no federal form for submitting the request. Each agency has a different method and procedure for dealing with requests. *Front Burner* spammed them over multiple DOJ departments and agencies. Several got forwarded to him based on the sender. Tierra Campos is trying to make a point.

"Oh yeah, about what?"

"Isiah Burgess."

DeAnna stops putting her coat on. "Why would you have any information on that?"

"I don't. Since when has that ever stopped *Front Burner?*"

"They're fishing, Conrad. You have nothing to worry about."

She starts to brush past him, and he lightly grabs her arm. "I'm not worried about it. The election will be over before I need to respond. It's just an unnecessary irritation."

"Why are you telling me this?"

"Because you hold Tierra Campos and *Front Burner* in such high regard."

She scoffs and crosses her arms. "When Oliver Jahn calls her the 'Great Pretender,' it's more complimentary than she deserves. Campos is a know-nothing tart who stumbled into a pair of prestigious awards. She can't investigate – an important skill for an investigative reporter – and writes about as well as a five-year-old. She belongs at *Front Burner.* They are the biggest bunch of journalistic losers this country can manage to assemble."

Conrad enjoyed every second of that rant. He happens to agree, but that really isn't the point. He leans in to her.

"Why are you telling me and not the world?"

"We did that. Or weren't you paying attention?"

"I watched as you had them on the ropes and stopped punching thirty seconds before the bell rang. Now, *Front Burner* is not only still in the fight but growing stronger each day."

"A few subscribers hardly makes them a media powerhouse," the aging business heiress argues. "And we still throw jabs at them every now and then."

"DeAnna, you run a media empire. You have people checking out your competition with ruthless efficiency. We both know that *Front Burner's* subscriber rate is growing."

Her eyes narrow. Conrad has seen the look before. The media mogul resents people telling her how to run her business and isn't bashful about bringing out her claws when she feels like she's being lectured.

"Their entire business model is flawed. You can't crowdsource the news. They have no legitimacy, their quality will suffer, and their subscribers will cancel. *That's* what my research analysts are saying."

"I forgot that the mainstream media is the bastion of legitimacy," Conrad says in a heavily sarcastic tone. "One can only wonder why pubic faith in journalism is at historic lows."

"Something that we are working hard to restore," DeAnna argues.

"And will never accomplish while *Front Burner* peddles their disinformation and lies…or exclusively reports information, like something Isiah Burgess might have given them."

DeAnna was slow to pick it up but now understands the point of this conversation. Just because she inherited a media empire doesn't mean she's all that bright. VH Media excels at establishing narratives. They tell the legions of uninformed Americans what their opinions should be. She gets to choose what information makes it to their eyes and ears and what gets "memory-holed," to pull a term from Orwell's *1984.*

"We'll take a hard look at *Front Burner* and take Tierra Campos down a few notches. Good enough?"

"Let's hope so. Thank you, DeAnna. Enjoy your evening."

She coldly turns and meets her party at the door before exiting. Conrad needs another drink. Having Oliver Jahn and her media assets take shots at them won't be enough. He needs to bring in the heavy artillery to handle *Front Burner*. It's time for him to turn up the heat.

CHAPTER NINETEEN

BRIAN COOPER

The Chadwick at Rittenhouse Square
Philadelphia, Pennsylvania

Long days grow longer the closer the election looms, and today was no exception. The doorman does his job, and Brian enters the hotel lobby, preoccupied with the thought of heading to his room and passing out. Taking off his clothes and brushing his teeth are optional at this point. When he sees Arran Duncan in the lobby before heading to the hotel lounge, he knows the day is about to get a little longer. Arran didn't come here to drink alone.

Brian edges up to the nearly empty bar and sits next to Arran. Nobody is within earshot except the bartender, who is about as disinterested in her job as a human being gets. He orders a scotch to match the one just poured for the senior producer at VH Media.

"I didn't expect to see you in Pennsylvania."

"This is where the action is. I came up to scout locations for remotes."

"And that led you in here?"

Arran turns slightly to Brian. "I'm holding up my end of our agreement."

That didn't need to be explained. A campaign manager's job isn't just about developing political strategies and managing resources. The most important part is accumulating information and analyzing important data points. That recipe for understanding trends is the key to victory in a close race.

Brian has sources all over the country. Reporters, opposition researchers, and pollsters are the tip of the iceberg. The best information comes from the higher levels, and Arran Duncan has proven useful several times. As a result, he gets adequately compensated for his services.

"What do you have?"

"DeAnna went to dinner in D.C. tonight."

"That's breaking news, I'm sure," Brian says with a scoff.

"It is, considering she rarely leaves Wolfwood, but that's not why I'm telling you."

"I would hope not."

"An email was sent to every executive, producer, and journalist in her empire the moment she returned."

Brian rubs his chin. That's a quick turnaround.

"I assume it wasn't about a company barbecue."

"Close enough. DeAnna instructed everyone to roast over a spit Tierra Campos, *Front Burner*, and anyone in the alt-media they are working with."

The alt-media is the chic term for any outlet not under the control of a business syndicate. It can be a traditional form, such as newspapers, magazines, radio, and television, but typically suggests newer online media outlets like websites, streaming, and podcasts. These alternatives usually offer a different perspective from what is presented in the mainstream media. Its roots can be traced to counter-cultural or underground media, which provided dissenting points of view and ideas to be shared outside the established media.

"You guys have been targeting Campos for a while now," Brian says, keenly aware that alt-media directly threatens DeAnna's stranglehold on information.

"That's been mostly Oliver over at TNT. Everyone just sorta followed his lead. This is different. This is a directive from the boss-lady herself."

"What more can you do to Campos?"

Arran shrugs. "I don't know. I work with a school of piranha. They'll nibble until they sink their teeth into something."

Brian sips his drink. That's bad news for Tierra. Journalists have become unscrupulous over the past decade. They parrot articles from other outlets without conducting any verification or doing due diligence. It's created an inability to separate lies from the truth, leaving Americans to believe whatever they want.

"Will everyone go along?"

He gets the dreaded look of disbelief from Arran. "You've met DeAnna, right?"

"Once or twice."

"Would you go against her?"

"With enough scotch and some chain mail armor, I would."

"Well, she isn't signing your paycheck. Everyone will be on board, except maybe Oliver Jahn."

Brian turns his head so fast that he almost sprains his neck. "I thought he would be leading the charge."

"Not this time," Arran says, taking a long pull of his drink and grimacing as it burns down his throat. "I spoke to one of the associate producers at TNT yesterday. Oliver isn't happy, and Mi Sun is taking a leave of absence."

"Ahn Mi Sun? As in his right-hand woman?"

"She's been with him since TNT was a podcast recorded in Oliver's basement. Apparently, they've had a falling out, and now she's taking a break."

"Falling out over what?"

"Nobody knows, although Oliver is at war with his EP. Rumor has it that he was assured he could control the show's content and direction."

Brian smirks. "Let me guess. That's not the case."

"Corporate is practically writing his monologue. If he plays ball, expect the 'Queen of Pretenders' rhetoric to reach new heights in the next day or two."

More bad news for Tierra. Oliver Jahn mustered so much resentment against her that she was attacked and badly beaten in broad daylight. It was those injuries that she showed off during the Republican National Convention. Oliver was humiliated, but he landed on his feet when DeAnna offered him an eye-popping contract to join her VH media empire.

"Who did DeAnna go to dinner with tonight?"

"How the hell should I know? She doesn't share her social calendar with me. What does it matter?"

"It doesn't. I'm just curious."

"I can try to find out," the VH producer offers.

"Nah, don't bother. It's not that important. Thank you, Arran."

"Thank me by upholding your end of our arrangement."

"You know I'm good for it."

Arran dumps the rest of his scotch into Cooper's glass. It's a little disgusting, but Cooper is tired and not about to waste good whiskey. He drains what's left, pulls out his phone, and composes a text:

411 for you. How soon can you make it to PA? LMK ASAP

CHAPTER TWENTY

TIERRA CAMPOS

Front Burner Washington Office
Washington, D.C.

I walk down the sidewalk, consumed by thoughts that my FOIA requests may have already rattled some cages. Brian Cooper has his fingers on the pulse of the media. It comes with his job as a campaign manager. His text didn't mention anything specific, but he thought it was critical enough to meet me in person tomorrow.

I enter *Front Burner's* empty main lobby like I have hundreds of times and make my way to the elevator. I stop at the turnstile to swipe my card, oblivious to my surroundings.

"A penny for your thoughts," the baritone voice says, causing me to nearly jump out of my skin.

I make a panicked turn to find Seth Chambers standing behind me in civilian clothing. My heart sinks back into my chest where it belongs. The Massachusetts State Police detective helped Victoria during the Brockhampton investigation and was instrumental in taking down the Sword of Freedom. He's the closest thing to an ally either of us has.

"You scared the bejesus out of me!"

"You should probably keep a little more situational awareness given your history, Tierra. You walked right past me without even noticing I was here."

He's right, although I won't admit it.

"I'm getting spoiled. Nobody has tried to kill me in a while. What brings you to Washington, Seth? Are you in town to see Vic?"

He looks around the lobby before settling his eyes back on me.

"I was due to drop in on her but needed to see you first. I'm on a mission from God," he says, doing his best, or worst, Elwood Blues impression. "Is there someplace we can talk privately?"

"Our building is more ghost town than office, so that won't be a problem. Follow me."

"Call Austin and have him meet us. He's going to want to hear this."

That arouses my curiosity, but I don't ask questions, and I make the call. Austin agrees to round up the team and meet us in the war room. Seth immediately heads to the whiteboard and begins studying it.

"You've been busy."

"Not busy enough. We're way behind."

"Maybe this will help."

Seth hands me a package wrapped in brown paper just as the team pours through the door. It looks like an old-school parcel package, right down to the string securing the flaps.

"What is this?"

"Your guess is as good as mine. This was hand-delivered to me by a man claiming to be a friend of Isiah Burgess. He said he owned the house Isiah met you in."

That gets everyone's attention.

"Hand-delivered?" Austin asks, staring at it.

"Those were his instructions. I don't know why he gave it to me."

"I do. Isiah knew that Victoria and I are friends. We were together for Brockhampton, and she was in the studio at Granite State when I interviewed Isiah, his father, and Andrew Li."

"So?"

"You're an outsider. They aren't watching you."

"You mean Conrad Williams?"

I nod.

"That's too small to be a bunch of files," Austin says, still fixated on the package. It could be folded paper, but it doesn't look flimsy enough."

"Open it and find out."

"Not yet. You need to leave, Seth," I say, causing the big detective to rock backward on his heels.

"That's rude."

"That's not my intention. We were afraid that whatever information Isiah possessed would be intercepted. You were entrusted with this because you're an outsider. The moment you showed up here, you popped onto their radar. You don't know much, and it's better if it stays that way. If you stay and watch me open this, you'll be more involved than you want."

Olivia, Tyler, Logan, and Austin all nod. Seth is a good man with a wife and a career up in Massachusetts. He has been a great help to us in the past. That's no reason to jeopardize his future.

"If they think I'm involved, does it matter if I know or not? They'll assume I know everything anyway. I can watch my own back."

I glance over at Austin, who nods.

"Enough with the suspense. Open it," Tyler prods.

I untie the string and carefully pull the wrapping off. I can feel the excitement in the room turn to dejection when they realize what I'm holding. It's a leather collector's edition copy of Machiavelli's *The Prince*.

"Is this for real?" Olivia asks.

"He's taunting us," Logan adds.

"Or he was the real Machiavelli all along," Tyler adds, even though we've ruled that out. There is no doubt in my mind that Andrew Li is Machiavelli.

I leaf through the pages and stop when I come across a piece of folded paper tucked into the middle of the book. I withdraw it and unfold it on the conference room table.

"What is it?" Austin asks.

"A note and a phone number."

Everyone gathers around me and reads over my shoulder.

Tierra,

You are a National Treasure that belongs in a sealed vault. All great thinkers have enemies, and sometimes exile in the dark is the only solution. For others, there is no Safe Haven. The key to their absolution rests in 1984.

May you find yours.

Isiah

"Did he channel Lizzie Schwarzer when he wrote this?" Tyler asks, leaning back away from the page.

I was the only outsider who spoke with Lizzie Schwarzer in the hospital. To check if I was listening, she gave me the key to a puzzle that was later revealed in a statement to the media. She said, "People only hear every eighth word after you've said two paragraphs' worth of them." That code allowed me to decipher her message. I was led to the location of her journals, which revealed the truth about the Brockhampton mass shooting and resulted in Ethan Harrington's demise.

I check the message. There is only one paragraph, and every eighth word is nonsense. Not that I expected Isiah Burgess to be quite that obvious. Everybody in America knows that story by now.

Austin studies the note. "Do you guys recognize the name of the hotel?"

We check the header on the stationery as he moves to the board and taps the location of the first attempt on Isiah's life.

"He wrote this from that room," Logan concludes.

"Or stole the pad from it for later," Olivia argues. "What about the number?"

"It could be a Chinese restaurant," Tyler quips. "For those late-night kung pao chicken cravings."

"That isn't an Illinois area code or a Chicago exchange."

"It's the U.S. Virgin Islands."

We look at each other and shrug as we take turns checking the board. That has no meaning to this investigation. Maybe Isiah visited there on vacation, or it has some other relevance to his life. It's worth digging into. Maybe.

"What do we do?" Tyler asks.

"Call it. Read it out to me," I say, pulling my cell phone.

"3-4-0…2-0-0…5-9-4-0."

I place the call on speaker and set the phone on the table. It rings once, and then nothing happens. Five seconds later, a series of tones sounds before the call disconnects.

"That was anti-climactic," Tyler moans.

"What the hell? Did the message get erased?" Olivia asks.

"Maybe he never got the chance to record anything," Logan says.

"Or it's a taunt meant to mess with us," Tyler offers.

"Could the tones mean something? Like Morse code?"

"They were too short for Morse code. It sounded like...noise."

"Either way, it's a dead end," I conclude.

A heavy silence blankets the room. If it is a taunt, it's a cruel one. A lot of effort was expended on a malicious joke. But there's no reason for that. Isiah was adamant that he wasn't Machiavelli. He was digging to uncover the truth before he was killed. There must be something to this. I just don't know what.

"I drove all the way down here for this? I feel like we just opened Al Capone's vault."

Thirty million viewers watched as Geraldo Rivera broadcast the opening of the mobster's walled-off room in the basement of Chicago's Lexington Hotel in 1986. The network hyped the event as potentially revealing riches, illegal Prohibition-era alcohol, or even a few dead bodies on live television. All they found were a few empty bottles and a lot of dirt. It was one of the most disappointing endings in television history.

"I'm sorry that it was a waste of time," I say, giving the man a hug. "Thank you for bringing it to us, Seth."

"No problem. Sorry it wasn't helpful."

Austin shakes Seth's hand and leans in to him. "Go see Victoria. She could use a friend right now."

Seth nods, and Tyler joins Olivia in walking him out of the war room. Logan writes the number down in a note app on his cell phone.

"I'll dig into the records and see what I can pull up on this number," he says before disappearing.

I stare at the small piece of stationery and the handwriting of a dead man.

"What's wrong?" Austin asks.

"Isiah thought that I liked puzzles because of what happened in Brockhampton. I can't help but think that there's more to this than a wild goose chase. I don't know if it's because there is or because I want it to be true."

"Put it on the board, and then go find out for sure," Austin commands.

I'm falling further behind. Nothing will stop the onward march of time, and there is precious little of it before Election Day. Maybe Dial Pirate can provide some assistance. The hacker can track stuff better than I can. I just hope he's willing to help. Whatever Machiavelli and Robespierre have planned, I feel powerless to stop it.

CHAPTER TWENTY-ONE
SPECIAL AGENT VICTORIA LARSEN

Arlington National Cemetery
Arlington, Virginia

It could be paranoia. It would be much easier for Victoria to pass it off as that as she checks to ensure that her phone is still off. In an interview with NBC's Brian Williams, Edward Snowden revealed that the NSA can turn a powered-down phone back on. It's not precisely true, but why take chances? That's where paranoia sets in. Why would they bother with hers?

It doesn't matter if they would or wouldn't. How many people have died wishing they had been a little more paranoid than they were? It's pointless to speculate, but it keeps her mind occupied as she switches from the Red to the Blue line at Union Station.

She rides it until reaching Arlington Metro Station. A five-minute walk along hedge-lined Memorial Drive brings her to the Women in Military Service for America Monument in Arlington National Cemetery. Seth Chambers is already waiting for her.

"We couldn't have met at one of the Smithsonian museums instead of outside? You realize that it's late October, right?"

"You live in New England, you big crybaby. You can handle chilly weather a few hundred miles south."

"I can, but I'm wondering why I have to," he says as Victoria hugs him. "I tried calling you. I wasn't sure you were coming."

"I'm sorry, I've been taking a few precautions. It's good to see you, Seth. What brings you to D.C.?"

He smiles. "You don't talk to Tierra much, do you? I figured she would have called you the moment I left *Front Burner*."

"We've been limiting our contact. Why did you need to see Tierra?"

"I had a package from Isiah Burgess. It was only a copy of *The Prince*, with a twist. You really need to talk to her."

"I will," Victoria says with a nod. "Thank you for bringing it."

"Like it or not, I'm involved in this."

"You shouldn't be, Seth. This is dangerous."

"So was not arresting you for murder and then taking down the SOF. We've been through a lot. I'm not about to quit on you now."

He's right. Seth took a massive risk by not hauling her in when she had an arrest warrant issued with her name on it. Then he was all too willing to help coordinate with Diego from the New Hampshire State Police to bring the SOF to justice.

"I appreciate that, but—"

"Where are you in your investigation?"

She relents. There is no talking Seth out of helping. "I have pieces, but none of them fit. Worse, nothing leads back to Andrew Li or Conrad Williams."

"Does that surprise you? They're smart and won't leave a trail that leads back to them."

"There's one lead they can't escape from – Ian Drucker. Of course, he has all but disappeared like some mirage in a damn desert."

Seth turns to admire the monument. The Women's Memorial honors military women of the past, present, and future. To his knowledge, it's the only major national memorial honoring the women who served in our nation's defense. That's a travesty. So many women have sacrificed for this nation. One of them is standing next to him.

"Has he? You know he's in Pennsylvania, and you suspect he was involved in the Allentown arson. I think you're right."

"How did you—"

"I saw the board in Front Burner's war room. That information came from you, didn't it?"

"It's speculation, not proof. Those are two different things," Victoria argues before turning to Seth. "It might not matter. The FBI is assigning me out of the country. Africa."

"They can do that?"

"When they want to. I'm either to report by the end of the month or resign."

"Just in time for the election," Seth grumbles.

"Hell of a coincidence, isn't it?"

"There's nothing coincidental about it, but you already know that. Resign. You could get a job at *Front Burner* as an investigative reporter."

Victoria shakes her head. "That doesn't help much, does it? Besides, they're broke. I'm better off leaving that world to Tierra."

"What are you going to do?"

"Hope for the best. It's all I can do."

Victoria gets unsteady and starts to wobble. Seth reaches out and grabs her arm to steady her. She opens and closes her eyes, trying to get them to focus before moving her hand to her temple.

"Are you okay?"

"Uh, yeah…I still feel the effects of that concussion every now and then."

"Are you medically fit to even go to Africa?"

"If I were any other agent…." He gives her a look. "No doctor's note is going to keep me off that plane. I don't think the Bureau cares as long as I don't stay anywhere near D.C."

"I still think you should get checked out. The doctors might find something."

She forces a smile. "I will."

"No, you won't," he says with a laugh. "The only reason you went to a hospital after a brick smokestack fell on you was that you were unconscious. You're stubborn that way."

He gives her a goodbye hug. "I need to stop in and see a friend of mine on the way back to Massachusetts. I'll talk to you soon."

"It was great seeing you again, Seth."

"You too, Victoria. Be safe."

CHAPTER TWENTY-TWO

IAN DRUCKER

"The Forge" Militia Compound
Liberty, Pennsylvania

Two Weeks Until the General Election

The order came in an hour ago, and he was pleasantly surprised. None of Ian's previous communications with Machiavelli and Robespierre hinted at this mission. Something unexpected must have happened to trigger such an aggressive response. It doesn't matter what. Christmas is coming early.

Ian immediately gets busy packing some equipment for the mission. This isn't combat. He doesn't need to worry about extra ammunition, rations, or full canteens. He needs to worry about stealth and escape. These tools will help with that should something go wrong.

The bunker is inconspicuous and looks unused among the lumber company's modern buildings. It passes as a storage area should any OSHA or state health inspector ever question why it's here.

Remy and Mike swing the steel door open and enter as Ian packs a flashlight and suppressed pistol into the black assault bag. About ten other militia members file in, led by Stag, who blocks the door.

"Where are you going, Ian?" Stag demands.

"Out." Ian slings the bag over his shoulder and walks up to the big man. "Out of my way, Tiny."

"Not until you tell us."

"I don't owe any of you an explanation."

"Then you don't leave."

Ian turns to Remy and Mike. Neither man jumps to his defense.

"I warned you that it would come to this," Remy says.

"You sold us out, didn't you? We got all those tanks, and now the feds have the evidence to take us down. Your job is done, so you're leaving. Are they on their way?"

"Not that I would tell you if that was true. Trust me, if the feds are on their way, it's because of me, not you."

"Maybe you struck a deal. This whole thing is entrapment."

"We shouldn't let him leave," one of the other militia members says.

"Yeah, let's tie him up."

"Or beat the truth out of him," a third man offers.

Ian can't stop himself from snickering. As the faces of the men grow angrier, his laughing becomes harder.

"What's so funny?" Mike asks.

"You should listen to yourselves. A militia pledging to uphold the Constitution and the American way of life is so willing to violate the rights it enumerates." He gets nothing but blank stares. "The Privileges and Immunities Clause? Have you guys even read the Constitution?"

Stag takes a threatening step forward. Remy stops him and turns to Ian. "You should tell us where you're going."

"Yeah, I can't do that."

"Why not?"

"Because those are my instructions."

Ian starts to move around Stag, who holds a hand up. "I'm afraid we must insist."

"Stag has a valid concern," Remy says, playing the role of peacemaker. "I don't think you're working for the feds, but that doesn't mean I trust you."

"I understand. It also changes nothing."

"Then you leave us no choice," Stag says as three men start to move around the sides of Ian.

This is a coup. Remy is losing control over his militia. These men are loyal to Stag for whatever reason. He's the one giving them orders, and that won't do. The last thing Ian has time to deal with is political infighting.

"I'm leaving to go kill somebody."

The men look at each other. "Who?"

"I'm not going to say, Mike. You don't need to know."

"Why are you killing someone?"

"Because it needs to be done. That's the difference between you guys and me."

"What the hell is that supposed to mean?" Stag asks.

"It means you guys are all talk."

"Careful, Ian," Remy warns.

"Why? Does that hit a little close to home? This group has been around since what…the nineties? What have you actually done to defend this nation? To preserve our democracy? Name one thing."

The militia members remain silent. He knew they would. There were a dozen groups in this state that Ian could have picked from. This one was the furthest off the radar because they *haven't* done anything. They're nothing more than toy soldiers, and that's an insult to the little green army men he played with as a child.

"That's what I thought. All you do is 'train.' Train for what? What mission requires over three decades to prepare for? Don't answer that because I'll tell you: this one."

The men all look at him. He has their attention, so it's time to make a move. These are the players in this militia. The rest of the minions will follow their lead.

"If you think Remy is a weak leader and Stag is the future, fine. Whatever. But you will miss the moment you've all been waiting for. I told you that this isn't an enemy you take head-on. You have to fight how they did in the American Revolution. You have to choose your fights and know how not to get annihilated."

"Who are you going to kill, Ian? A politician?" Remy asks.

"That would be stupid. The entire state would be crawling with federal agents. No, another target will cause the needed distraction without raising our profile."

"Distraction for what?" Stag demands. "We don't even know your plan. If there is one. All we've done is collect propane tanks. What are we going to do, have a barbecue?"

Ian shrugs. "Kinda."

"We've been patient, Ian," Mike pleads. "We've sheltered you from the FBI. We've trusted you this long. Now we need to know."

"You're right. You have given me your hospitality, and I've held out on you. The reason is that we're too far from the election to risk it. This isn't something that can be taken lightly. What we are about to do will shake this country to its foundation and set the stage to rebuild this Republic. All I ask is for a little more patience. I need to do this. When I return, I will tell you everything. Good enough?"

Ian scans the faces of the men in the bunkroom. Most seem to have accepted his explanation. Remy does the same thing and gets nods in return. The coup has been avoided, at least for now.

"You held a gun to my head," Stag says, realizing that he no longer has the support of the militiamen who followed him in here. "Don't think for a second that I've forgotten that."

"Oh, I haven't," Ian admits. "Don't forget why I had to."

The two men eye each other. Remy nods, as does Mike. Stag crosses his arms and shakes his head but doesn't stop Ian as he passes.

"How will we know that you succeeded?" Mike asks as Ian reaches the door.

"It will be the lead story on the news tomorrow morning. If you hear nothing, then shoot me when I get back. If I fail to kill the bitch, I'll consider it an act of mercy."

CHAPTER TWENTY-THREE

BRIAN COOPER

Reading Terminal Market
Philadelphia, Pennsylvania

Brian walks in and is bombarded with a thousand aromas and an invigorating atmosphere. The Reading Terminal Market first opened in 1893 and is heralded as one of the nation's oldest and largest. It reminds him of Quincy Market in Boston. Over one hundred merchants offer fresh produce, meats, books, crafts, and clothing.

And then there's the food. Brian isn't here to eat, although his grumbling stomach may have something to say about that. There is a wide selection of different cuisines, from soul food to Asian and Middle Eastern dishes to authentic Philly cheesesteaks.

He looks around and spots Tierra before he gets too distracted. The stalls are laid out in a grid pattern, so it's a matter of negotiating his way through the crowd to her side. She turns and is startled to see him standing next to her.

"I'm surprised you came," Brian says, taking in the sights around them.

"I'm surprised you found me in this crowd."

"You stand out more than you think you do," Brian says, lying. It was dumb luck, nothing more.

"That's depressing. I took pride in being invisible for most of my adult life."

He knows some of the story. Tierra was victimized by the events at Summerville High School in Arizona. She barricaded herself in a closet with several classmates while the gunman tried to force his way in. Police arrived just in time to save their lives. Under those circumstances, Brian would have spent a decade trying to be invisible.

"A Pulitzer and a Peabody on your mantel should have shattered that illusion. I'm hungry. Do you want to join me for a cheesesteak?"

"How many calories do you think I can afford to consume in a day?" she asks.

Tierra isn't in horrible shape. Brian is far soggier around the middle, but that's not about to stop him from chowing down.

"Have you ever had one?"

"Sure."

He grins. "Have you ever had one in Philadelphia?"

"I can't say that I have."

"Then you've never had a real one. Come on."

He leads the way to a stall and orders them plain cheesesteaks with whiz and a couple of drinks. He pays, and they move to the center court to find seats. Neither says a word until the first third of the hoagie is demolished.

"I didn't think you were a food purist. Pizza from Naples, wings from Buffalo...."

"Did you know the first plate of wings was served at the Anchor Bar in 1964?" Brian asks. "It was a family-owned joint. They coated the wings in their special sauce and served them with blue cheese and celery because that's what they had available."

"Of course you know that. Why did you invite me up here?" Tierra asks, looking around.

"There's no need to be paranoid, Tierra. A journalist sitting with a campaign manager isn't that uncommon, assuming anyone even recognizes me. Too many Americans can't name both candidates, let alone recognize their campaign managers."

She smirks. "You didn't answer my question."

He returns her grin. "You have cheese on your chin."

"Thanks," Tierra says, wiping it off with a napkin. "Why did you invite me up here, Brian?"

Her focus is one of the things he loves about her. Too many people don't have it. It's a good trait.

"I spoke to a media contact on Sunday. What did you do?"

"What are you talking about?" she asks, sipping her Coke.

"The FOIA requests."

"How did you know I submitted them?"

Brian cocks his head. "I was Alicia Standish's chief of staff. You don't think I developed extensive contacts in the Justice Department while she was trying to pass gun control legislation? What are you hunting for?"

Tierra shrugs. "I think someone is going to interfere with the election."

"That's true in every election cycle."

"Yes, but those were isolated incidents. I think this is an organized effort to throw the country into chaos," Tierra says, studying his face. "You don't look surprised."

"I spent a few days in a New Hampshire jail cell because the SOF decided to rig a primary. Nothing surprises me anymore. The FOIA requests were all targeted at the DOJ. Do you think someone there is involved?"

Tierra dabs the corners of her mouth and tosses the napkin on the sandwich wrapper. "No, but the DOJ runs the FBI. They are searching for Ian Drucker somewhere out West, but Victoria is convinced that he's in the state. There's a chance he could be getting protection from someone in the government."

"That's a hell of an accusation, Tierra. Do you have any proof?"

"Don't you think we would have published it if we did?" she snaps.

"Fair enough. How close are you?"

Tierra leans back in her chair. "Why are you asking, Brian?"

He sighs and rests his hands on the table with his interlaced fingers in front of his mouth. "Because of the reason I asked you up here. I have a source inside VH Media. Your old boss has it in for you."

Brian watched from afar as Tierra was yanked from her anchor duties on *Capitol Beat* and then drummed out of DeAnna Van Herten's company. It was a mistake to force such a prodigious talent out the door, and the error was exacerbated by Wilson's high-profile departure during his convention broadcast. It made for great television but was a net loss for VH Media.

"That's hardly news. DeAnna hired Oliver Jahn because he attacked *Front Burner* and me nightly."

"It's about to get worse."

It only takes Brian a minute to relay what he was told. It's disconcerting but isn't earth-shattering for a young woman who has already been through so much. It's just a harbinger of more fights yet to come.

"Why are you telling me this?"

"Because I want you to watch your back. The stakes are going up, and I think you rattled someone's cage. It will get worse by the end of the week if you are on to something. This race is about to get nasty."

"What do you mean?"

He looks around. "Bradford is going to lose if he doesn't get aggressive."

"The solid blue city swing you have him on. I have to admit, holding rallies in your opponent's voter strongholds is—"

"Ballsy?"

Tierra smiles. "I was going to say desperate."

"It's not as desperate as it sounds. How much do you know about Alicia Standish's past?"

"Probably more than I want to," Tierra moans.

"Did you know that she's a closet racist?" That earns Brian a skeptical look. "Yeah, I wouldn't have believed it either. Except she is one. She never co-sponsored a single piece of legislation that supported people of color."

"That sounds like the argument she makes against Bradford."

Brian slurps some soda up the straw. "Funny how that works, isn't it?"

"Why would Standish ignore one of her most dependable voting blocs?"

That is the question Brian needs the media to start asking. They will if he plays his hand right. The mainstream media favors Democrats over Republicans and has been known to bury inconvenient stories, but this targets an intersectional demographic that they won't readily ignore. The woke like to eat their own.

"Because two black men killed her parents."

Tierra looks unmoved. "I was shot at by a white boy in Summerville. Does that make me a racist?"

"I hope not. Then again, did you write a letter to his family blasting an entire race as uneducated thugs?"

"You have a letter Standish wrote?"

"A copy of it."

"What did it say?" Brian only smirks, happy to let her have an appetizer but not the entrée. "You've been holding the letter as a trump card in this race. I get it. If Alicia had just lost her parents, then she would have been emotional. That's what she'll say."

Brian nods. That's precisely what her argument will be. The counter to that is most people are more honest when under severe emotional stress. They lose the ability to lie and they betray their true feelings. That's what Bradford is set to argue.

"No doubt. But couple that with the senator's legislative record, and you have a trend. It doesn't matter if it's true. Suddenly she's a racist who tries to cover her misdeeds by hiring a black campaign manager. Perception is everything, Tierra."

"And if minorities start to doubt Standish, they stay home. Are you telling me this because you expect me to write a hit piece on Standish on your behalf?"

"I know you won't, even though *Front Burner* could use the exposure. I just wanted to give you the information I have and wish you luck tracking down whatever is going on. I staked my political career on winning this election. I would hate to lose it because someone is rigging the game."

"I'll do the best I can," she says as Brian stands and collects their two trays to bring them to the trash and recycle bin.

"This has been fun. We should do it more often."

"It was good seeing you, Brian. Good luck on the campaign trail."

CHAPTER TWENTY-FOUR

SPECIAL AGENT VICTORIA LARSEN

Independence Square
Philadelphia, Pennsylvania

The greeting is what Victoria imagines most old friends would have after not seeing each other for a while. It hasn't been that long, but Tierra is as close to a female friend as she has ever had. She wishes this were more about catching up on dating adventures than the business of stopping a dangerous plot.

They walk toward Independence Hall, passing the statue of the father of the U.S. Navy. Commodore John Barry. The plaza is filled with people, even in these cool late-October temperatures. Everybody is going about their lives, oblivious to the dangers that await them in just a couple of short weeks.

"Vic, I appreciate the girls' day out, but why are we here?"

"Remember when we started working on the Ethan Harrington case in Boston?"

Tierra nods. "Yeah, it simultaneously feels like a lifetime ago and yesterday."

"I was at the kitchen counter in your hotel room, and we agreed to trust each other."

"I remember."

"I need you to trust me now."

"I do," Tierra confirms. "What's this about?"

Victoria tells her about the transfer. She wasn't sure where to start this conversation. Her friend needed to know that the cabal had made their next move.

"It sounds like Robespierre is pulling some strings at the Bureau. Do you think the FBI director is involved in this?"

"I don't know. Krekstein is friendly with Conrad Williams, and it may be nothing more than that."

"Or he could be just as involved."

"Yeah, he could."

Victoria stops and presses her fingers against her temples.

"Are you okay?" Tierra asks, placing a hand on her shoulder.

"Yeah, I've just been getting dizzy lately. It's nothing."

"Have you had it checked?"

Victoria needs friends and allies, not another mother. She isn't sure who is worse, Seth or Tierra. They make a headache and some dizzy spells sound like she's dying.

"I'm fine, Tierra. There's another reason they want me out of here."

"Why?" she asks as the two women continue walking.

"Because of what happened in Allentown. Austin told me."

Victoria smiles. Of course he did.

"The three men found there were killed with high-caliber, high-velocity weapons. Multiple hits on most of them. They were gunned down before that inferno was started."

Tierra purses her lips. "That's why you think it's Drucker."

"I don't know what Ian has been up to the past couple of months, but I'm betting that he recruited some minions and is doing Machiavelli's dirty work."

"Do you have any proof?"

"Proof. Does either of us know what that is anymore?"

They barely had any proof of Ethan Harrington's complicity in the massacre until Tierra located Lizzie Schwarzer's journals. They had only gut instinct to go on when she incorrectly fingered Isiah Burgess as Machiavelli, although it was a safe bet at the time. Their relationship has been defined by the never-ending search for evidence that seems to become more and more elusive to uncover.

"Fair point. I can't believe Drucker's escaped capture this long."

"The Bureau is looking for him out west in the Rockies. Mysterious eyewitness accounts and grainy video footage are all the justifications they need to search for him in the wrong place. It's not the agents' fault. Conrad Williams is running a sophisticated effort."

"So, what are you going to do?" Tierra asks as Victoria grabs her head again. "Maybe you should sit down."

"Uh, yeah, that may be a good idea." They start walking in the direction of a bench. "What did the note Seth give you say?"

"Nothing good. Tyler said that Isiah was channeling Lizzie Schwarzer."

Victoria lets out a laugh. "That bad?"

"Worse. I had the key to unlock that puzzle. This one…not so much. I'm going to keep digging. I submitted a slew of FOIA requests to the Department of Justice."

"You did what? Are you crazy?"

"The election is in two weeks, Vic. I have to do something."

"Tierra! I don't think you realize how dangerous this is!"

"Calm down!"

"No, I won't! I think—"

Victoria's legs give way, and she collapses straight to the ground. Tierra rolls her onto her back, and Victoria finds herself staring straight up at the sky. Everything gets fuzzy.

"Vic! Someone call 9-1-1!"

Bystanders gather around her. Half of them look like they're on their cell phones. A policeman fights through the crowd and barks into his radio. Victoria feels consciousness slipping away when the wet splash of a tear hits her forehead. She can see the anguished look on Tierra's face as she cradles her head. Best friend. It feels good to have at least one.

CHAPTER TWENTY-FIVE

DEPUTY AG CONRAD WILLIAMS

The Courses at Andrews South
Andrews Air Force Base, Maryland

A stone's throw from the nation's capital, the fifty-four holes of the Courses at Andrews Air Force Base is the grandfather of military golf facilities. The links on the three courses are frequented by everyone from U.S. Presidents on down. Mere mortals need not apply, as the complex is managed and maintained in a relaxed "country club" atmosphere only for government bureaucrats and military personnel.

The golf courses are normally open for play seven days a week, which is convenient. They offer patrons two eighteen-hole, par seventy-two championship golf courses known as East and South and a nine-hole course known as "West." All except South have shut down, so it's on one of those solitary fairways that Conrad and Vice-Admiral Davis Mullin find themselves pulling up to a green.

"This is close to being tundra golf," the admiral complains.

"Quit your whining. It's not that cold."

"The ground is."

Conrad shrugs. "It means there are fewer divots to repair."

"You're desperate to get in one more round before winter, aren't you?"

"The election is right around the corner. I'm going to have my hands full at the DOJ."

Conrad searches through his golf bag for his putter. Mullin does the same, and they walk onto the green.

"The pundits are saying the race will come down to PA."

"Since when does a career sailor believe anything reported in the media?"

Mullin scoffs. "Since I gave up driving ships to drive golf balls. Sometimes their intelligence is more actionable than ours."

"That's terrifying coming from a man whose organization can read the Kremlin's e-mail."

"We can read everyone's e-mail, Conrad, including yours."

"That's reassuring," he says before putting for bogey.

The National Security Agency leads the government's efforts in signals intelligence and cybersecurity. They are the vanguard of the digital communications battlefront and help the United States gain a decisive advantage against its adversaries.

Facebook, Google, Apple, and other leading online services have publicly admitted to sharing customer data, emails, messages, and documents with the NSA under the obligations outlined in the PRISM program. As a result, the NSA is decried by many for its ability to hack devices and exploit computer code vulnerabilities in the name of national security. Outside of the conspiracy theorists and privacy activists, most Americans have no clue that the government can learn about every aspect of their lives through their digital footprint, including their location at any given time.

The admiral is about to attempt a long putt for par when Conrad's phone rings. He excuses himself and walks back to the cart.

"Yeah?"

"I have news about Larsen."

"Is she alive?"

"Yes," the man says, causing Conrad to grimace. "She was admitted to the Philadelphia Hospital for Neuroscience and diagnosed with brain aneurysms. That's not uncommon after experiencing explosive overpressure. Larsen was lucky to survive that blast in the first place."

Conrad presses his lips together, wishing the chimney collapse had finished her. His life would be easier if it had.

"So, it's legit?"

"I think so. It's odd that she was transported straight there, but the EMTs who responded could have recognized the symptoms and made that call."

"Okay. Keep me informed. I want to know the second she's discharged."

"Problems?" the admiral asks after Conrad ends the call and walks to the golf cart.

"No. Routine business. Did you two-putt?"

"Missed par by six inches," he says, looking around. "Here's some more routine business you asked for."

Admiral Mullin digs into his golf bag and retrieves an envelope. Conrad accepts it with a nod and stashes it in his own.

"Any highlights?"

"You can read for yourself. *Front Burner* has decentralized their operation, but they're reachable in a pinch. Their web servers have been moved offshore, but we have a relationship with the hosting company."

"What about their communications?"

The admiral shakes his head. "Not without a warrant, and for that, you need just cause. My favors don't extend to breaking the law."

"Since when?"

Mullin scowls. "Did you join some right-wing militia before our tee time, Conrad? Because that isn't a question that the number two man at the DOJ should be asking."

"I have it on good authority that *Front Burner* is going to try to manipulate this election using foreign assistance. Campos has it in for Alicia Standish, and the Russians and Chinese are eager to help."

"That may be true. Convince a FISA judge of that, and I'll do whatever you need me to."

"It takes too long."

"You sound like Director Krekstein. FISA allows wiretaps to begin immediately in emergencies so long as the court is petitioned within three days. Of course, FISA judges are available at all hours, so I'm not sure why that would be necessary."

"The targets are journalists. Or at least pretending to be. No judge will rush to sign off on that."

"You're not getting an argument from me, Conrad. I have no interest in defending Campos or her agenda. She represents everything wrong with this country. I'm only telling you how it is. I'm not about to risk my career or my agency's reputation by failing to follow procedure."

"I'm not asking you to. I'll get the FISA judge's order. Consider this a warning order."

"Duly noted. Now, can we finish this game before frostbite sets in?"

The two men load into the cart to head to the next tee. Conrad's thoughts aren't on finishing their game. They're on the contents of that envelope and how he can use it to destroy *Front Burner* and Tierra Campos once and for all.

CHAPTER TWENTY-SIX

TIERRA CAMPOS

Philadelphia Hospital for Neuroscience
Philadelphia, Pennsylvania

Waiting rooms are depressing. The best hospitals try to make them comfortable, but no amount of décor, uplifting music, or pleasant aromas can overcome the worry of concerned family and friends. I'm in my own little world, so anguished that my vibrating cell phone barely registers. When I finally feel it, I check the caller ID and accept the call.

"Hey, Austin."

"Where are you?" he asks, his voice laced with worry.

"Still at the hospital. Victoria is undergoing another evaluation. Nobody is telling me anything."

"It might not be that bad," he says, unsuccessfully trying to be the optimist.

"She collapsed right beside me and was brought straight to this neuroscience hospital. This is very serious."

"We can only hope and pray for the best. Give me a call as soon as you know something. Please give Victoria my…. Tell her I was asking about her."

I smile, knowing what he was about to say. "I will. What are you doing? What's that obnoxious noise in the background?"

"Believe it or not, I'm watching Oliver Jahn again."

My blood pressure edges up. The doctors may need to admit *me*.

"Mhmm. Why?"

"Don't be like that. The show is so horrible that I made popcorn during the first commercial break. The graphics are all wrong, and Oliver's all over the place. A friend called me after the first two minutes and told me to turn it on. It's like watching a train wreck."

"Couldn't happen to a nicer guy," I say as a man in a white lab coat appears and walks toward me. "The doctor's here. I have to run."

"Tierra Campos?" he asks as I end the call. "Victoria would like to see you."

"Is she okay?"

His face remains completely passive. "I'll let her explain."

I'm about to pepper the doctor with questions when he abruptly turns and strides out. I hurry to follow him to her room. He isn't the talkative type. Typical.

"Victoria? Your guest has arrived. I'll give you some privacy."

He steps out. She doesn't look that bad inclined in her bed wearing a hospital gown. There is a heartbeat monitor on her finger, but no tubes or anything else. Not even an IV for fluids stuck in her arm.

"Vic, what's going on? You're not dying, are you?"

"Look for yourself."

She nods at some imagery sitting on the rolling tray next to her bed. The pictures mean nothing to me, but the paper with the diagnosis does.

"A brain aneurysm?"

"Five of them, to be exact. Two are ready to burst. If I hadn't gotten admitted, I'd be lucky to have lived another week. At least, that's what the CT scan says."

I'm floored. Victoria said that with the emotion of a lecturer reciting the tax code.

"Why are you being so nonchalant about this? You could die—"

"It's not my scan, Tierra," she says with a devilish grin. "This woman is in bad shape. I'm a little rough around the edges after the explosion, but otherwise perfectly healthy."

"What? I don't...you're faking this?"

"Surprise! I should have gone into acting."

My mouth hangs open. "I don't know whether to hug you or choke you! You scared me half to death!"

"I'm sorry for that, but it had to look authentic. I'm sure the FBI secured the footage of my collapse in the square within an hour. Your freaking out would compel even the most ardent skeptic. I'm touched, by the way. I mean that," Victoria says, reaching out and taking my hand.

"This is how you plan on getting out of the assignment," I say, coming to the only conclusion I can reach about why she would pull off this feint.

"And going on medical leave for a while longer. I can't investigate while the Bureau keeps me chained to a desk before shipping me off to Kenya to play with giraffes."

"How...I mean...how? The hospital lied for you?"

"No, but the doctor did. It turns out that he and Seth were best friends in high school."

I nod slowly. "That's why you wanted to meet in Philadelphia. It had to be his hospital. You're scary brilliant sometimes."

"The credit goes to Seth. After he left Washington, he came up here to set this up. The doctor agreed immediately. All he needed was for me to play ball, and then I needed you to make the drive. There is also another perk to being here. We can talk about our next steps without worrying about surveillance."

"What are you talking about?"

"They're watching me, Tierra. I'm going to bet they're watching you and everyone else at *Front Burner*."

"That's—"

"Insane? Yeah, I agree, but it's happening."

"Why would they be watching us?"

"Because they know Isiah had information on the cabal, and they figure he would have made arrangements to get it to you. I bet they know what color his lawyer's bowel movements are."

"That's…disgusting. The FBI would need a warrant for that kind of surveillence."

"That's true, but Conrad Williams knows the heads of all the three-letter agencies. They don't need to be shadowing you to keep you under surveillance. Assume everything you say or transmit electronically is being intercepted."

I have been through a lot. I've been doxed, assaulted, stalked, almost shot, berated on television, and publicly ridiculed. Covert surveillance by my own government is just another square on my life's bingo card.

"They're wasting their time. There is no Isiah information. The information Seth gave us is worthless. The note was nonsense."

"I'm willing to bet that it isn't. Maybe Isiah gave you the key to the lock, but not the lock itself."

"Or it was just a final taunt."

I sigh. My God, I'm beginning to hear Tyler's voice come out of my mouth. I can't let myself get that cynical.

"Like Lizzie Schwarzer's letter? A bunch of nonsense that had no meaning?"

I give Victoria a look of disapproval. "That was different."

"Was it? Look, my career is as good as over. If Conrad Williams gets his way, my life may as well be. I'm all in on this, just like you were once. I need to know if you're with me. I don't know if we'll succeed, but I know I can't do this alone."

"You're not alone. Austin is rebuilding *Front Burner* for this reason. We're the only ones with a sniff about what's going on. What good is it if not for something like this?"

Victoria gives a sharp nod. "Good. Let me review everything I know. Then we need a secure way to talk to each other."

"We could use pre-paid phones."

"No good. They can be tracked."

"Okay, let me reach out to someone I know. How can I reach you in the meantime?"

"Agent Imani Bangura. B-A-N-G-U-R-A. She works at the Philadelphia Field Office and can get a message to me in the DL."

"What are you going to do?" I ask, curious as to what her next move is as I retrieve my pen and jot the name down.

"I will be in the hospital for the next week, or at least that's what their records will indicate. I'm going to slip out and get to work. Something is about to happen in Pennsylvania, and Ian Drucker will be involved. I need to find him and make him talk. We need to know who else is in this cabal."

"Okay. What do you need me to do?"

"Keep applying pressure. The FOIAs were a really nice touch, by the way."

"You were yelling at me over them."

Victoria beams. "I thought it would be a believable moment to start this charade. You did open yourself up by sending them, but I need you to do more of that. We have two weeks to solve this puzzle. The only way to stop them is to force them into making a mistake."

I pull up a chair next to her bed. This is the best I have felt in a long time. I'm relieved that one of my closest friends isn't going to die, and encouraged at the prospect of making any progress. I just hope it isn't too late.

"All right. Let's get started. Tell me what you and Imani know."

CHAPTER TWENTY-SEVEN

IAN DRUCKER

In the Shadows
Philadelphia, Pennsylvania

It's dangerous being in the open and exposed like this. Ian is top dog on the FBI's most wanted list, and is skulking around a large city brimming with police. Cities have cameras everywhere, and despite his best efforts, Ian may not have seen all of them in this area.

Fortunately, he has a few things going for him. It's late at night, dark with streetlights providing shadows, and his target has no idea he's here. As tactical situations go, he's been in worse. The hardest part was getting into position.

He picked up a few things from Vassyl in the short time they worked together. The assassin may have been arrogant and not as skilled as he thought, but he used effective tradecraft that the FBI has no reason to teach. Ian watched and learned some of his techniques. It's the least Vassyl could do for planning to betray him. He who laughs last is likely the only one left alive in this business.

A man steps out after the building's doors open, pulling his coat closed against the bitter air. A cold front has moved through, sending the temperatures plummeting closer to something that feels like late November. That could be a problem. If his target calls a rideshare, this will get far more complicated.

Killing a person is easy. Making it look like an accident in this age of hyper-surveillance and cutting-edge forensics is far more challenging. He would just as soon put a bullet in her head. It's fast, clean, and almost ensures an easy getaway. Unfortunately, Machiavelli is into appearances, so an "accident" it is.

He wants this to be a message to Victoria Larsen. Her time is coming. That can't happen on this mission. There's too much risk, and he's come too far to blow it now. Ian outlived Marx and Vassyl and is sure to survive longer than Remy, Mike, and the lemmings that follow them. This is his time.

He spots her coming out of the building and looks around. It's late, and the coast is clear. It won't stay that way, so he must be fast. It's showtime.

Ian slips out of the comfortable anonymity of the shadows, walking lightly on his feet to avoid heavy footfalls. She's twenty feet away, heading toward the concrete stairs. He calculates the intercept and quickens his pace as the woman walks, oblivious to the danger. After the events in New Hampshire, one would think she'd know better.

Ten feet...five. She still doesn't feel Ian's presence. Now, it's too late.

He reaches her at the top of the stairs. After one final glance behind him, Ian shoves the woman hard in the back. She catapults forward, and her things fly in every direction. She slams into the concrete and tumbles down the stairs, coming to rest at the bottom. Ian hustles down the steps and rolls her onto her back. It would have been easier if the fall had done the job, but he's going to get his wish after all.

Ian squats next to the woman, carefully avoiding the blood from a nasty gash on her forehead. Her head is resting against the bottom step. He couldn't have planned that any better. She stares up at him, trying to make out his face.

"Don't think for a moment that this isn't satisfying."

He lifts her head, and with as much muscle as he can muster, slams it into the lip of the concrete stair. The crunching sound of her spine lets him know the job is done.

Ian looks left and right. Seeing nobody, he removes her shoe and scuffs it against the sidewalk at the top of the stairs. It would have been easier had there been ice or snow on the ground, but this will have to do. After replacing the footwear, Ian retreats to the shadows to make his way out of the area.

It's another tragic trip and fall accident in the City of Philadelphia. Only this one will lead the morning news broadcasts. It's not every day that such a high-profile figure meets her end.

CHAPTER TWENTY-EIGHT

BRIAN COOPER

The Chadwick at Rittenhouse Square
Philadelphia, Pennsylvania

The news broke overnight. The governor asked the senior campaign staff to assemble in his suite at six a.m. to discuss the campaign's response. The morning news is already on the television, and everyone watches in stunned silence.

"Metro police are treating the death as accidental and have indicated that there is no evidence of foul play. We'll continue to follow this story as it develops. To recap, Angela Mays, the campaign manager for Senator Alicia Standish, was found dead at the bottom of a concrete stairway after leaving a meeting with a prospective donor in Philadelphia."

Bradford mutes the television and sets the remote on the coffee table.

"You must be doing cartwheels, Brian," Joel says from his seat in one of the suite's high-back chairs.

"Why?"

He shrugs. "You didn't like her."

"That's true. I didn't. Not liking someone doesn't mean I want to see them dead. For example, I don't like *you*."

"Okay, that's enough," the governor interjects as the two men glare at each other. "How are we going to deal with this?"

"We are drafting a statement expressing your condolences," the communications director says.

"What's on today's schedule?"

"Nothing," Brian says.

"What do you mean?"

"I mean, all our scheduled campaign events are canceled. I've been waking people up since four this morning. It's already taken care of."

Bradford puts his hands on his hips. "Without consulting me?"

"We had to move quickly, and I'm not going to debate this with you, Governor."

"Then perhaps you should be the one running for president," Bradford says, his tone matching the temperature of his anger. "Last I checked, that's *my* decision to make."

"Yes, sir, except when it isn't. Here's what would have happened. You would have asked the question, and Joel would make a full-throated argument that you should take full advantage of this tragedy. He'd likely convince you because the allure of being the only candidate campaigning today would be irresistible."

"Because it's logical."

"Except it will make the governor look callous and uncaring. It will undo everything we're building, resulting in a two-point hit nationwide. That's the election. So, I removed the temptation."

"I want to gaze in your crystal ball sometime, Zoltar," Joel says, a smug look plastered on his face.

"The Zoltar machine didn't have a crystal ball in *Big*, you moron."

"You want me to sit on my hands?" Bradford interjects as the smile gets wiped off Joel's face.

"No. You're going to call Senator Standish and offer your personal condolences. Then you're going to quietly reach out to Angela's family expressing the same."

"We'll release the details on social media."

"That defeats the idea of doing it quietly," Brian snaps. "Outside of a message of admiration for Angela and her contributions to American politics, we go completely dark. Pull all ads for the next twenty-four hours in all markets. We have less than two weeks until the general election. This will be the last day off any of you has for four years, so enjoy it."

"That's insane!" Joel exclaims, rising from his chair. "Let me guess. You think this is one of Andrew Li's traps."

"No, this is a tragedy. If we are seen exploiting it, or seem the least bit insincere or uncaring, then Andrew won't hesitate to set one."

"I'm sure you're right, Brian," Joel argues. "Just let them milk this until the election."

"Mays's death alters our messaging," the communications director says. "We can't go after Standish after her black campaign manager dies. We need a new tactic."

"Like what?"

"We're going to talk about Angela Mays."

"Wh-what?" Joel asks with shock and disbelief on his face. "She's a liberal Democrat! Hell, she's a socialist."

"Exactly. We spend a lot of time burning down bridges. It's a useful political tactic, but we can't do that now. If we can't destroy Standish, we'll have to outrace her to the finish line."

"How do you plan on doing that?"

Brian smiles. He's been working on this since his phone woke him up four hours ago. He almost wishes he had come up with it a month ago.

"By causing her to trip as we enter the home stretch."

CHAPTER TWENTY-NINE

SPECIAL AGENT VICTORIA LARSEN

Cobbs Creek East Rowhouse
West Philadelphia, Pennsylvania

Victoria pulls her Phillies cap down to shield more of her face. She has a ponytail hanging out the back, just as she does when wearing FBI headgear. Nobody is eyeing her on the "El." SEPTA's Market-Frankford Line takes her to 56th Street in West Philadelphia. From there, she walks south, searching for the house and checking to ensure she isn't being tailed.

This part of the city is nothing but densely packed rowhouses. Most have numbers on the front, making the address easy enough to find. She climbs the stairs, knocks, and waits. A couple of men make catcalls from a porch across the street. Victoria pays them no attention.

"You made it," Imani says, opening the door and letting her in. "Any problem finding the place?"

"Piece of cake. Could we meet in a more conspicuous neighborhood?"

"I'm sorry, I sublet my hundred thousand acre Wyoming ranch. There is anonymity in numbers, Victoria. This neighborhood is more densely populated than ninety-seven percent of communities in the U.S. Nobody will rat you out to the FBI, and the police have better things to do."

"You live here?"

She shakes her head before heading to the refrigerator, pulling out two beers and popping the caps. "It was my grandfather's house."

"How many blue markers are in this area?"

Imani smiles, thrilled that Victoria remembered the story she told at the print shop when they first met. "West Philadelphia has about seventy-five of Philadelphia's nearly two hundred."

"Thanks," Victoria says after Imani hands her the cold brew. Both women sit on the sofa and take a long swig.

"I was surprised you contacted me. I thought you were hospitalized."

"So does the Bureau, and we're going to keep it that way. I faked it."

Imani laughs, impressed. "That's a boss move. Was your friend Tierra in on it?"

Victoria feels a pang of guilt. "No. It was more authentic that way. Is anybody living here?"

"Not at the moment. Most of the houses in this area are a mixture of owners and renters. There are a lot of vacant homes on this street – like seventy percent of them.

I swing by every couple of days to ensure there are no squatters. Nobody will think twice about either of us being here."

"Okay. What do you have?"

"Besides a headache? A solid lead. The Bureau has a mountain of information on the SOF and hasn't bothered sifting through it."

"Rigo's team was."

"I know. They did good work. I've spent weeks going through it and didn't find anything until I realized I was looking at it wrong. Your team was trying to follow the money. They weren't looking at where the money was coming from."

"Okay, you have my attention."

"Let's start from the obvious. The Hooksett safehouse was leased by a shell corporation."

"Yeah, it was a dead end."

She holds a finger up. "The check came from an account in Allied Republic Bank. Not really a red flag, except that name comes up a few times. Ian Drucker received several large deposits in his domestic bank account before starting at Quantico. It was dismissed as an inheritance according to his security clearance. Can you guess what bank had the accounts the funds came from?"

"Allied Republic."

"Could be coincidence, right? Then we get to Vassyl Strachenko and his Back Bay safehouse. It was a high-end online listing, and the owners only accepted electronic payments. In this case, it was a wire transfer from an account at…"

"Allied Republic Bank."

"Bingo. The account was closed immediately after you introduced Vassyl to the afterlife. The account owner is another shell corporation."

"Another dead end?"

"That's why everyone stopped looking. Makes sense. I would have too, except I was curious, so I called one of the account managers at the bank. Nice woman. Very helpful. Banks keep tidy records because of all the federal laws, but there wasn't any information on these companies. Then she said they were coded."

"Coded?"

"Apparently, the bank codes accounts with a designation when they're special. In this case, they were coded 'PC.' That stands for 'parent company.'"

"Which we don't know."

Imani leans back and smiles. "We do. Kratos Holding Corporation."

Victoria's jaw drops. "How did you find that out?"

"Because of the coding. It's the same as the bank's accounts for *their* parent company. Kratos owns Allied Republic Bank."

Victoria exhales and leans back into the couch. That's too many coincidences for a woman who isn't a big believer in them.

"What do we know about Kratos?"

Imani hands her a couple of sheets of paper containing the standard business information and disclosure documents. A holding company doesn't sell goods or conduct any business operations. It exists to own assets. Any corporation where it has a fifty-one percent stake becomes a subsidiary. Johnson & Johnson is technically a holding company. The most famous is Berkshire Hathaway.

"It's an LLC in Delaware, not a public company, so information is limited. It does pay taxes and files its paperwork on time. They have about a dozen companies under their umbrella, but here's the mystery: I can't figure out who's backing them. They don't generate enough revenue to fund their corporate purchases."

"They have an investor," Victoria says.

"Bingo. I just haven't figured out who yet. Here's the best part. Kratos is headquartered right here in Philadelphia."

Victoria leans forward and steeples her hands. Imani made more progress in a few days than Rigo's team did in months. She was right about having a fresh perspective. It allowed her to take an avenue that nobody else explored.

"We should go visit them."

"Not yet," Victoria says.

"Why not? It's the last thing they would expect."

"That's true, but we would only startle them and won't get squat without a warrant. Whoever is running Kratos will know we're on the trail the moment we walk through the door. The CEO is likely only a stooge. We need to know who the man behind the curtain is. Did you bring a second laptop?"

Imani's face lights up. "I was hoping you would ask."

CHAPTER THIRTY

DEPUTY AG CONRAD WILLIAMS

Office of the Deputy Attorney General
Washington, D.C.

Conrad doesn't know if the FBI still maintains hardcopy personnel records or whether this was printed out for his benefit. Probably the latter, but it doesn't really matter. What's in this folder does. So far, he's happy about what he sees. Krekstein picked the right man for the job.

The FBI director and one of the Bureau's rising stars sit opposite Conrad's lacquered oak desk. The agent is tall and lean, with an athletic build, chiseled face, and square jaw that makes him look like he was plucked straight out of Central Casting. He also has the bright, capable eyes of a man who graduated from the school of "been there, done that."

"Impressive. Very impressive. But records don't tell the whole story, do they, Special Agent Murphy?"

"They rarely do, no."

"What's not in here?"

"That list is too long to discuss in an uncomfortable visitor's chair, sir," Agent Murphy says. "You've seen what I've done. If you want to know who I am, it's simple: someone who gets the job done."

"Ah. Superman."

"Hardly. The FBI isn't skiing. It's a team sport. I'm only as good as the people around me, and they deserve as much credit as I do for our successes."

Conrad nods. "You were in the same class at Quantico as Victoria Larsen?"

The FBI's world-class training facility in Quantico, Virginia, is where all recruits become future agents. They endure twenty intensive weeks of classroom, firearms, and defensive tactics training by experienced FBI instructors.

"Yes, sir, she was in my class."

"How well did you know her?"

Murphy's head bobs left and right on his shoulders. "Not that well."

"Why not? You were there with her for five months."

"With all due respect, sir, I knew her, just not well. That's how Quantico works. We started with fifty NATs in my class, and friendships were made early. By the time the dropout rate whittled that number down, we were a month in and already rivals."

"NATs? You guys and your acronyms."

"We speak the foreign language of acronyms at the Bureau," the director says. "It stands for 'new agent trainees.'"

"Larsen kept to her herself," Murphy continues. "The only guy she spent time with was Audie LeClair. They were close. I heard they had a falling out during the Brockhampton investigation."

"How would you compare yourself to her?"

The agent grins. "I beat her in the classroom."

Conrad looks down at the file. "And she beat you in Hogan's Alley."

Universal Studios has nothing on the federal government in the set building department. Hogan's Alley isn't just a fictional town with fake buildings. It has its own ZIP code and features amenities, including a bar, billiard hall, pharmacy, and the Bank of Hogan. If there was any complaint from a fictional townsperson, it would be that the movie *Manhattan Melodrama* starring Clark Gable and Myrna Loy has played in its theater for over thirty years.

Trainees are run through countless real-world exercises on these streets and in the buildings. There is no substitute for practical experience, and forcing decision-making in the heat of the moment is a useful skill to build. It worked for Victoria Larsen.

"I've learned a thing or two since then. Sir, what's this about?"

Conrad eyes the director, who offers a slight nod. "We're opening an investigation into Victoria Larsen and Tierra Campos."

"Investigation for what?" Agent Murphy asks.

"Election interference. Treason. Possibly murder."

The agent eyes his boss before turning back to the deputy AG. "You can't be serious."

The comment earns him a nasty look from the director. It's not something he shies away from. It takes more than a glare from the head of the FBI to faze him.

"Sir," he finishes.

"I wish I wasn't." Conrad produces a thick file and hands it to him. "That's the information we have so far. On top is a warrant for wiretaps and surveillance. This government needs to know if Tierra Campos and Victoria Larsen are colluding to keep Alicia Standish from becoming president of the United States."

Murphy opens the file and scans the court order before closing the folder and resting it on the edge of the desk.

"I have a hard time believing Larsen would do that."

"We all do, but that's where the facts take us. We know that Campos and Standish have a history. We also know that Larsen has a bad habit of being in the same neighborhood as trouble. She was at the South Hooksett raid on the SOF and in the thick of the Loughborough disaster. I don't believe in coincidences."

"Why me? You think because we were rivals at Quantico that somehow I hold a grudge against her?"

"No, nothing like that. The director hand-picked you because it will take our best to stop her. You and your team are it."

"And if I say no?"

Conrad warily eyes Krekstein. He expected the agent to jump at any opportunity given to him by his director and the deputy attorney general of the United States. This is a sensitive assignment. Krekstein said he follows orders without question, and Conrad is counting on that. The last thing he wants is the Victoria Larsen situation made worse by introducing her male clone into the mix.

"This isn't something you say no to, Special Agent Murphy," Director Krekstein warns. "This is your assignment."

"And if I find that neither Campos nor Larsen is involved in anything illegal?" Conrad smiles. "I'll sleep better at night. The election is twelve days from now. If nothing happens, then we can wrap this up quickly. If something does happen, we need you to be all over it."

"Okay. Who is the priority?"

"Larsen is laid up in a Philadelphia hospital," the director says. "She has an assignment waiting for her in Africa once she's medically cleared to resume her duties."

"Campos is a journalist," Conrad adds. "But she may be planning something in the background or operating in Larsen's stead. She hasn't written an article in days but spends all her time at *Front Burner*. I need to know why."

"She could be helping them rebuild."

"A possibility. Find out if that's the case."

Agent Murphy nods. "Okay. We'll get to work."

"Agent Murphy? You are to keep your assignment quiet. Only you and your team know about this. You report to me directly," Director Krekstein says.

Murphy nods before leaving the office. Conrad looks at his old friend.

"Keep your eye on him."

CHAPTER THIRTY-ONE

TIERRA CAMPOS

Front Burner Washington Office
Washington, D.C.

Coffee has become my best friend. I sit down with my latest mug of liquid nirvana and stare at the board. So many pieces. So few of them lead to anything. Something has to break our way, and soon. I just can't figure out how to help that along.

Logan swings the door to the war room open and collapses into a chair. He's been working as hard as the rest of us, wearing five different hats in our struggle to keep the lights on at *Front Burner*. He was hired as a researcher for Austin's investigative team. He's so much more than that now.

"Long day?"

"Aren't they all?" he moans. "We're digging on the Angela Mays story."

"Is everyone still calling it an accident?" I ask, harboring reservations about that. My experiences in New Hampshire have made me jaded.

"Her shoe was scuffed, there was no sign of a struggle, her injuries were consistent with hitting her head, video surveillance had her leaving the building alone, and she was carrying a bunch of stuff. It leads the police to conclude that it was a tragic slip and fall."

"Maybe it was," I say, not really believing that.

"It's possible. Nothing from Dial Pirate?"

"Radio silence," I say, checking my phone again. "It's been days, and he won't call anytime soon. He's probably still sleeping."

Logan checks his watch. "It's nearly three in the afternoon. Who isn't awake at this hour?"

Hackers don't keep normal working hours. I wonder if DP ever gets more than a couple of hours of sleep at a time. Work, rest, work, rest. Time has no meaning for him. At least, that's how I interpret what his schedule looks like.

The phone vibrates in my hand. The look on my face gives away the caller.

"Did we say his name too many times?" Logan asks.

"It's not Beetlejuice. It's from Master Splinter," I say, showing Logan the screen.

"I wouldn't have pegged Dial Pirate as a Teenage Mutant Ninja Turtles fan," Logan says as I answer.

"What can I do for you, Tierra del Fuego?"

I smile at the handle I used once to enlist the hacker's help. Dial Pirate has dropped the annoying voice disguise. There's a level of trust growing between us. That's good because I genuinely like him despite how our relationship started. Thanks to Ethan Harrington, he teamed up with some fellow hackers to dox me. Once I learned from Brian Cooper who they were, I enlisted their help in finding the SOF safehouse in New Hampshire. Only Dial Pirate has stayed in contact since.

"Is this call secure, DP?"

"Duh."

"Sorry, I almost forgot who I was talking to. I hope I'm not bothering you."

"I called you. I'm not into anything that can't wait. What's up?"

"I was hoping you could help us with something. We obtained some information that came with a phone number. When we call it, all we get is a series of tones, then nothing. It's not a normal 'call cannot be completed as dialed' or 'number no longer in service' thing. We don't know what to make of it."

"What's the number?" Dial Pirate asks, rustling what sounds like a potato chip bag.

"DP, you need to know that the information I'm trying to track down is sensitive. People high up in the government have killed to protect it. I'm asking for help, but it could put you at risk. I want you to know before you decide to help."

"I appreciate the warning, but it isn't necessary. I've spent my life staying one step ahead of the government. If someone tries to backtrace me, it will take them through three satellites and lead right to the door of a Hoboken, New Jersey bakery."

"Okay," I say before reading him the number.

The hacker places me on speaker as he dials and listens to the series of tones. I hear an amused purr and then a series of keystrokes. Then mouse clicks. Then more keystrokes.

"Anything interesting?"

"I'm running it through software. Hold on…okay, it's a recording played at ten times speed. This is what it sounds like normally."

I hear the beeps and the pauses between them clearly. Slowing it down made all the difference. I wish I had thought of that. Maybe this isn't a wild goose chase down the rabbit hole for the red herring, after all.

"Is that Morse code?"

"No. The tones are ones, and the pauses are zeroes. It's binary. 101-110-1-1-1-11-1000-1001-1…give me a couple of minutes. It's easier if I do the conversion for you."

He can take all the time he needs. Logan had started writing it down on the whiteboard and stopped. He has the same expression I do. It's the rare look of optimism in this office.

"It's a string of numbers coded in binary."

"Read them to me."

He complies as Logan jots it on the whiteboard. I read it back to ensure accuracy. My eyes wander over the numbers. I look for patterns, dates, or anything else that sticks out. Nothing does.

"Does that have any meaning?" Dial Pirate asks.

"It could be anything."

"Is it a safe combination?" Logan asks, leaning against the table while holding the dry-erase marker to his lips.

"Not for any safe or vault I've ever heard of," the hacker concludes.

"It could be an alarm code."

"That's one hell of a PIN to memorize. If it was, it wouldn't have a 'twelve' button. PIN pads are zero through nine."

I frown. He's right. "I'll figure it out. Thanks, DP."

"You're welcome, Tierra Del Fuego," he says before disconnecting the call.

I lean back and reread the jumble of seemingly meaningless numbers.

5-6-1-1-1-3-8-9-1-4-9-2-4-3-3-4-7-1-2-12-4-4-9-2-2-8-5-3-5-3

Logan takes a seat and does the same. Neither one of us speaks. The numbers can't be meaningless. Isiah would never go through the effort unless this is the greatest prank of all time. He knew someone had framed him and that his life was in jeopardy. No, these numbers are somehow the digital key that unlocks Isiah's cache of revealed secrets. I just have to find the lock.

CHAPTER THIRTY-TWO

BRIAN COOPER

The Chadwick at Rittenhouse Square
Philadelphia, Pennsylvania

Not actively attending rallies, meeting with campaign contributors, or greeting voters doesn't mean Brian has the day off. A campaign is a machine with a lot of moving parts. It requires oversight, maintenance, and quality assurance. Taking even a few moments, like to meet with Tierra Campos or sleep, means that much more work is waiting for him.

The good part of knowing people isn't just understanding their routines but having insights into their internal clocks. Are they morning people or night owls? Do they hit a wall at two o'clock or get hungry early? Everyone has an ebb and flow to their energy, and he knows hers. He times this call perfectly to coincide with one particular cycle.

"Senator Standish?" Brian asks after the call connects, but he can't hear anything other than light breathing.

"Brian Cooper," a male voice replies.

"You're definitely not Alicia Standish. Andrew?"

"You have some balls calling this number."

He must have guessed right. "And you have some stones answering her personal cell phone."

"The Senator is busy becoming the next president of the United States. This phone number isn't as personal as it once was."

"Gotcha. So, she tosses it to you when she isn't using it. Let me be the first to say that you're doing a marvelous job as her personal assistant."

"I'm her new campaign manager," he hears Andrew say, his tone changing. His teeth must have been clenched.

"I guess that makes sense. I've always said that someone would have to die for you to get that role."

"What are you trying to say?" Andrew asks, offended.

"Where were you between the hours of—"

"What do you want, Brian?"

"Let me talk to the Senator."

He expects protests or an outright refusal. Brian was sure it would take some convincing to hand the phone over and war-gamed several different approaches. Instead, the compliance was almost immediate. Curious.

"Brian."

"Senator Standish. I'm surprised Andrew handed you the phone."

"I instructed him to in case you were stupid enough to call," she says, causing the corner of Brian's mouth to curl up.

"I don't want to start an argument with you, Senator. I called to extend my deepest sympathies. I know you and Angela were close."

"Stow it, Brian! I know you don't give a damn about my pain over losing her any more than you cared about her life."

Brian checks his watch. Clockwork. She always gets cranky and belligerent in the late afternoon. He always tried to avoid appointments at this time when he served as her chief of staff. The most irrational decisions she ever made were right before the work day ended.

"That's not true."

"Yes, it is! You hated—"

"We disagreed. That's all."

"Well, at least she'll be useful to you in death," the senator says.

Brian counts to five in his head. "What's that supposed to mean?"

"Do you really need to ask after Bradford's spectacle this morning? Really? Pandering to blacks using the death of my campaign manager is awful, even for you."

"We aren't pandering to anyone. We pulled ads and canceled events as a sign of respect. The governor's public message was heartfelt and honest, not political. It was also all true."

"Right."

As expected, the tactic worked like a charm. The governor's warm statement, coupled with sincere comments to the cameras outside the hotel, struck a nerve with Alicia. She probably expected them to make political hay out of this.

"What did you want us to do? Spend the day on stages pointing out how your bankrupt policies will destroy this country? Pretend that nothing happened to Angela?"

"I see you're chugging the Republican Kool-Aid like a frat kid at a kegger."

"Yes, well, we don't have the luxury of calling everyone a racist while the media does the heavy lifting for you."

"Maybe if you had a single idea that benefited the nation instead of the top one percent, the media would."

"We both know better than that. And it's astounding that you think making Americans poorer through high tax rates and forcing them to rely on government handouts somehow *benefits* them. It benefits you. We all know the tricks Democrats use to get votes and stay in power."

"Same old Brian," the senator says with a sarcastic laugh. "There never was any point in arguing with you."

"I could say the same. You're still as clueless as you were when you threw in with Ethan Harrington and Ryan Baino."

Brian almost winces at his words. That was below the belt. It's true, but still a low blow. He tried talking her out of working with them countless times. It was another of her late-day decisions in action.

"As your candidate has reminded voters for months now," she says, sounding like she's struggling not to lose her temper.

"Voters deserve to know. I'm sure that's how you justify trying to implicate me in sabotaging your New Hampshire campaign."

"I never said that!"

"You implied it. Would you like a list of the speeches?"

"An implication…it's…it's not the same thing!"

She's flustered. Brian decides to wrap this up. "Well, Senator, this has been fun."

"Why did you really call me?" she demands.

Brian makes a show of sighing heavily. "Because I sincerely wanted to give my condolences. I'm not a monster."

"No. You're an enemy that needs to be vanquished."

"Only you can take a condolence call and turn it into hyper-partisan rhetoric. You need therapy, Senator."

"And you need to stop turning a tragedy into political gain!"

"As much as I would love to continue going in circles with you, I know you have to get busy lying to the commoners."

"Screw you, Brian!"

"You're not an unattractive woman, Alicia, but what would your husband think?"

There is no response. Brian checks to see that the call was disconnected. He expected to get hung up on after that.

Brian pockets the phone, almost feeling bad for Andrew. He's been there before. The senator is about to go on a legendary tirade and then demand him to do something stupid. That's how she operates, like clockwork. Brian checks his watch again. It's almost bad decision time, and he's counting on this one being a doozy.

CHAPTER THIRTY-THREE

IAN DRUCKER

"The Forge" Militia Compound
Liberty, Pennsylvania

Ian pulls the borrowed late model Chevy pickup into the access road and past the debarker and head saw in the semi-automated lumber mill before slamming on the brakes. He's not even going to get a chance to park. The company is usually busy conducting its legitimate business at this time. Not today. The men at the Forge are in militia mode. They surround the truck while Remy, Mike, and Stag wait for Ian to climb out.

"What's going on, fellas?"

"I thought you said we weren't killing politicians," Stag says, jamming a finger at Ian's face. He doesn't react.

"We aren't."

"What is Angela Mays?"

"A campaign manager. She isn't running for office."

"It's the same thing!"

"School wasn't your thing, was it, Stag?"

The big man is starting to move toward him when Remy jumps between them. Stag settles down, and the militia leader turns to Ian.

"Why didn't you tell us?"

"I explained that before I left. I also said you'd see it on the morning news, which you did. So, what's the problem?"

"You're going to attract attention," Mike says, standing beside Remy while keeping an eye on their loose cannon.

"Whose? Local police are calling it an accident. The FBI doesn't appear to be questioning that. What attention did I draw?"

"You could have," Remy says.

Ian crosses his arms. "You were all ready to kill Standish and Bradford a week ago. I don't think attention is what this is about."

"You don't run this militia."

"Neither do you, Stag," Ian says, causing him to get red-faced.

"Okay, everyone cool down," Remy says, again trying to de-escalate the tension. "Ian, if this had gone wrong, it would have been disastrous. We would've been caught off-guard with no means to defend ourselves."

Ian looks around. That's why all the militiamen are armed. They were expecting company that never came. He hates to disappoint them, but nobody is coming for them. At least, not yet.

"You're right. I should have told you to establish a watch in case I failed."

"Why didn't you?" Remy asks.

"Napoleon Hill."

"What?"

"Who, actually. Napoleon Hill wrote the book *Think and Grow Rich*! He said, 'Every person who wins in any undertaking must be willing to burn his ships and cut all sources of retreat.' I was focused on succeeding. Angela Mays's death needed to look like an accident. Murder would have jeopardized everything."

"Then why do it?"

"Like I said, it needed to be done."

"Any other surprises waiting for us?" Stag asks.

"For us, no. The government is sure going to get one."

"So you keep saying. I don't trust you," Stag says, puffing his chest out.

"You don't trust me because you're a coward who hides behind brave words and has incontinence at the thought of taking any action."

That was the last straw. Stag pulls his gun and points it at Ian's forehead.

"Am I a coward now?"

"Yes. A real man doesn't hide behind a firearm when his opponent is unarmed."

Stag clenches his jaw. Ian moves forward until the barrel is pressing against his forehead.

"Do it. I'm hunted by the FBI, and they'll never stop searching for me. My life is already forfeit. Is yours? I'm your best opportunity to strike back at our oppressive government. Are you willing to pass this up, Summer Soldier?"

Stag regrips his weapon. He clenches his jaw as he moves his finger to the trigger. Ian stares him dead in the eye. A revolver is pressed against Stag's temple, and the hammer is cocked.

"If Ian dies, so do you."

"What the hell are you doing, Remy?"

"Defending Keystone's interests. I don't completely trust Ian either, but I'll give him the benefit of the doubt until he proves otherwise. You should do the same."

Mike pushes down Stag's weapon with his hand. The man relents.

"Good," Ian says, smiling. "Friends again?"

He scowls.

"Fun time is over. You've all done a great job gathering the needed supplies. Remy, can you assemble everyone when work is over? It's time to start making preparations, and you need to understand the plan's next phase. As we get closer to execution, I will tell you what we'll accomplish. I'm going to explain how the Keystone Militia will make it into the history books."

CHAPTER THIRTY-FOUR

DEPUTY AG CONRAD WILLIAMS

Philadelphia City Hall
Philadelphia, Pennsylvania

Investigators are ready to present the query's results into Angela Mays's accident only fifty-five hours after the first 9-1-1 call came in. The governor wanted to make the announcement himself, with state and federal authorities flanking him.

Conrad finds his mind drifting as Governor Fox speaks. Americans have short attention spans but long emotional memories. The countless allegations of fraud and cheating in recent elections have scarred the nation's psyche. Then the New Hampshire Primary happened.

The result of the SOF's attempt to subvert the political process has people looking for scandals around every corner. That's the real danger for him, Machiavelli, Robespierre, and Rasputin. People looking for scandals tend to find them. Conrad's job is to steer people in the wrong direction. Once the election is over, there is nothing anyone can do to thwart their plan. They will own the president.

After the governor speaks, Bernard Mercado of the FBI Philadelphia Field Office provides more details about their findings. He lays out the case step-by-step, explaining events while carefully eliminating other possibilities based on the evidence. His words are compelling, though they won't be enough.

The director introduces Conrad, and he takes the podium. There is no glee in his voice. This isn't a day for smiles, or so he keeps telling himself.

"I would like to thank Governor Fox for his outstanding leadership in these difficult times. I also would like to credit the Federal Bureau of Investigation Philadelphia Field Office, Pennsylvania State Police, and Philadelphia Police Department for a fantastic job investigating this tragedy with speed and thoroughness.

"I have a serious conflict of interest here," Conrad says, causing the reporters to look at each other. "I knew Angela Mays. We weren't close friends, but she was a staple in political circles. I had the opportunity to meet her on numerous occasions.

"She was a brilliant political mind and an even better person. That's why Attorney General Lisa Ehler sent me here. I insisted that we determine the true nature of what happened beyond any doubt, reasonable or otherwise. I have reviewed all the evidence and am satisfied that investigators have cause to close the case.

"What happened was an accident. There's no evidence to indicate foul play, and I will admit that's difficult for me to hear. It was a senseless death. Part of me didn't want to believe this could be an accident. So much has happened, beginning early this year in New Hampshire. It had to be something more. But an accident is what this was.

"That may be hard for people to accept. Some won't. We've become jaded. In New Hampshire, erroneous conclusions led to procedural missteps and false arrests. All of that happened during a contentious primary. It's easy for us to believe this is much of the same. While the circumstances may feel familiar, they aren't. This was not an act of sabotage or murder for political advantage. It was a tragic end for a lovely woman who took a fall down some stairs and hit her head.

"Senator Alicia Standish's campaign has many competent people working on her behalf, but Angela is irreplaceable. We cannot honor her by conjuring up false stories about her demise. Conspiracy theorists will do just that, so I am asking the FBI to make public all evidence regarding this investigation. I do not want to see such a great woman become a focal point for conspiratorial minds looking to advance an agenda.

"Angela Mays deserves to rest in peace, and her family must be confident that her death was only a tragedy and not part of some nefarious ploy. They need the time and space to mourn her loss. So do I."

Conrad steps back. The governor returns to the podium to take questions, but he tunes them out. Ian Drucker may be far better at this than he ever thought. There wasn't a single piece of evidence left at the scene. That made this easier.

It may have been better for Conrad had he let him have another shot at Victoria Larsen. It's something to consider for later if things go wrong. The former SOF member has other missions to accomplish first, and they are all counting on his success.

CHAPTER THIRTY-FIVE

TIERRA CAMPOS

Front Burner Washington Office
Washington, D.C

We have no life. It's Friday night, and everyone in this room is either in their twenties or early thirties. We should be out in Adams Morgan or Georgetown, meeting with friends and enjoying ourselves. Instead, we are all in a conference room at a staff meeting. We're either the most dedicated people in this city or the dullest.

"My meeting with Tom Swim went well today," Tyler says.

"Are you serious?" Naomi asks. "I didn't think there was a chance of that."

"He likes the idea of expanding his audience by leveraging our platform. He's been a fan of *Front Burner* for a while and sees the media becoming increasingly hyperpartisan. He firmly believes there's a thirst for actual agenda-free news, and the first outlet that runs to the middle will win in the ratings."

"I believe that as well," Naomi says, beaming.

Swim hosts a podcast and livestream called "Let's Go Swimming," where they "dive" into current events. News is delivered in short videos, while substantive discussion is reserved for longer livestreams. He has an array of guests with him on the podcast, and both sides of an issue are typically represented. In a polarized world, he's doing what *Front Burner* is: targeting the moderate middle.

"I also had my first meeting with Radio Free America," Tyler continues. "They love the idea of partnering with us. Their growth has plateaued because of technical limitations, and they have been pigeonholed by the mainstream media as far-right."

"They're as moderate and balanced as the news gets these days. They may be more motivated by the reporting of factual news unswayed by agendas or narratives than we are," Olivia adds.

"I know that Jerome is enlisting contributors all over the place. Where are you, Austin?" Naomi asks.

"I think Alétheia is going to come on board. They don't want to rely on video publishers and social media platforms that constantly threaten to shadow ban them or shut them down entirely."

Alétheia is Greek for "true to fact." They explain at the beginning of their documentary videos that it is not spoken truth, but the truth of an idea or reality. They do undercover exposés to highlight corruption, ulterior motives, and conflicts of interest in government, business, and society.

"That could boost our subscriptions into the stratosphere. What's the timeline?"

"Our legal team is working that out with them," Austin says, eliciting snickers around the table.

"You mean our one lawyer?" Logan asks.

"Yeah, so don't stress her out by getting into any trouble that will get us sued. She has enough on her plate."

Everyone laughs except me. I'm barely paying attention.

"You don't look enthusiastic, Tierra. What's wrong?" Austin asks.

"Sorry, I'm just lost in thought."

"The Isiah mystery?" Naomi asks.

"Yes…well, no."

"If you need a sounding board, we all have…. Austin checks his watch. About ninety seconds of free time."

There are chuckles around the room. Even Olivia cracked a smile, but I didn't find it funny. I know that I'm in this alone. They don't need to rub it in.

"What if Angela Mays's death wasn't an accident?"

"Everybody says it is," Naomi argues. "Everybody."

"Well, then, it must be true because nobody *ever* lies."

"You're right, Tierra, but no conspiracy could be that extensive. We're talking local, state, and federal authorities, medical examiners, forensics experts…."

"No, I'm sure it looked like an accident. I'm asking, what if it wasn't?"

"To what end?" Olivia asks.

I lean forward and stare at my clasped hands resting on the table. "We all agree that Andrew Li is Machiavelli, yes?" Heads nod. "What if he needed to be in a higher position for whatever they are planning?"

"You mean like campaign manager?" Tyler asks.

"Angela and Alicia Standish were BFFs, so Andrew wouldn't ever replace her because of incompetence or lack of results," Olivia says, getting with the program.

"It would take her dying, and voila!" I exclaim, making a lame magic gesture with my hand. "She takes a tumble down concrete stairs when the closest icy sidewalk is in northern Canada."

"Sometimes coincidences happen," Logan argues.

"When was the last time we saw one of those?"

"You think it was Ian Drucker," Austin says.

All eyes turn to me. "It makes sense. Victoria thinks he was behind the Lehigh Valley Printers arson, and he's definitely behind the ballots found there. What if he's hiding out in Philadelphia? How hard would it have been?"

Austin rubs his chin. "I think you may be right, Tierra. I also think that there's no way to prove it."

"How do you know? We haven't looked."

"Are you volunteering?" Austin asks.

"She isn't," Naomi decrees. "We agreed that uncovering Isiah Burgess's information is the priority."

"Then assign someone," I fire at Naomi.

She spreads her arms out. "Who? We're all trying to keep *Front Burner* above water."

"Then hire someone."

"Same problem, Tierra."

I sigh loudly. It was pure theatrics, and the reason isn't lost on anyone.

"I understand your frustration," Naomi says. "I do. I wish we had an army to help you. This is a story worth chasing, and your argument makes sense. Unfortunately, we don't have the bodies or financial resources. We have to cede this round."

I slam my hand on the desk, causing everyone to jump. "The election is a week from Tuesday! We can't cede rounds!"

"We have to pick our battles."

"Then what's the point of any of this! Who cares about Mike Swim, or Alétheia, or RFA if we fail in the one thing we are here to do? Yeah, we'll rebuild *Front Burner*. Great. You can be the next DeAnna Van Herten if that's what you want. You'll be remembered as the one person who could have stopped a direct attack on our democracy and didn't."

Naomi purses her lips and glances at Austin. The others are in stunned silence. Slowly, everyone looks at her for the verbal beating she's bound to issue. Instead, she rises from her seat and leaves the room. Sensing that the meeting is over and it's Austin's turn for an intervention, everyone follows her. I bury my face in my hands, knowing what's coming my way.

Austin pulls up a chair and sits next to me without a word.

"I'm sorry," I whisper.

"I know. I'm not going to yell at you. Naomi didn't take it personally."

"How do you know?"

"Because she's an incredibly bright woman that knows what we're asking of you. You're trying to solve a thousand-piece jigsaw puzzle yourself in pitch darkness. I'm amazed at your progress. I couldn't have sleuthed out that binary code if I had three years to work on it."

"I didn't. Dial Pirate did."

"And who enlisted his help? Would any of us have been able to convince a hacker who doxed you to team up with us?"

I appreciate the pep talk. It reminds me of the old days and is a stark contrast to what happened in New Hampshire.

"We've come a long way," I mumble.

Austin nods. "It's been a long road."

"I'm going to fail, Austin."

"Are you giving up?"

I shake my head. "I'm sharing how I feel. Even if we find Isiah's information and it, by some miracle, contains anything useful, what can we do about it? Without hard evidence, it's speculation. Lisa Ehler has Williams practically running the FBI. Andrew

Li will become Standish's chief of staff. Rasputin could be the president himself, for all we know. How do we beat this?"

"I don't know."

"That's helpful," I moan.

"Would you like me to lie?"

"No, I guess not."

"We may get help from Alétheia if we can get them on board. Radio Free America will bring it to their subscribers if it's solid. Until then, just do the best you can. It's all anyone asks."

"And if my best isn't good enough?"

He smiles. "It's still better than most journalists can muster. Don't just think that. Know it. We do."

CHAPTER THIRTY-SIX

SPECIAL AGENT VICTORIA LARSEN

Cobbs Creek East Rowhouse
West Philadelphia, Pennsylvania

Coffee, sore fingers and back, a headache, and bloodshot eyes. Those are the trademarks of any FBI researcher. Only Victoria isn't one. She considers herself a woman of action who would trade a computer for a service weapon, her wits, and a healthy dose of adrenaline any day. This work is not for her, and she isn't good at it. Luckily for her, Imani has some skills.

"Kratos is an interesting mythological figure," Imani says, leaning back in her chair. "It's agreed that he's a Greek god of strength and power, but there are conflicting stories about almost everything else. There are competing versions of his parentage. In many myths, he's the son of the titans Pallas and Styx. That would make Kratos a relative of the Olympian gods."

"None of that is helpful," Victoria says, rubbing her eyes.

"I know. I'm running out of ideas for where to look. Kratos is a complete black hole."

"All right. What do we know about the CEO?"

"He's an absentee landlord. He doesn't do much for the company. Hell, his primary residence isn't even in Philly or its suburbs. It's in Martha's Vineyard."

"Maybe that's normal." Imani looks at her like she just stepped off a flying saucer. "I deal with men like the Devil Rancher. I'm not familiar with how things work in corporate America."

Imani smiles. "I had a case where I had to work with the CEO of a holding company. Their job is to manage the assets. Kratos owns all of the companies under its umbrella. Each has its own chief executive officer, but he should still be a busy man."

"So, we have a holding company that makes no money and a CEO that does nothing. This has to be about the parent company."

Imani makes a mouse click or two and a few keystrokes to call up her notes.

"Actyv Private Equity, spelled A-C-T-Y-V – I like that, by the way – formed twelve years ago and based out of some swanky Midtown Manhattan skyscraper. It has three principals, all founding members, and manages…damn, more than $750 million in assets."

"Is that stock?"

"Private equity is having an ownership stake in a company that does not have publicly traded shares on a stock exchange. These could be well-established companies whose owners retain control but need a cash infusion. It may also be a new company not valuable enough for a public offering. Sometimes, a private equity firm like Actyv will purchase all outstanding shares at a premium and remove a company from public exchanges, called de-listing."

"It sounds like they're a successful company."

"I'd say."

"So why have an underperforming nothing burger like Kratos on the books?"

Imani looks back at her screen. "I don't know. Private equity investors tend to be highly selective. They target companies with unrealized potential or distressed companies with valuable assets. Kratos has neither of those."

Victoria stands and stretches. "Diversification?"

Imani smiles. "You know what that is?"

"I have a retirement account."

"Maybe, but the private equity game usually requires hundreds of millions of dollars in liquidity. It doesn't make sense to have garbage like this. Even if it was an investment that didn't pay off, they would have cut their losses long ago."

"All right. Who's running the show at Actyv?"

Imani clicks over to more notes. "There are three principals, all founding members. Roman Muratova was a Russian media exec before coming to the States. He is still chummy with Russian oligarchs. They were big investors in the first two Actyv funds."

"That explains where some of the cash came from."

"Our second contestant is Xinming Qi. He is a former Chinese Communist Party member who fled to the States to keep his tech fortune. He was big into artificial intelligence research and advanced computer processing."

"That makes sense."

"You're going to love this last guy. Garrett Brewer."

"Wait. I know that name."

"You would. He is a registered foreign agent with the Justice Department who lobbied Congress for various Chinese, Russian, and Syrian foreign interests. Shady stuff. He was also a rival of, wait for it…Dylan Spencer."

Victoria sits back down. She doesn't believe in coincidences. Dylan Spencer committed suicide months before the New Hampshire primary. She had always thought that was suspicious, and her investigation led her to Marx and his Sword of Freedom thugs. Her interest in Spencer is a big reason she followed a path that led her to Imani's grandfather's old house.

"You have a look in your eye," Imani observes. "Before you go all 'shooter on the grassy knoll' on me, they might be involved. Or this could all be about the CEO."

"The absent one living large in Martha's Vineyard?"

"Or maybe someone in the office."

Victoria closes her eyes. She's right, it could be, but that feels too small. Anyone behind what's happening would have to be a heavy hitter, and neither the CEO nor manager at a crap holding company would have that kind of juice. It shouldn't be ruled out, though.

"It's time to pay them a visit."

"I thought it was a risk."

"It is, but we're running out of time and need to start shaking some trees. I have to do something first. And I need a big favor."

CHAPTER THIRTY-SEVEN

BRIAN COOPER

City of Brotherly Coffee Lovers Cafe
Philadelphia, Pennsylvania

Political operatives have a love-hate relationship with reports. They love them when stories help their cause and hate them the rest of the time. It's a historical distrust that dates back to the American Revolution. Today's hyperpartisan political world has done little to mend their relationship.

They use each other, plain and simple. It's the unspoken basis of every relationship. Reporters need articles with headlines that compel readers and viewers to click or watch segments. Politicos need help with messaging, smear campaigns, and occasionally, publishing disinformation.

Of all the reporters on the political campaign beat, Marvin Theiss is among the most legendary. He's been following candidates since Bill Clinton played the sax on the Arsenio Hall Show. He's to electoral politics as Wilson Newman is to political television. He has another thing in common with the old anchor: He despises Brian Cooper.

"Long time, Marv," Brian says, joining the AP reporter in the corner with a tall cup of freshly -brewed coffee.

"Not since Manchester. Weren't you locked up?" he asks with a smirk.

"Weren't you getting bad information from Andrew Li at the Jittery Jack?"

That has to hurt, but Marv smiles at the slight. "I liked that place. I only get to go every four years. How did you know I met Andrew there? He certainly didn't tell you."

"You know better, Marv. It's my job to know those things."

The reporter lets out a laugh. "You had someone tailing him during the primary."

"Interns are all so eager," Brian says with a smirk of his own.

"It wasn't bad info."

"You're right. It was an outright lie from the Standish campaign, and you ran it without vetting other sources."

It was a good play. Standish's campaign was teetering, and Andrew Li, then working for Governor Luther Burgess, leaked misinformation to Marvin that Angela and much of the senior staff were planning to quit the campaign and join the opposition. It's dirty politics, but you could fill volumes with the devious ploys candidates use to win races.

"Welcome to modern journalism. My editors insisted on running it."

"I'm glad to see you all maintain such lofty standards."

"The world has changed, Brian. Modern reporting is a race to be first, not right."

"That's sad."

"It's reality. A lie travels around the world before the truth gets to the airport. News at the speed of electrons beamed to personal computers that people carry around in their pockets. Don't blame me. Blame the Internet. Or Al Gore."

Leave it to Marvin to punctuate the point with the perfect example. Commentators on the right once accused Al Gore of claiming to have invented the Internet. The former vice president actually said he "took the initiative in creating the Internet," referring to legislative matters and making the accusation false. That didn't stop the spread. Derisive references to the quote continue to be proffered regularly.

"I've been in politics forever," Brian says. "I know that better than anyone."

"Is this a nostalgic visit?"

Brian offers a look of bizarre disbelief. "Do you think I pine to spend my day reminiscing with a reporter?"

"You tell me. I'm not chummy with Tierra Campos."

Brian can't hide his surprise. Marvin may be a bottom-feeding hack, but he's well-informed.

"I respect her."

The reporter shrugs. "Or you're hot for her."

"You have issues, Marv."

"Hey, it's lonely on the road. Nobody understands that better than I do."

The AP reporter leads a lifestyle best reserved for a bachelor who has a girl in every port. Unfortunately, the years haven't treated him well, and the wrinkles don't benefit the face only a mother could love. Brian assumes Marvin pays for his companionship, but he has never been bold enough to ask.

"Did you see Conrad Williams's press conference?"

Marv sips his coffee. "I was there."

"Then you were one of the lemmings. Is there an inquisitive reporter left in this country, or do you all just accept what's spoon-fed to you?"

"Okay, now you're insulting me."

"I'm disappointed it took this long."

Marv leans back and folds his arms. "What questions do you think I should have asked?"

"Where Ian Drucker is, for starters."

"You like turning everything into a conspiracy, don't you?"

"Not really. A conspiracy almost cost me my freedom."

Brian has a right to be bitter about that. The SOF did their level best to frame him for their activities, including the arsons of Luther Burgess's campaign offices. He had to deal with the embarrassment of the FBI cuffing him and escorting him out of Standish's campaign office in full view of the media. The jail wasn't fun, either.

"Is that why you're here? You want to prod me into questioning the official narrative on Angela Mays's accident?"

"No, you should want to do that naturally," Brian says, leaning forward. "I want you to ask hard questions about election security, starting with confirmation that blank Pennsylvania ballots were found at the print shop fire in Allentown. Then ask if the workers there died of smoke inhalation or the multiple high-caliber bullet holes found in their charred remains."

That gets Marv's attention. He studies Brian's face for any hint of deception and finds none. His eyes narrow.

"You're serious about this. Where did you get that information?"

"The FBI."

"They briefed the campaign?"

Brian chuckles. "Are you kidding? That would leak in less time than it takes to make microwave popcorn. You're not the only one with sources inside the Bureau."

"How many ballots?" Marv asks in a near whisper.

"Firefighters found dozens littered around the parking lot."

"That's nothing, Brian."

"Do the math, Marv. It was an industrial high-volume printer, not a Staples. Do you need an abacus to figure out how many there could have been?"

Marvin rubs his chin. "To what end?"

"You follow campaigns and read polls. How many mail-in ballots do you think it will take to rig the election here?"

The reporter exhales sharply. "That's a hell of an accusation."

"You're right. It is. Ask the FBI what they think."

Marvin lowers his eyes. It's what a salesman would call a buying signal. He's searching for objections but wants to run with this story. There's no question as to why. This would be clickbait gold. It would raise his profile, earn his company a mountain of money, and give him the chance to scoop his cutthroat peers.

"They're not going to tell me anything, and I can't run that story without corroboration."

"All evidence to the contrary. Take it to your editors and see what they say."

Brian raps his knuckles twice on the table, snatches his coffee, and stands.

"If you're lying to me, Cooper, I will eviscerate you."

"Ask them. When your sources start to lie, press them harder. When they clam up, you'll know that I'm not. Good seeing you, Marvin."

Brian walks out of the shop and onto the bustling Philadelphia sidewalk. That was almost too easy. Then again, modern journalism is more rumor mill than anything. Break the story first and confirm it later. If they need to retract, they will when nobody cares anymore. It's a lousy model for a healthy democracy, but it serves his purposes just fine.

CHAPTER THIRTY-EIGHT

IAN DRUCKER

"The Forge" Militia Compound
Liberty, Pennsylvania

The meeting room at the Forge was probably once an old cafeteria or lunch room for the mill workers. It has long since been converted into a shrine for the American Revolution. The walls are decorated with Gadsden, Betsy Ross, and Grand Union flags. There are portraits of the Founding Fathers and framed replicas of newspaper front pages screaming about the Maine being sunk in Havana's harbor, the outbreak of World War II, and the twin towers falling.

Ian has converted the hall into a production facility filled with free labor. Most militiamen eagerly perform their tasks, even if they don't know the reason behind them. That doesn't extend to Remy, Mike, or Stag, but they are currently going along with the program. Ian checks his watch. They're on schedule.

"We're almost done," Mike says, supervising the effort alongside Remy.

"Good. Did anyone lick an envelope?"

"No."

"You're sure? Because if they did, they are going to prison for a long time."

"How?" Remy asks, joining them at the back of the meeting room.

"The moment anyone scrapes their tongue over the glue, they leave skin cells. Skin cells have DNA. These ballots will end up with the feds and that's the second thing they check for after prints. The DNA will be matched quickly, especially for any militia who are former service members. Then they will get a home address and employment records, leading them straight to here. When they see this room, the Forge will be overrun by three-letter agencies."

Remy looks around. "Then why do this at all?"

"Because it needs to be—"

"Stop it, Ian!" Remy snaps. "Tell me why. We all feel dirty marking down Alicia Standish's name on these ballots. She is the antithesis of everything we stand for."

"Bradford isn't much better," Mike adds, "but at least he isn't trying to disarm us. Why not fill the ballots out for him?"

Ian wondered when his "because it needs to be done" excuse would finally fail. It took them long enough to really challenge him on it. They are close enough to executing their plan now that he can share some details. Or versions of them.

"Because you want to save the Republic, not choose the lesser of two evils. This isn't about putting our thumb on the scale to elect one party over another. It's about bringing change. The system is rigged. Every four years, we elect charlatans masquerading as representatives from the parties that rigged it in the first place. The only way to fix America is to destroy the two-party system and start over. This will help with that."

"I don't see how," Stag says, joining the three men after spotting them from his table. "It looks to me like you're working for Standish."

Ian scoffs. "I'm not. Trust me."

"We don't trust you, Ian. We've made that clear," Stag says.

"Because you don't see the big picture, not surprisingly," Ian says. Stag balls his hands into fists. "Ballot scanners."

"What?"

"Were you not listening to Governor Fox's press conference the other day? He was talking about the countermeasures they employed to prevent election tampering. One of the technologies is a ballot scanner that recognizes phony or mismarked ballots."

The three men look at each other. Ian grades his presentation of the lie as a solid B+. He rehearsed this conversation in his head for days and reached the point where he believed it was true. It sounds more authentic that way.

"So, we're gonna get caught?" Remy asks.

"Not unless you lick envelopes or handle envelopes without gloves."

"What good is them finding the ballots?" Stag asks.

Ian fights hard not to sigh. "Once they realize the system is compromised, it will create chaos. Everyone will begin questioning the mail-in system's integrity. In a close race, like what we have here, the results will be in doubt. The winner's legitimacy will be questioned."

"That's not bringing about change," Mike argues.

"No, but it creates the circumstances for it. We need the people with us. It's why Paine wrote *Common Sense*, Lincoln penned the Emancipation Proclamation, and the United States let the Lusitania get torpedoed so we could enter World War I. The will of the people is a powerful thing. Imagine our strength when we enlist every patriotic American in our cause."

"Half the country won't join," Stag argues, forever playing the pessimist.

"The other half will; those are the true patriots we need."

"Okay, we'll go along with this," Remy says, getting a nod from Mike and a scowl from Stag. "Where are we taking these? The post office?"

"Ballot drop boxes across the state. We will use two vehicles to transport them to a central point and then distribute the ballots in personal vehicles from there. We need a wide dispersion so they can't be traced back here."

Remy nods and turns to Mike. "Instruct the men to gas up their vehicles."

CHAPTER THIRTY-NINE

DEPUTY AG CONRAD WILLIAMS

Office of the Deputy Attorney General
Washington, D.C.

The investigation isn't strictly legal. It's also not unprecedented. The Federal Bureau of Investigation searched troves of international communications for information on American "racially motivated violent extremists" without a court order. A widely disseminated, declassified report from several years ago revealed they demanded access to massive amounts of electronic communications harvested by the National Security Agency.

Of course, those all involved foreign cases, thus falling within the NSA's mandate. The Campos matter is strictly a domestic investigation. Special Agent Murphy will never learn that this is tantamount to violating countless constitutional rights. Conrad only needs to keep the lid on this until after the election. Then it won't matter.

"Sir, I know you didn't want to be disturbed," his admin says over the intercom, "but I have a call from Director Krekstein. He says it's urgent."

"Okay. Put him through." Conrad punches a button and places the call on speaker. "What's up, Mike?"

"We have COMINT on Victoria Larsen. Agent Murphy found something interesting."

COMINT, or communications intelligence, is acquired through the intercept and analysis of wireless communications such as voice and data. Much of that is done through the FBI's Data Intercept Technology Unit, or DITU. They are responsible for intercepting terrorists and foreign intelligence target telephone calls and e-mail messages inside the United States. Now they have another assignment. That means Special Agent Murphy and his team are working quickly. Krekstein chose well.

"What's he got?"

"Larsen asked Campos about a private equity firm named Actyv and a subsidiary named Kratos Holdings. Ever hear of them?"

Conrad stops reading as the blood drains out of his face. "I can't say that I have. What specifically was she looking for?"

"Mostly background intel on the CEO of Kratos and the founding partners of Actyv. Murphy hasn't determined why she's interested in them but is digging into it."

Conrad curses under his breath. "I'll look into it. Anything else?"

"We cast the net over *Front Burner*. We have their comms via CellSpoof. They won't be able to order a pizza without us knowing the toppings."

CellSpoof is a mobile device that eavesdrops on mobile phones by impersonating cellular base transceiver systems. The device tricks phones into connecting and intercepts any communications before passing them along to a carrier's tower. CellSpoof has a decent range but still requires the device to be located near the target. That isn't a problem in a metropolitan area like Washington, D.C., but it can have its limitations in other parts of the country.

"Anything of interest?"

"One thing. *Front Burner* doesn't appear to believe that Angela Mays's death was an accident."

"I hate conspiracy nuts. Crack one Ethan Harrington case, and suddenly they question whether the world is round. How much more evidence and testimonials from law enforcement do they need?"

"More than we've offered, apparently. Campos seems to think Ian Drucker is in Pennsylvania."

"Yeah, he's hiding in Independence Hall with Elvis, D.B. Cooper, and the Roswell aliens. These people are unbelievable. Outside of that, is there anything we could consider subversive?"

"Nope. Everything is aboveboard."

Conrad rubs his chin. "Could Campos be running something behind their back?"

"Agent Murphy doesn't think the *Front Burner* staff is into anything overtly illegal, so it's possible. Naomi Merritt seems to be making a go into running the outfit. Nothing remotely shady has popped up on her."

"It's early. Have your agent keep an eye on Merritt and the rest of them, but focus on Campos. Get her search history. Intercept anything coming through. I have the NSA working on accessing their overseas servers in case they're hiding something on them."

"Okay, I'll let Murphy and his team know."

The FBI director hangs up, and the deputy AG returns the phone to its cradle. He leans back in his chair, wondering how the hell Larsen came up with those names. They were so careful. The only reasonable explanation is that she has Isiah's files, but that's not likely. There's no telling what information he could have acquired, but it would have to be more damaging than just shady companies.

None of that changes what needs to be done. Conrad retrieves an encrypted cellular phone from his desk drawer and makes a call he never thought he would have to. Not this close to the election, at least.

"Yes?"

"Kratos is blown. Actyv is on the radar. Take precautions."

There is only breathing on the other end of the line as Conrad waits for an acknowledgment.

"Okay."

The line disconnects. That's all that needed to be said. They'll know what to do next.

CHAPTER FORTY

TIERRA CAMPOS

Front Burner Washington Office
Washington, D.C.

The traditional workday ended hours ago. Dinnertime is in the rearview mirror despite my not eating. The conference room is as quiet as a graveyard, but that's nothing new since I work in a mostly empty office. All I have to show for the time I've spent gazing at this board is something new I've learned: Staring at a problem for hours on end with no break doesn't help solve it. I need to file that away for future reference.

"Knock, knock."

"Josh! How did you get up here?"

He points over his shoulder. "You haven't had anyone manning the desk for months now, Tierra. I jumped the turnstile."

I laugh. It's sad but true.

"I brought you dinner."

"How did you know I didn't already eat?"

"Because you're you. There isn't much room for anything else when you're dialed into a problem. It's your favorite."

Josh knows about my weakness for piping hot Neapolitan pizza with pepperoni, peppers, and onions. At least my eating habits will never be as bad as Victoria's. She never met a cheeseburger she wouldn't devour. That's of little consequence to my hips and waistline.

"You are a godsend," I say, yanking open the box and jamming the pointy end of a loaded slice in my mouth.

"This is a little more filled in since the last time I saw it."

"Victoria has a lead," I say between bites. "We think Rasputin may be a finance guy with a company called Actyv, with a 'y' and no 'e.' Ever heard of them?"

His head jerks around. "It's a big money private equity firm up in New York. They have hundreds of millions in assets under management. You think they're involved?"

"No idea. Victoria is pulling on that string. It makes sense, though. We know whoever running this cabal is a heavy hitter."

"Is this the infamous note that Seth gave you?" Josh asks, pointing at a copy of the slip of paper as he reviews the board.

"The very one."

He reads it out loud. It sounds even more absurd in my ears than it did in my head when I first read it.

"Nonsense, right?"

"Not really. Didn't you ever see the movie?"

"What movie?"

"*National Treasure*. The Nicholas Cage film where he was solving clues to find a lost treasure that the Founding Fathers ended up hiding under Trinity Church."

"Um...spoiler alert. You are such a dork. What does that matter?"

Josh looks bewildered. "He mentions it right here."

That grabs my attention, and I move next to him to see the note. "That could be anything."

"Then why did he capitalize it? That bit was in the movie, too, by the way."

It could be. But what would that reference mean? Isiah often quoted 16th-century philosophers, not Hollywood action-adventure flicks.

"Did the movie have a sealed vault?"

"Not in the traditional sense. But that movie had riddles. They used an Ottendorf cipher to solve it using a—"

"A what?"

"It's a numerical cipher that decodes a message from a book or article. If you know the source and the cipher, you could turn the Bible into a code book."

"Numbers?"

"Yeah, usually the page, paragraph, line, and the number of letters."

"Numbers like those?" I ask, pointing to what Logan wrote on the whiteboard hung on the side wall.

"Yeah. Where did you get that?"

"It was the recording on the phone number Isiah gave me. It was binary code sped up to sound like static noise."

"Then all you need is a source."

I hurry over to the credenza and pick up the book. "It came with this copy of *The Prince*."

"Let's try it."

We rush to sit at the table and start working through combinations. The obvious ones don't work, so we try different variations. After fifteen minutes, it's obvious that we're on the wrong path.

"That's not the source, which makes sense. It's too obvious. If Isiah wanted only you to crack this, it would be something more personal. Did he have access to your journal?"

"I don't have a journal."

"Yes, you do. That pink book with the cute little gold lock that a three-year-old could pick."

I shoot him a stern glare. "If you ever read that, I *will* kill you."

"I'll make a beautiful corpse. It'll be the only time in my life I wear makeup."

A klaxon sounds in my head. Makeup. When Isiah gave me the nonsensical slip of paper, I stored it behind the makeup tray of a compact so that it wouldn't be found. I walk over and pluck the copy off the board.

"Like this? Isiah gave me this. It's lyrics to Nas's *New York State of Mind*. It doesn't have pages…just lines."

"Let's try skipping the page number. What're the first three numbers?"

"Five, six, one."

Josh traces his finger along the paper, moving down five lines, over six words, and stops at the first letter. "M."

"One, one, three."

"E."

"Eight, nine, one."

"Another M."

We repeat the process for the next seven groups of numbers. My stomach starts doing cartwheels. I know what it spells three letters before we finish.

"Whoa," Josh says.

"You are an absolute genius!"

My excitement gets the best of me. I grab him and kiss him. It isn't a peck on the lips. I didn't mean it to turn into the kind of kiss romance novelists write about, either. That's what it turns into before I finally pull away.

Josh is one of my oldest and dearest friends. I owe him my life in a literal sense. My fear has always been that any sort of romantic endeavor would shatter the bond we have between us. I fear I may have just crossed a line from which there's no turning back.

"Remind me to show up and save the day for you more often," Josh says, his face flushed and his smile full of teeth.

"I need to call the team."

"I'll leave you to it."

"Josh? Thank you."

"Happy to help. Don't forget to eat a couple more slices of that," he says with a wink.

I send a cryptic group text message to the team and leave a voice message for Dial Pirate. I write the two words in big black letters on the board and stand back. It's not nonsense, after all. It's Orwellian, and it has a purpose: MEMORY HOLE.

Now I have a new problem to obsess over: knowing what to do with it.

CHAPTER FORTY-ONE

SPECIAL AGENT VICTORIA LARSEN

Philadelphia Hospital for Neuroscience
Philadelphia, Pennsylvania

Hospitals are not anyone's favorite place. Doctors and nurses might work here to save lives and mend the ill, but they would never want to be a patient themselves. Despite the strong smell of chemical cleansers, Victoria knows this room is a petri dish. That's why she wants to make this stay as brief as possible.

Austin and Tierra have their own bad experiences, especially the latter. Tierra got her introduction to the medical profession as a teenage trauma victim. Nothing has helped her overcome that experience since. Victoria is partly surprised she came and is pleasantly surprised that she brought her boss.

"The flowers are a nice touch," Victoria says from her borrowed hospital bed as Austin searches for a good place to set them down.

"It seems you don't get to appreciate the bouquets I buy you."

He didn't mean any harm by the comment, but it did sting a little.

"Nice gown. You're taking this charade a bit far, don't you think?"

Victoria looks down at the ridiculous pattern. She's uncomfortable wearing anything other than her pantsuit and heeled boots, including sundresses and this absurd garment.

"It's comfortable, at least."

"I thought you were breaking out of here to do some digging," Austin says, finally setting the flowers on the windowsill.

"I did. Now I'm back. I need to show myself to the cameras once in a while."

"The FBI is monitoring the hospital's CCTV?"

"I doubt they're watching it twenty-four seven, but they'll give it a cursory check. Besides, this is the best place for us to meet."

"You're the best-looking patient I've ever seen," Austin says. Victoria beams.

"Get a room, you two," Tierra moans after rolling her eyes.

"We're technically in one. I'm glad you're okay. When Tierra first called...well, let's say that you scared the crap out of us."

"I'm sorry. It had to be done the way I did it."

"For appearances?" Austin asks, getting a silent nod.

"We stopped at your place last night and picked up some things."

Tierra hands her a large tote bag filled with clothing and the few essential hygiene and hair care products she owns.

"Did you see anyone at my apartment?"

"No, but you didn't really expect me to, did you?"

"We're surveillance experts, so it would have been surprising. You may have walked past an agent and didn't know it."

"I can't believe the hospital is letting you pull this off," Austin says, looking around the room. Everything is set up to make it look like she's a patient, right down to the nurse's notes on the small whiteboard.

"The ward is, not the hospital. My doctor is beloved here."

"Seth's friend?"

"Yeah. As for the hospital, they don't know the difference."

"Isn't that insurance fraud?" Austin asks, getting a wry smile in return.

"Add that to my list of transgressions. I'll have a problem to deal with when they figure it out, but that issue's for another time. Speaking of problems, I have a couple of things for you."

Victoria hands her a phone. It's not a smartphone and looks like a device people used in the 1990s.

"I already have a cell."

"Yes, and it's easily monitored."

"They're spying on me? Why?"

Victoria shrugs. "I don't know if they are or aren't. I'm not taking chances. This is an encrypted satellite phone. My number is already programmed in it, and the battery is charged. We can use that to communicate. Don't tell anyone you have it or let anyone see you using it."

"They're watching me?"

One of Victoria's complaints about modern society is that people wander through life without any situational awareness. They walk around with earbuds and stare at screens, oblivious to what's happening in their surroundings. Tierra isn't the worst offender, but she is hardly the poster child for alertness. With all that she's been through, it's surprising that her head isn't on a swivel.

"Tierra, we have to assume the worst. Conrad Williams is the deputy attorney general of the United States. He knows everybody and has everything to lose if this fails. I wouldn't put anything past him, and you shouldn't either. You too, Austin."

They both look at each other before nodding.

"You said you had a couple of things."

Victoria pulls out a Glock 43X and shows it to Tierra. She checks to ensure the chamber is empty and retrieves two more loaded ten-round magazines. There is no manual safety on the gun, and she would prefer her best friend not to have an accidental discharge since there isn't a spare holster.

"Whoa. I don't want that."

"Take it."

"I barely know how to shoot!"

"We went to the range."

"Yeah, once, and I could barely hit the back wall."

That's not true. The back wall is all that Tierra managed to hit. Victoria decides not to further erode her confidence and walks her through the weapon's functions.

"It has a Trijicon RMRcc Red Dot sight, and the battery will last four years. Put the dot on the target and squeeze the trigger. The grip is smaller than the normal Glock, so you should be comfortable firing it."

"I doubt that," Tierra mumbles.

"Don't forget to rack the slide back to chamber a round first."

Tierra accepts the weapon and holds it like it's an alien artifact. With that muzzle discipline, Victoria is glad she double-checked the chamber.

"Whose is this?"

"It belonged to a fellow agent's grandfather. It was reported stolen. He was older, thus the smaller grip. She bought it for him before he died."

"Do you think I need this?"

"I hope not, Tierra, but it's there if you ever need it."

"It's illegal for me to have this. I don't have a permit."

"Just keep it at your bedside. Don't carry it around."

"Do I get one?" Austin asks with a grin as Tierra studies the Glock before tucking it in her purse.

"Sorry, they were fresh out of squirt guns. Tierra, do you mind if I have a minute alone with Austin?"

"Sure. I'll go get a couple of drinks from the vending machine."

"I'm sorry about all this," Victoria says after she leaves. "Tierra was really upset with me for faking my episode. I didn't want to deceive her…or you. How is she?"

"Stressed."

"Try to lighten her load. She's not in this alone. She needs to know that."

"She understands but is putting a lot of pressure on herself. I'll do what I can."

It's amazing how quickly things change. There was a point when Austin was so angry with her that he was ready to toss her out in the street. He was reckless. Victoria always thought that it was out of character for him. It's good to see that she was right.

"You've come a long way since New Hampshire, Austin. What changed you?"

He sits beside her in a chair. "I don't know. A lot of things. You played a part. I thought you were going to rip my arm off and beat me with it at the hospital in Nashua."

"I never mastered diplomacy. I'm protective of Tierra. I don't know why. She's a big girl and can take care of herself. It's just something that I'm compelled to do."

"Protecting people is in your DNA, Victoria. That's why."

She levels serious eyes at him. "This is going to get worse, Austin. A lot worse. This could get dangerous if Tierra proves who the conspirators are. You need to be ready for that."

CHAPTER FORTY-TWO

BRIAN COOPER

Franklin Baptist Church
Allentown, Pennsylvania

Brian isn't religious. Neither is his candidate. Appearances matter in politics, and Bradford has a base to appease. For that reason, he has been attending Sunday services at churches across the country since the campaign kicked into high gear. The time worshiping the Lord also gives the candidate time to decompress and maybe even pray for his soul. More politicians should do that.

Brian feels his coat pocket vibrate and retrieves his phone to read the text message. Trying to be as inconspicuous as possible, he slides along the back wall and eases out the door. He looks around and sees Adika's bright purple hair before noticing her leaning against her rental car in the parking lot.

"You could have come in."

She looks back at the small church. "Oh, no. I didn't want to be struck by lightning."

"That's a little melodramatic, don't you think?"

"Why tempt fate?"

Brian fights with himself but has to ask. "What have you done that would cause God to smite you?"

"Wouldn't you like to find out?" Adika asks, running her finger down his chest. "Once services are over, I can show you."

"What do you have for me, Adika?"

"You're no fun, Cooper. Here."

She slaps a folder against his stomach and looks at her nails as he takes a peek.

"Anything good?"

"You could do something novel and read it to find out."

"That would take the fun out of you telling me. Are there any skeletons in his closet?"

"Everyone is hiding something."

"And you're the best in the world at finding out what," Brian says, quick with the praise for the eccentric opposition researcher.

"When I get paid enough to bother. The SparkNotes version? He's a sexual deviant."

"Sexual dev—are we talking about, like, being a furry?"

Adika chuckles. "Oh, he wishes that's all it was."

"Do you have art?"

"Turn a few pages and see for yourself, Cooper. Jeez!"

Adika watches as Brian does just that. His facial expressions go from amused to horrified, to incredulous, and back. It amazes him what people are into these days.

"He did a good job hiding his profile. That may work to hide his…oddities…from his wife, but it's not good enough to hide from me."

"Excellent work, Adika."

"Why do you care about the Pennsylvania secretary of state anyway? It seems beneath you."

She's right. In most cases, Brian couldn't care less. However, when that individual promotes the integrity of the electoral process in a tight race, it's time to pay attention. This man will be responsible for certifying the presidential vote totals after all sixty-seven Pennsylvania counties submit their tallies.

"Noah built the ark before it started raining. It pays to be prepared."

"Okay, while you're collecting pairs of animals, tell me how his being a sexual deviant matters?"

She sounded sensitive about that. Brian can't imagine why.

"It doesn't matter to me. It may bother the voters in this state when he runs for governor next cycle."

"That's stupid. Why does politics always have to get so personal?"

Brian shrugs. "Because character matters. At least, it matters to people who don't blindly support one party or another."

People start filtering out of the church. Brian checks his watch and sees that the service ended a few minutes early.

"You think there will be a problem with certifying the vote, don't you?"

"There usually is in a close race. This one will be decided by less than a percentage point."

"So, you're going to extort him to get the outcome you want?"

Brian shakes his head. "I'm going to ensure nobody else can. If the presidency is decided by a couple of thousand votes in Pennsylvania, you couldn't pay me enough to have the secretary of state's job. He'll be under enormous pressure. It's good to have an ace in the hole."

"All right," Adika says, satisfied. "Good luck. You know where to find me if you need anything else. *Anything* else. See you around, stud."

She winks and smacks him on the ass as she breezes around the rear of her car and pulls the driver's door open.

"You know, there may be a day I take you up on your offer," Brian says, grinning.

She rests her arms on the car's roof. "You know. I'm not sure your heart could handle what I bring to the bedroom. I don't want you dying on me, Cooper. You pay too well."

CHAPTER FORTY-THREE

DEPUTY AG CONRAD WILLIAMS

The Allegheny Industrialist Luxury Hotel
Pittsburgh, Pennsylvania

Conrad has never been to the Steel City. He expected it to be a polluted bastion of underpaid workers, dilapidated buildings, and crime-riddled streets. He was wrong. It's actually a shining metropolis – at least the downtown area is.

Located directly across the river from PNC Park, the Industrialist, as it's known to the locals, caters to the high-end business and tourist crowd. Conrad isn't here for the onsite spa or two Michelin-star restaurants as he enters the hotel lobby and presents his identification to a man dressed in a suit and wearing an earpiece. That's not a normal greeting for a four-and-a-half-star luxury hotel in the city's cultural center. Then again, it's the only hotel in the country where the president of the United States is sleeping tonight.

Pollsters are hyperventilating over the tightening race in the state. As a result, mainstream media pundits have openly questioned why the president isn't taking a more active role in supporting his party's candidate. Some have even leveled sexism accusations at him.

The pressure was enough to schedule joint campaign events with Standish over the next three days. That doesn't mean the business of running the country stops. One of the top agenda items is the AP report that ballots were found at the arson site in Allentown. The timing of that was unfortunate but not unexpected.

The president has demanded a briefing today, so Conrad will be joined by Director Krekstein in explaining what's happening in the state and what federal agencies are doing about it. Election interference is a serious business, and his administration took a serious hit after the shenanigans in New Hampshire. The president has a legacy to protect, and this has the potential to unravel it.

The hotel lobby is teeming with Secret Service, both visible in suits and milling around in plain clothes. Conrad takes a seat by the fireplace to wait. He checks the note from his administrative assistant again:

Allegheny Industrialist lobby - 2pm.

Ten minutes pass before an attractive young woman dressed in the hotel uniform approaches him. "Deputy Attorney General Conrad Williams?"

"Yes."

"You have a phone call. I will transfer it to the lobby phone."

He points at a modern phone sitting on a nearby table, and she nods before returning to the long check-in counter. He relocates to a leather high-back chair and stares at the phone. A moment later, it rings.

"Williams."

"You've been a busy man," Rasputin says.

"As have you, no doubt. Using the house phone is a neat trick."

"I thought so. Would you rather I just show up in the lobby for this?"

Conrad frowns. "We agreed that there would be no contact after the convention."

"I know. I was the one who made the rule. Now I'm breaking it. Efforts need to be coordinated."

"Everything is going according to plan," Conrad says, carefully keeping his voice low.

"Not everything. Why did you open an investigation into Tierra Campos?"

"How did you know?"

Rasputin sighs. "It's my business to know."

"I think she has Isiah's files."

"No, I can assure you that she doesn't," the cabal's *de facto* leader assures him. "If Isiah managed to get communications and financial records to Campos, we'd be reading about it."

"Then how does she know about Actyv and Kratos?"

"I don't know. I'm not the one tapping into her communications. You tell me."

"Larsen told her."

"Then that's how she knows. Since Victoria Larsen is laid up in a hospital, we can assume she doesn't have the files either."

"If that's true, she made the connection another way. That's even more unnerving."

"Handle her. She should have been taken off the board months ago."

"She's being transferred overseas."

"I know. Africa. Yet she's still here, causing problems. I meant handle her *permanently*. You know where your target is. It shouldn't be that hard."

"It's not that easy. We don't have the resources. Drucker will drop everything to take her out, jeopardizing our plan. Agent Murphy is too much of a boy scout to conduct an assassination."

"Machiavelli has other contacts that know people who can take care of her quickly."

Conrad clenches his teeth. He hates relying on that arrogant ass for anything. Unfortunately, he needs a backup plan. That's the best option, as distasteful as it is.

"Okay. What about Campos and *Front Burner*?"

"Nietzsche is handling them."

"Yeah, that's working out real well," Conrad says, laying on the sarcasm. "Media attacks are not going to dissuade her from digging. She's a serious threat."

"We're in the endgame now. Everything is a threat. Being rash is a bigger one. Let me worry about Tierra Campos. The FBI can have eyes and ears on her but keep them on a short leash. Is Drucker on track?"

"Yes. The ballots are being delivered according to plan."

"Good. Once that story breaks, the president will take a keen interest in what you have to say."

Everyone will tune in to that drama. The media frenzy alone will make it the top story on every broadcast, and sensationalized clickbait headlines will vie for America's digital attention. It will be the opening act in what is bound to be a circus.

"Don't worry about that. Did you know about Angela Mays? Machiavelli didn't see fit to inform me," Conrad complains, changing the subject. He doesn't need Rasputin telling him how to do his job.

"It was necessary. Is the lid still on?"

"*Front Burner* is questioning the narrative, but it's only speculation that they won't run with, even with their low standards. Are we done?"

"Tread lightly with Campos. Your investigation is illegal, so don't get caught. It'll blow up in our face."

"Noted," Conrad says, hanging up the phone.

Secret Service begins shifting their positions in the lobby. The president must be on his way. Conrad checks his watch again. It's time to get back to work.

CHAPTER FORTY-FOUR

IAN DRUCKER

Butler Roadhouse
Butler, Pennsylvania

Ian hands the plastic and metal U.S. mail crate full of ballots out the back of the van to the last pair of militiamen. He climbs out and closes the rear doors as it's loaded in the trunk of the car parked alongside. Half of the ballots will be on their way to drop boxes across the western part of the state. After the first run, they will load up again, and as the militia moves to deposits at closer locations, Ian will head back to the Forge.

He looks around the area. The roadhouse is dark, and the hotel and convenience mart parking lots are quiet for the time being. There are a million spots he could have picked for this. It's Western Pennsylvania - there is no shortage of secluded places to make this transfer. Not that this is at all necessary from a strategic standpoint. It was planned this way more for what comes next.

The Butler Roadhouse, with an unimaginative name, sits off an intersection of State Highway Eight and U.S. Route Four Twenty-Two. It's closed, but people are used to seeing cars here, so they won't stand out. Best of all, there is a motor lodge across the street. Transients rarely question what's going on around them.

Butler would be a strategic town if a war were ever fought on American territory because it's at a critical crossroads. It's not unlike Gettysburg that way. The Army of the Potomac squared off against Lee's Army of Northern Virginia outside that town because roads led there. Butler isn't a big city, but it's far from being a quaint village, either.

"Are you guys all set?" Ian asks.

"Yeah, we're good."

"Any last-minute questions?"

"No."

"Then get to it. I'll see you when you're done."

Ian slaps the roof of the car and watches the pair drive off. He doesn't expect the first team to return for a couple of hours, giving him plenty of time to kill. He climbs into the driver's seat and settles in.

He wonders if Victoria Larsen will find a way to get involved with this. He has no confidence that Robespierre can handle her. The bureaucrat doesn't appreciate what she's capable of, in the field or otherwise. She has no equal in the Bureau. Anyone who thinks they are one is just fooling themselves, making every agent the FBI employs a fool.

Ian knows because he was one of them. He was convinced that Larsen was a pretty face with long legs and no brain. He started developing respect for her when she neutralized Marx, Sartre, and Trotsky. That conclusion changed for good when she pinned Vassyl and him down behind an old boiler in Loughborough. She got the upper hand, and it took his selling Vassyl out just to survive. He cannot let that happen again if they ever meet.

Ian looks at his watch and does some mental calculations. It's time. He moves a mail crate full of ballots to the front passenger seat and turns over a bunch of envelopes so they can be read from outside the window. Satisfied, he wipes down the steering wheel and shifter. Despite wearing gloves, he refuses to make a simple mistake.

He makes a final survey of the van's interior, locks it, and treks over the access road, through a grassy area, and across another street to the motor lodge. It's a misnomer, in his opinion. The name makes it sound like a run-down motel occupied by vagrants and hookers. This is anything but, and the cars in the parking lot attest to a solid middle-class clientele.

Only a couple of cameras are watching the entrance and parking lot. They have narrow fields of view, and Ian is careful to avoid them. He presses the unlock button on the key fob, but nothing happens. He curses and tries again in a different direction, and a set of lights on a Toyota flashes two cars over. Perfect. Robespierre came through.

With his exit strategy confirmed, Ian rehearses the next call in his head one final time. It has to be believable without sounding panicked. Content that he has it down, he reaches into his pocket, retrieves a cell phone, and powers it on. The number is easy enough to remember.

"9-1-1, what's your emergency?"

"It's not an emergency, just a…I'm at a hotel in Butler, and…I don't want to get anyone in trouble, but there's a van parked across the street, and…well, I think someone is selling drugs out of it."

Ian presses his lips together. The cadence was right, but the voice may have sounded too cartoonish. Oh well, it's too late to change it now.

"What is your name, sir?"

"I…uh, I'd rather not say. I don't want to get involved. I just thought you should know."

"You said you're at a hotel?" the 9-1-1 dispatcher asks.

"Yes, ma'am. I saw the man in the van hand something to a guy who put it in his trunk and left when I arrived. Then it happened again a couple of minutes later as I was getting ready to leave."

"Thank you, sir. Are you outside now?"

"Yes, I am."

"Can you see a sign across the street?"

"Yes, ma'am. It says Butler Roadhouse."

"Okay, sir, thank you for your vigilance. I will send a unit to check it out."

"Thank you, ma'am. Have a good night."

That landed right where he wanted it to on the priority list. Drugs are taken seriously in this area, especially if it's fentanyl. The call will be a priority but not urgent.

Ian climbs into the Toyota and makes a left out of the hotel parking lot. He then takes a right onto an access road the roadhouse parking lot dumps into. He follows the street as it winds in a one hundred and eighty-degree arc before stopping outside a medical clinic. Ian kills his headlights and has a perfect line of sight to the entrance. All he can do is wait. It doesn't take long.

A squad car pulls into the roadhouse parking lot with its lights off. He can't see the front of the building from this vantage point, but their reaction will tell him what he needs to know. The car's lights come on a minute later, bathing the area in red and blue. Five minutes later, two more units come screaming off the main road, strobe lights on and sirens blaring.

"Perfect," Ian mumbles.

There is no reason to stay any longer. He points the Toyota toward the main road and makes a right up the ramp for the Benjamin Franklin Highway for the journey back to the Forge.

His story for Mike and Remy is solid. Ian stole this car from the motor lodge when he saw the police converging on him. It's plausible, albeit suspicious. That sums up most of Ian's time at the Forge. All that has to happen now is for the militia to remember his instructions at the briefing. That's a coin flip.

Either way, this mission is successful, and he can report that to Robespierre and Machiavelli. The fun part will be removing a pair of rooks covering two towns on his map when he returns.

CHAPTER FORTY-FIVE

SPECIAL AGENT VICTORIA LARSEN

Cobbs Creek East Rowhouse
West Philadelphia, Pennsylvania

Imani placed the call from her grandfather's study. The solitude wasn't really required. Victoria had no intention of speaking while she was on the phone. She doesn't want anyone to know that she's here any more than her partner in crime does.

"There were no prints in the van," she says upon returning. "It was completely wiped down."

"I'm not surprised," Victoria says, rubbing her eyes.

"Do you think this was Drucker?"

"There's no doubt about it. The question is, how many people does he have working for him, and where did they come from?"

Imani sits in the recliner opposite the couch and sets her cell down on the end table. "He could be a solo act."

"Sure, it's possible. Then why park at a closed roadhouse? He'd just drive around and make his deposits."

"Maybe he got tired," Imani says, helping Victoria war game reasons.

"Then he would have been fast asleep when the police rolled up. The only reasonable conclusion is that the van was a distribution point. Ian found some worker bees to bring the ballots to separate drop-offs to avoid detection."

Imani rubs her throat. Victoria watches as she tries to come up with an alternative solution. It doesn't look like she's having much success.

"Okay, that sounds like the most plausible explanation. Ian isn't from around here. Who would he get to help, and with what resources?"

Victoria shrugs. "Good questions. Anyone could be helping him: illegals or hired thugs...anyone. As for money, I'm going to bet it's coming from someone through Kratos, probably via an account at Allied Republic Bank."

"Not that we can get a warrant to check. I guess we should be grateful that the ballot distribution got interrupted," Imani says.

"That bothers me, too. Any news on the person who dialed 9-1-1?"

"Nope. Agents talked to the hotel the call was placed from. The manager cooperated and gave them a list of registered guests. The number doesn't match any contact information."

Victoria rubs the back of her neck. "It could have been someone staying with a friend."

Imani shakes her head. "You read the transcript of the call. Everything was in the singular. 'I'm staying at....' 'I was heading to my car....' "It didn't read like someone part of a pair or group. Curious, right?"

Victoria exhales. She's right. Knowing who the caller was might provide additional insights, but they'll likely never find out.

"A little. It doesn't matter. The damage is already done. Drucker is still a couple of steps ahead of us."

"I found out that the Bureau is asking the media to pipe down about the potential impact on the election. So far, they seem to be listening. VH Media has yet to even air a story."

Victoria grimaces. Since when does the media adhere to requests from the Bureau, especially about a story as juicy as this one? Scandals sell, and this one would guarantee attention. The nation is already on edge. That the press is taking a pass on reporting this story makes no sense.

"I'm not sure that's a good thing."

"Why not?"

"Because this is clear voter fraud. The people have a right to know."

"It could cause a panic, Vic. You know that as well as I do."

"Yeah, but what do you think will happen if this comes out *after* the election?"

The road to hell is paved with good intentions. There have been times when a news blackout made perfect sense. People's lives or the successful completion of an investigation was at stake. That isn't the case now. The news of the ballots will eventually capture public attention. When it does, the shouts of a cover-up by the Bureau to manipulate the election will be deafening. That's the last thing the FBI needs.

"I see your point. What's the next move?"

"We're not going to get anywhere playing defense. We need to make a move that will apply pressure."

"Like pay Kratos a visit and shake a few trees? I'll get my gear."

"No, don't."

The request startles the young agent. "What do you mean?"

Victoria sighs and leans forward on the couch. "Imani, I'm radioactive. Even talking to me could spell the end of your career if the Hoover Building finds out."

"I already told you that I'm willing to take that risk," she says with an annoyed tone.

"So were others. It didn't end well for them. I don't want you to regret this. I appreciate all the help you've already given me. It's been invaluable, but I think you need to walk away."

Imani is about to protest when her phone rings on the end table. She snatches it up and checks the caller ID.

"The office," she says before punching the icon to accept it. "Agent Bangura."

Imani has a series of expressions that causes Victoria to imagine what is being said on the other end of the line. Her face betrays her emotions as it moves from anger to annoyance, to surprise, to something that makes her look constipated.

"Okay. I'll be right there," Imani says, ending the call. "That was my supervisory agent. There may have been another van distributing ballots in the eastern part of the state. It's all hands on deck in our field office."

"I'll go to Kratos," Victoria says, partially relieved.

"No. Don't. You need backup, Vic."

"I'll be fine."

"No, please. Don't take that chance. You're the best hope to catch Drucker and expose this cabal. Walking into that place blind could get you killed. You're no good to anyone if you're dead. Kratos isn't going anywhere. We can go tomorrow."

"Imani…."

"Promise me, Vic."

She nods, and Imani heads out to her car for the drive to the Philadelphia Field Office. Victoria watches her out the window and thinks about going to Kratos anyway, but a promise is a promise. She's short on friends. Outside of Tierra, Imani is the closest she has to one. There's no point in alienating her because of impatience.

CHAPTER FORTY-SIX

TIERRA CAMPOS

Front Burner Washington Office
Washington, D.C.

It's a late night for everyone. Most of the *Front Burner* team is still in the office as the clock passes midnight. The coverage of Angela Mays's "accident" dominates the news cycle. There isn't much coming from the authorities to report, so media outlets are filling their airtime and social media feeds with filler about campaign impact. I think it's much ado about nothing. The worst is certainly yet to come.

Tyler and Olivia drop in to say goodnight. We begin chatting about nothing in particular as I stall for time. Dial Pirate hasn't called. I need to sleep, but I can't seem to pry myself away from the war room. Despite Josh's breakthrough on the binary, I don't know where to go from here. Nobody does.

My cell phone rings, and I jump. Both of my friends grin at the reaction.

"A little jumpy, Tierra?"

"It's been a long day," I say, checking the caller ID.

Rosco P. Coltrane. It's about time. I'm not a big *Dukes of Hazzard* fan, but I appreciate his sense of humor. I'm not sure what compelled him to choose the bumbling sheriff, but here we are.

"Hi, DP. You're on speaker with Olivia and Tyler."

He groans. "Great. A crowd."

"How's Boss Hogg?"

"Still up to his usual tricks with the Duke boys. Don't mock my love of '80s television. I'm sorry it's taken so long to get back to you."

"What company are you swindling this time?"

"It's not like that. I was busy taking down a call center full of scammers in Bangalore, India."

I smile. "Were they trying to sell you an extended warranty on your car or something?"

Dial Pirate laughs. "No, they said I needed additional computer support. Bastards."

"That's rich," Tyler muses.

"They tried to hijack my computer by getting me to install an application, so I invaded their network and locked their databases and call scripts with ransomware."

"Poetic justice," Olivia says, impressed.

"You have a fan, DP."

"It's nice being appreciated. What can I do for you?"

"Help, I hope. We found the key to the lock."

I explain how we used the Ottendorf cipher based on the binary code he uncovered to deduce the MEMORY HOLE password from the song lyrics Isiah gave me. He almost sounds impressed.

"That's not an accident."

"Yeah, but we don't know what to do with it. There's no next riddle to solve."

"You said a message came in the package you received from Isiah Burgess. Read it to me."

'Tierra, you are a National Treasure that belongs in a sealed vault. All great thinkers have enemies, and sometimes exile in the dark is the only solution. For others, there is no Safe Haven. The key to their absolution rests in 1984. That's it, outside the phone number you already know about. My friend Josh figured out the National Treasure clue."

Dial Pirate lets out an amused laugh.

"What's funny?" Tyler asks.

"You should have read me that earlier."

"You know what it means?"

"I'm a hacker, Tierra Del Fuego. It pops right off the page. Exile in the dark alludes to the dark web."

The dark web is a hidden part of the worldwide web accessed using a Tor browser. Dark web pages don't appear in search engines, so a user needs to know the exact address of a website. This part of the Internet is described as "dangerous." Outside of nefarious black markets for stolen identities, it also happens to be a place we lowly journalists can have conversations with whistleblowers.

"Okay...."

"Safe Haven is an anonymous storage system based on the Free Haven Project," DP continues. "It's designed to ensure the privacy and security of documents by emphasizing persistence rather than accessibility."

"Have you ever heard of it?" I ask Tyler.

"Yeah. It's a distributed peer-to-peer system with servers that hold fragments of documents."

"It's a little more complicated than that, but basically," Dial Pirate says, "it uses a dispersal algorithm such that a file's contents cannot be determined by uncovering any one piece. It's like writing a book and storing each chapter in a different bank safe deposit box. For greater security, Safe Haven periodically moves the location of shares between nodes."

"Isiah wanted to ensure the FBI could never find these," Olivia says, getting nods from Tyler and me.

"How do we get them?" Tyler asks.

"The shares are stored along with a unique public key. You need to broadcast that key to find fragments and recreate the file."

"The key to their absolution lies in 1984. So, MEMORY HOLE is the public key?" Tyler asks.

"No way. It's too simple. Without getting too technical, the generation of key pairs depends on cryptographic algorithms based on mathematical problems termed one-way functions."

"That's not technical?" Olivia asks.

"I *could* go on for hours if you'd like. The public key is a long string of letters and numbers. Your Orwellian reference is likely a way to access the file that will get you the public key."

I rub my temples. "If Isiah wasn't dead, I'd kill him myself."

My comment is tongue and cheek and meant metaphorically, but I know it probably sounded crass. He was a paranoid man, but not paranoid enough. I know his loss has gutted his father.

"Where do we find the file?"

"In a sealed vault."

I bristle at Dial Pirate's matter-of-fact response. "You're jerking my chain now, DP."

"I can't help it. You're cute when you get all worked up."

"Bite me," I say as Tyler and Olivia snicker.

"He mentions a sealed vault. The Vault is a simple file storage system on the dark net. All you need to access the share is a plain text username and password."

"We have the password, most likely, but we don't have a username," I complain.

"Yes, we do," Tyler says. "It's in the letter. Every great thinker has an enemy. We're dealing with Robespierre, Rasputin, Machiavelli, and Nietzsche."

"Robespierre was a lawyer. Nobody would accuse one of being a great thinker," Olivia says.

"Rasputin was a mystic and holy man, so he's out," Tyler concludes. "That leaves Machiavelli and Nietzsche."

"It has to be Machiavelli," I say. "Isiah has a personal connection with him after my accusations on *Capitol Beat.*"

"Who were his enemies?" Dial Pirate asks.

Olivia opens the browser on her smartphone and begins a search. "You mean there's something you don't know, Dial Pirate?"

"I'm far better with ones and zeros than philosophers and Renaissance political strategists."

"Machiavelli was removed from the Chancery because of his close association with the head of the republican government, Piero Soderini. He was confined for a year to his smallholding in Sant'Andrea, located just outside Florence."

"Informative but not helpful, Olivia," Tyler says. "Who exiled him?"

She stares up from her phone. "The Medici family."

"Good enough for me. Try Medici, Tierra."

I open up a Tor browser.

"Your systems aren't nearly as secure as mine," Dial Pirate says. "You should let me do this."

"DP…," I say, staring at the phone. "Powerful people would kill to ensure these files are never seen. This is too dangerous to involve you any further."

"It's no safer for you. The feds can just waltz into your office. They'd have to find me first. Holy crap…it worked. I have the public key…sending it now."

Nothing happens as a minute goes by. Then two.

"This is anti-climactic. How long is this gonna take?"

"I'm not sure," Dial Pirate says. "Not instantly, apparently. The data is coming in small chunks over ridiculous network routes. This will take a bit. It gives me time to think of a secure way of getting this to you."

I'm so excited that I wring my hands as I bounce in my chair. I've been dreaming about this moment since Isiah's death. I needed this shot in the arm to keep pushing forward, and it couldn't have come at a better time. There's still a chance to stop this.

"I'm going to hug you when I meet you!" I screech like a tween talking to a boy band member.

"You'll never meet me, Tierra Del Fuego," Dial Pirate advises. "I'm a cyberwarrior, which means I'm a ghost. You can't hug a ghost."

CHAPTER FORTY-SEVEN

BRIAN COOPER

Lake City Hotel & Suites
Erie, Pennsylvania

The campaign is back in Erie. Brian actually has the same room he occupied the last time they stayed here. So does the governor. Brian knocks on the door a minute before the requested six a.m. meeting. Colin Bradford answers, already showered, dressed, and ready to go. Whatever this is about, it's a private conversation. No other staff is present, including Joel.

This has to be about the results of their barnstorming tour of the liberal cities. It's difficult to measure the results, but the polls in the state have tightened. The governor did a fantastic job on messaging, and his refusal to get distracted has helped shape the narrative. Black communities across the state are questioning how much Alicia Standish will benefit them. According to their internal numbers, enthusiasm for her is waning. Of course, when you pay someone handsomely for information, you usually get what you want to hear, not the actual reality on the ground.

"Coffee is on the counter," the governor says, retreating into the living area. "How much do we have left in the campaign coffers?"

"Enough."

"That's not an answer."

"Governor, just keep doing what you're doing," Brian says, pouring a mug.

"I plan to. I don't have much choice at this stage, do I?"

Brian sits on the sofa across from him, his hands wrapped around the warm mug. "There are always choices, sir. Your decisions are the difference between victory and defeat."

"Did you see the AP article about Butler this morning?"

"I did."

"You don't look surprised," Bradford observes, taking a sip of caffeinated heaven. Even hotel coffee tastes good this early.

"After what happened in Manchester, nothing surprises me."

"Something is up in this state. If Democrat operatives are printing ballots, what faith do Americans have that the election isn't rigged?"

"None."

Bradford presses his lips together. "Do I say anything at today's rally?"

"We will release a statement to the media. Don't mention it at the rally."

"Why not?"

"Two reasons," Brian says. "One, it will look like you're starting to make excuses for losing. It will sound like a lack of confidence. Two, because the crowd you're speaking to won't be sympathetic. These are Standish voters. You won't change their minds, and the point is for them to stay home. Let the media run wild with speculation. Focus on your message, and don't step on the cycle."

"Polling doesn't have this swing making a difference."

"The polls don't accurately measure a voter's likelihood of voting. They are trying to demoralize your supporters with these nonsensical push polls."

"The base is already demoralized. Instead of lighting a fire under conservatives, I'm talking to their enemies. They think I'm a sellout."

"There is too much at stake in this race for your base to abandon you. Your running mate is doing a good job reminding them of that. A few rallies in red districts aren't going to help them turn out. At this point, they either will or won't. You can affect Standish's turnout here, and this race is the election."

"So you keep saying. Best case scenario, what is the margin of victory if the election were held today?"

"A half-point."

The governor frowns. "And worst case?"

"We lose by one."

Bradford rubs his chin. "What was Pennsylvania's margin of victory in 2020?"

"Eighty-one thousand, six hundred and sixty votes."

"Why am I not surprised you know the exact number?"

Brian shrugs. "You pay me to know those kinds of things. It was a 1.2 percent margin, and this will be closer. Twenty thousand voters will decide the presidency. Why are you asking, Governor?"

Bradford stands and retreats to the kitchen to refill his mug. Politicians on the campaign trail feed off voter excitement and caffeine. The first is an emotional high, and the second is a chemical necessity. That's not why he moved to the other room. He's about to drop a bomb that Brian begins to brace himself for.

"Because, no matter who wins, there will be a protracted legal battle. We don't have the cash on hand to fight one."

"Do you want me to pull back advertising?"

"No, we need every dime we can spare. I was presented with another option yesterday. A group of businessmen in New York has offered a sizable contribution to the RNC's legal fund set up to deal with the aftermath of this race, no matter which way it turns out."

"Out of the blue?"

He nods. "Word travels fast. The DNC also set one up for Standish, and this group may have also offered to finance her."

"What's the name?"

"Actyv Private Equity. Ever heard of them?"

"Vaguely. I don't recall them making a contribution to our campaign."

"They didn't. They didn't make one to hers either, making them apolitical."

"So, why now?"

The governor smiles. "That's what I want to know. I'm sending you up to New York tonight. You have a meeting at their Midtown offices tomorrow morning."

The order catches Brian off-guard. He's not a fundraiser for the campaign. He deals with electoral strategy and oversees the staff that specializes in raising money. It's not something he does well.

"Why me?"

"Because you're a closer, Brian. If this is legit, take their money. If it isn't, then walk away. There is nobody I trust more to do that than you."

"Sir, I appreciate the vote of confidence, but I need to be by your side."

"Joel can handle that," the governor says, sipping his coffee as he leans against the kitchenette counter. "You don't need to listen to the same speech over and over. This is important."

"What if they're donating to Standish as well?"

"Find out why, but so long as their cash is green, take it. We can't afford to fall behind the Democrats coming out of the gate."

"Understood. I'll handle it."

"No."

Brian's head pops up. "No, what, Governor?"

"No, I'm not doing this to get you away from the campaign. No, Joel is not whispering in my ear about your strategy. No, I haven't lost confidence in you. Those are the questions rattling around your head. I wouldn't have gotten this far with Brevin. I liked him, but he didn't have a strategic vision. You put us in a position to win. Now I need you to start thinking about what happens after next Tuesday."

"Okay, sir, I will."

The governor's words are reassuring, but the man is a politician. That makes him a born liar. This could be legitimate or a convenient excuse to get him out of town so changes can be made. Brian guesses that he'll find out either way.

Governor Bradford nods at the door as Brian sets his mug down on the end table. "I'll handle today's staff meeting. Get some rest, and then get to New York. Let me know how the meeting goes tomorrow."

CHAPTER FORTY-EIGHT

IAN DRUCKER

"The Forge" Militia Compound
Liberty, Pennsylvania

Yesterday was a long day. Ian didn't return until after five and immediately crashed out. Since then, he has made it a point to avoid interacting with the militiamen. They all know what happened in Butler last night, and outside of a cursory explanation to Mike and Remy, Ian hasn't elaborated.

The militia gathered in the meeting hall, and Remy started taking their temperature. It's hot. Very hot. These men are angry for all the wrong reasons. Ian walks into a burning cauldron of anger. The leadership duo is trying to douse the flames, but it's whipping into a firestorm threatening to consume everything.

"Someone tipped them off!"

"We have a mole in the group!"

"We need an inquisition!"

"We're all in danger!"

Those were among the most decipherable shouts from the men standing and pointing fingers.

"When I find out who it is, I'll put a bullet in them myself," Stag bellows over his peers.

The pot is about to bubble over. Ian walks up the center aisle, causing the volume of threats and promises of retribution to wane. When he reaches Remy and Mike up front, he turns to face the now silent Keystone Militia.

"Very nice work on the ballots. Now we can move on to our next phase."

"What the hell are you talking about, Ian? We failed!" Stag shouts.

"Yeah, they found a truck before we could deliver half of them," one of his disciples adds.

"So? How does that change anything?"

"What do you mean?" Remy asks.

"I mean that the authorities made our job easier. I told you this wasn't about getting the ballots counted. They *need* to be discovered to cast doubt on the election. The police did us a solid by finding our truck and kickstarting the process."

"We have a rat!"

Another spate of accusations begins to crescendo. This is becoming counterproductive.

"You don't have a rat," he shouts when there is a natural pause in the yelling. "I tipped off the police."

The meeting hall plunges into silence.

"What are you talking about, Ian?" Mike asks.

"I gave them the truck's location in a phony 9-1-1 call. Then I leaked it to the media while I was returning here. That's why the police and feds couldn't cover it up."

"Why didn't you tell us?" Mike asks in a hushed voice that sounds like a megaphone in the quiet hall.

"Compartmentalization. None of you needed to know in case someone got caught."

Stag erupts in a sarcastic laugh. "You're such a fraud. I don't know why we're listening to you."

"Because I did in one day what none of you have in a decade. I'm bringing change."

"You're delusional. What do you think you changed?"

Ian grins and grabs the remote. He presses the power button, and the flat-screen television mounted in the corner comes to life. It's already tuned into CNN.

"Police are not speculating who is behind the ballots, only that nearly seven thousand have been recovered."

Ian presses the channel up button.

"The election is already tainted," a guest at the desk responds to the anchor at FOX News. "No matter what happens, this election is in doubt. Police recovered seven thousand ballots. How many did they miss? They could have hauled off a semi-trailer full of them at that industrial print shop. This is election fraud, plain and simple. The Democrats are trying to steal this election!"

Ian changes the channel again.

"Is there any discussion of this being a false flag operation by the Republicans since they are losing in the state?" the anchor asks an on-scene reporter.

"Police are not publicly speculating, but it is a possibility. Given the events in New Hampshire, the ballots may have been planted there to throw the election into turmoil. Those are the same kind of shady tactics the Bradford campaign has been employing for months. This election appears to have just gotten dirtier."

"Thank you, Domingo," the anchor says. "We are still awaiting comment from the Pennsylvania secretary of state and federal officials within the FBI. We turn our coverage now to—"

"Seen enough?" Ian asks, muting the television. "Congratulations, gentlemen. The Keystone Militia single-handedly killed mail-in voting in this country. Now we bury its body."

CHAPTER FORTY-NINE

TIERRA CAMPOS

Front Burner Washington Office
Washington, D.C.

There is nothing for me to do but wait. Dial Pirate will send the files when he has them. The puzzle is solved. All that's left is to wait for the prize to be delivered. It's excruciating. Fortunately, Olivia pokes her head into the war room to punctuate my boredom.

"You busy? Everyone is gathering in the conference room."

"What's happening?"

"Nothing."

Her response was too canned. "Olivia, I've known you for a while now. What's wrong?"

"Nothing's wrong. Come on. Join us."

She's lying through her teeth, but I decide not to press her. Everyone is there when I get to the main conference room, including Wilson. There is one more person here than usual. I immediately recognize the Asian woman sitting at the table and know why Olivia is being so cagey.

"What the hell is she doing here?" I demand.

"Tierra, this is Ahn Mi Sun from—"

I fold my arms across my chest. "Tomorrow's News Today. I know who she is. She's Oliver Jahn's sidekick."

"Former sidekick," Mi Sun corrects. "I quit."

"Whatever. What is she doing here?" I ask Austin, refusing to speak to my nemesis' enabler.

"Applying for a job with *Capitol Beat*," Wilson deadpans.

"You can't be serious!"

"I told you that TNT was going to hell," Austin adds. "Now we know why."

"And Oliver can go with it. She can join him."

I mean those words. Oliver Jahn is a despicable human being. Anyone who supports him as he spews his vitriol has no place in my life. Mi Sun is the worst of his supporters. She has been with him from the beginning. In my mind, they are one and the same.

"If you're waiting for an apology from me, you won't get one, Tierra."

"Imagine my surprise."

"Not because you don't deserve one. An apology won't begin to atone for what Oliver did to you."

"Don't make it sound like you aren't complicit!"

Oliver Jahn's viewers are impressionable, and he motivated them to commit violence. I was returning to my apartment from a Navy Yard grocery store when I was attacked. Had it not been for the acts of some random pedestrians, I could have been killed. That wouldn't have torn him up. Mi Sun probably would have put up some funny picture over his shoulder mocking my death.

"*Wasn't* complicit. Past tense. Things haven't been good at VH Media. That's why I took a leave of absence. I quit when I heard that Oliver is planning more brutal personal attacks on you."

"Gee, there's something to look forward to."

"He never used to be like that."

"Neither was Hitler. Ask the Jews if that matters," Logan mutters.

Mi Sun ignores the jab. "He told me in Times Square what his plan for you was. I was shocked. He was never about that kind of thing. Most of his attacks were in jest."

"Why did he do it?" Austin asks.

"Ratings. We were in contract negotiations, and Oliver wanted a bump to justify a higher price."

"That sounds about right," I say.

"This is different, Tierra. This came down from higher up the food chain. Even Oliver doesn't want to go along with it."

"Then why is he?" Austin asks.

"You all know how this business works. What choice does he have?"

I give her a disapproving grin. Guards at Nazi concentration camps used the same argument. People are faced with choices every day. Some of them have lasting impacts and financial implications. So what? Sometimes the right path is the most difficult one. Oliver has chosen his.

"What are you really doing here, Mi Sun?"

"I want to be part of something special again. That's why I showed up at Oliver Jahn's house when he was podcasting to fifty thousand subscribers from his basement. TNT was different, and that was exciting. Now it's more of the same."

"Are you guys really falling for this BS?" I ask my seemingly riveted coworkers.

Naomi leans back in her chair. "We wanted to hear her out."

"You should have *shown* her out," I retort.

"Honestly, that's what I expected," Mi Sun says in her sweetest innocent voice.

"So, why come here at all?"

She lowers her head in thought before looking me in the eyes. "Because I realized Oliver was attacking the one thing I wanted most to be a part of. I'm the daughter of immigrants. My parents came here because they believed in the American dream. That you can be anything you want if you work hard enough for it. I still believe in that dream."

"Good for you," I say, not trying to hide my disdain.

"I see the direction you're taking *Front Burner* in. It's going to be the news outlet that people not only want but need. I want to take that journey with you. Wilson is doing a great job adapting an iconic cable show into a new medium, but it could be much better. Podcasting has a different audience that's used to a different style."

"Like what Oliver did?" Tyler moans.

"No, he was unique."

"That's one word for it," Logan mutters.

"Wilson knows how to be a host, but the show needs to be more visual than it was on television."

"Like showing pictures of a rat with a crown?"

Oliver Jahn coined me the "Queen of the Pretenders." He claimed that my brand of journalism was phony and that the non-partisan approach in my reporting was just a ploy to gain readers and viewers. As he made the accusation, there was a picture over his shoulder of a rat wearing a bejeweled crown. That had to be her idea.

"No," Mi Sun says, shaking her head. "That was campy. I mean stimulating the viewers by using images to punctuate the point. It doesn't have to be clever or funny…or demeaning. It just has to be present."

I check to see Wilson's reaction. Most men with his pedigree and accomplishments would bristle at any criticism of their life's work. He remains completely stoic. His eyes shift to me as I wait for him to chime in and end this ridiculous conversation. He doesn't say a word.

"I appreciate your coming to us," Naomi says. "Objections stemming from your participation in attacks on our staff aside, we can't afford you."

"How much do you make now?" Logan asks, likely more out of curiosity than a need to know.

"My salary tripled when I went to VH," she explains, causing Tyler to whistle. "Salary isn't everything in life. I'll work for free until *Front Burner* gets on its feet, just like the rest of you are."

"How noble," I mutter.

"We have a lot to discuss, Mi Sun," Naomi says. "I'm sure you appreciate that."

"Of course. Please let me know what you decide." She rises and stops alongside me at the door. "I don't expect you to like me, forgive me, or ever trust me, Tierra."

"That may be the one thing we agree on."

Mi Sun nods. "You left *Front Burner* before coming back. I know the story. You found it in your heart to give Austin a second chance. I hope you'll consider doing the same for me."

CHAPTER FIFTY

DEPUTY AG CONRAD WILLIAMS

Office of the Attorney General of the United States
Washington, D.C.

One Week Until the General Election

The early morning summons to the attorney general's office wasn't unexpected. In fact, Conrad expected it sometime yesterday after the news of a van full of completed ballots broke. The media initially jumped on the story before moving on to other more important things like the latest celebrity divorce drama and viral TikTok trend.

Conrad meets Director Krekstein in the corridor at seven a.m. sharp before heading into the office. Lisa Ehler is in a foul mood, likely having received an earful from the president. His political legacy is at stake in this election. Years of successful policies can be whitewashed in the court of public opinion if a negative perception persists in the minds of the American people.

There are no pleasantries. The two men brief the AG about what the FBI and local authorities have learned about the discovered ballots. The briefing doesn't seem to impress the AG, who scowls and shifts in her seat when the director finishes.

"That's all the details you have? You've had an entire day to investigate."

"Yes, ma'am. Nobody was taken into custody, and no physical evidence outside of the ballots was uncovered at the scene. The van had a phony registration and plates. This investigation is going to be a grind."

"We're certain they were the ballots from the printing company fire?"

"They were perfect matches, so it's a reasonable conclusion. The Philadelphia Field Office has teams dusting every ballot for prints to see if we can identify who handled them. They are testing every envelope seal for DNA. It will be a time-consuming process."

"How many were found?" Ehler asks, leaning back in her chair.

"Almost eight thousand."

"And some were missing?"

"Given the van's cargo capacity, yes, we believe several mail crates of ballots weren't present," the director answers, his voice remaining even and dispassionate.

"Gentlemen, you're saying that the Pennsylvania election has been rigged. Do I understand that correctly?"

"Not exactly, ma'am," Conrad says, taking the reins from the FBI director. This is a political conversation now. "The Commonwealth of Pennsylvania has employed significant measures to secure this election. There are safeguards against fraud, especially in their vote-by-mail system. I'm confident they'll identify any forged ballots that may have been submitted."

"No countermeasures are one hundred percent effective, Conrad."

"Yes, ma'am, but even if some slip through, it won't be a sizable number."

The AG scowls. "Oh, yeah? Convince the American public of that."

Michael and Conrad share a look, and the director takes the lead. "I don't think they should be told."

The attorney general shifts her eyes between the two men. When they settle on the FBI director, she squints and wrinkles her brow.

"Come again?"

"All this information should be kept classified for the time being."

"It will leak," Ehler argues.

"Then we'll deal with it then. There should be no official statement from the Bureau until we have all the facts."

Conrad watches his boss study their faces. He imagines she is hoping that the two men are joking. Unfortunately, nothing about this is a laughing matter.

"Withholding information from the public until after an election isn't unprecedented," Krekstein continues.

"How's that been working out for the FBI in recent years, Michael?"

"The director is right. With what we know, all we're certain to accomplish by releasing details of an incomplete investigation is to create doubt and panic."

Lisa glares at him from across her desk. "And invite ourselves to be accused of a cover-up."

"That can be defended as a prudent measure given the matter's sensitivity. Determinations have to be made. We don't know the scope of this breach. It could have only been a couple of hundred ballots."

"It could have been tens of thousands!" the exasperated AG counters.

"That's exactly my point. If we go public with this now, it will only worsen matters. Let the FBI do its job, and then we can present a complete set of facts."

"Investigating reports of voter fraud, intimidation, and manipulation is the FBI's highest priority," the director assures her. "This is the highest profile instance of interference. We're working with state and local officials to uncover the group or individuals behind it and will get you answers."

Lisa wiggles her fingers and flexes her hands. One of the most difficult parts of her job is knowing what and what not to tell the president. It can't be a regurgitation of events and facts. She needs to provide the context and the path forward. That's what he demands from the country's top lawyer.

"The president isn't going to want to hide this. He'll want to get in front of it."

"As any good leader would," Conrad says, steepling his hands. "You need to explain to him that it will compromise the investigation and could unnecessarily endanger election integrity and confidence. There is no point in sounding an alarm without knowing the precise reason."

"Damned if you do, damned if you don't," Ehler mutters.

Conrad usually would opt to do in those circumstances. He fancies himself a man of action, but not in this case. Inaction at the federal level is critical to their success.

"Gentlemen, find out who is behind this and take them down. People are already rattled after what happened in New Hampshire. Any attempt to subvert this election is a clear and present danger to our Republic. Leave no stone unturned. Do you understand?"

"Yes, ma'am," the two men say in unison.

"We are a week away from the general election. I may be able to convince the president to remain on the sidelines, but it's a stay of execution. He will want results. Get them for me."

"We will," the director says as he and Conrad rise and leave the AG's office.

Conrad pledges Krekstein his support, and the director peels off to have his driver take him back to the Hoover Building. When he reaches his office, he settles into his chair and leans back. That was almost too easy. Lisa Ehler is weak and impressionable, but there is no way she agreed with the course of action they laid out. That's what happens when you don't have a backbone.

Rasputin, Machiavelli, and Nietzsche had better handle their business. At this stage, their responsibilities are easy by comparison. Conrad feels like he's carrying all the water in this effort. They had better not let him down.

CHAPTER FIFTY-ONE

BRIAN COOPER

Actyv Private Equity
Midtown Manhattan, New York

It was a short walk from Brian's Times Square hotel to Actyv's office on this brisk late October morning. At a whisper over fourteen hundred feet, One Vanderbilt is Midtown's tallest building and the city's fourth-tallest.

Brian checks in at the security desk and takes the elevator up to the 55th floor. This is easily the nicest office he's ever seen. Its modern design is beautiful, and the view of the island through the floor-to-ceiling windows is spectacular. It must be nice to be filthy rich and own a company that is basically a printing press for money.

An attractive receptionist shows Brian into a high-tech conference room before offering him a beverage. He declines, despite being under-caffeinated and needing a jolt. It can wait until this meeting finishes. He admires the view out the window until he hears the door open behind him.

"The infamous Brian Cooper," an impeccably dressed man says in a Russian accent as he makes his way into the meeting area.

"I don't know about that," Brian says, shaking his hand.

"I do. Roman Muratova. This is Xinming Qi."

"Good to meet you, Brian," he says as they shake.

"Garrett is running a few minutes late and should be here shortly. Please," Roman says, gesturing at a chair.

"We have been very impressed with what you've done with Colin Bradford's campaign," the Asian man opens.

"I can't take all the credit. I have a good candidate."

"Yes, but one who had a lousy strategy after the primaries."

"That belonged to my predecessor. Mister Muratova, I think—"

The Russian smiles. "Please, call me Roman. How is Brevin Hawkins doing these days?"

"You know Brevin?" Brian asks, already knowing that he does.

"I do."

"He's a clown," Garrett Brewer says, striding through the door and into the room.

The men rise, and another formal introduction is made. Garrett apologizes for his tardiness and takes his place to the right of Roman. The table is now set. Each of these men has almost unimaginable wealth and power. They're also very polite and excellent hosts.

"The governor's best move was kicking Hawkins to the curb and putting you in his place," Garrett concludes.

"Your candidate may be promising," Qi surmises, "but your strategy is proven. You've done a magnificent job competing in states that most pundits had written off."

"I appreciate the kind words. Thank you."

"Do you think it will be enough?" Roman asks, rubbing his hands in front of him.

"It all comes down to who gets out the vote in Pennsylvania."

"Interesting," Garrett says, leaning back. The other two men join him.

"What is?"

"That you didn't immediately say 'yes,'" Qi explains. "Instead of a canned answer, you provided a one-sentence analysis."

"The three of you don't strike me as the type of men who appreciate nonsense. Offering a hollow assurance of a certain victory is nonsense."

"Indeed."

"Do you know why you're here?" Roman asks.

"My understanding is that you're taking an interest in funding the RNC's post-election legal team."

"We're interested in funding the teams for both candidates," Garrett says.

Brian suppresses a grimace. That answers that question.

"You don't look surprised," Roman observes.

"I'm not."

"Why?" Qi asks, cocking his head slightly.

"I looked around this place when I got here. Your workplace is magnificent. It must cost a fortune per square foot, which means you generate more than enough revenue to cover its expense. You didn't reach that point by wagering your loose change on one pony. You're hedging your bet."

"I told you he was sharp," Garrett says, elbowing Roman in the ribs.

"Do you disagree with the tactic?" Qi asks, continuing to look at Brian like they're in a therapy session.

The political strategist is conflicted. He doesn't want them supporting Standish or any legal challenges or defenses the Democrats mount. But he is also in no position to demand their support at her expense. He needs to secure their financial contribution, not offend them by using lousy salesmanship. That's what Brevin would do and likely the approach the governor wants Brian to employ.

"No."

The three men lean forward as they glance at each other.

"I don't believe you," Roman finally says.

"You asked if I disagreed with your approach. Looking at it from your perspective, it's perfectly reasonable. In fact, it's probably likely. You didn't ask if I liked the approach, which I obviously don't."

"I can see why you're in politics," Garrett muses.

"And I can see why you gentlemen are in business. Regardless of the outcome of the election, you win. That's not a bad position to be in."

"It is a costly one," Qi confesses.

"Unless it buys you the influence you're seeking. Then it's not a cost. It's an investment."

Garrett smirks. "You want to know why we're doing this."

"I know why."

"No, Mister Cooper, you don't. All three of us are immigrants. We came to the United States to create a better life for our families and succeeded beyond our wildest expectations. We believe in America. Unfortunately, the aftermath of this election is going to be…ugly."

"Why do you say that?" Brian asks, knowing how dumb that question is.

Roman wags his cell phone. "We read the news. If the election is close, there is no reason to believe there won't be legal challenges to the results."

"There is historical precedence," Qi adds.

"Recent history," Garrett corrects.

Brian waits for a beat before speaking. "How does funding both sides help that?"

"From your perspective, it doesn't. We believe it will give the American public confidence that the results are accurate. We can fund recounts and investigations into improprieties. Both of those endeavors require considerable money."

"We have money."

"Do you not want ours?" Qi asks.

Now it's Brian's turn to show some discomfort. "I'll be honest. I don't like the idea of a check that comes with an obligation."

"Do you think we're extorting you?" the Russian asks.

"Aren't you?"

The three men look amused. "You don't know us very well," Garrett says.

"In fairness, I only met the three of you about ten minutes ago."

"Then you must get to know us better!" the Russian exclaims, slapping the table. "It will allow us to talk in a place with excellent vodka and walls that don't have ears."

Brian can't help but look around the room and then at the sleek conferencing unit in the center of the table. For the first time since he arrived, it dawns on him that they could have recorded this entire interaction. That's the advantage of playing the game on their home court.

"You must come out with us this evening. Perhaps we can discuss this further over a meal and some drinks afterward. My assistant will make the necessary arrangements. We can pick you up at your hotel at, say…seven?"

"That's very generous, Qi," Brian says. "However, I really have to get back to Pennsylvania."

"Are you that indispensable to Bradford's campaign?" Garrett challenges, narrowing his eyes.

Brian offers a slight shrug. "I'd like to think so."

"And we would have to think twice about supporting someone so…reliant on others."

"What Roman is trying to say is that you should think twice about declining," Qi says.

Brian nods.

"Good man. We'll meet you at the restaurant," Garrett says, slapping his shoulder.

As if through extrasensory perception, the receptionist materializes at the door and holds it open as the three men depart. Maybe this room is monitored after all. She escorts him to the elevator bank as Brian starts making mental preparations for spending another night in the city.

CHAPTER FIFTY-TWO

SPECIAL AGENT VICTORIA LARSEN

Kratos Holdings Corporate Offices
Elkins Park, Pennsylvania

This isn't what Victoria expected. As a holding company with a big-money private equity backer, she expected Kratos' offices to be located in a skyscraper downtown. When Imani steered her car north of the city, her expectation changed to a small three-story building in a well-manicured office park.

Instead, she pulls up outside a bleak brick and concrete structure with small windows and hideous pale blue awnings. It's a building that could have been plucked out of Bratislava in 1970s communist Slovakia, not situated outside one of America's most historic cities.

"How do you want to handle this?" Imani asks.

"Let's just walk in and see who's home."

They enter the unguarded building, check the directory, and head upstairs to the second floor. Of the five companies who call this building home, only Kratos occupies the second floor. Victoria does some math in her head to determine the approximate square footage. The office can easily accommodate up to a hundred people, assuming they have the requisite conference and break rooms and a spacious office for the CEO.

The lights are out in the short corridor leading to the double doors. The Kratos logo is illuminated beside them, such as it is. It looks like something purchased for ten bucks off some online logo website.

Victoria reaches for the handle and pulls the door open. Most companies would have a receptionist to greet visitors. Not here. There are no overhead lights on, no computer or phone on the desk, and no décor. Not even a plant in the corner.

"Creepy," Imani whispers.

Victoria draws her weapon, with Imani following suit a second later. They sweep past the reception desk and through the doors into the main office area. Except for cubicles, office chairs, and wires for computers and telephones, the space is completely empty.

The two women split up and take different paths around the cubes. Motion sensing lighting overhead clicks on as they move deeper into the bowels of the office. Victoria sticks her head into an empty conference room. Imani checks the CEO's office to find that completely cleared out, desk and all. The two women converge at a break room at the far back. It's also empty.

"Clear."

"Clear," Imani confirms.

Victoria opens the refrigerator. It's spotless. There are no five-day-old sandwiches, wilted salads, or expired yogurt. Even the coffee machine has disappeared from the stained counter it once rested on.

"Was this place ever occupied? It's completely empty."

A noise from the other side of the office causes them to jump. Victoria regrips her weapon and moves to the door to peek out.

"Not completely."

Both women retrace their steps, moving swiftly and quietly down the carpeted space between cubicles. A man appears in the doorway to the reception area holding something in his right hand. Victoria immediately stops and takes up a shooting stance.

"Federal agent! Drop it! Do it now!"

The man complies immediately, raising both hands to shoulder level. A Kobalt cordless drill clatters to the floor.

"Who are you?" Victoria demands.

"I'm…I'm the building manager. I came to change the locks. What are you doing in this office?"

"We're with the FBI." Imani removes her gold badge from behind her body armor and lets it dangle on the chain. Victoria's badge is clipped to her belt, and she's certain it's visible.

"What's your name?"

"Angel Mendoza."

"You don't look Latino, Angel," Victoria observes, looking for a verbal cue that will confirm the man's identity.

"My mother was Filipina."

"Do you have identification?" Imani asks.

Angel reaches for his back pocket.

"Stop right there!" Victoria barks. The man looks like he's about to piss his pants. "Where is your ID?"

"My back pocket."

"Left or right side?"

"Right."

"Turn and face my partner," Victoria calmly commands, lowering the volume of her voice but still speaking with authority. "With your finger and thumb, pull it out. Do it slowly. Quick movements will get you shot, Angel."

The man does as instructed, and Imani takes the wallet and moves back a few steps. She nods. Victoria gestures at the building ID badge on his belt. Imani checks that as well. It matches.

"Okay, Angel," Victoria says, holstering her weapon. "Do you have an office in the building?"

"It's down on the first floor."

"Take us there. Leave your tools. You can change the locks when we finish."

Angel looks at the two women while remaining frozen in place. "Am I in trouble?"

"Not if you take us to your office."

The trio takes the stairwell back down to the ground floor and walks down a corridor. Angel unlocks his office, and the women follow him in. It's only a cramped space with a desk and two chairs, but it's not claustrophobic, either.

"What is this about?" Angel asks, sitting behind his desk.

Victoria sees the pictures of him and his family on the desk. Another hard-working man trying to earn a living. She needs to go easy on him.

"How long has Kratos Holding Company been a tenant here?"

Angel rubs his stubbled chin. "About two years. They signed a five-year lease for the entire second floor and moved in when construction finished."

"When did they move out?"

"They started two days ago. They didn't provide notice or nothin'. I saw them moving boxes, and they said they were moving out. That's it. They finished up yesterday."

Imani and Victoria share a look. Either it was one hell of a coincidence, they were tipped off, or someone is monitoring Victoria's activities. Either way, Kratos' quick exit has everything to do with her.

"Is breaking a lease common?" Imani asks.

"No, it's unheard of. The early termination penalty is obscene."

"What can you tell us about their CEO?"

"He drives a Bentley," Angel says with a grin that smacks of admiration.

"That's it?"

"It's a really nice car."

"It's overrated," Victoria says, not knowing if that's true. She's never been inside a Bentley, much less owned one.

"It's nicer than my Honda Civic."

"Civics are nice," Imani says.

"They're girl cars."

Victoria tries to suppress a smile. "What about the man himself?"

"He's a douchebag. Fortunately, he's rarely here. Not too many people are. I've only ever seen a dozen people up there, and they come and go."

"There are cubicles for about eighty people up there," Imani says, drawing on her mental picture of the office.

"Most were never used. What's this about?"

"We can't tell you that, Angel. We need you to dig up every piece of paperwork that relates to Kratos Holding Corp."

The building manager looks at the stack of papers on his desk and then at the overstuffed file cabinet.

"That could take a while."

"We can wait."

CHAPTER FIFTY-THREE

IAN DRUCKER

"The Forge" Militia Compound
Liberty, Pennsylvania

This is not how Ian drew it up. Livestreams are a far more effective way to record the truck's journey from Liberty to Philadelphia. He could have strapped cameras all over the thing and played the part of a video producer in a control room. It would have been fun and entertaining.

Unfortunately, technology was Sartre's department, and the men here can barely turn on a computer. Ian cannot replicate what Marx and the SOF did to force Dylan Spencer to drive his fancy supercar onto the tracks in front of a speeding locomotive. Instead, he had to use the most insecure method imaginable: a video chat from a cell phone. At least he managed to share it on the meeting room's television.

"We are about forty miles from Philadelphia," Remy informs the group as he stares at the camera. "That was an important city in the American Revolution. It will be more important for the next revolution – the one we are about to start. This is our Lexington Common. This is the Old North Bridge. We are the new minutemen, and these are the first shots of the Second American Revolution."

A cheer goes up from the group of assembled militia members seated in rows in front of Ian. He is content to sit at the folding table in front of the room and choreograph this adventure in domestic terrorism.

"We the People will no longer be ignored," Mike says from behind the wheel. "Unlike that day, no historians will argue over who fired this 'shot heard round the world.' Remy and I took on this mission because we bear it as our responsibility. We are committing the Keystone Militia to war against an oppressive government. We—"

"Wait! What's that?"

"What's what?" Mike says, noticing Remy staring at the mirror.

The video gets shaky as Remy adjusts his position in the passenger seat. Ian sits more erect in his chair. Almost everyone sitting in the Forge's meeting room does the same thing.

"Behind us! Aw, hell. Ian, we have a problem."

"What is it?"

There is a murmur in the room. Ian settles everyone down.

"We're getting pulled over."

Ian curses to himself. "Were you speeding?"

"Negative," Mike says, checking the dash. "I've been driving five miles per hour under the limit. What do we do?"

"Keep going," Remy orders.

Ian leans forward in his chair and picks up the phone so the two leaders can see his face on the video. Remy is holding his device near his lap. His face ducks in and out of the camera view every time he checks the mirror.

"Pull over!" the police order, changing the tone of their siren to command the two men's attention.

"We could pull over and play it cool," Mike says, presenting an option. "It may be nothing."

"Crap. There's another one," Remy says, staring hard at the side mirror.

"This isn't a routine stop, guys," Ian says, doing some mental calculations.

Mike and Remy could pull over, but it'd be risky, considering their cargo. If they turn this into a chase, it may buy time, but they'll never make it into the city. The best option is to elude capture and then try to flee the vehicle, but that will be tough on this section of the interstate.

"Ian, how far are we from the target?" Remy asks with a sense of urgency.

"Too far. You've got about another hour of travel time, easy."

"We're not going to make it."

Ian unfolds a map and spreads it out on the table. He traces his finger along the Pennsylvania turnpike and stops at the truck's approximate location just past the Brandywine Travel Plaza. They are still some distance from the next exit in Exton. There is no way the police will let them reach it.

"They're backing off! They're backing off!" Remy excitedly shouts.

"Whoa!" Mike exclaims, slowing the vehicle dramatically.

"What is it?" Ian asks.

Remy points the camera out of the windshield. There is a roadblock about a half mile ahead made up of squad cars and a pair of armored vehicles. The truck's size and weight could conceivably get them through the cars, but there is no way those trucks are budging.

Ian leans back. Armored cars. This is no ordinary stop. They belong to SWAT, and that team would only be involved if the authorities knew what Mike and Remy were carrying.

"We're screwed," Mike concludes. Remy points the camera at his face.

"Those who expect to reap the blessings of freedom must, like men, undergo the fatigue of supporting it," he says, quoting Thomas Paine. "It has been an honor leading you brave men. Continue the fight."

"You don't need to do this, Remy," Ian argues. "We can find a way—"

"There is no way out. Finish this for us, Ian. Make good on the promises you made me. That's how you can reward this sacrifice."

"Remy, don't!" Ian barks.

The two men aren't listening. Mike slams the truck into drive and guns the engine. The camera shakes as the vehicle lurches forward and picks up momentum. The action isn't lost on the men at the barrier. They open fire with their rifles as the truck hurtles at them. The windshield begins taking hits before pieces start giving way under the pressure of the air hitting it. Glass is flying everywhere.

"Aw, dammit!"

The video turns to Mike, and Ian sees him clutching his shoulder before taking another round. His hands drop off the wheel, and the side of the truck slams into the steel guardrail before grinding to a halt. The police are still shooting, forcing Remy to duck behind the dash. It's only a matter of time. Everyone knows it, including him.

"Sic semper tyrannis!" Remy screams as he stares into the camera, the detonator close to his face.

A second later, the video goes dead.

Ian closes his eyes. Thus always to tyrants. He can see the fireball and imagine the police ducking for cover to avoid the shrapnel and concussive wave of the blast. He knows the two militia leaders weren't close enough to the roadblock to take anyone with them. It's a waste of perfectly good plastic explosive, fertilizer, and diesel fuel. No tyrants perished in that blast. Their deaths were for almost nothing.

"We were betrayed!"

"We have a mole!"

It's the same song and dance with this group. "We don't know that."

"Yes, we—"

"We don't know that!" Ian exclaims, slapping his hand down hard on the table.

"Yes, it could be a betrayal. It could also be a thousand other things."

"They were waiting for us there!" Stag says, preparing to lead the crusade against Ian.

"Yeah, and the vehicle could have been spotted."

"Was it you, Drucker?"

Ian's eyes narrow at his accuser. "If it was me, that truck never would have left the Forge. Agents would have rolled in here and stopped the truck bomb before we could find the keys to start the engine."

"So, what do we do?" a man asks before Stag has the opportunity to press his challenge.

"Continue our mission."

"What mission?" Stag asks.

"The one Remy and Mike were working on. The explosives we procured weren't all packed in that truck. Did you see all the small boxes in the storage shed?"

"Yeah."

"They're going to be addressed and mailed to senators and congressmen across the country. The Semtex in them is rigged to explode when the box is opened."

"That will never work!" Stag exclaims. "Packages are screened."

"Yes, they are. Except when a code is affixed."

The men in the room instantly calm down. They begin quiet conversations with each other as Stag folds his arms.

"What code?"

Ian smirks. "Each politician and top bureaucrat is issued a special secret six-digit alphanumeric mail code. They only share it with people close to them. It means that packages and mail are subject to reduced screenings. Authorities may intercept some of them, but they won't get all of them."

"Where did you get the codes?" a man in the back asks.

"Mike and Remy didn't invite me here for my devilishly good looks. I was an FBI agent. I had access to lots of information not available to the general public."

That makes sense to the militia as Ian sees the nods of approval.

"When do we mail them?" Stag asks, his arms still welded across his chest.

"I've arranged for shipment on Saturday. They'll arrive at campaign offices across the country right before the election."

"What's the point of that?" someone asks.

"Fear. It's a powerful weapon. Scared people do irrational things. That will allow us to capitalize on their mistakes," Ian says as he stands. "Gentlemen, tonight was a setback. We lost two good men in our battle against a despotic government that will chisel away our freedoms until we have none left. Now it's time to fulfill our promise to them. We will honor Mike's and Remy's sacrifice by making it mean something."

Words of agreement ripple through the militia. Their confidence is restored, so Ian walks down the center aisle, shaking hands and slapping backs. He stops when he reaches the door.

"Double the guard tonight and be on high alert," Ian says to the man he saw assisting Mike and Remy on countless occasions. "If there is a mole in this compound, we don't want to be caught with our pants down."

CHAPTER FIFTY-FOUR

TIERRA CAMPOS

Front Burner Washington Office
Washington, D.C.

The team assembles in the conference room a little before seven in the morning to discuss the coverage of the alleged truck bomb in Pennsylvania. Specifically, they want to discuss its lack of coverage. Most news sources never made mention of the explosion that rocked the Pennsylvania Turnpike and closed the road for four hours.

That's the kind of story that earns national attention even when a state isn't ground zero in a presidential election year. It's a terrorist act, and those get attention. Not this time. The local Philadelphia stations mentioned the incident but have corrected their early reports that claimed it was an attempted bombing.

Front Burner's growing list of alternative sources thinks differently. Logan is coordinating stories and researching their material and won't be joining them in the conference room. Nobody is surprised by the sloppy reporting, but it usually flows in the other direction. Austin seems surprised that the initial reports didn't involve an Iranian briefcase nuke carried by Sasquatch in a car driven by Fred Flintstone.

Once we finish commiserating over our competitors' lack of diligence, I explain that Dial Pirate still hasn't rebuilt the files. We have nothing to build on, and that's not the worst of it.

"Let's assume these files are the smoking gun. What are we going to do with them?"

Naomi glances over at Austin. I already know I'm not going to like what comes next.

"Publish them."

I shake my head. "An uncorroborated report by a man indicted for rigging an election? We need to investigate, and for that, we need investigators. I can't do this by myself."

"Nobody is expecting you to, Tierra," Naomi says, still annoyed with me after I insulted her the last time we met.

"That's *exactly* what you are expecting."

"I understand your frustration. I know you don't believe that, but it's true. But we're still barely squeaking by. We are trying to bring on more people—"

"Like Ahn Mi Sun?"

Everyone averts their eyes. I meant it as a joke, but it's less of a laughing matter than I thought.

"Why are…oh, hell no! You can't be serious?"

"She would be an asset to *Front Burner*," Naomi says.

"She's a despicable human being who worked for an even more despicable one."

"The latter part is certainly true, but we believe—"

"No, no, no! I don't care what you *believe*. I was beaten on a sidewalk and left for dead because of that woman."

"That was Oliver Jahn, not her," Austin says, causing me to shift my glare.

"I don't draw the distinction."

Austin should know better. He was the one musing about how Oliver's show had gone downhill. Mi Sun is Hermann Goering to Oliver's Adolf Hitler. He may have been the face and voice of the movement, but she was the one whispering in his ear.

"I understand how you feel."

"You clearly don't, Naomi, so stop saying that you do. Have you ever been doxxed? Had thugs in masks storm your apartment? Been chased while running or beaten within sight of your apartment? No? Then stop pretending you in any way understand how I feel!"

"Tierra, it's—"

"It's not just a business decision, Austin," I say, anticipating his defense. "It's personal to me. I know Mi Sun is talented, but so are countless other people. Hire someone else."

"The decision has been made," he states before pressing his lips together.

I look around the room. I can't believe I'm hearing this. It feels like yet another betrayal. I'm hurt, and maybe even wounded, that Austin and Naomi would consider bringing her to *Front Burner*.

"Then maybe I—"

"They weren't going to hire her, Tierra," Wilson says. "I wanted her. It was my call."

I'm at a loss for words. I feel my body instantly go numb.

"Can you all give Tierra and me the room, please?" Wilson waits patiently as everyone leaves, and I try to recover emotionally. "I know that look on your face. You think I stabbed you in the back."

"You did," I whisper because my mouth has gone dry. "I expected it from Naomi and maybe even Austin, but you?"

"I did no such thing," he says, shaking his head slowly. "It only feels that way."

"It *is* that way, Wilson. Why can't you understand that?"

"I do. More than you know. The difference is that I believe in second chances. You did once, too."

I close my eyes as some unwelcome memories rush back. I should have died on the library floor in Summerville when one of my fellow students opened fire. If not for Josh, I would have.

I got another second chance with *Front Burner* after my interview with Ethan Harrington got me fired from WWDC News. It was the rebirth of my career in journalism. Wilson could even argue that I got another when I joined him at *Capitol Beat*.

"I still do," I say, opening my eyes. "I gave Austin one, and look what's happened!"

"For the record, he was dead set against this because he knew how you would react."

"He was right. So, why?"

"Because she's talented, and I think she has the right to prove herself. Really, it's because I need you to let go of your anger."

"I'm not angry!" I snap.

He makes a disapproving face. "Yes, you are. You enjoyed watching Carl Brennan bumble through hosting *Capitol Beat* because of what he did to you at WWDC News. You relished the idea of taking Oliver Jahn down a peg at the Republican National Convention. You enjoyed sticking it to DeAnna Van Herten when I walked off the set at Granite State. You want people who wronged you to suffer."

"That's not true!"

"It is, and you know it. You're not only emotionally invested; you're obsessed. That's why you're taking everything personal, and it will consume you. I don't want to see that happen."

Nobody likes having a mirror thrust in their face. I wanted to be angry and resentful and lash out at the betrayal. Wilson is showing me how unhinged I appear to others. I didn't think my anger was irrational. Now, I'm not so sure.

"Wilson, do you think hiring Mi Sun will fix that?"

"I believe finding some forgiveness in your heart will be a start. Your battle isn't with her or even Oliver Jahn. They're only pawns in this game. If you want to uncover who is working with Andrew Li and Conrad Williams, you need to tackle the problem with a clear head. You need to set emotion aside and be the journalist this country needs. Otherwise, you're pushing an agenda just like everyone else."

"Passion isn't a bad thing, Wilson. You taught me that."

"I did. It's critical, but it needs to be channeled."

I lower my eyes and focus on the table. Wilson's right. I know in my heart he is. Why can't I accept that? Is it because I shouldn't or because I won't?

"We work in a jaded business surrounded by skeptics. I know that better than anyone. I've been doing this since before you were born. You gave me hope for the future, Tierra. You're more than my favorite journalist; you're my favorite *person*. I will always love you like the daughter I never had."

I have to fight the tears forming in my eyes. "Wilson…."

"If you don't want me to hire Mi Sun, I won't. But I'm asking you to consider why. I would be grateful if you find it in your heart to give her a chance. Not because it benefits Mi Sun. Because it will benefit you."

The aging anchor stands and squeezes my shoulder. He gives me a reassuring look before walking out of the room.

CHAPTER FIFTY-FIVE

BRIAN COOPER

Union Square Park
New York, New York

Hangovers are a cosmic force – they have a unique ability to bend time. Everything is slower, duller, and foggier until the human body can shake the effects of the poison that led to it. Brian had every intention of rising early and getting on the road back to Pennsylvania. The late night was a problem but not his worst enemy. That honor goes to the vodka.

Since he's still in the city, there is no reason not to take the time to pay someone a visit. Brian steps off the Broadway express N train and heads into Union Square Park. The former burial ground is the honored home of statues depicting George Washington, Abraham Lincoln, Mohandas Gandhi, and Marquis de Lafayette. He's not here for any of that.

In the southwest corner of the park are some of the best chess masters in the city. He's heard mixed reports about the legitimacy of the games, but the people there beat opponents straight up. Being good at chess means playing a lot, and these hustlers play from sunup to sundown. They don't cheat unsuspecting tourists out of their hard-earned vacation money. They beat them without breaking a sweat.

"Still victimizing tourists, Abe?"

"As I live and breathe. Brian Cooper. What brings you to the Big Apple?"

"Campaign business. I had to meet with some big financial guys."

"Oh, and you call me a crook."

Brian laughs. Abe has a point. Wall Street is demonized in every form of media imaginable for good reason. While he doesn't doubt that there are a few honest men and women working for colossal financial firms, finding one would be the equivalent of finding a leprechaun having inappropriate relations with a unicorn.

"I could have used a hustler like you in that meeting."

"Meh! It's not a hustle. Your father used to call it a reappropriation of excess financial resources."

Brian smiles at the memory. "He was good with words."

"He was full of shit," Abe grumbles.

"That too," Brian says with a laugh.

"You wanna be my next victim?"

Brian takes a seat. "I don't plan on losing to the Sausage King of Chicago."

"Hey, now! Don't start that again. For that, I'm just going to make you sit there. That damn movie ruined my life."

Abe's last name happens to be Froman. Any classic film connoisseur or child of the '80s will recognize the Ferris Bueller's Day Off reference. Abe Froman was the reservation Ferris, Cameron, and Sloan hijacked to get a table from the absurd maître d' at Chez Quis.

"Shouldn't you be wooing voters instead of money guys?"

"I would be in a functioning democracy. Money is the lifeblood of modern politics. Every candidate is a slave to cash, right down to the guy running for city dog catcher."

"Just like the Founding Fathers envisioned it," Abe says, heavy on the sarcasm. "What do you think of what's happening in Pennsylvania?"

Brian grimaces. "Democrats will stop at nothing to win."

Abe scoffs. "As if Republicans are angels."

"Well, that's true, but we aren't using political shenanigans to cover up our conspiracy to influence the election – fake ballots, rioting, threats – those are right out of their playbook."

Abe lowers his head and eyes him. "You know I'm a Democrat, right?"

The corner of Brian's mouth curls. "You know that I used to work for one, right?"

"Do you enjoy what you do, Brian?" Abe asks, setting up the chessboard.

"Not as much as I used to. The game has changed too much."

"Has it?"

He has a point. Dirty politics in this country dates back to when the Founding Fathers were fighting to succeed George Washington as president. Maybe it's the invention of the World Wide Web or the advent of cable news, but it feels much worse now. After two and a half centuries of rule-making, all legislatures have done is give candidates more laws to break.

"All right, they never used to be so overt about it."

"That's the system," Abe laments. "We have to deal with it."

"Why? Why should we?"

"I didn't peg you as a revolutionary."

"I didn't peg you as a chess hustler, yet here we are," Brian says, his arms outstretched. "The game is rigged, Abe. Republican, Democrat…it doesn't matter. Politicians stopped acting on behalf of the people long ago. The divide between red and blue in this country is the greatest feat of deception ever devised. The ideologies are different, but the political nobility on both sides is the real enemy."

"You're implying that we're serfs?"

"Isn't that how you're treated?"

Abe scowls. "Be careful, Brian. I served my country in Vietnam. Two tours."

"What did it get for you? What did it do for the American people? Other than free love, how did it benefit anyone other than defense contractors and politicians? The rich got richer, and everyone else got the threat of being drafted. The system is set up to serve itself, not you or me."

"Is Bradford any different?"

"He's more of the same. They all are."

Abe laughs. "You're turning into your father. One man can't change the system, Brian. Many have tried. Some came close and are worshipped for it. Most fail miserably. All end up dead one way or another. Will you be any different?"

Most children grow up with an expectation that they will conquer the world. Young men distill the abundant energy of youth into raw ambition. Much of that fades over time. The special people in this world never see it ebb. Despite not wanting the praise and criticism that come with the public stage, Brian considers himself one of those special few.

"'All that is necessary for the triumph of evil is for good men to do nothing.'"

Abe offers Brian an amused look. "Yes, the brave words of a politician who never had to sacrifice anything. Assuming Edmund Burke even said it at all."

Brian turns to watch a group of Asian tourists meander toward the park. "You have fresh victims. I'll leave you to it."

"Brian, fate whispers to the warrior, 'You cannot withstand the storm.' The warrior whispers back..."

"I am the storm."

Abe smiles and nods. "You're a bright young man. You always were head and shoulders above your friends. That makes you special, and special people don't sit in parks and play chess while life passes them by. Go out and be the storm, Brian."

"It was good seeing you, Abe."

Brian makes his way out of the park to go uptown and check out of his hotel. It was good seeing the old man again. He has always found his chats with him inspiring, this one included. *Be the storm.* That's exactly what he intends to do.

CHAPTER FIFTY-SIX

DEPUTY AG CONRAD WILLIAMS

U.S. Department of Justice
Washington, D.C.

Conrad gets remarkably little mail for a high-ranking United States government official. Most of his communications come via email or text message. The fan or hate mail all goes to the attorney general herself. He doesn't spend much time in the spotlight as a lowly deputy.

The overnight letter envelope on his desk catches his attention, not because he received it but because of the marking in the corner. Rasputin started a system where any package he needed to send would be marked with a highly stylized "R." He has a flair for the dramatic and far too much time on his hands. Conrad thinks the practice is absurd but can't argue against its effectiveness. He spotted it right away.

The return address in New York City doesn't ring a bell. There is no way that it's Rasputin's actual residence. It is likely a legitimate location, just not one he will be at. At least it isn't Yankee Stadium. Their East 161st Street address is too recognizable.

Conrad opens the envelope and slides the single sheet of letter paper out. The typed note is straight to the point.

Hope this helps.
-R

CyberOreo – Lucas Rella - 34-37 42nd St Unit 2L, Queens, NY
Dial Pirate – Brian Phillips - 441 E Erie St, Chicago, IL
AnarchyBooster – Nikolas Danek - 1610 W James Pl, Kent, WA

"I'll be damned," Conrad says as he pulls out his cell phone. He scrolls through recent calls until he finds who he's looking for.

"Mullin."

"Good evening, Vice-Admiral. Where are you?"

"I'm out to dinner, Conrad."

"Home or at a restaurant?"

There's a pause as if the head of the NSA doesn't want to answer the question. "I'm at Ferrandino's. What's this about?"

"I'll explain when I get there," Conrad says, ending the call. He immediately punches his intercom button. "I need a car out front immediately."

The car is waiting by the time Conrad makes it outside. He gives his driver instructions, and the man wastes no time pointing their vehicle southeast toward the Anacostia River.

The timing of the names couldn't be more fortunate. The FBI has learned that Campos is working with someone from outside *Front Burner* but they could not trace the calls. The degree of sophistication required to defeat the trace is found only in hacker, espionage, or counterespionage communities.

Rasputin must have a source inside *Front Burner* to acquire that information. According to Victoria Larsen's field reports in New Hampshire, Campos has a history with these hackers. She didn't know their names, or at least never reported them.

If Conrad can neutralize these hackers, it may be harder for Campos to conduct any investigation. The last thing they need is for her to uncover Isiah Burgess's research, assuming he had some. It's plausible and needs to be treated as a threat.

"Wait here," Conrad says, opening the rear door. "This will only take a few minutes."

The deputy attorney general enters the restaurant and scans the tables. The vice admiral is along the far wall, his back against it so he can watch the door. Conrad has never met anyone in the military that likes to have their back to an entrance or exit if it can be avoided.

The admiral spots him and excuses himself from the table. He straightens his uniform jacket as he weaves between the tables. The man has an impressive number of ribbons designating campaigns and decorations. Military personnel wear their resumes on their chests. Too bad most people have no idea what any of it means.

"All right. What's so important that you drove out to Anacostia?"

"I'm repaying a debt," Conrad says as he hands him the sheet of paper.

The names mean nothing to Conrad, but Davis's eyes light up like it's Christmas morning. He clearly recognizes the hackers.

"Where did you get this?"

"Call it an anonymous tip."

"Conrad…."

"Don't look a gift horse in the mouth, Davis."

He shakes his head. "The NSA can't legally act on this. They're stateside."

This man needs to get up to speed on how things work in this city, or he'll get eaten alive. Ordering dinner is a political act in the nation's capital. He needs to understand how to use leverage, bend rules, and game the system. What good is power if you don't use it?

"You have a liaison in the NCIJTF, right?"

"Yeah."

"Give it to him."

"Her," the admiral corrects him.

Conrad smirks. "Whatever."

Communication, commerce, and how government interacts with its citizens forever changed with Internet connectivity and the convenience of smartphones. Unfortunately, these advancements introduced a new breed of technologically savvy criminals engaging in everything from ransomware attacks to identity theft.

The National Cyber Investigative Joint Task Force was established to address these evolving cybersecurity challenges. Thirty agencies spanning law enforcement, the intelligence community, and even the Department of Defense, have assigned representatives to accomplish the organization's mission. It's an impressive government response to an increasing threat. That doesn't mean all the participants are regarded as equals.

"They're going to wonder where she got it."

"Make something up."

"I can't just—"

"You work in Washington, now, Davis! That's all we do here."

"I work in Maryland."

Conrad is starting to lose his patience. "Then give it back to me. FBI Cyber will be doing cartwheels if I—"

"No, I'll use it."

Conrad frowns, but it's only for show. "Fine. Whatever. Just keep my name out of it."

"This had better pan out," the admiral says, folding the paper and tucking it in one of the pockets in his service uniform.

"It will. Check it out first if you need to."

"Those three hackers are on the cyber most wanted list. I don't think the information I gave you on the links was an even exchange."

Conrad slaps his shoulder. "Then you owe me one. I need to head back to Justice. Enjoy your dinner."

Mission accomplished. He climbs back into the car, knowing that a problem solved tonight is one fewer that he'll need to deal with tomorrow. Larsen and Campos. Those two women should have been taken out long ago. The failure to do so is an oversight that needs to be addressed. This is a positive step in that direction.

CHAPTER FIFTY-SEVEN

IAN DRUCKER

"The Forge" Militia Compound
Liberty, Pennsylvania

Having the deputy AG on the team is important. He gained access to important information that was required to accomplish this mission. Ian assumed that the FBI had an infiltrator in the Keystone Militia. They embedded agents in most anti-government groups to monitor their operations. Once Robespierre confirmed that there was an agent present, Ian had to hatch a plan to figure out who. Now, it's a matter of springing the trap.

It wouldn't be enough if Ian knew the agent's identity. He's still an outsider here. Any accusation he flings is likely to boomerang back at him. The informant has to be caught in the act of contacting the Bureau in a public way. That means he needed to be given an urgent reason – one Ian was quick to provide.

It's dark, but the night isn't impenetrable. Ian can still see the silhouettes of the lumber mill's buildings and the shapes of the trees at the woodline. He has no problem spotting the lone figure moving between the piles of logs. The man isn't being overtly stealthy but isn't advertising his movements either. It's a smart tactic for a snitch. His actions provide plausible deniability should a militiaman stumble upon him.

These piles of logs along the southern edge of the storage have been here since long before Ian arrived. He's not sure whether there isn't a market for the boards the huge trunks would yield or if they were just forgotten. It doesn't matter. The crevices between them are the perfect place to hide communications equipment.

The man takes one more look around and starts groping in a space between logs. Ian watches him feel around and then start getting agitated when his hand touches nothing but wood and air.

"Come on, come on, where are you?" the man grumbles in a near whisper.

"Right here," Ian says from his spot atop the pile.

Stag freezes in place. He clicks on his flashlight and shines it at Ian.

"Lower it a bit, will ya?" The man complies. "I never would have found this here. It's hidden yet easily accessible. You were well-trained, Stag. What class were you at Quantico?"

"I don't know what you're talking about!"

"Let's be adults and not play make-believe. You got caught reporting on the militia's activities via this sat phone. Your mission is over, Stag."

He looks around. "How did you find it?"

"I followed you before Remy and Mike left. I knew you would call that in. The device was too big not to, and you had no idea what the target was. You had to ensure it was intercepted."

"Where were they going?" he asks. It's the curious mind of an investigator.

"Standish's campaign office in Philly."

"You're a liar," Stag says. "You never intended it to make it. You set it up as a mole hunt."

"You must have some experience with that kind of counterterrorism operation. I figured that the trap would be laid closer to the target area. Mike and Remy had an escape route planned farther down the road," Ian lies.

There was never going to be an escape for the two men. Ian just can't say that. The militiamen in the camp would appreciate hearing that their leaders were used as bait. By eliminating them and snagging Stag, Ian is the *de facto* leader of the Keystone Militia. That's how it needs to be.

"And the letter bombs to politicians?" Ian only smiles at the man's gullibility. "It's over, Drucker."

"How do you figure?"

Stag pulls his gun and points it at Ian. "You're under arrest for domestic terrorism. We can do this the easy way or the hard way."

Ian tightens his jaw, presses his lips together, and offers a disapproving shake of his head. "I don't like either of those options."

Men pour from around the woodpile. Stag doesn't have time to shoot any of them, including Ian. They are on him in seconds. He is disarmed and hauled to the ground. Ian can hear the percussive sound of thuds from kicks and punches. He lets the boys have their fun before he climbs off the pile to stop them.

"Enough. That's enough! Give me some light."

A handful of flashlights turn on. Stag is prone and stares at the dozen militiamen looming above him. He knows he's in deep shit. It's written on his face.

"Get this scumbag on his knees."

The men do as instructed. Stag is bleeding profusely from his mouth and nose. His right eye is beginning to swell. They worked him over well in the short time they had. Ian bends down to look him in the face.

"Any last words?"

"They know you're here," Stag says, his eyes filled with hatred. "I reported it. You won't make it out of here alive."

"I'm sure you did. It doesn't matter. And don't be so sure about that second part, not that it should matter to you. 'It is the just decree of Heaven that a traitor never sees his danger till his ruin is at hand.' Pietro Metastasio. I don't know who the dude was, but his words are spot on, don't ya think?"

Stag spits blood in Ian's face. "Screw you."

"What are we going to do with him?" one of the militia members asks while another offers him a handkerchief. Ian accepts the cloth but doesn't use it.

"Give him a traitor's death."

Ian draws his weapon and aims it at Stag. The agent is about to protest when a round punches through his forehead. Brain matter splatters on the logs behind him as he rocks back before planting face-first into the dirt. That's one more problem solved.

"Rotate the guards. I want everyone to see this," Ian says, setting the satellite phone on one of the logs next to the body. "Once they have, dispose of him."

"We didn't know," one of the militiamen says, acutely feeling the betrayal.

"Our enemies are well-trained. Pick your head up, and don't ever lower it again. You couldn't have known."

"Is this what you meant by operational security?" a man asks as Ian starts to walk away. He stops.

"Exactly. Now that the FBI spy has been neutralized, it's time for you to learn the real plan. Assemble the militia in the meeting room tomorrow night. It's time to reclaim our nation."

CHAPTER FIFTY-EIGHT

SPECIAL AGENT VICTORIA LARSEN

Cobbs Creek East Rowhouse
West Philadelphia, Pennsylvania

Victoria closes her eyes. Sleep hasn't come easy despite the mental fatigue. She is starting to drift off on the couch when the shrill ring of a cell phone pierces the silence. She glances at her dormant device before registering that it's coming from the other room.

"Hello," she hears Imani answer.

Then nothing. Victoria tilts her head and points her ear toward the bedroom, but her fellow agent isn't saying anything. It's a one-way conversation.

"Okay, I'll be right there."

A light comes on, and Victoria can hear movement. She isn't a stranger to these late-night calls. No FBI agent is. That doesn't mean she isn't curious to know what that conversation was all about.

Victoria throws the blanket off and heads down the hall. Imani is already dressed and sliding into her suit jacket.

"Has the alarm been sounded?"

"Something like that. A task force has been thrown together to determine where that truck bomb came from."

"I thought the tip came from a militia source."

"It did."

"Okay...doesn't anyone know the source's location?"

Imani frowns. "Yeah, we should, but nobody does."

That level of incompetence is unheard of at the Bureau. Despite the mistakes the FBI has made over the decades, it is very tidy about operational details. There is no way that information is missing. Someone knows, and that information is being suppressed.

"That doesn't make any sense."

"Tell me about it. Instead of finding out who reported the tip and from where, the brass has agents poring over surveillance videos from the interstate and local businesses. It's labor-intensive, and they need more bodies."

"That's stupid."

"No argument from me," Imani says as she hangs her gold badge around her neck. "They have it narrowed down to two possible anti-government militia groups with the manpower, expertise, and resources to pull this off."

"But?" Victoria asks, sensing Imani has an opinion on the matter.

Imani holsters her weapons and looks at her. "Both are in the eastern part of the state."

"Which would have made Pittsburgh a more likely target."

"Bingo. Why risk driving a bomb clear across the state if you don't need to?"

You wouldn't unless the target is specific to Philadelphia. Victoria doesn't believe for a second that it was. This feels like deliberate misdirection. Someone has the FBI looking in all the wrong places.

"Robespierre."

"What do you mean?"

"What if the militia group who sent that bomb is being protected? It explains why nobody knows where the agent is."

"That's crazy, Victoria. Williams may be a bigwig at Justice, but he doesn't *run* the FBI."

"That's true, but if you think of anything that makes more sense, let me know. That truck bomb never should have left the garage it was built in. The presence of that much explosive is more than enough cause for a raid."

"You think this is all connected?"

Victoria stretches her neck. "I do, but I can't prove it."

"I can stay and help you," Imani says, starting to shed her jacket. "I'll find a reason—"

"No, you need to go in. It will raise suspicions if you don't."

Imani stares hard at the senior agent. "Victoria, you have that look in your eye. Please don't do anything stupid."

"No promises."

Victoria follows her host into the kitchen, where she digs through a junk drawer and produces a set of keys. She holds them up and lets them dangle.

"If you need to go anywhere, take my grandfather's car. It's unregistered and uninsured, so don't get pulled over or hit anybody."

"It'd be the least of the laws I've broken lately."

The women hug. It feels like a goodbye, even though neither should think it is one.

"Keep me in the loop," Victoria says.

"Keep that sat phone close. I'll let you know if I come up with anything. Are you sure you don't need help?"

"Just watch your back, Imani."

She nods. "It's not mine I'm worried about. Don't forget to lock the door when you leave. This isn't America's safest neighborhood."

Victoria watches her "partner" climb into her car and drive away. She's right. This isn't a safe neighborhood. If Ian Drucker, Conrad Williams, and Andrew Li pull off this conspiracy, there won't be a safe one in the entire country.

CHAPTER FIFTY-NINE

BRIAN COOPER

Outside Smethport
McKean County, Pennsylvania

The campaign bus looks wildly out of place here. McKean County, with its population of under fifty thousand, is about as rural as Pennsylvania gets. There are neighborhoods in medium-sized American cities with more people. It's friendly territory for Republicans, and Bradford is concerned about turning out the base on Tuesday. A swing through cherry-red areas is probably appropriate before he goes back to campaigning in blue cities.

Brian climbs aboard and finds the governor chatting with his communications director and Joel Graham. It doesn't look like it's anything overly important. Most likely, the two are engaging in small talk as the governor scarfs down a cheeseburger and onion rings.

"Could you excuse us for a moment?"

Joel follows the communications director out, both nodding as they pass Brian. He takes a seat across from the governor.

"Healthy dinner."

"I think this is breakfast. Don't tell my wife. I'm surprised you found us out here. I'm not even sure where we are."

"That was the easy part," Brian says with a smile. "I microchipped Joel while he slept."

"Don't they do that to dogs?"

Brian taps his nose and points at the governor, who grins.

"How was New York?"

"Busy, as usual. I met a lot of angry Jets fans. You would think—"

"I meant the meeting, Brian," the governor says, not in a mood for playful banter.

"Actyv is supporting both legal efforts."

The governor dabs his mouth with a napkin. He doesn't look surprised. He also doesn't look happy.

"Why?"

"They said they want to ensure a fair and free election by ensuring every vote is counted accurately."

"Do you believe them?"

Brian shrugs. "They spent dinner at Cipriani and drinks at the Carnegie Club trying to convince me of that."

"Did they?"

"No, it's complete bullshit. They want access."

Brian stated that as a fact, even if it's more of a conclusion. The three wealthy men were excellent hosts and said all the right things. They had conviction behind their words, but none of what they said rang true. The uber-wealthy don't care about the democratic process or fairness in elections. They like to win.

"This is how it begins, isn't it?" the governor asks.

"How what begins?"

"The path that leads every honest politician down the trail to ruin."

"Yes, it is. Money is the dark side of the force in politics, and there are no Jedi in Washington."

"That's reassuring," Bradford says, pushing the remainder of his meal away from him.

"It's the price of admission, Governor. It's the system, like it or not."

"You think I should instruct the RNC to take their money."

Brian grimaces and rubs his hands together to relieve the tension. "I don't think you can afford not to. The 2020 election cost fourteen billion dollars before the legal costs for lawsuits and recounts."

"The RNC will cover most of our legal expenses. How much is Actyv offering?"

"Millions."

Bradford's eyebrows arch. "Isn't there a limit to what they can contribute?"

"Not for donations to the party."

Campaign finance is among the trickiest sets of laws in the country. It's a minefield, and any mistake usually makes it to the front page of newspapers and the lead story on cable news. That's why Brian hired a dozen specialized lawyers to manage campaign finances. He may be the boss, but their word is gospel.

"What about our campaign? What do we have left?"

The law states that candidates may use any money left over from campaign fundraising to cover post-election legal and recount expenses.

"There won't be much."

"And Standish already has more," Bradford says, getting a nod. "Then maybe there is no point. Why fight if we can't win?"

"This isn't about being a sore loser or feeling a sense of entitlement to the White House. Pennsylvania margins will be razor-thin. There will be fraud, and that could be the difference between winning and losing."

The governor shakes his head. "All this for fewer than two-dozen electoral votes. Sometimes I'm beginning to think the left isn't wrong about the popular vote."

"You're a Republican?" Brian asks, causing the governor to offer a weak smile. "Despite the many problems with the Electoral College, there's one very good reason to keep it. The system prevents nationwide chaos when the popular vote is close. Our system partitions the popular vote among the fifty states and D.C. That restricts recounts in close elections to the few states with sufficient electoral votes and a close enough tally to affect the outcome."

"Standish supports the National Popular Vote movement. It's democratic."

"We don't live in a democracy, sir. The United States of America is a republic. Anyone who ever recited the Pledge of Allegiance should know that."

Brian shudders at the thought of what a close popular election would mean to the country. The way the game of modern politics is played, it would be a complete disaster. Countless elections have been decided by less than a percentage point.

Al Gore led George W. Bush by a half percentage point during the Florida debacle. It's a cautionary tale. A national popular vote system would have triggered a nationwide recount, requiring tabulation of the over one hundred million votes cast in the country. Then the games begin. Rejected ballots in every precinct would be scrutinized and argued over. Questioning signatures, voter identity, and ballot box stuffing would be the easy tactics to predict.

Worse, the 2000 election wasn't an anomaly. The 1960 contest was decided by two-tenths of a percent, and the popular vote difference between Richard Nixon and Hubert Humphrey in 1968 was less than a percent.

"I know you're right. It's just…I don't want to be that guy."

"There is an alternative."

"What?"

"Win. Win by a lot."

"We have a week, Brian. Mail-in voting has already started in most states. Let's not pretend what I say now makes that much difference."

Brian folds his arms. "I disagree. It might make all the difference. There are just over one hundred seventy-five thousand precincts in the United States. If you change two minds in each of them, you'll gain four after you reduce Standish's tally. That's seven hundred thousand votes nationwide that could move swing states to your column. That's an election."

"Okay. I need to stretch my legs."

The governor rises and walks toward the front of the bus.

"I owe Actyv an answer, sir. If I wait until tomorrow, they may find your lack of timely acceptance rude."

Bradford stands at the stairs leading down to the door for a long moment without looking back. "Take the money."

CHAPTER SIXTY

TIERRA CAMPOS

Front Burner Washington Office
Washington, D.C.

I can't stop fidgeting. The last day has been brutal. It's hard to keep my mind distracted while waiting for something to happen. Anything. There's an old adage that a watched pot never boils. The modern version of that is a watched cell phone never rings.

I don't understand how the dark web and Safe Haven work or what's taking Dial Pirate so long. I'm in the population segment that can turn on a computer and open Microsoft Word. While I understand why someone would want to distribute parts of files worldwide for security, I question whether it's worth it when it takes this long to get them back.

Olivia enters and sits down at the table. "Still nothing?"

I gesture at the phone in frustration. "No, not yet. How are things going upstairs?"

She sighs. "Have you ever heard of a truck bomb going off on a major interstate and the media not covering it?"

"Nothing surprises me anymore," I say, meaning it. "There has been no follow-up at all?"

"There has been some coverage on the local murder, arson, and rape report, and a couple of networks gave it a thirty-second mention. Then the story completely disappeared."

That harsh moniker for the local news is based on the observation that it's what regional telecasts specialize in covering. Sprinkle in a few human interest stories and maybe a local politician bloviating about this or that, and you summarize almost every newscast in the country.

It's odd that this isn't national news. It has clickable interest and is happening in a state that's ground zero in this election cycle. Hundreds of reporters are already in Pennsylvania, and most have their own satellite trucks. Why would they not cover an explosion if terrorism is mentioned in the same breath?

"What have we found?"

Olivia shrugs. "Not much. Local police only confirmed whatever was in the initial reports. They claim it was a possible domestic terrorist attack and handed the investigation over to the—"

"FBI," I finish for her. "Who hasn't uttered a word about it."

Olivia nods. "Their only comment was something along the lines of, 'what truck bomb?'"

I shake my head. I stand and walk over to Logan's conspiracy tracking board. He should have created a category for "unconfirmed but likely."

"You think this is Williams," Olivia concludes.

"Indirectly, yes. Or this guy." I tap the board with a marker on Michael Krekstein's box. "It looks more and more like the FBI director could be involved."

My cell phone rings, and I jump. I head over to the phone. If this is a telemarketer, I'm going to chuck it against a wall. Instead, the caller ID reads, "National Biscuit Company." That's not as cheeky as his usual name spoofs.

"Hello?"

"Tierra Del Fuego?" the electronically altered voice asks.

"Dial Pirate?"

"No. This is CyberOreo."

I put together the clues. It makes more sense now. The National Biscuit Company is better known as Nabisco, the maker of Oreo cookies.

"It's been a long time. Why are you contacting me?"

"Not long enough. I'm doing a favor for a friend even though I think it's stupid."

"DP asked you to contact me? What's wrong?"

"Other than him being BFFs with a journalist? He was raided. FBI Cyber broke down his door with a SWAT team early this morning."

I feel sick to my stomach, and my mouth goes dry. I sit down at the table and stare at the phone.

"Is he okay?" I ask, bracing for the worst.

"He was lucky. He wasn't there when the windbreakers stormed in like they owned the place. They shut down his entire operation and confiscated everything. They know who he is. It's only a matter of time before they catch up to him. He's a good hacker but will make a lousy fugitive."

I rub my forehead. "DP said our conversations couldn't be traced. I mean…did…did what we were working on lead them to…oh, my God."

"As much as I want to blame you, I don't think so. Anarchy Booster agrees. The feds got their information from somewhere else. The hacker community is trying to find out how, while anyone who knows him takes precautions. I've relocated just in case."

"Good. If you talk to Dial Pirate, tell him I appreciate his help with everything and hope he stays safe."

"Interesting," CyberOreo says after a long pause.

"What is?"

"I lied. I thought maybe it was you. I figured you would ask me about the Safe Haven files because that's all you cared about. I was wrong. You're actually worried about him. Voice stress patterns don't lie. That, and you haven't even asked about the files."

"I tried to warn him that we're working against some dangerous people. I didn't want him to be more involved than he was, but he insisted."

"That's what he told me. I didn't believe him, either. I figured that he just thought you were hot."

Olivia rolls her eyes. A slight smile creases my lips. I feel like hell and probably look worse. I'll take the half-compliment from a hacker I've never met. It's been one of those weeks.

"I'll get the files another way, CyberOreo."

"There's no need. I have most of them and will find a way to get them to you."

My heart does a cartwheel in my chest. "Email works."

CyberOreo laughs. "No, it doesn't. I think there's a high probability that you're being monitored, Tierra Del Fuego. They are intercepting your email and cellular communications. All of you."

Thanks to Victoria, I already knew that I was a target,. I've been careful about my conversations and Internet searches ever since. I didn't realize that they would be watching all of us.

"Without a warrant?"

"Why do you think I'm a hacker? This has been happening for years. If the people really knew what the government is doing, there would be rioting in the streets. Instead, they're kept oblivious. Maybe you and *Front Burner* can do something about that someday."

"Count on it. When will I hear from you?"

"When I have a plan. Soon. Just be ready to act."

The line disconnects, and I lean back in my chair. That was a rollercoaster ride. Now I'm on the way down. DP may be a hacker, but he's a good man. He helped me when he had no reason to and asked for nothing in return. He deserves better than this.

"He's smart. He'll be okay, Tierra."

"I hope so."

I add overwhelming guilt to today's range of emotions. I'm a walking, talking, one-woman reality television show right now. I can't do this for much longer. Something has to give before I have an emotional breakdown.

CHAPTER SIXTY-ONE

DEPUTY AG CONRAD WILLIAMS

U.S. Department of Justice
Washington, D.C.

There was no doubt that this would be the hard part. The end of any race is the worst part. That's doubly true when the race isn't some infernal 5k or triathlon. Political contests may be between two or three candidates, but they are a vacuum that sucks everyone and everything in.

That normally wouldn't impact Conrad directly. In this case, he convinced his boss to let him run point for security in an election that will, by design, be anything but secure. He knew that would result in a lot of yelling and finger-pointing. All he needs to do is endure it and keep his eyes on the prize.

"Mister Williams," his assistant announces over the intercom, "Michael Krekstein has an urgent call for you on line two."

"Thank you," he says, picking up the handset and punching the appropriate button. "What can I do for you, Director?"

"We have a problem. Two men showed up at the Philadelphia Hospital for Neuroscience forty minutes ago. A local cop didn't like what he saw and started questioning them. It turns out that they are MS-13. Both men had outstanding warrants and were taken into custody."

The Mara Salvatrucha, better known as MS-13, was formed in the 1970s in Los Angeles, California, to protect El Salvadoran immigrants. They eventually grew into the most violent and deadly gang in the world, with a reputation for killing with machetes. They now boast over fifty thousand members worldwide, of which around ten thousand reside in the United States.

"That doesn't sound like much of a problem."

"They were there to see Victoria Larsen."

Conrad stops what he's doing and stares at the phone like it's about to grow legs and run off his desk. MS-13 wouldn't pay an FBI agent a social visit unless they were there to deprive her of life. Machiavelli. He found goons to do some dirty work, and they didn't even make it to her room.

"Why would thugs be visiting Larsen?" Conrad asks, needing to find out how much the FBI has learned.

"We don't know, so we went to her room to ask her."

"What did she say?"

Krekstein sighs. "Nothing. She wasn't there."

It takes Conrad a moment to process that short sentence. "What do you mean she wasn't there? Did you check with the nurses' station?"

"She hasn't been there for days, Conrad."

The deputy attorney general rubs his temples. "Are you telling me that she's not a patient?"

"Oh, she's still listed as a patient. I'm telling you that she's not physically there. The records we've been obtaining to monitor her condition were fabricated. I don't believe her diagnosis. She doesn't have aneurysms. It was all made up."

Conrad swipes the legal pad off his desk. Larsen played them. The FBI is supposed to be the nation's premier law enforcement arm. Their work was sloppy. An agent could have been sent each day to pay her a visit, but that was never done. She made everyone in the Bureau look like fools.

Now she's out in the wind, but why? Using the medical excuse to get out of her African assignment makes sense. Leaving the hospital doesn't. The action does provide an opportunity…

"Arrest anyone involved in covering for her. That means nurses, doctors, administrators…anyone. It's obstruction of justice."

"Conrad, I don't think—"

"Don't you see it, Michael? Larsen is orchestrating the election interference. She is behind everything going back to New Hampshire."

There is a short silence on the other end of the line. "It's suspicious, but there is no evidence to draw that conclusion."

"If you wait for evidence, it'll be too late," Conrad says. "Larsen is working with Drucker. Find her, and you will likely find him."

"I don't think there's any evidence that makes that connection."

"Are you defending Larsen's actions? Her insubordination?"

"No, I'm not. But there is a vast difference between that and treason. Despite her talents, I despise Victoria Larsen and think she's a liability to the Bureau. But Agent Murphy hasn't found any evidence that either she or Tierra Campos is involved in anything illegal."

Conrad's jaw tightens. Hard evidence is often hard to come by during investigations. Successful ones require good luck or a break that opens the floodgates. That doesn't mean the FBI can't take certain measures, and Krekstein knows that. Maybe a little encouragement will help.

"I consider Victoria Larsen as a person of interest regarding the interference activities in Pennsylvania and a possible threat to national security. I want her taken into custody."

"There is going to be blowback."

"I'll handle it," Conrad snaps.

"I mean from within the Bureau. Larsen is highly regarded by many agents."

"So highly regarded that none of them visited her in a hospital to find an empty room? Get your agents in line. I will handle the rest. Find Victoria Larsen and put her in a cell."

Conrad hangs up and rubs the back of his neck. He thought Larsen was out of play. This changes things. It also creates an opportunity to succeed where Machiavelli failed. There's no point in informing the others of his plan. They'll hear on the news about what he's about to do.

CHAPTER SIXTY-TWO

IAN DRUCKER

"The Forge" Militia Compound
Liberty, Pennsylvania

Ian scans the room full of mopey faces. The militiamen parked in seats feel betrayed. He understands. It's natural to feel that way after they lost the two leaders who powered and steered the ship. The men here relied on them for their livelihood. Mike Brescia and Remy Mitchell ran the lumber company and the militia, both of which are now in jeopardy.

"You all look defeated."

"How should we look?" one of the men shouts back.

Ian shrugs. "Mournful about our losses, but with a glint of vengeance in your eyes."

"Mike and Remy were more than our leaders, Drucker. They were friends, and Stag sold them out."

"I understand. Everybody waxes poetic about revolution or civil war on social media. They scream that it's coming and even hope it does. Then it reaches their doorstep. When it does, they realize how turbulent their cushy lives will become. I guess you're no different."

"We were betrayed. Our revolution is over."

"No. It has only just begun."

"You and your missions," another man says with a sneer.

"Our missions."

"What do you expect us to do?"

Ian points back at the television. "Honor Remy's wish before he gave 'the last full measure of devotion.' Finish this by starting it."

"How?"

"By rattling some cages and then unleashing hell. Stag was a scumbag informant, but he didn't know our real plan. Mike and Remy have been molding Semtex into small sheets and placing them into ballot envelopes. The detonator is tricky, but the letter bombs will fit in ballot drop box slots. We're going to blow fifteen of them up in three different waves ten minutes apart."

The militiamen look at each other. It's concrete action for a group whose bark is far worse than its bite. For all the grandstanding and posturing about a revolution, they don't look like they have the stomach for actually fighting one.

"You will be grouped into pairs and assigned a different part of the state. One of you will get dropped off blocks away from the target. You'll slide the bomb in the slot and hustle out of there. It is timed so that you'll all be on major roads by the time they detonate. Each of you will be provided a safe haven in either a hotel or a rented apartment. Some of you will reassemble here. Others have a follow-on mission to capitalize on our victories.

"Gentlemen, this is a dangerous mission. Each of these ballot drop boxes is monitored. You'll have to contend with video surveillance and police patrols. You must be quick without looking suspicious and then be able to blend into your surroundings without people giving you a moment's thought."

"What about the five teams we already deployed?"

"They are the 'rattle the cage' part of this plan."

There is grumbling in the ranks. Ian thought militias were supposed to be tough, but they're anything but. This one is no different. They're all talk and haven't done anything to back up their words. It was his biggest concern when he talked this plan over with Robespierre and Machiavelli. He convinced them that he could make this work. Now, he needs to deliver.

"We've been living in two nations for more than a decade. The government has done everything in its power to divide us. The media have parroted their propaganda and deepened the divide. We'll leverage that to bring real change to this country."

"We don't want civil war."

"Most Americans don't. That's the tragedy of the modern age. The government divides its citizens to prevent unity against them. It's a ploy to preserve power. Racial tension, class warfare, ideological rifts…it's all means to an end that preserves the power of the political aristocracy in both parties."

"I don't see how this works. Your plan will divide us further."

Ian climbs off the platform and stands in front of it. He wants to be among them…one of them…for this talk. This isn't a leader pushing his subordinates. It's a brother supporting his brothers.

"I've seen the library of books you have. Have any of you read them?" he asks, causing about half the group to lower their eyes. "To have a revolution, you need five factors: mass frustration leading to uprisings, dissident elites, powerful unifying motivations, a crisis that paralyzes government authorities, and a tolerant global order that won't intervene."

Ian counted off the five factors on his fingers before lowering his hand. "We are creating those conditions. The electoral votes from this state will push one of the major candidates over the two-seventy threshold unless the election is tainted. Then it won't. While the two parties turn on each other and their supporters clash in the streets, we start our revolution by offering an alternative guaranteed to return America to a government of the people, by the people, and for the people.

"This election sets the stage for everything that follows. We can either sit here and complain about our country, or we can act. You can mourn Remy and Mike or honor them by fulfilling their dream. You can seethe at the traitor Stag or seek retribution against the political apparatus that sent him here.

"I know what I'm doing. That's why Remy brought me here. This is the last election where the American people are forced to choose between the lesser of two evils. This is the New American Revolution, and you're the reincarnation of the minutemen at the Old North Bridge. Or are you?"

Ian grimaces and walks down the center aisle. Half the militia track him with their eyes. The other half hang their heads. He still needs their help to complete his mission. After that, he doesn't care what they do. Another week is all it will take. Fortunately, nobody likes being called a coward or a quitter. He knows the result of that speech.

"I'll be back in a half hour to issue your assignments. If you're here, you'll help start the revolution. If you aren't, well, you can watch from the sidelines as we save America."

CHAPTER SIXTY-THREE

BRIAN COOPER

World War II Memorial
Washington, D.C.

This memorial is not the most iconic in the capital, but it is one of the most symbolic. The World War II memorial opened to the public in 2004, making it among the newer monuments in the city. It's located on the National Mall, flanked by the Washington Monument and Lincoln Memorial. That makes it one of the most visited, and why he chose this spot to meet Nathan.

Brian appreciates anything that honors the sixteen million men and women who served in the armed forces of the U.S. Four hundred thousand of them gave their lives, and countless millions more supported the war effort from home. It was a simpler time when everyone knew who the enemy was and what it would take to defeat them. The nation was unified in that goal. That's a far cry from what we experience today.

Nathan and Brian go way back. They met at a bar when they were both new to the city. The former went on to find a wife and have a nice career in the FBI, while Brian became a player in Washington's political circles. Despite the separate paths, they still remain in contact and exchange information from time to time.

They don't hug or pretend they haven't seen each other like the last time they met at Memorial Plaza. They also aren't making it obvious that they're meeting there on purpose.

"Are your kids still driving you crazy?"

"They're back in school," Nathan says, staring up at one of the fifty-six granite pillars. "Now it's shuffling schedules and helping with homework."

"The trials and tribulations of a family man."

"And I wouldn't change it for anything. What brings you back to D.C., Brian? Don't you have an election to win?"

"The election *is* why I'm back."

Nathan grins. "You don't need to babysit the candidate? Isn't it the campaign manager's job to tie his shoes, put on his bib…things like that?"

"Nah, I staff that out. The governor is making a quick tour of the red states, so I'm running the show from here. I have a meeting at the RNC tomorrow."

"I was wondering if you guys were going to leave Pennsylvania or if he was just going to get an apartment and move in."

"We have a good reason to spend time there, and you know it."

"The ballots."

It's amazing how few pundits on television recognize the importance of this. It might explain why the coverage is so scattershot. What few brave souls discussed it offered little more than perfunctory analysis. It's nice to hear that the FBI recognizes the potential problem.

Brian nods. "More specifically, the apparent lack of media interest in them."

"I assume you heard about the truck bomb that the FBI and Pennsylvania State Police intercepted on the turnpike."

"Yeah, only because I read every shred of news coming out of that state. Nobody else in the country knows about it."

Nathan turns his head and looks at Brian. "Including the SIOC."

The FBI's Strategic Information and Operations Center is a fancy name for its global command center. The SIOC was created so the Bureau's leadership could maintain situational awareness and share information about investigations and tactical operations. They are the FBI's brain and should be aware of everything.

"What do you mean?"

"Pennsylvania has almost every agent in the state dedicated to election security. Yet, we aren't getting timely information from anyone."

"Does that happen often?"

Nathan shakes his head. "It never does. There's something else that's odd. A small task force is looking into Victoria Larsen and Tierra Campos."

"What? Why?"

"Nobody knows for sure. Rumor has it that the investigation came directly from the DOJ. Something about subversion, or so we think."

Brian presses his eyes closed and shakes his head. "Wait…hold on. You're telling me that the FBI is wasting resources investigating a fellow agent and a journalist while someone is trying to make Pennsylvania the next New Hampshire primary debacle?"

The wounds from what happened there between Alicia Standish and Luther Burgess still haven't scabbed over, let alone become scars. National confidence in the electoral process has been shaken. Another breakdown could destroy it forever. Yet, the FBI is more interested in chasing ghosts.

"I don't know if it's a waste or not, but it is odd. Someone at the DOJ has an ax to grind."

"Nathan, please tell me that the FBI isn't withholding critical information on an election."

"Why would we be?"

"It's not unprecedented. Targeting a journalist who doesn't like Alicia Standish very much makes it look like the Bureau is playing favorites again."

Nathan's posture straightens instantly. "I don't think that's the case."

"What else would it be?"

"I don't know. Something isn't right, and that's all I can say."

"Can, or will?"

"Is there a difference? Look, I need to head back before I'm missed. It was good seeing you again, Brian," Nathan says, giving him a pat on the shoulder.

"Give my best to your wife and kids. Hopefully, we can get together after the election."

"I'd like that."

Nathan moves off in the direction of the White House, and Brian returns to staring at the campaigns in a war that changed world history and the trajectory of nations. This memorial was designed to inspire future generations by deepening their appreciation of what World War II accomplished in securing freedom and democracy.

Only, the men who fought and died in the sands of Europe and the Pacific didn't secure it. They only bought it time. Freedoms are getting eroded at a frightening pace. Democracy takes a back seat in an age where dark money campaign contributions from special interests reign supreme. The worst part is that the people don't seem to care.

He can't imagine what life will be with Alicia Standish in the White House. She can't be counted on to do the right thing. The government has repeatedly failed to do what's in the people's best interest. This election could change that, but will it? That's the greatest question of all this November.

CHAPTER SIXTY-FOUR

TIERRA CAMPOS

Lettuce Indulge You
Washington, D.C.

I have been chasing the Isiah files and researching Andrew Li and Conrad Williams at the expense of most other parts of my life. I'm not exercising or eating well. It comes with being chained to a desk for hours on end. With nothing to do now until CyberOreo gets me the files, I decide to eat lunch out.

This salad bar isn't close to the *Front Burner* office. The walk gives me an opportunity to stretch my legs and get some semblance of physical activity on the way to eating a wholesome lunch. After arriving at Lettuce Indulge You, a clever wordplay that causes me to smile, I move to a table and dive in.

Two men and a woman dressed in suits enter the small restaurant, and I eye them closely. It's Washington, and that attire is hardly rare in this part of the city, but there's something about how they carry themselves. It reminds me of Victoria. I don't need to see gold badges to assume they're government agents.

Two of them pull out chairs and sit at a nearby table. One of the men peels off and makes his way over to me. I expect him to say something, but instead, he pulls out the opposite chair and sits down without an invitation. They're definitely in the FBI. I have a few seconds to figure out how I'm going to address this while I finish chewing. Before meeting Victoria, I would find this incredibly intimidating. After what's happened in my life, it's anything but.

"That's very forward of you, Special Agent…?"

"Murphy. How did you know I'm with the FBI, Miss Campos?"

"I didn't. You have the swagger. And while you're fit and obviously don't eat poorly, I'm guessing that you prefer more protein in your meals than the grilled chicken they top salads with here."

"You're observant."

"I'm a journalist. That comes with the territory."

"That's not my experience with reporters."

I smile at the slight against my profession. He isn't all wrong. "You should get out more then. To what do I owe the pleasure?"

"I think you already know the answer to that question," he says, studying my face for expressions.

"Humor me." I stab some of the salad with my fork and put it in my mouth to let him know I'm done talking.

"We're conducting an investigation."

"Isn't that typical in the FBI?" I say after I swallow.

"It's kinda our thing, yeah. Do you want to know the subject?"

"Not really, no. I think you sat down at my table because you're dying to tell me."

Agent Murphy slightly shifts his weight in his chair. "Here's the thing, Miss Campos. Special Agent Larsen is in some trouble. We believe she's working with Ian Drucker to interfere in the presidential election."

I can't help but laugh. "Have you read Victoria's file?"

"Cover to cover."

"Then, if you had any common sense at all, you'd know how ridiculous those words sound coming out of your mouth."

"Have you had any contact with her?" Agent Murphy asks, ignoring the comment.

"So, you think that because Victoria and I are close, I could be involved as well?"

The agent cocks his head a little and raises his eyebrows. That's exactly what he thinks, but I know there is more to this story than he's letting on.

"Am I under arrest, Agent Murphy?"

"Should you be?"

"I asked you a direct question," I say, placing my fork down and leaning forward.

"No, you aren't."

"Good. Then go pound sand."

He smiles. "I was warned about you."

"By whom? No, wait, let me guess…the deputy attorney general of the United States. He likely also had Director Krekstein with him. How am I doing so far?"

Murphy raises an eyebrow. I'm over the target.

"You're well-informed. I'm curious how you could know that."

You seem like a decent guy, Agent Murphy, so I'll be straight with you. You're being manipulated."

"I doubt that."

"It's your prerogative to believe me or not. You'll learn the truth eventually. Why did *you* get assigned this investigation?"

"I'm asking the questions," Murphy says in a stern voice meant to sound threatening.

"Dispense with the tough guy act, will you? You confronted me here so I would know you're watching me. You knew I wouldn't answer any questions, so why tip me off? Unless publicity is the end goal, I can't think of why the FBI would announce to someone that they're the subject of an investigation."

Murphy is well-trained. He doesn't fidget or flinch. There are no telltale signs of nervousness in his body language. He can't mask his eyes, though. They're conflicted. I know the look because I've seen it staring back at me in the mirror countless times.

"You're not the subject of it."

"I'm one of them. Don't pretend I'm not."

"Okay, Miss Campos. Enlighten me on why you think I'm here since you seem to know everything."

I ignore the dig. "Because this investigation doesn't make sense to you, either. You were handed this assignment, but you're having difficulty stacking the facts up and can't figure out why. The reason is that you're being lied to."

"Fascinating."

I miss doing interviews, even though this technically isn't one. The last time I sat at a table and had to outmaneuver someone was in front of a live television audience on *Capitol Beat*. Part of me misses those days. Watching someone powerful squirm in their seat is intoxicating.

"Not really. I think you're one of the good ones, Agent Murphy. Maybe a little too ambitious. But you're likely an excellent agent who follows orders without question and gets results. You're an FBI poster boy."

"Flattery will get you nowhere."

"And your defense mechanism won't hide you from the truth."

"Why would the deputy AG and the FBI director send me on a wild goose chase?" I point at him. "That's the question you're desperate to answer."

"Do you know why they did?"

I lean back and fold my arms. Murphy is fishing for information. Nothing I say will convince him I'm right. It's something he can only learn for himself. I only hope Victoria keeps him off her tail long enough for him to recognize that.

"Are we done here, or do I need to announce to everyone in this restaurant that you're sexually harassing me?"

"Cute tactic, Miss Campos, but completely unnecessary. Enjoy your lunch. I'm sure we'll be talking again, Tierra del Fuego."

I freeze as he offers a smile and leaves the restaurant with his two sidekicks. For the first time in this conversation, he got a reaction from me. But he also gave me a critical piece of information. The question is, was it a slip of the tongue or by design?

Murphy couldn't have known the handle I use when talking to my hackers. It's not a nickname used around the office. The only people who know it are some of the *Front Burner* staff, Josh, and the hackers themselves. The FBI can access my computer, but it also means that they may have a mole on the inside. The thought of that is terrifying.

CHAPTER SIXTY-FIVE

SPECIAL AGENT VICTORIA LARSEN

Cobbs Creek East Rowhouse
West Philadelphia, Pennsylvania

Victoria stands abruptly and shakes her hands as she paces around the living room. The hands of the wall clock haven't stopped their relentless march around its face. Every minute she wastes is another closer to Ian Drucker escaping for good. She can't let that happen. Not again.

She needs to put her mind to something. Being idle isn't in her nature. She walks down the short hallway and into Imani's grandfather's study. It was once a bedroom that he repurposed with bookshelves chocked full of dusty tomes. The man was a voracious reader. Bravo.

A political map of Pennsylvania is pinned to the wall over a small antique writing desk. The towns are depicted in different colors, and all the county boundaries and major roads are labeled. It doesn't seem to have sentimental value, so Victoria pulls it down and brings the map into the living room. She spreads it on the coffee table and retrieves a black magic marker from the kitchen's junk drawer.

Checking the FBI data Imani printed about fraudulent ballots found by state election officials, she plots the precincts with the marker. She cross-references the information with reports on a blog she trusts more than any mainstream media outlet. She should tell Tierra to have *Front Burner* consider reaching out to the contributors. They have excellent sources.

Victoria stares at the map when she finishes. "Clarice, doesn't this random scattering of sites seem desperately random – like the elaborations of a bad liar?"

She frowns at her horrible Hannibal Lecter impression. She's in the FBI, so, of course, *The Silence of the Lambs* is a favorite. This isn't the first time some part of that movie was applicable.

"Desperately random," she mumbles, finishing with Clarice Starling's next line.

Buffalo Bob was trying hard to make his murders look random, meaning it was a well-thought-out plan. Humans are typically horrible at determining what's random and what isn't. Our brains like order, not chaos.

The boxes Drucker had his minions deposit the fake ballots in are desperately random. He avoided cities and suburbs, likely because of video surveillance and police concerns. They are all in rural areas of the state…except the north-central part. Victoria leans back and presses the marker against her lips.

"It could be a coincidence," she mumbles before remembering that she doesn't believe in them.

Victoria pulls her notebook computer off the end table and sets it on her lap. She's tempted to open any of the countless FBI resources she could use to research this but decides it's not worth the risk. The Bureau runs multiple operations to infiltrate extremist groups around the United States.

With Conrad Williams involved in this plot, any search for field reports could lead the FBI to her doorstep. Or Imani's grandfather's, in this case. She'll have to find out the hard way what she wants to know.

Fortunately, the Internet is a vast ocean of information, and someone fishing can reel in a good catch in the right location. There's no shortage of open source information on militias. She opens up a promising one and begins scanning the page. Pennsylvania is home to five main anti-government groups and several upstarts.

Only one fits her first criterion of location: The Keystone Militia. The group is headquartered in Liberty, a small Tioga County borough situated in the North-Central part of the state. She surfs over to Wikipedia to see what she can learn about the town. Tierra would have a fit if she knew. It may not be a useful reference for journalists or academics, but it serves her purposes fine.

The borough's population was two hundred thirty-two in the 2020 census. The racial makeup is over ninety-nine percent white. That makes it a candidate for a militia. While not all have roots in white supremacy, anti-government groups typically segregate themselves into groups along racial lines. There weren't any white Black Panthers. They had their own group that supported them, called the White Panthers.

Victoria opens up the online maps and searches for Liberty. She moves her mouse around, scouting the surrounding area. What did people do before satellite imagery of nearly every point on Earth? As lousy as modern times can feel, the amount of information at our fingertips is mind-boggling.

"Okay, where are you guys hiding out?" Victoria asks herself.

There are no obvious old military bases, camps, or compounds anywhere in the area. The greater Liberty area features a few structures in town and plenty of farms. There's a lumber company, a gun range, a trucking company, and a few churches. The Keystone Militia could be in any of them or none of them. There's no way of knowing.

She checks social media and comes up with snake eyes. Most militias use it to actively recruit, but this one runs a low profile. It helps them stay off the radar, but how do they increase their membership? Maybe she should find out.

Victoria leans back into the sofa as she works out some details in her head. Imani will be pissed, but she'll have to get over it. It requires shopping, which Victoria despises, and makeup, which she has little practice applying. She smiles, knowing that she can make this work. It's time to shake some rust off her undercover skills.

CHAPTER SIXTY-SIX

DEPUTY AG CONRAD WILLIAMS

U.S. Department of Justice
Washington, D.C.

There are welcome sights and unwelcome ones. Attorney General Lisa Ehler walking into his office falls into the latter category. When he notices her wearing sneakers and a fall coat, Conrad knows he should have come up with a third category. This is going to be far beyond unwelcome.

"Come take a walk with me, Conrad."

The tone of her voice was reason enough not to argue with the directive or come up with a weak excuse as to why he doesn't have the time. Instead, he eschews donning his own coat and follows her out. It's only early November, and his suit jacket provides enough warmth to combat the chilly autumn air.

They leave the building without speaking and walk across the street to the corner of Ninth and Constitution. The National Gallery of Art Sculpture Garden is a six-acre public attraction on the National Mall. Conrad has been here on a few occasions. The landscaped grounds are adorned with over twenty monumental works of modern sculpture by internationally renowned artists. Conrad doesn't think his boss is here to admire the craftsmanship.

"What the hell is happening in Pennsylvania?" Lisa asks as they reach the path.

"The FBI is investigating the ballots found at the arson site and determining the penetration of the ones distributed."

"What about the truck bomb, and why did I hear about it from someone other than my own deputy? And don't say you're protecting me."

"Keeping that from you wasn't my intent."

Ehler glances at her subordinate out of the corner of her eye. "Conrad, you're no fool. Your brain is not a sieve. I expressly told you to keep me informed of any developments. A domestic terrorist attack using explosives falls into that category, regardless of whether it was successful. Tell me everything you know, or the next job you'll hold will be as a public defender in Barrow, Alaska."

The threat could have been worse. Conrad likes the cold weather better than hot and humid. Miami would have been pure torture.

"The FBI has penetrated most of the dangerous anti-government militia groups in the country. An agent infiltrated a militia in Pennsylvania years ago and contacted a field office with information about a planned truck bombing."

"What's this agent's name?"

"I don't know," Conrad honestly answers.

"What militia?"

"I don't know that either."

"How could you not know?" she presses.

"I didn't receive the report, ma'am. The FBI did."

"Are you saying they don't know, either?" she asks, annoyed.

"It's a sensitive operation. Communications are coded, and infiltrators don't report to the operation's supervisor for security reasons. They check in with local field offices, but agents have no idea who they are or where. They only receive actionable intelligence and pass it along."

Conrad exhales slowly. It was a reasonably good lie.

"That's stupid."

Conrad shrugs. "That's deep cover. I don't establish Bureau tradecraft protocols. If the militia uncovers an informant, he's as good as dead. The FBI goes to great lengths to protect—"

"What was the target?"

"Alicia Standish's Philadelphia campaign headquarters."

"Are you…what?"

"There was never any threat to them," Conrad tries to reassure her. "The truck was intercepted long before it reached the Philadelphia city line."

His boss stops walking and turns to face him. "And if it hadn't been?"

Lisa and Conrad are lawyers and look at things as black or white. That's how the law works – you're either innocent or guilty. You broke it or didn't. Most of life isn't that way. There's a gray area, and Lisa is lousy at recognizing the nuance of it. Actions have consequences, especially now.

"Did you want me to tell a national campaign to evacuate an office right before an election?"

"To possibly save lives, yes."

"And, in the process, provide an issue that she could use for political gain, while the Bradford campaign accuses the FBI and DOJ of putting our thumbs on the scale in a tight race."

"It's being diligent and transparent!" Ehler screeches.

"No, ma'am. It'd be framed as a conflict of interest because of your relationship with Alicia Standish."

"Most people in this city know her, including you."

That's true. Alicia Standish is a very visible senator with friends and contacts in almost every governmental department. Conrad worked with her during the Ethan Harrington fiasco. Well, it was more like she tried to use and manipulate him during it.

"I'm not the one who is going to get scrutinized. You are. We handled the issue quietly and can release all the information after voters go to the polls."

Her eyes narrow at Conrad before she turns and continues walking. "Any other nuggets you want to get around to informing me of?"

"The FBI thinks that Victoria Larsen and Ian Drucker are working together to sabotage Alicia Standish."

She stops again. If this is meant to be a power walk, she's failing miserably. "Why?"

"Bad blood. They have a history going back to Ethan Harrington and Brockhampton. *Front Burner* may also be involved. That's being looked into."

"Victoria Larsen is hospitalized for brain aneurysms in Philadelphia, last I checked. How could—"

"She's not there. Agent Larsen left the day after she was admitted and convinced a doctor and nurses there to cover for her."

Lisa hangs her head. She takes a cleansing breath and looks up at the sky. When she wrestles control of her emotions, her eyes settle back on her deputy.

"Okay, Conrad, this is what's going to happen. I'm going to get a cup of coffee and fight the urge to choke you. You will meet me in my office at the top of the hour and tell me everything you know about what's happening in Pennsylvania. I will make the decision as to how to proceed. Understood?"

"Yes, ma'am."

She strides toward the small shop on the edge of the sculpture garden as he heads back to the office with a smile. He dreaded having whatever conversation would accompany the Beltway's version of a nature walk. Instead, he managed to get everything he wanted. He's leading a charmed life.

CHAPTER SIXTY-SEVEN

IAN DRUCKER

"The Forge" Militia Compound
Liberty, Pennsylvania

Ian has always been an early riser. Despite the lack of windows in this converted bunker, he knows it's morning. There are two reasons for that. The first is his internal clock. While not nearly as good as Jack Reacher in Lee Child's novels, he can still pinpoint a time within an hour. The second reason is how sore his back is. The thin air mattress doesn't have much in the way of support. After the next few days get crossed off the calendar, he swears to never sleep on the ground again.

Ian flips the light on and powers up the decrepit old coffee maker. This will be a day of preparations for him. How much will depend on what happens when he turns on the television. Finding the remote, he presses the wrong button three times before finding the correct one. The television comes to life and is already tuned to VH Media's network.

"It's racist, and everyone knows it," one of the talking heads spouts. "Governor Bradford should be ashamed of himself for pandering to blacks for the past couple of weeks while his supporters scrawl hateful messages in public places."

"There's no reason to believe that he or his supporters were behind this."

"Okay, yes, you're right, Scott. Please, tell the audience which left-wing groups did that," the man says, pointing at the screen off to their side.

The network is showing footage of swastikas in red spray paint. There are dozens of them in this park, and they weren't rush jobs. The lines are thickly applied and won't be easy to remove.

The video cuts to another shot of the n-word painted on storefronts in black neighborhoods. There are also a few instances of "F*** BLM," the n-word, and other hateful rhetoric that the network partially blurred out for broadcast.

"I never said it was a left-wing group! I'm saying that these might not be Bradford supporters," Scott argues.

"They certainly aren't Standish supporters. This is a binary election. There are only two sides."

"Why would these messages of hate appear now?" the host asks as more footage appears from Philadelphia.

"Intimidation, pure and simple."

Ian takes a sip of his coffee and almost spits it out. The guys in Philly screwed up painting one of the swastikas. He's not sure what that is, but it isn't the ancient religious symbol appropriated by the Nazi Party. The ones nearby are better, so at least they got the hang of it.

"Intimidation by vandalizing black and Jewish areas with hate symbols? That will only motivate them to vote, not intimidate them."

"I disagree, Scott. The intent is to cow people in fear at the thought of the Gestapo waiting for them at the polls."

"Aw, c'mon…you can't be serious! This could just as easily be the left making it appear they're being targeted. That isn't unprecedented."

"It's also a ridiculous assertion considering what Standish went through up in New Hampshire during the primary."

Ian changes the channel. Scott annoys him. He is VH Media's token Republican but is more liberal than most moderate Democrats. His role on the network is to set up the others to beat down his message, and he's very good at it.

The other left-leaning news outlets are covering the incidents with similar gusto. The first has a field reporter live from one of the locations in Pittsburgh. The other has an interview with a political expert about the fallout for Tuesday, calling this the fabled "October Surprise" and claiming it will backfire for the GOP.

As expected, the conservative outlets don't have much to say. They want to see if the narrative burns itself out before going on the offensive. Ian shakes his head. The media are just glorified cheerleaders for their respective parties, and their reaction to events is predictable. This is what our political process has become.

Ian moves to the chessboard. Four cities were targeted for the graffiti, although only two seem to have made it to air. He will wait before contacting the teams to find out about the others. Social media will give him an inkling. The fact that none of the cable news channels report any arrests is encouraging.

He takes the bishops and knights from the map one by one, almost celebrating each removal. They're closer. The queen was removed when Remy and Mike met their fiery end on the Pennsylvania Turnpike. Now, only the pawns and the king remain in play. Once they're gone, the game ends, and Ian can retire.

CHAPTER SIXTY-EIGHT

BRIAN COOPER

Republican National Committee Headquarters
Washington, D.C.

The Republican National Committee is the party's brain. It develops and promotes the party's political platform, formulates election strategy, and conducts fundraising activities. It also plans, organizes, and holds the Republican National Convention to select a presidential candidate.

Its headquarters is an unassuming white brick structure on First Avenue in the heart of the nation's capital. The last time Brian was here, he rode the Metro and arrived in time to ambush Monica Stengel outside. He needed to convince her to not interfere with Colin Bradford hiring him. They've come a long way since that tense conversation. Now, it's his turn to get ambushed.

"Long time, Brian," Brevin Hawkins says from beneath the green awning.

"Not long enough. What brings you here?"

"I'm working for the RNC now."

Brian rubs his chin. "Not campaign strategy, I hope."

"Still patting yourself on the back for getting me removed from the campaign, I see," Brevin says with a smirk.

"Nah, it's not like that. You got yourself removed."

"So you say. Well, it won't matter. You're going to lose the election by ninety electoral votes because of your bone-headed moves."

It's a bold proclamation. Brevin is standing outside the RNC, reveling in a loss that has yet to happen. That's petty, even by his standards.

"Says you."

"Say the polls. Have you seen the Real Clear Politics average lately? It's over."

Real Clear Politics aggregates polls for political races into averages for public consumption. An individual survey may be an outlier, but the reasoning is that an aggregate of reputable polls paints a more accurate picture. The RCP average is widely cited by media outlets. Unfortunately, it doesn't fix the underlying issue.

"That's always been your problem, Brevin. You don't even think like a Republican. You accept a rigged system at face value."

"Polls are polls."

"Yes, but did you check the cross tab data or just read the results like most people?" Brian asks, getting Brevin to cock his head. "Each one of the polls in the RCP oversampled democrats. That's what they do, and the results get skewed."

Brevin shakes his head. "You're drinking your own Kool-Aid."

"Am I? In 2016, the Democrats led by five points going into Election Day. What happened? How were they so off? Sampling, that's how."

"That's a convenient excuse when it benefits your argument," Brevin says, standing a little straighter.

"Because it always does. Take the last election. The president was up by eight. He won by less than two percent when the final vote was counted. That's a six-point swing for an *incumbent*. Do you really think there were that many undecideds going into Election Day?"

"I've seen the internals," Brevin sputters.

"So have I. We're going to win the states we need. Standish and Bradford will both be in reach of two-seventy. Pennsylvania will determine the election."

"My God, you really think you can win this."

"You work for the RNC now, Brevin. You were Bradford's campaign manager. You should never have stopped believing that he could win."

Brian slaps Brevin on the shoulder as he passes him.

"I never thought the GOP would put our fate in the hands of a Democrat. It's embarrassing."

"That isn't what should embarrass you, Brevin," Brian says, stopping. "You'll need therapy once you realize that your wing of the party has a massive inferiority complex and a fear of being anything other than a permanent obstructionist minority. You don't want to lead. You want to whine, and that's why Bradford fired you. That's why you're comfortable losing, and it's why I will always beat you. See you around, Brevin."

Brian smiles as he enters the building. That was an unexpected gift he got to unwrap early. Nothing amuses him more than demeaning an arrogant bastard like Brevin Hawkins. These are the moments when he loves his job.

CHAPTER SIXTY-NINE

TIERRA CAMPOS

Front Burner Washington Office
Washington, D.C.

The war room is like a second home at this point. I don't know what to do with myself. I'm waiting for a call that may or may not ever come, and it's excruciating.

CyberOreo has never been my biggest fan. When I extorted the hackers into helping me uncover the site owner on the dark web during the SOF investigation, they relented to avoid exposure. Dial Pirate was the only one remotely enthusiastic about helping, but it was conditional. I was forbidden from advertising he was helping. CyberOreo couldn't have been thrilled when Dial Pirate asked him to contact me.

I quietly enter the room to see Logan toiling away. He's so focused that I don't dare interrupt him as he creates a spiderweb of boxes, lines, and names on the whiteboard. I only speak when I see him pause to read something.

"What are you doing down here, Logan?"

"I needed a break," he says, not turning to face me as he continues drawing boxes and lines.

"So, you came here to do more work? A break traditionally means letting your mind relax a little."

"This is relaxing," he says, not understanding my comment. I don't argue with him.

Logan isn't a researcher because it's his job. It's something he enjoys and also happens to be very good at. Janey was probably more thorough, but Logan is better at finding obscure information. That's exactly what the doctor ordered to unravel this conspiracy.

"You've been busy," I say, taking in his extensive work on the whiteboard affixed to the long wall in the conference room. "What exactly is this?"

He caps the dry-erase marker and steps back. "I wanted to understand the size and scale of this conspiracy."

Now I understand what he's doing. It's an org chart. All of the boxes are filled with names and connected to larger squares with the names Conrad Williams and Andrew Li.

"I hope you're not suggesting that all these people are involved?"

"No, not really. A dashed box indicates a strong association with a known conspirator. Take Vice-Admiral Davis Mullin. He runs the National Security Agency, and I've found a dozen pictures of him and Williams together. Or Michael Krekstein. He's in charge of the FBI. Same thing."

"The Deputy AG is bound to know a lot of people."

"Tell me about it," Logan moans. "I'm already running out of real estate on this whiteboard."

"So, what do we do if we find out they're a part of this cabal?"

Logan points with the marker. "We change the box to red."

"There won't be many," I argue, sensing that anything this dangerous wouldn't be far-reaching.

"It doesn't have to be many. Look at the board. Even the power of the two players we know about is ridiculous. There are still two more to account for to understand the full scope of the cabal's dominion."

I'm legitimately impressed. This took a lot of effort, and I'm kicking myself for not having started the process earlier. It would have given me something to do and allowed him to dig deeper than I ever could.

"This is great work, Logan."

"Thanks."

"I don't think...whoa. Senator Alicia Standish? Seriously?"

He grins. "I doubt that box will turn red, but it was fun to write down. Can you imagine how terrifying this will be with Machiavelli as her chief of staff?"

He's right. The White House chief of staff is the highest-ranking member of the president's executive office and is the senior aide to the president. Legally, the position holds no official authority. Unofficially, the chief of staff has a ton as the president's gatekeeper. Anyone who watched *The West Wing* understands how much power and sway Leo McGarry had. And that was television.

"How complete is this list?"

He shakes his head. "Not very. It's what I dug up in a couple of hours. That was all the time I could afford. There could be countless more people."

I exhale as he joins me at the table. We stare at the spread of names in front of us. The list that Logan admitted is incomplete is already daunting, and that's with two key people still missing.

"Tierra, this isn't just four players. We're going up against the backbone of the federal government. Even when we uncover the other two names, what the hell are we going to do about it?"

"I don't know."

That's the honest answer. Even if we uncover this conspiracy by some miracle, proving it is another thing. These men have already killed. They have manipulated. What can *Front Burner* do? Who would believe us? All good questions that we aren't close to answering. At least, not yet.

CHAPTER SEVENTY

SPECIAL AGENT VICTORIA LARSEN

Block House Creek Bar
Liberty, Pennsylvania

The Block House Creek Bar is right off Liberty's main street next to a convenience store and across from a quartet of run-down multi-family houses. It's the type of dive bar you would expect to find in a rural town home to a thriving militia.

Victoria checks herself in the rearview mirror of Imani's grandfather's vintage Oldsmobile. She applies a little more fire engine red lipstick to compliment her provocative clothing. This is definitely not the classy sundress and strappy heels look that Tierra once envisioned for her. She looks like an available skank looking for johns. The outfit might be overkill, but it's too late to do anything about that now. Her story is the key to admission. The lie about why she is passing through Liberty, Pennsylvania, is what needs to be convincing.

Victoria struggles walking in the high heels as she moves around the side of the building and enters the bar. There are a dozen men here, and every last one stops what he is doing to behold the train wreck that walks through the door. She can feel eyes undressing her as the men don't try to mask their ogling.

She slinks up to the bar and orders a beer, making herself feel upset and angry to sound that way. Not hard to do considering the direction her life and career are going. The bartender pours a cheap brew from the tap as Victoria climbs onto a stool, fighting to keep her short skirt from revealing too much. She was counting on getting attention, and now she has it.

A man from the corner approaches her first, checking back with his friends every few steps. He must have won whatever game they played to see who gets the first shot at bringing her home. That, or he is the only one who's downed enough liquid courage to try.

"You're not from around here," he says, trying to look cool as he leans against the bar.

She eyes him coolly, as any jilted woman would. "What gave it away?"

"Oh, no need to be hostile."

"Men are pigs. Get lost," Victoria says, turning her head away from him.

From the corner of her eye, she catches the man staring back at his friends. He's not off to a good start, so he recalibrates his approach.

"You must not have a real man in your life."

"You can say that again," she agrees in a touch warmer tone than her greeting.

"Single?"

"Am now. My ex-boyfriend's an asshole."

"Where you from? It ain't around here."

"It ain't in this state. Richmond."

Victoria leaves off the name of the state. She assumes this guy has probably heard of the capital of Virginia.

"What brings ya to Liberty?"

"Nothing. I got in my car and started driving. I got tired and stopped here."

The man beams. "Lucky me."

Her eyes give him the onceover. She's horrible at flirting because she's never really had to. Her mother always said that she was graced by God with her beauty and would never have to try earning male attention. Her only experience playing hard to get is when she actually means it.

Victoria offers him an amused smile. "Not yet."

"Can I buy you a drink?" he eagerly asks, having received the iota of encouragement.

She points at the half-filled glass. "You're sweet. You can buy me a second one."

"Wanna talk about it?"

Victoria shakes her head. "I shouldn't talk to strangers."

"My name's Billy, but everyone calls me Strohs. There. We're not strangers now."

"Stroh's? Like the beer?" Victoria asks, acting like that's a hip name.

"Without the punctuation."

"I'm Tammy. You sure you wanna hear this?"

"More than anything," he says, pulling the stool beside her away from the bar and plopping himself on it.

Victoria, aka Tammy, launches into the completely fictional yet highly detailed story about what happened between her and her former beau Cody. She complains that he's a deadbeat with delusions of greatness working at a dead-end job because he has no real ambition. She channels Tierra's troubled work relationship with Austin in New Hampshire as a source of angst. The man is riveted. From the look of the haggard men at the corner table, his friends can't believe he's made it this far with the new bimbo in town.

"Last call," the bartender bellows.

"I like you, Tammy. You're my kind of woman."

"And I like talking to you. You're a good listener. I bet you do all kinds of things well," she says, questioning the line's effectiveness until a smile creeps across his lips. "You have a place we can go?"

"Nah, I've been staying at work lately. I can't bring you there."

"You sleep at work?"

"I work at the lumber mill. I'm a big deal around there," he says, likely inflating his worth.

Victoria puts on her best "Tammy is unimpressed" look and then starts looking around the bar. He works at the mill. That piece of information got her halfway home. Now she needs to compel him to divulge if he does anything else there.

"We also have some other things going on," he says, responding to her sudden disinterest.

"Like what?"

"I really can't talk about it. We're protecting the country."

"Like a soldier?" Victoria asks, perking up to encourage him further.

"Something like that. The Army has been corrupted. We are preserving freedom and democracy."

Victoria leans forward, showing more cleavage than she's normally comfortable with. "That's so honorable. I like that. My ex-boyfriend certainly didn't have any honor. What do you do for them?"

"Whatever I need to," Strohs says, his eyes lingering on her chest. "I'm like a leader there now. We lost our two the other day."

"An officer and a gentleman," Victoria squeals, grabbing his knee.

The squeal was legitimate, even if the flirtation was anything but. Strohs is a confirmed member of the Keystone Militia, even if she doubts he plays an important role. She has her target. Now comes the tricky part.

"I'd love to show you what kind of gentleman I am," he says, pressing his luck.

"I bet. Since we can't go to your place, we can talk more in my car."

Strohs' eyes light up. He's hooked and pays the tab before walking over and giving the news to his friends. As Victoria leads him to where she parked behind the building, his buddies head for a car across the street. He's alone, isolated, and completely hers. He moves to the passenger side and waits for her to unlock the door.

"We'll be more comfortable in the back."

Strohs practically sprains something as he quickly moves to get in. Victoria savagely kisses him, tugging at his shirt in an unmistakable signal. His hands start to wander, first to her breasts, then down her side, and then to her toned stomach. They don't make it any lower.

"Ow! What the hell was that?" he barks.

"You don't like having a woman nibble on your neck?"

Strohs rubs a spot, checking for blood on his hand. "It felt like you…jabbed me with…something," he says, spotting the syringe Victoria's holding. "What did you…?"

"It's Propofol. It slows brain and nervous system activity. Hospitals use it as a sedative or a general anesthesia for surgery. You'll be fine."

"I thought…I thought you liked talkin'…to me?"

"I do, Strohs, I do. You'll have plenty of time to talk to me when you wake up. Until then, sleep tight."

CHAPTER SEVENTY-ONE

IAN DRUCKER

"The Forge" Militia Compound
Liberty, Pennsylvania

Ian stretches his arms and rolls his head to loosen up his neck. This metal folding chair is as uncomfortable as furniture gets. It gets the job done. He will have a plush recliner to sit in soon enough. This mission is almost over.

The feed finally refreshes, and Ian leans closer to the laptop screen. Despite being boosted via an extender, the wi-fi signal still isn't strong here. Luckily, he doesn't spend much time online, and even slow download speeds still work for his purposes.

The wait for results isn't because of a slow connection. Ian thought about having the militia record the bombings and ruled it out. Digital signals can be traced, and he didn't want to prematurely lead the FBI to the Forge. Then he realized recordings weren't necessary because social media would take care of it for him. Everyone has a camera on their mobile phone these days, and that footage will force the media to report the incidents. That should be enough.

After another refresh, the first shared tweets pop up. A few minutes later, a video is posted. Ian switches over to other social media sites. After reports of the second, third, and fourth bombing surface, the snowball they rolled down the hill turns into an avalanche. Hashtags like #PABombing #PAInterference start trending. Reddit is lit on fire. Thanks to America's infatuation with social media, momentum slowly grows.

So far, there's no sign that any Keystone Militia members have been taken into custody or were arrested before making their deliveries. He was willing to accept a failure rate of up to twenty-five percent. The later waves were riskier due to increased vigilance. That fear hasn't been realized. Everything is going better than planned.

Ian surfs over to local news and sees he caught a break. A local reporter was live on the air across the street from a polling station when one of the ballot boxes exploded. She has an obvious reaction to the detonation and is shaken up, but the camera continues to roll. She jumps back into the frame with a harried explanation of what just happened. Perfect. There are no obvious signs of collateral damage, and that's a good thing. This isn't about maiming or killing Americans. Innocents have no reason to die today.

The video streams across the country at the speed of electrons. Ian flips through the cable news channels until he sees the footage already picked up by one with a breaking news chyron. There is no mention of the blast on any other.

Ian checks his watch. All the bombs have detonated by now. He leans back, knowing that the real Sunday morning entertainment will be in studios as producers have aneurysms. The media will be caught between hyping the story for higher ratings and not wanting to be seen influencing an election. That's why he timed the attacks for early morning.

That's how ridiculous America has become. This is news, plain and simple. It doesn't require analysis. They should report it to inform the masses and compel the police to investigate, identify the perpetrators, and make arrests. It's simple. That's not how this will shake out. Candidates, politicians, activists, law enforcement, and ordinary Americans will offer political posturing and excuses. Those in power will deflect blame, and those seeking to take advantage will assign it to their chosen target.

Depending on the ideological bent, the main culprits will be right-wing militias, Antifa, and maybe foreign operatives. Ian can only imagine who will get caught in the verbal crossfire. Robespierre and Machiavelli are brilliant. They know how to manipulate Americans and the system itself.

He has done his part. All he needs to do is sit, watch, and wait for federal authorities to play catch-up. Then he can escape to a warm country with a beach and no extradition treaty with the United States. He will live like a king and spend every night toasting his fallen friends who will never get to enjoy the spoils that come with victory and a job well-done.

CHAPTER SEVENTY-TWO

DEPUTY AG CONRAD WILLIAMS

U.S. Department of Justice Press Briefing Room
Washington, D.C.

Almost every press room in Washington has a podium with a seal on the front. Behind the speaker, a rendition of the building with the department name on a blue background is mounted on a curtain. An American flag is posted on the speaker's right, per U.S. Flag Code. Since this is the Justice Department, the DOJ flag, with its eagle, shield, and scroll, is on the left.

The Latin motto for the Department of Justice is *"Qui Pro Domina Justitia Sequitur."* Notwithstanding alternative translations, it means, "who prosecutes on behalf of justice," or Lady Justice. It is taken from a proceeding by the attorney-general at common law, who during Elizabeth's reign would say, "who prosecutes on behalf of our Lady, the Queen."

Conrad is announced and steps to the podium for this briefing. Further musings about mottos can wait. It's close to an election, and the room is only half-filled. Governmental business is rarely covered on a Sunday. That is especially true right before voters prepare to go to the polls in a presidential election year.

"Good afternoon. Thanks for being here today. I'm Deputy Attorney General Conrad Williams, and with me are Director of the FBI Michael Krekstein, Assistant Attorney General for National Security Charlie Campbell, and Assistant Director in charge of the FBI's Philadelphia Field Office Bernard Mercado.

"As part of a focused investigation into potential election fraud, a complaint has been filed and an arrest warrant issued against former FBI agent Ian Drucker. Mr. Drucker is also suspected of interfering with the New Hampshire Democratic Primary and has been indicted by a federal grand jury for the murders of two FBI agents assigned to the Boston field office. He is also complicit in the murder of federal agents in Loughborough, Massachusetts."

Under the United States Constitution, federal felony charges must proceed with a grand jury indictment. Getting one against Ian Drucker was easy. He was a confirmed member of the SOF and was present at the dilapidated mill attack. There is also evidence that he was complicit in the murders of two agents in Boston. The next piece is the tricky part.

"Through a special investigation run from Washington, we've determined that there is a probability he isn't working alone. We're developing a list of possible accomplices and expect more to be identified. At this time, we have also filed a complaint against current FBI Special Agent Victoria Larsen."

The reporters in the room perk up and begin looking at each other. Everyone remembers the name. *Front Burner's* stories made her name recognizable enough for eligibility to become a contestant on *Dancing with the Stars*. Her reputation only grew in New Hampshire and the reporting of the aftermath in Massachusetts. This news will hit the media like an anvil.

"This was not a direction that any of us expected. Agent Larsen has been a valued asset to the FBI and the American people for a decade. To think that she could be involved with Ian Drucker is almost unfathomable. Unfortunately, we are compelled to follow the evidence the investigation has uncovered.

"Reports that she was admitted to a local Philadelphia hospital and is resting comfortably while awaiting brain surgery are false. Agent Larsen is not at the hospital, and the doctors and nurses are being questioned about allegedly falsifying medical records. Her location is currently unknown, and we ask that any member of the public with information on her whereabouts contact the FBI tip line. Director Krekstein can provide more details in a moment."

Conrad hangs his head. He wants to look conflicted and even emotional. Most of what happens in this city is theater. Press conferences are no different.

"We are committed to working collaboratively with those on the front lines of elections. That includes state and local governments, election officials, and federal partners. Together we must manage risks and subdue threats to our electoral process. Our goal here at the Department of Justice is to remain transparent about our efforts to the public, and agile in our response to those threats. With that, we can let Director Krekstein provide more details."

The deputy attorney general steps aside. Victoria Larsen can't run now. She won't even be able to show her face. By the end of tomorrow, she will wish she had taken that assignment in Africa. It's going to look a lot more appealing than a jail cell.

CHAPTER SEVENTY-THREE

BRIAN COOPER

Independence Mall
Philadelphia, Pennsylvania

The national campaign swing may have been necessary, but it has some poignant downsides. The hours in the air, bouncing between cities and states in different time zones, made the governor cranky. He puts on a stoic face in public, but behind the scenes, he is short-tempered, agitated, and mentally exhausted.

Most people don't realize how much energy it takes to run for office. The governor shakes thousands of hands a day. He gives no fewer than three speeches, and has countless meetings and conversations with donors, and even more with voters. From the moment he opens his eyes in the morning to when he closes them at night, he's campaigning or working to further the campaign. There is no rest.

The governor has been on stage for the past half hour. The crowd gathered near Independence Hall isn't hostile, but it isn't friendly, either. Standish had a rally here, and Brian thought it was a nice symmetry to hold their last one in the state here. That was then. The events on Saturday changed the algebra on that decision.

Bradford started his remarks by addressing the racist and anti-Semitic graffiti, knocking him off his message and making him play defense. He had to do it, but Brian didn't like it. The fact that he has circled back to it at the end of the speech isn't sitting any better with him.

"I hope they catch the people who did this. I want their mug shots shared online and in every newspaper in the country. I want them paraded into a trial where the evidence against them is outlined for a jury of their peers. Then I want them found guilty and imprisoned for their crimes.

"Much has been made about my governance concerning people of color. I have made mistakes. I accept and learn from them because that's what leaders do. I will tell you here, now, that I reject any notion that I support what happened here on Saturday. Such messaging is inappropriate to think, much less write with spray paint. If the cowards who did this consider themselves my supporters, rest assured, I have a message for them: Cast your vote for someone else. I don't *want* it."

It was a good line. Brian nods at Joel, who returns it. The consultant didn't want to hold this rally. He argued with Brian, crying that it would inflame the situation. He may be right, but the optics of canceling are even worse. Public figures can't run from incidents like this. It makes them look weak. Americans respect those who stand and face the music.

At least Joel took the time to prep the governor. He needed to speak to this using the right tone. It had to be genuine. Joel clearly gave Bradford ideas but stopped short of providing him lines to recite. That's why the words sound real. He is speaking from the heart.

Governor Bradford ends his remarks and receives a warmer, more enthusiastic response than Brian expected. It's time to get out of Dodge. The senior campaign staff piles into the bus, and junior staffers load into rental cars. A small detail of Secret Service agents rides with the governor while the rest of his protective detail climbs into Suburbans for the ride to the airport.

The convoy lurches forward for the trip out of town. The staff begins talking about the last rally in Raleigh when a sound causes everyone to stop talking and look around. An egg hits the window, exploding and running down the side of the bus. Then it happens a third and fourth time.

The crowd along the sidewalk begins to grow as the bus slowly makes a left turn. It feels like they veered straight into a demonstration. There are more people here than at their rally.

"We're getting pelted by unborn chickens," Joel says, grinning. "Does anyone have bacon? We can make breakfast."

"Can you bring a bus through the car wash?" another staffer asks.

"Sure, but it's not in the budget," a third chimes in.

Brian smirks as they all share a laugh. It's a needed tension breaker that doesn't last. A loud thud against the window causes everyone to turn. That wasn't an egg. Then another. Then there's a crash as the window explodes. The communications director yelps as a brick hits her before dropping to the floor.

People pour into the street and block their path. The bus halts and the crowd starts banging on the bus's sides. Two beefy men start trying to pry open the door. Others are hitting the sides of the bus with hammers and tire irons. The Secret Service jumps into action as another window is shattered, and the huge windshield is cracked. They move Governor Bradford to the back and begin to bark orders into their sleeve mics.

The senior staff huddles in the middle of the bus, immobilized in terror. Police in riot gear move into the street and struggle to push people away. The bus lurches forward when the driver taps on the gas. The left side toward the front erupts in a sheet of flame, which quickly burns out. Brian looks at Joel.

"Molotov cocktail."

For the first time, Brian starts to feel panic. The police step up their crowd-clearing efforts with palpable urgency. They hit people with ASP retractable batons, knocking them to the ground. Brian sees plumes of tear gas. People get hit by rubber bullets and pepper spray balls, causing them to fall to the ground. Teams move in pairs to drag them off.

The bus follows a Suburban as the path in front of them is finally cleared. When they reach the open street, the driver floors it. Everyone holding their breath finally lets it out. They are out of immediate danger as they follow their escort to the airport.

"Are you okay, sir?" one of the Secret Service agents asks.

"I'm fine. I'm fine. Is everyone okay?"

There is a smattering of yesses and nods. Brian rubs his temples. Holding this rally today was all for nothing. He knows not a single word of what the governor said will be aired. Every report in conservative media will be about the barbaric attack while the left trumpets criticism of the egregious police response against a "peaceful protest." They will show bloodied men and women without mentioning anything about bricks or Molotov cocktails.

A Secret Service agent checks out the communications director. She's okay. The laceration on her arm doesn't require stitches and is bandaged. Brian puts his hand on her shoulder.

"How are you?"

"I'll be okay, thanks."

"When we get to the airport, I need pictures and video of the outside of this bus. We need to document every scratch."

"Why?"

"Because the narrative will be that we tried running down a group of protesters and forced the police to beat the crap out of them. We need to show just how 'peaceful' it was."

"That's ridiculous."

"Yeah, it is, but it's what left-leaning media will run with two days before an election. Trust me. Document everything."

She nods, and the agent finish his work as Brian collapses into a chair. He stares blankly out one of the unshattered windows. Images will help but won't solve the issue. Pennsylvania just slipped from their grasp, and it will take a miracle to get it back.

Bradford sits down across from him without speaking. "I'm not going with you to North Carolina, Governor."

"Why not?" he asks, cocking his head.

"I need to do damage control here. The media doesn't want to do their jobs, so I need to do it for them. I will meet you in Raleigh late tomorrow."

"Who will—"

"Joel can walk you through tomorrow's agenda. He's more than capable of handling it."

Joel nods, appreciative of the support from a man he's been at odds with since the day he was hired. Brian may disagree with Joel's tactics, but he is competent. That's high praise coming from the campaign manager.

"Okay. Good luck. Keep me posted."

Brian returns to staring out the window, knowing he will need all the good luck he can get.

CHAPTER SEVENTY-FOUR

SPECIAL AGENT VICTORIA LARSEN

Random Cornfield
Outside Liberty, Pennsylvania

Day Before the General Election

This is beautiful countryside. Victoria sips her coffee as the sun rises over the sweeping cornfield. Tourists visit large cities and play in the urban jungle. Progress is measured by the height of skyscrapers and how efficiently population density can be increased. Most never see the majesty of the rural areas. It's a shame. This is America.

Without even looking, Victoria can hear Strohs beginning to stir behind her. She slides off the Oldsmobile's hood, careful not to spill her coffee. His eyes open, and he struggles to process what he's seeing. It must still be confusing that the floozie he was chatting up at the local watering hole is dressed in tactical gear.

"Good morning, Strohs. Did you have a restful sleep?"

"Where are we now?" he asks with a moan.

"How the hell would I know? I'm not from around here, remember? Do you want some coffee?"

She watches as he struggles to break free from the handcuffs secured around his wrists with a tree in the middle. It's a compromising position, and it doesn't take long for him to figure out it won't work.

Victoria spent much of yesterday changing from one remote location to another. Strohs isn't going to be easy to make talk. Most fanatics aren't. He needs to realize that there is no hope of escape. This isn't Afghanistan or Iraq. He knows he has legal protections and needs to understand that they don't matter to Victoria.

"I'm never going to talk to you."

"Okay. I tried my best, but you're a tough man. I'm going to leave you handcuffed with your arms around that tree. I'm sure someone will find your corpse sooner or later."

"That's not legal!" he shouts.

"You're part of the Keystone Militia, right? I don't think you and your friends are concerned about what's legal and what isn't."

"Let me go!"

Victoria sips her coffee and stares at him until he begins to get unnerved. "Tell me what I want to know, starting with the leadership and number of members."

Strohs figures he has nothing to lose by telling her about the Keystone Militia's command structure. Most of them are already dead. He tells her how Remy and Mike recruited him and what they were preparing for. Then he explains what happened when Ian came to the camp and started turning their words into actions. All of Victoria's suspicions are confirmed. Ian is using them as hired thugs without their knowledge. It's a smart plan. She's about to press further when the ring from her satellite phone interrupts them.

"You're being very helpful, Strohs. Hey Imani," she says, walking a distance away from her captive.

"We found the information on the agent who infiltrated the Pennsylvania militia. The name of the group is—"

"The Keystone Militia in Liberty, Pennsylvania."

There's a long silence on the other end of the line. "Okay, you're spooky. How do you know that?"

Victoria recaps the last thirty hours. She doesn't bother omitting any details. Imani needs to know what she's caught up in. Victoria is a fugitive now, so she needs to start acting like one.

"That's gutsy, girl."

"What good are feminine wiles if you don't use them every now and then?"

"It's also blatantly illegal," Imani adds.

"So are cabals trying to take over control of the government. I have nothing left to lose at this point."

"What are you going to do now?"

"Sneak into the Forge and find Ian Drucker."

"Okay, there's going to be a complication. HRT has mobilized. They're forming a joint task force with the ATF to execute a warrant issued by the DOJ."

"Williams?"

"You got it. Your name's listed on the warrant. Williams and Krekstein have convinced the Bureau that you're working with Ian Drucker. If you're spotted at the compound, it will only confirm everything they've told the public."

Victoria lowers her head and stares at the ground. Imani's right. Williams will hang everything since New Hampshire on her if she's there when the task force moves in. The best defense lawyer in the country wouldn't be able to keep her from serving a life sentence. That might be the price for winning.

"If I don't go, Ian will escape. I'm not letting that happen again."

"You need to forget Ian Drucker, Victoria. They will bring everything when they assault that camp, including helicopters and drones. Even if you manage to get past the militia and find Drucker, you aren't getting out of there."

"I have no choice. Ian left himself a way out. He must have. When is the assault team moving in?"

"I heard an HRT guy mention it could happen tomorrow evening. I'm supporting the operation from here, so I'll know soon enough. The country will be watching the returns, and the media covers presidential elections like they're the Superbowl. It will get buried in the news cycle if it goes wrong."

Victoria grins. That's a smart play. Nobody will notice if it goes south. If it's a success, they get to trumpet it on Wednesday as the nation wakes up to find out who the new president is.

"Keep me informed, and thanks, Imani."

"You're welcome, but I'll do one better than that. I'm going with you."

"No way. I appreciate everything you've done, but I can't let you put yourself in that position. I'm a fugitive, and if you insist on helping me, you're more valuable feeding me inside information."

"You can't do this alone, and you know it. You're afraid I'll end up dead like Takara or wounded like Diego. I won't."

Victoria hates being profiled. Unfortunately, Imani's good at it. She could use the help, but there would be no living with the guilt if something happened to this bright young woman. The FBI is a better organization with her in it.

"Don't make assurances you can't possibly keep. What happened to Takara and Diego wasn't your fault. Risks come with the job. Diego couldn't have anticipated that SOF ambush any better than you could. Stop blaming yourself. People help you because they believe in you, Victoria. I believe in you."

"I'll talk to you on the flip side."

Victoria hangs up and powers down the phone. She has almost two full days to plan.

"You're going into the Forge by yourself? My guys will eat you for lunch."

"No, they won't. You're going to tell me where every position and OP is. You're going to give me every detail about the layout of the mill, including emergency escape routes."

The man scoffs. "What makes you think I'm going to tell you that?"

"I admire your loyalty, Strohs. Tell me something. If the FBI shows up, will your men fight?"

"Hell yeah, they will."

"Then they'll die. Tell me what I need to know, and you go free. You'll get to live a long, pathetic life."

"And if I don't?"

Victoria glares at the man with a heartless contempt that countless criminals have given her. She walks over to him, bends down, and looks him straight in the eye.

"You'll join them."

CHAPTER SEVENTY-FIVE

TIERRA CAMPOS

Charlton Service Plaza - Eastbound
Charlton, Massachusetts

Massachusetts has several rest areas and roadside facilities maintained by the state government's transportation department. I had to stop at a few during the Brockhampton investigation and when I was on my way to New Hampshire to cover the Burgess arsons. I've never been to this one.

The Charlton Service Plaza is located near mile marker eighty on Interstate I-90. Despite being on the last leg of our journey to Boston, we needed a break from the car and a chance to stretch our legs. After a bathroom break, Austin, Olivia, and I decide to get coffee and not sit in something moving for a while. Tyler seizes the opportunity to grab a steak and cheese sandwich and soda from a chain deli restaurant. I was the first to pay for my coffee and move to the sitting area.

My phone chimes and I read the text message from my new buddy Nabisco.

> *Contact not available until tomorrow.*
> *Still working on xfer. Sit tight.*

I want to smash the phone. The others see my frustration as they take seats at the table.

"This can't be good," Tyler concludes.

I look around the seating area. The plaza isn't crowded, and none of the people waiting in line for food or trekking to the restrooms look like federal agents. I should wait until we get back in the car, but what the hell. I feel like I can talk freely here.

"We can't make the pickup today."

"Why not?" Austin asks.

"I don't know. CyberOreo's message was vague."

"Crap. Now what?" Olivia asks.

"We work. I booked us at the Seaside. We can help the team back in Washington with election coverage until we're ready."

Tyler and Olivia nod at Austin. I just scowl.

"You don't look pleased, Tierra."

I rub my forehead and push back into my chair. "We drove up here because we didn't want to book flights that could get us reported by TSA to DHS and over to the FBI. Now, we've wasted hours."

"You couldn't have foreseen this," Tyler says between bites.

"I know, but we're going to need a new plan if we assume the FBI will follow us up here."

"Would they involve the Boston Field Office?" Olivia asks.

I shrug. I hope not because that would mean tangling with Victoria's former colleagues. Having a team from Washington stalking me is bad enough. I don't also need a field office full of agents on my trail.

"Austin, why did Naomi send the three of you with me? I could have done this by myself."

Olivia and Tyler stare at him as he sips his coffee. "She knows that."

"Then why?"

I think it may be guilt, but I want to see if there's a better reason. I've had words with Naomi for not helping me with this investigation. I don't want them here at *Front Burner's* expense because of my complaints.

"Would you believe me if I told you that I insisted?"

"Maybe."

"What about me?" Tyler asks.

"Maybe."

"What about me?" Olivia finishes.

"Yes, that I'd believe," I say, cracking a smile.

"Hey!" Tyler says, throwing a wrapper at me. "The truth is, we all insisted."

"Guys, this isn't a four-person job. We already don't have enough bodies to—"

"We can't rebuild *Front Burner* doing what the mainstream media does," Austin says. "We can't write all the articles. The 'newssharing' needs to work for us to survive."

"Newssharing?"

"It's a new word I created. Do you like it?"

I do, but I refuse to say so. "I thought maybe Naomi was worried about my safety."

"She is," Austin assures me. "That's why she agreed to our demands without an argument. None of us were letting you come up here alone."

"I don't think Machiavelli or Robespierre would be reckless enough to do something to me," I argue.

"I don't want to take that chance," Austin says. "They've already killed FBI agents, civilians, and possibly even Angela Mays. We'll watch your back for anyone wanting to add you to their body count."

"Tierra, the information in that file could destroy them," Olivia adds.

"Or so we think."

"Either way, it's worth killing to protect."

Austin is right. I'm at risk…again. Worse, the three of them are placing themselves in harm's way by supporting me. This is becoming an unfortunate habit.

"How far are we from Boston?" I ask.

"I don't know…about an hour, maybe, depending on traffic. Why?"

"Then that's how long we have to devise a plan to get these files if the FBI is tailing us."

"Are you getting a little paranoid?" Olivia asks.

I nod, staring at her with serious eyes and no hint of a smile. "Until this is over, we all need to be. It might be the only thing that saves us."

CHAPTER SEVENTY-SIX

BRIAN COOPER

Triangle Oaks Hotel
Raleigh, North Carolina

Election Day

The alarm on Brian's phone rings its shrill tone. Unlike most mornings, he doesn't fumble around trying to silence it. He simply turns it over in his hand and punches the screen icon. He was already awake and spent much of the night that way.

He hops out of bed and opens the curtains to his Raleigh hotel room. The sun hasn't even started penetrating the inky darkness of the night sky. The artificial lighting in the capital of North Carolina still glows in the windows of silhouetted skyscrapers set against the horizon.

As he checks his phone, he punches the brew button on the preloaded coffee maker. He answered all the late-night and early-morning text messages. At half past midnight, polls closed in midnight voting for two New Hampshire towns that cast their ballots as the clock struck twelve. Standish won four to three in the first, while Bradford won the other by a twelve to nine tally. That's the first story the media will air as Americans wake up on Election Day.

Polls will be closing in Guam in about an hour. Not being a state or the District of Columbia, they don't send electors to determine the winner. Their presidential straw poll receives media attention from the talking heads who use it to suggest how the rest of the country will vote. Historically, it's not a good indicator.

At six a.m. Eastern Standard Time, polls start opening across the fifty states and Washington, D.C. Brian doesn't need to go to a polling place to cast a ballot. He mailed his absentee ballot weeks ago. He's a D.C. resident but knew he would be with the governor in North Carolina to watch the returns.

The candidates will spend the morning making a show of voting in their home districts. The media come out in force to cover the events, as dull as they usually are. It is their last chance to gain some free airtime, and no presidential or vice-presidential candidate passes up the opportunity.

Standish will cast her ballot in Cambridge before heading to her hotel at the Boston Convention Center. Bradford spent last night at the governor's mansion in Raleigh and will go to the polls after she does. He'll retire to spend some time with his family this afternoon before heading to the convention center to watch the returns alongside the key staff and party leadership.

They both have it easy. The campaigns are running the show today, and Brian will be posted in their war room to make phone calls and coordinate activities. This will be the beating heart of the GOP's get-out-the-vote effort. That's all they can do now.

The debates are long over, and advertisements reaffirming their message will run throughout the day. This election is about voter turnout, especially in Pennsylvania. Whichever side does it better will win. It's that simple.

Brian logs into his computer and checks the overnight internal polls. Nothing has changed. He leans back and smirks. Cubic called it months ago. The race will absolutely come down to whatever happens in Pennsylvania. The man is a wizard. He sees things in numbers and trends that mere mortals can't.

The coffee finishes brewing, and Brian pours a cup before settling down at his open laptop on the small hotel stationary desk. He clicks on the news sites and opens them in different browser tabs. He rubs his chin after checking the first and sips his coffee while scanning the others.

There is almost nothing about the destroyed ballot boxes. The truck explosion is only covered on two networks, and they label the attack an assault from a "right-wing militia." The anti-black graffiti in Philadelphia is getting coverage from left-leaning sources, while conservative outlets are covering the anti-American stuff supposedly scrawled by Antifa.

Welcome to modern America, where the news is all propaganda all the time. He doubts either account is true, but facts don't matter on Election Day. Only winners and losers do. The media has a role in making sure their preferred candidate wins.

He can't help but feel that he contributes to that. Neither campaign is innocent when it comes to courting the media. Something changed in this country where everyone feels they need to choose a side. Journalists used to be considered the Fourth Estate – a term used to signify their advocacy and implicit ability to frame political issues. The derivation arises from the three estates of the European realm: the clergy, the nobility, and the commoners.

Media outlets have more in common with the Soviet state media Pravda than a free press presenting facts so that the people can make informed decisions. Now they want to think for the people. It's sad, but it's the system. Not even *Front Burner* is going to change that.

Brian checks the time on his screen. He has time for a quick shower, a shave, and a second cup of coffee. This is going to be the longest of all days. Whether it ends with the fairy tale ending that he wants is up to the voters and the media that influences them.

His cell phone rings, and Brian checks the caller ID. "What's up, Joel?"

"How fast can you get here?" the consultant asks with an unnerving urgency tinging his voice.

"Less than an hour. What's up?"

"Something is going on up in Pennsylvania."

CHAPTER SEVENTY-SEVEN

IAN DRUCKER

"The Forge" Militia Compound
Liberty, Pennsylvania

About two dozen men mill around the meeting hall as Ian enters. The lumber company has been shut down. Outside of loading a few trucks to fulfill previous orders, the business has been shuttered. He has these men preparing for revolution. There isn't time for anything else.

"Where is Strohs?" Ian asks, realizing he doesn't see the man among the faces in front of him. He doesn't know all their names, but that one sticks out. He wonders if the man has a dog named Alex. It would be a nice homage to the old commercials.

"He hasn't come back."

"How long was his furlough?"

"He should have been back last night," one of Remy's lieutenants says.

Ian frowns. He needs every man he can muster. "Have you tried calling him?"

"A few times," the lieutenant confirms.

"He ran off with some broad from New Jersey," one of his friends confirms.

"What?"

"Some skank came into the Block House, and he was set on charming his way into her panties. Haven't seen him since."

Ian shakes his head. Some dedication to the cause.

"All right. Do you guys understand the modified defense plan?"

Heads nod. "Yeah. What makes you think we'll need it?

"Are you serious?" Ian says with a chuckle. "Haven't you been watching the news?"

"Yeah, but they don't know any of that is because of us."

"Yet. Don't underestimate your enemies. They'll find out, and when they do, they'll take quick action to prove to the people that they are capable."

"We only have half our guys," the lieutenant says. "Where are the others? They finished up yesterday and should be here to help. What are they doing?"

Ian smiles broadly. "This."

He clicks on the television. CNN is showing footage of men in black outfits, helmets, goggles, and face coverings walking down a street.

"What the hell? You turned them into communists?"

"Deception is a key component in the art of warfare, gentlemen. Even the patriots dressed up like natives for the Boston Tea Party."

"We have a report that shots have been fired by masked men outside a precinct in Chester County," the anchor says, cutting away to a video of two men dressed in black firing from a vehicle at a crowd in line to vote. "Fortunately, there are no reports of any casualties, but this certainly has shaken the small town. Let us turn to our expert, Myles Marandza. Is this Antifa?"

They leaped to that conclusion as fast as Machiavelli hoped they would. Antifa brands itself as a left-wing anti-fascist and anti-racist political movement. It is decentralized, and the groups under the movement's banner act autonomously, using nonviolent means and violent direct action to achieve its aims. They have an established legacy of causing chaos in the streets, and the masks they wear makes them easy to mimic.

"It appears that is the case. Chester County is a historically red area in voting, so it would make sense that they would be targeted."

"We have gotten several unconfirmed reports of intimidation and harassment in Pennsylvania as the polls open. Could this be a coordinated effort in response to what happened Saturday?"

"That's a fair conclusion," the expert says. "It could be considered political—"

"I'm sorry to cut you off, Myles, but we have more breaking news now out of Somerset County, where four people have been injured by a pipe bomb thrown at a polling station at an elementary school. We have a local reporter who was reporting on the scene at the time of the incident."

Ian mutes the television and turns back to the awed faces of the militiamen.

"Some of our guys are likely to get caught today."

"Then they'll know it wasn't Antifa!"

"For our purposes, it doesn't matter. These attacks are disruptive and will undermine the system. That's what we need and why we need to defend ourselves. Keep a minimal guard at the OPs today. When the feds come, it will be after sunset. We need one hundred percent security tonight to thwart the attack. After they pull back, we'll use the escape route out of the Forge."

"What about our guys in the Antifa costumes?" the lieutenant asks.

"They've been briefed on where to meet up with us. Let's get to it."

Ian smiles at the lie. He doesn't care what happens to these men. They'll be reluctant to leave the Forge, but they can stay and defend it with their lives if they want. It's a free country, at least for now. The fallout isn't his problem. He'll be on his way to a new life in twenty-four hours.

CHAPTER SEVENTY-EIGHT

TIERRA CAMPOS

Mike's Pastry
Boston, Massachusetts

Mike's Pastry is located on Hanover Street in Boston's historic North End. Founded in 1946, the owner created a one-of-a-kind cannoli that keeps Bostonians and flocks of tourists streaming through their doors. I was first introduced to the pastries when Victoria brought some down to Washington after the Brockhampton investigation.

Since visiting Mike's has become a Boston tradition, the line stretches outside the bakery and is perfect for what I need. This is a plausible destination should the FBI be lurking in the shadows. A woman directs people into twin parallel queues to keep it moving, one for cash payment and the other for debit or credit cards.

I engage in small talk with a group of five tourists from North Carolina and chat with some visitors from England. I make a show of being friendly and talkative to mask what happens next. I don't know what my source looks like. I only have a name. When a woman closer to the front of the line falls back, I assume it's her.

"Miranda?"

"It's me, Jimmy Olsen," she says, making a show of tying her shoe. I was warned about her love affair with the Marvel and DC superhero universes. "Are you being followed?"

"I don't know. Austin took my cell on a scenic walk along the Freedom Trail. I haven't spotted any Men in Black so far."

"Good, that makes this easier."

"Thank you for doing this, Miranda. Victoria told me that you didn't want to be involved."

Miranda was key to uncovering the possibility that the elusive Robespierre was none other than Conrad Williams. She used geolocations from government-issued phones to place him and Machiavelli in the same D.C. park. It was no coincidence.

"It's not every day I have a world-class group of hackers hijack my personal computer and contact me. Cyber would be forever jealous if I told them. How's Superwoman doing?"

"She's doing her best Harley Quinn impression."

Harley Quinn, formerly Dr. Harleen Quinzel, was a promising psychologist and intern at Arkham Asylum in Gotham City. She was assigned to study the Joker and became obsessed with her subject. After she fell for Batman's nemesis, she helped him escape. It's not the perfect metaphor. Victoria may have an unhealthy obsession with Drucker, but her plans don't include dating him.

"None of that stuff the Bureau said is true," Miranda says with a sneer as the line inches forward. "No way."

"And you know why they're saying it. Do you have the file that CyberOreo sent?"

"I already slipped the drive into your coat pocket. Don't feel for it. It's too obvious if my colleagues are watching us."

"You got it. Won't they know that you're FBI?"

Miranda chuckles. "Field agents don't talk to tech geeks unless they need something from us."

"Did you look at the files?"

The computer forensics expert grimaces. "I shouldn't have but couldn't resist. You already know who Machiavelli and Robespierre are. The files implicate both of them."

"Williams and Li. Who's Nietzsche?"

"You should sit down for this, Tierra."

I look around after getting the feeling that she's serious. "We're fresh out of park benches. Just tell me."

"DeAnna Van Herten."

Tierra's jaw drops. "Wow! I…I can't…I *did not* see that coming."

The implication is massive. DeAnna heads a media empire with unprecedented access to government leaders, an enormous payroll, and one of the most influential news organizations in the country. She has her name laminated on nearly every list of the top ten most influential figures.

"You used to work for her, right?" Miranda asks as I recover from the shock.

"*Capitol Beat* aired on her network. She forced me out."

"And now you know why."

"What about Rasputin?"

Miranda sighs. "There's a problem with that. CyberOreo never got the file from Dial Pirate. Apparently, he was raided before the Free Haven transfer was completed. There's no information about Rasputin."

The excitement of finally solving Isiah's ridiculous riddles and getting my hands on these files after all these months collapses into a feeling of utter despair. A knot forms in my stomach. This may not have been worth the effort after all.

"Damn it."

"I'm sorry, Tierra. There's something more you should know. Isiah found the money trail. He has records tying all of them together through a holding company called—"

"Kratos."

Miranda turns her head at me. "How did you know that?"

I shrug. "Victoria's been busy."

"That woman never ceases to amaze me. Isiah managed to get their financial records. I think he found someone to hack into their network because these weren't IRS documents. He also traced Kratos' funding. Do you know where that came from?"

"Actyv Private Equity."

"Damn, you guys are good. They are up to their eyeballs in all this."

After twenty minutes of being tortured by the aromas wafting out of the bakery, we finally make it through the front door. The inside is almost as packed as the outside. There are a couple of metal tables between the L-shaped counter and the entrance, but good luck getting one. This place is designed for take-out and enjoyment on the streets of Beantown.

"Is there enough on that drive to prove anything?"

"In a court of law, no. In the court of public opinion, maybe. Luckily, you're a journalist."

"I'm not sure that helps. This conspiracy is bigger than we thought it was. If we move too soon without solid proof, this thing will come crashing down on us."

"Well, good luck. I've done my part."

"Thank you, Miranda. For everything."

We are served by two separate clerks, each of us buying an assortment of amazing-looking pastries. I eye the masterpieces as they are boxed and I slide over to pay at the register. Miranda is already gone by the time I reach the door.

I feel for the USB drive in my pocket. Isiah's research may help prove the conspiracy, but the biggest piece of the puzzle is still elusive. We need to know who's seated at the head of the cabal's table before the bell rings for dinner.

CHAPTER SEVENTY-NINE
DEPUTY AG CONRAD WILLIAMS

State Capitol Building
Harrisburg, Pennsylvania

Conrad wasn't surprised by the order to get to the state capitol. His only directions from Lisa Ehler were to be visible. He would have thought she was more concerned about calming the masses, but that's part of her problem. She's more concerned with perceptions than solutions.

That works in his favor. He can be as visible as needed without actually forcing authorities to do their jobs. Press conferences are tightly controlled events that require media credentials. Press gaggles are a different story and are often more effective during times like these. Gaggles are what people see on television, usually preceded by an official or political figure leaving an office and stopping to talk to the press. This is the latter.

The governor is making a show of combating fraud. It's a political tactic that the White House is eager to play along with. The real work is being done behind the scenes. The public face of this crisis, at least in terms of federal assistance to Pennsylvania, is Conrad's burden.

To say that the state capitol is a busy place would be an exercise in understatement. That's why the media are omnipresent in and around the building. Upon entering the historic Beaux-Arts style structure, Conrad told the press that he would have something to say after speaking with the governor. As he departs, he's true to his word and stops to address questions. They are mostly softballs, and his answers are vague promises. He's about to wrap things up when he hears a familiar voice.

"Why are you suppressing information about the fake ballots, Mr. Williams?"

"I'm not suppressing…."

Conrad realizes who he's speaking to. Brian Cooper is standing among the gaggle, wearing an overcoat to blend in. The last time he heard, Bradford's campaign manager had returned to Raleigh with the candidate. What the hell is he doing back up here?

"Have any arrests been made?" Cooper presses. "Suspects identified? Did you even discuss it with Governor Fox?"

"We spent much of the time discussing the hate speech in the state's urban areas, Mr. Cooper."

"I'm glad to hear that because it's despicable, and the people should demand justice from its government leaders. But hate speech doesn't impact an election like thousands of ballots would."

"We don't know there were thousands of them," Conrad argues as the cameras roll.

"Ballots were found at an *industrial* printer in Allentown specializing in mass mailings. They were found completed in a van in Butler. There is suspicion that there were more in the eastern part of the state. Are you suggesting—"

"Election authorities have assured us that any illegitimate ballots have been identified and removed."

"That's good news, sir. How many were there? Has that been reported?"

Conrad stares at the political operative. "I don't have those numbers. Are there any other questions?"

"Yes," Cooper says, interjecting. "The ballots found in the van…who were they filled out for?"

"I'm not sure—"

"You're the deputy attorney general of the United States. You talk to the FBI and the governor every day. They didn't tell you?"

Conrad feels his anger rising. He's getting boxed in and is hoping someone from the media will throw him a life preserver. They don't seem inclined to do that. These reporters smell a story and are content to let this play out.

"I'm sure they did."

"Then you forgot? Who were they filled out for, Mr. Williams?"

There is no escaping the question. "My understanding is that the ballots all benefitted Senator Standish."

There's a grumble in the press corps. The liberal media would have preferred the opposite, but this is something reportable. The conservative media will be jumping all over this in a matter of minutes.

Cooper outstretches his arms at shoulder level. "Why would you not release that information?"

"Because the investigation is ongoing."

"And today is Election Day. Ballot boxes have been bombed. Fake ballots were known to be submitted. People need to go to the polls knowing their vote is secure; that the election they are voting in isn't tainted."

"We don't believe either incident will materially impact the result."

"Then prove it by divulging what you know."

Conrad feels the shift among the journalists gathered around him. They're beginning to eye him with suspicion. He needs to make this look like a desperate political stunt, and quickly.

"Mr. Cooper, I understand why you're here. You have an agenda that doesn't include electoral fairness or relaying information to the American people. This is about propping your candidate up after what happened yesterday and on Saturday."

"Yes, it is. I don't suppose you discussed the attack on our campaign van with the governor."

"The response was discussed at length."

"The response. That's an interesting choice of words. It makes it sound like the attack on the bus wasn't worthy of mention, that somehow, we all overreacted. Would you like to see one of the bricks thrown through our window?"

Brian tosses the piece of masonry, and Conrad moves to avoid it hitting his feet as cameras snap away and record it on video to be replayed on air across the country. The deputy AG stares at Cooper like he just hurled it at his head. He doubts that the brick is from the bus. That would have been collected by the Secret Service as evidence. It doesn't matter. The media got their visual, and they'll run with it.

"I look forward to hearing the results of your investigations. I'm sure all Americans do. Why don't you start with some of the highlights now."

Conrad smirks. He lost this round and needs to get out of here.

"No more questions. Thank you, all."

He begins moving down the sidewalk with reporters shouting at him. The State Police effectively keep the journalists at arm's length as they escort Conrad to his vehicle. He stares out the window as the car pulls out for the drive back to the airport. Ehler is going to be pissed.

"Well-played, Cooper. Well-played."

CHAPTER EIGHTY

SPECIAL AGENT VICTORIA LARSEN

Ridge & Hollow Gun Club
Trout Run, Pennsylvania

Political maps have their advantages. They depict geographic borders, bodies of water, highways, railways, and secondary road networks. That's helpful, but Victoria realized driving up here that a topographic map would have been more helpful. She had more than a full day to prepare for this. After checking the terrain, she wished that she had more time.

The lumber company is located on a plateau south of Liberty with streams carved into it, creating spurs. The terrain is steep on the front slopes and is only gradual along the main driveway leading to the mill. Getting in and out without being detected will be problematic.

Strohs' information is proving useful. To the south of the Forge is a wind farm that runs east-west along the plateau. A dirt service road snakes to each windmill and is served by two accesses at each end, likely secured with gates. A single worker inspects and maintains the site. He's a part-time militia member who hasn't been recently active. He only keeps their secrets and drinks a lot after work, which is why she wasn't here at the crack of dawn. That's her way in.

Victoria kills the headlights and parks up the road from the Ridge & Hollow Gun Club. She doesn't see a range but assumes there's one here somewhere. She sneaks up to the front of the building and spots the man drinking at the rustic bar. From his movements, he'd have problems standing erect.

She hopes she doesn't find out. Her helpful date claimed that the maintenance worker leaves his keys in his truck to find them after tying one on. It's rural Pennsylvania, not South Philly. He wasn't wrong when he said nobody was around to steal it. That much is true. This is the middle of nowhere.

Victoria climbs in, finds the keys in the center console, and drives the utility truck without headlights to the northwest. She takes it slow, using what ambient light the moon provides to navigate the bends in the road. She comes to the service road and uses the key on the ring to unlock the gate before swinging it open. Windmills stand like sentries, the whop-whop of their blades punctuating the dull noise of the wind and sounds of nature. She wonders if Don Quixote could have tilted at one of these. Probably not. Cervantes would have picked something else.

She parks three windmills past her target, not wanting to get too close to the Forge. She looks up and scans the night sky. The FBI likely has drones up by now. A truck close to the perimeter will draw attention. This is already risky enough.

Victoria walks over to the windmill with a tool bag draped over her shoulder. She sets it down and slips into the woods. Moving as swiftly as she dares, Victoria skirts along the tree line, tripping over roots and low vegetation. She doesn't want to pull her flashlight out. White light is visible for a long distance.

"All right. Where are you?" she whispers, searching the perimeter of the clearing around the target windmill.

Victoria takes five steps when her foot catches something, causing her to tumble to the ground. Climbing to her knees, she finds the culprit. The concrete lip is well-camouflaged. It would literally have taken someone tripping over it to find it.

The access isn't locked, which makes sense. Nobody would ever find it anyway. She opens the iron door to reveal a tunnel that travels due north. She looks up. Bingo, it heads right for the militia compound. Victoria carefully climbs down and lowers the door. Once inside, she risks turning on the light. There is no way she is going to grope her way to the end in the pitch darkness.

The passage is cramped and shallow, but effective for an escape route. It must have taken the militia forever to build this. Victoria travels over a thousand feet before she comes to a door above her head and kills the flashlight.

Victoria listens in the darkness for any sign of movement. Nothing. She cracks the trap door open an inch, willing the hinges to be oiled. Still nothing. She half expects to see Ian waiting with a gun pointed at her head. Instead, she opens the hatch and is greeted by an empty room.

She climbs out of the tunnel with her weapon drawn. The lights are on, and this feels more like a bunker than a building. The concrete walls are windowless, and the only exit is via a steel door. There are empty energy drink cans, ramen noodle packages, and protein bar wrappers on the far table next to an unrolled sleeping bag and pillow on an air mattress.

"Very cozy, Ian."

She glides over to the map laid on the table with cities and towns marked by chess pieces. Only black ones are used, with some removed and set off to the side. Without a legend, they have no meaning other than the rogue former agent being up to no good.

She looks around some more. There are no radios, walkie-talkies, or other means of communication. There is no efficient way to get orders out. This isn't the militia's command center. It's more likely their Alamo. They can barricade themselves here, and while authorities search for a way to breach, they could use the tunnel to mount an escape. It's not a half-bad approach.

Victoria moves to a map taped on another wall. It's filled with military symbols that she only vaguely understands. She doesn't need to know the exact meaning to understand what this represents. The Forge isn't a lumber company where a militia meets – it's a fortress. They have set up a layered defense with strong positions, heavy weapons, and interlocking fields of fire. She remembers the feeling of the SOF firing their M240B machine gun, and felt the effects of the same weapon at the mill in Loughborough. This would be even worse.

She pulls out Strohs' map and holds it up next to the one on the wall. He was pretty accurate but didn't tell her everything. She almost feels bad about keeping him handcuffed to the tree. At least she remembered to tell Imani where to find him.

The tactical team only has a couple of options to storm this location, and all the approaches are covered. There is no way to come in from the rear or west without being spotted unless they use the tunnel. That won't happen, leaving the north and east as the probable avenues. Both require a climb of over three hundred feet in elevation.

She pulls out her phone and powers it on. It gets a signal, albeit a weak one. She places the call and waits as it rings.

"Come on, Imani, pick up…pick up…damn!"

She's about to try again when she realizes what all the black dots with the dashed arrows are. She checks the legend of this map to be sure and rubs her chin. Anti-personnel mines.

"My God. This is going to be a bloodbath."

With that one realization, she is now a victim of Murphy's Law: No plan ever survives first contact intact. Any assault will get decimated, and she can't reach Imani to warn her. Victoria may be a fugitive now, but she's not about to let her fellow agents walk into a buzzsaw. She could never live with herself if she let that happen.

CHAPTER EIGHTY-ONE

BRIAN COOPER

Raleigh Convention Center
Raleigh, North Carolina

The big party is in the thirty-two thousand square foot main ballroom. At least, that's what the GOP faithful hope it will turn into. The room buzzes with anticipation as they wait for the first results from the East Coast states.

Brian shows his badge and makes his way to the executive suite, where the governor is holed up to watch the results. This one has vaulted ceilings and wood paneling that he imagines would be a perfect setting for corporate board meetings if there were a table in the center. He slips into the back unnoticed. That doesn't last long.

One of the senior staff spots him and starts applauding. Within fifteen seconds, he's getting an ovation from everyone in the room, including North Carolina's governor and first lady. He's used to being behind the scenes. Accolades like this are a new experience.

He walks toward the Bradfords, getting high-fives along the way. Joel Graham stops him before he gets there.

"We haven't always seen eye-to-eye, Brian, but what you did with Conrad Williams was absolutely brilliant."

"Thanks, Joel."

"I know it's November now, but it was a little warm for an overcoat, wasn't it?"

Brian smiles. "I didn't want to make it obvious that I was carrying a brick around Pennsylvania's state capitol."

"The Secret Service took the ones that crashed into the bus. Where did you get it from?"

"Home Depot," Brian says with a shrug, causing Joel to shake his head and smile.

"Did Williams speak to you after the ambush?" the governor asks after he walks over.

"Nope. He got an escort back to his helicopter and returned to Washington."

"He must have more important things to do," Joel moans.

"Thank you, Brian."

"For what, sir?"

"Making a scene."

Brian looks down at his hands. "I figured you would think I embarrassed the campaign."

"You know, I might have back in the summer," the governor admits with a nod. "We're way beyond that now. It was needed."

"Has it gotten any airtime?"

"Some," Joel says. "More than any previous reporting."

Brian frowns. He needed the media to be talking about this. He wanted awareness for all the people going to the polls after work. Casual mentions won't be enough to move the needle.

"Too little, too late, from that perspective."

"Don't be so sure," Joel argues. "Exit polls in Pennsylvania have the race dead even. Turnout in urban areas is lower than expected, and it looks like the governor has gained three points with people of color. That could be the margin of victory."

The governor nods. Brian doesn't like exit polls. The media love them because they're indicators of an election's direction that they get to talk about all day. Exit polling began forty years ago in a Kentucky gubernatorial contest. They've been unreliable ever since, with the 2000 election being an infamous example. Exit pollsters and news organizations awarded Florida to Al Gore and were forced to retract it.

They have even less meaning in the age of mail-in voting. Exit polls don't count absentee votes, and pollsters' election models are often flawed. In 2000, a data entry mistake inflated Gore's vote total. After that election, networks vowed to hold results until all the polls in a state had closed. It's a rare instance of the media showing self-restraint.

"The results are about to come in," the governor says, pointing over his shoulder. "Grab some food and come join us."

Brian plans on doing precisely that. He's famished, and there's nothing more that he can do other than enjoy the moment the best he can. There will be plenty of work for him after the election. That much he knows for sure.

CHAPTER EIGHTY-TWO

TIERRA CAMPOS

Outside the Olde Towne Exhibition Hotel
Boston, Massachusetts

I rendezvous with the rest of my small *Front Burner* team outside the hotel adjacent to the Boston Convention Center and look up at the gleaming glass tower. This place must cost a fortune to stay in, especially when there's an event next door. I can't imagine the rates for attendees of a presidential victory celebration.

Detective Seth Chambers exits the hotel and strides in our direction. He looks resplendent dressed in his state police uniform. I'm about to compliment him when I notice the dour look on his face and know it's the first sign of trouble.

"What's wrong, Seth?"

"We have a development," he says in an ominous tone. "We need to change our plan. The race is tilting toward Standish. VH Media has made some questionable state calls."

"We got the alerts," Olivia says, wagging her phone.

"DeAnna Van Herten is jumping the gun, not that it's unexpected," Austin moans. "It will pressure other outlets to do the same shortly."

"So what?" I ask. "Why does our plan need to change?"

Seth gnashes his teeth. "She's heading down to the convention center ahead of schedule. She might not be in her suite when I sneak you into the hotel."

"Can we intercept her on the way?" Tyler asks.

"Do you enjoy getting shot at by the U.S. Secret Service?"

"Okay, so, now what?" Olivia asks.

Seth pulls a pair of laminated press credentials with lanyards out of his pocket. "I…uh, liberated these."

"Where did you get them from?" I ask.

"A pair of unfortunate reporters are subdued and tied up in a utility closet."

I share a look with Austin. I'm not entirely certain if Seth is serious.

"I'm kidding, Tierra. There's no reason not to have some fun while I'm committing career suicide. Now, I can escort two of you in, but I don't know if I can get you close to Standish."

"You and Austin should go," Tyler says. "Olivia and I can keep a lookout for the FBI."

"That shouldn't take long," I grumble.

"FBI?" Seth asks.

"Long story."

"You're as bad as Victoria. I look forward to hearing about it, but we need to go. You have until we get inside to concoct a plan to get the senator to speak with you. It had better be good. I'm going to lose my job over this."

Austin and I hang the media credentials around our necks and follow Seth to a side entrance. Magnetometers manned by the Massachusetts State Police are set up and overseen by Secret Service agents. They check our credentials, and we pass through the screening. An officer directs us to the press area, and we head in that direction.

"There's one more thing. That checkpoint is where my authority ends. The Secret Service is running the show in this venue."

"Could you get a note to Standish?"

Seth shrugs. "Possibly."

I walk over to a counter with Standish for President pads and borrow one. I scrawl out a quick note and sign the bottom. It's unnecessary and even a little campy, but I don't feel like rewriting it.

"Hand her this."

Seth opens the folded note and reads it. "Are you kidding?"

"Trust me."

I can feel my phone vibrating but don't hear the ringer over the noise from the main hall. I check the caller ID and put the phone up to my ear while plugging my finger in the other.

"What's up, T?"

"Your FBI buddy is here, and he looks pissed. They just rolled up in force with about a dozen other agents and are heading to the entrance."

"Okay, thanks." I turn to Austin. "Company's coming."

"I have a place that you can stay out of sight, but I need to set it up," Seth says. "Can you avoid getting arrested for a bit?"

A huge roar goes up from the crowd. I thought that maybe the senator took the stage to introduce herself as the next president, but there was no introduction. Another news outlet may have called the race. Either way, the roaring audience must have given Austin an idea.

"There's safety in numbers. What do you think, Tierra? Have you ever thought about becoming an ardent Standish supporter?"

CHAPTER EIGHTY-THREE

SPECIAL AGENT VICTORIA LARSEN

"The Forge" Militia Compound
Liberty, Pennsylvania

Victoria kills the light in the bunker and inches open the steel door. The Forge compound is dark. That would normally benefit a tactical team with night vision capabilities. In this case, the militia probably has them, too, negating the advantage. She needs to give her guys a reason to halt their advance.

She closes the door and sprints west before stopping between two piles of logs. There's no movement around the lumber mill. Most of the men must be manning the perimeter. Taking a chance, Victoria sprints up the dirt road until it becomes crushed gravel, and she stops when she reaches a large building.

Most of the structures Strohs described are loading docks and covered wood storage areas. This one stands out. The side door is unlocked, and she slips into the dark building. A few glowing exit signs for the fire code and some small accent lights provide the only available illumination.

Victoria makes her way over to a control room on the main floor. She looks around and decides to hazard turning on her small flashlight, pointing it at the panel full of switches and buttons. She then aims it at the machinery on the floor. Her jaw drops.

This place must crank out lumber at a ridiculous rate. Victoria expected to see large saws, but this is more manufacturing plant than sawmill. Much of the work in this facility is automated. That takes a sizable capital investment, and this lumber mill must have healthy enough revenue to justify it.

"Okay, how do I turn this thing on," she mumbles, searching the panel.

Most of the buttons and toggle switches are labeled with terms she doesn't understand. She flips one, then two, then three. Nothing happens. Victoria begins pressing buttons, and still nothing. The panel is dead.

"Where are you?" she asks, looking for an on-off switch before finding a promising candidate on the panel's side.

The machinery roars to life. Victoria claps her hands and starts flipping toggles. Saws spin, and hydraulics actuators begin to move. The noise is deafening. Victoria checks the door before aiming the flashlight behind her. A pair of breaker boxes on the wall are labeled "plant lights" and "site lights."

"Perfect," she says, throwing both levers into the "on" position.

Night turns into day as hundreds of fluorescent lights bathe the mill floor and white-hot LEDs flood the surrounding grounds. If the machines powering up didn't get the tactical team's attention, the lights did. It undoubtedly got the militia's, too.

Victoria ducks in the control room. "Time to go."

The noisy plant covers her retreat out of the building. She stops in the doorway and looks around. The cover of darkness is gone. There isn't even a shadow. It's going to be hard to stay out of sight. She moves across a gravel driveway separating the mill from a loading area and ducks behind a large forklift.

There is still no movement or shouting. The equipment isn't as loud out here, but it could stifle the sound of shouts or voices. Victoria is about to move when she hears a crackle over her head. She tucks in closer to the body of the machine and stares through the glass cab. A head pokes over the eave of the roof.

"Shit."

The man disappears, but that doesn't solve her problem. He'll have a commanding view from up there and will likely be watching the area. There is no way she'll get back to the bunker unseen.

Moving swiftly, Victoria comes up alongside the building and rounds the corner. There is a metal ladder leading to the roof. Keeping her weapon drawn, she moves slowly and deliberately up the ladder. She could be spotted, but that will be the least of her problems if the target hears her coming. One clang against the metal siding, and it's over.

Victoria pokes her head above the roofline and sees a plywood platform built near the peak. It's a crow's nest that wasn't on Strohs' map. Now she's glad she kept him chained to the tree. A lone figure is lying prone with his feet toward her. There is no doubt that the FBI's drones have seen him. If he's a sniper, he chose a lousy spot. She slowly creeps along the metal roof to it.

The short wood ladder made of two-by-fours is quieter, and Victoria steps onto the platform without making a sound. She's careful not to hit the man's feet, but it doesn't matter. He senses her and turns, growing wide-eyed as he starts to reach for his weapon.

"Don't," she warns.

The man was only armed with a Colt six-shooter. There is no rifle. Whoever this guy is, he isn't a sniper.

"What are you doing up here?"

He glances at a black device resting on the platform next to his gun. "Screw you, fed."

"I don't take requests." Victoria moves fast. He reaches for the gun and almost has his fingers on it before she crashes the butt of her weapon onto his temple, knocking him out cold. She stares at him, happy that she didn't need to shoot him.

Victoria lies down to reduce the size of her silhouette. The crow's nest has a view of the northern approach. There's almost no visibility to the west, thanks to a stand of tall evergreen trees. It's not the best spot, but it's what they have.

She picks up the black device. It's a detonator, most likely for the minefield. This is the best place to trigger it if they require line-of-sight. That explains why he's up here without any cover and little concealment.

Victoria stares at the tree line, faced with a choice. She can't assume there is only one detonator for the mines. Destroying the device might not render the field useless. She needs to eliminate the threat before a lot of agents' wives become widows. Unfortunately, doing so could send men to their deaths by her hand. She closes her eyes, summoning the courage to make an impossible decision.

CHAPTER EIGHTY-FOUR

IAN DRUCKER

"The Forge" Militia Compound
Liberty, Pennsylvania

Ian stares at a map of the Forge's defense. He has a similar one back at the bunker and knows each position by heart. But there's something nostalgic about studying a real map. It's very World War II. Modern battlefield intelligence is displayed digitally in real-time. This is anything but.

Using a physical map requires imagination to understand movements, but it also doesn't have distractions of icons moving around a screen. That means Ian needs to anticipate his enemy's moves. That forces him to think tactically.

He had no training on this at Quantico. The skillset required to be an FBI agent differs from that of a soldier, despite the occasional similarities between the two occupations. He was in the Army, though. He learned a few things despite not being in a combat arms military occupational specialty. Western militaries, particularly America, understand the value of tactics, strategies, and logistics. He has employed all three of those precepts.

"Command, OP Two. Targets moving in from the northwest."

"This is OP One. Same from the north."

Ian checks the map. The feds aren't coming in from the south or east. They will most likely rotate men to form a perimeter. Advancing from the wind farm was the most likely approach because of the flat terrain. As a result, Mike and Remy constructed robust fortifications in that area. But a wise enemy doesn't strike where you expect it.

"OP Three, OP Four…leave a small force to watch the rear and redeploy to the north. Don't do it at once. Stagger your movements."

"Roger."

"Acknowledged."

The sound of spinning blades and heavy machinery fills his ears. A few seconds later, light pours through the windows.

"What the hell is going on?"

One of the militiamen here in the command room rushes to the window. "Someone powered on the plant!"

"Go turn it off. Watch your back."

"What about the lights?"

Ian thinks about night vision capabilities. The militia has civilian models and a couple of surplus military units charitably considered ancient. The FBI has state-of-the-art military devices.

"Leave them on. It doesn't matter now."

"Command, OP One. The feds have stopped advancing!"

"Same at OP Two! They're falling back."

"Eagle Eye, this is Command," Ian says into a walkie-talkie. "Hold off on the mines."

"All right. I'm waiting for your order."

Ian puts the walkie-talkie down. He doesn't like not having control of the minefield. It's their best defense, and these guys are bound to screw it up. Unfortunately, the meeting room is on the south side of the mill and doesn't have line-of-sight. The detonator needed to be closer and higher, so he posted a man on the roof of the northern loading area. He can watch from that location but doesn't need to. That's why they have observation posts on the perimeter.

By now, the FBI has used its drones to fix their locations. The heat of the plant and the LED lights may have done them a favor. He should have activated them before sunset to avoid having the assault team stop to evaluate before entering the kill zone, but it's too late to fret about that now.

"Everyone hold tight. See what the feds do next."

CHAPTER EIGHTY-FIVE

TIERRA CAMPOS

Boston Convention & Exhibition Center
Boston, Massachusetts

Seth leaves to go make some magic happen. Austin and I look around, feeling like fish out of water. I'm about to suggest we head for the media area, but that may be too obvious. It's the first place I would look if I were in the FBI.

The convention center is packed with people eagerly awaiting the final result that pushes Standish over two hundred seventy electoral votes. They could be waiting a while. With all the problems in the state, and considering how close the vote is, it's reasonable to think it may take days to determine a winner.

That's not our immediate concern. Seth has two missions to accomplish: Find a place for us to meet with Standish that isn't her waiting area among family and friends; and ensure Andrew Li is nowhere near her when we do. Neither is an easy task.

"Okay, we need to find a good place to lie low to wait for Seth," I say, feeling exposed out in this hallway. "What's your plan?"

"Come on," Austin says, waving me to follow.

The ballroom is rocking. Chants for Alicia Standish are so loud that they can be heard in Connecticut. Her supporters are in a festive mood, anticipating her victory. We come up on a swag table for the people waiting inside for a victory speech.

"Put your hair up," he commands.

"Why?"

"You always wear it down on camera. It's recognizable."

"What about you?"

"My hair's too short to put up, and I wasn't an anchor on *Capitol Beat*."

"Austin…."

He hands me a ballcap, pin, and a Standish for President sign.

"Take these."

"Seriously?"

"We need to blend in, Tierra. If you can think of a better way, I'm all ears."

I tie my hair in a ponytail and run it through the back of the hat. I pull it down close to my eyes and fasten the pin on my shirt. I carry the sign, tempted to use it like Wilson staring over the fence in *Home Improvement*.

Austin puts on a cap and several pins, even grabbing a pompom. I hope nobody recognizes us. I've spent my life railing against partisan journalists. The last thing I want is a picture portraying me as one. If the FBI catches us, they'd likely make me wear the pin for my mug shot.

We enter the crowded ballroom after showing our passes. The area near the stage is jammed with people standing shoulder-to-shoulder. We're in the back, far too close to the exits for comfort. An agent could easily spot us here.

We try to move forward but meet with limited success. These people have been here for hours and aren't keen on moving. I look back and spot a woman in a suit. She has to be FBI. If they watch the exits, we'll be trapped in here. Luckily, there's safety in numbers. The problem will be getting out.

I tug on Austin's sleeve and point at her. He scowls. "Just play along for a while. We need to give Seth more time."

A cheer erupts when a staffer comes on stage for an announcement that the senator has arrived and will be speaking soon. I look at my watch and frown. We're running out of time. We continue to cheer along with the crowd for another ten minutes.

"Where did Seth want to meet us?"

"The main lobby," Austin says, checking the exits.

"We need to get there."

The woman in the suit is gone. I don't see any other agents, but there is a man who could be one moving along the far wall on the other side of the stage.

"All right. It's time to go."

We move to an exit and slip out. So far, so good. The corridor isn't empty but isn't packed with people either. Supporters are returning from bathroom breaks, and we high-five a couple of them. It's the most awkward thing ever.

An agent emerges from the men's room. Austin keeps walking and starts chanting, mimicking the singsong coming from the ballroom. I join in from alongside him as we pass the agent.

"Standish! Standish!"

I let out a hoot as the people in the corridor join in. More high-fives and fist bumps are offered. When I turn, the agent isn't paying us any attention. I glance at Austin, and we begin walking a little faster to the lobby. It doesn't have as many people as we hoped. Everyone is clearing out to make their way to the main ballroom.

"Now what?"

I spot two agents coming from one direction. They stop suddenly and turn away from us. Another agent is coming from the far end.

"We hide."

Without thinking, I flip up the white linen skirt for the registration table and scurry under it. Austin joins me. This is the worst idea imaginable, but it's all I have.

A man stops in front of us. I can see his shoes in the two-inch gap between the fabric and the carpet. He stops. What is he doing? I look at Austin, waiting for him to pull up the fabric to look underneath the table.

Then a cell phone rings seconds before a massive roar fills the lobby. I feel my phone vibrate with news alerts and stare at Austin. He nods. They just called more states for Senator Standish.

"I can't hear you, sir! Hold on."

The pair of shoes moves off. We just dodged a bullet, but other agents are still looking for us.

My phone vibrates again. This time I pull it out of my pocket to check.

"It's Seth," I inform Austin before answering. "Where are you?"

"The lobby. Where are you?"

"Twenty feet away."

"Huh? I'm standing in the middle of the lobby. You're not here."

I can actually hear his voice over the din. "Yes, we are. We had to duck away from the agents."

"They're gone. Duck where?"

"You see the registration tables?"

"Yeah," the detective says.

"Walk over to them."

I give him a few seconds, then lift the linen skirt. "Hi, Seth."

Austin pokes his head out, and the detective grins. "There's so much I could say right now. Nice pompoms, Austin."

"Go, America!" he says, waving them.

"You guys are too much. Follow me. I have the meeting room ready, and we don't have much time."

CHAPTER EIGHTY-SIX

SPECIAL AGENT VICTORIA LARSEN

"The Forge" Militia Compound
Liberty, Pennsylvania

Victoria closes her eyes. She may either regret pressing this button or regret not pushing it. This is no time for indecision. The team would have halted when she hit the lights, if not pulled back and waited for more intelligence from drones and air support. That's what she keeps telling herself. They could have hastened the attack thinking they were spotted. It's a crap shoot.

"I hope you guys fell back," she mumbles before pressing the button.

A roar erupts from her front and left. There are no flames or billowing plumes of smoke. This isn't Hollywood. The concussion from the blast rolls over her and dissipates into the darkness beyond the sawmill. Thousands of bits of metal shred the trees in front of the mines. That's the only evidence that anything happened.

Victoria scrambles off the platform and hurries down the ladder. She needs to get into a position that she can defend. The militia counted on the mines to cause massive casualties and halt the attack. The FBI and ATF would be forced to establish a perimeter, much like they did at Waco. It would become a siege that the militia wouldn't survive since they don't have numbers on their side. That means they have an alternative plan. Who knows what it is?

With the minefield neutralized, they'll have to adapt. Victoria assumes many of these guys have military experience. They'll want to consolidate their defense. She'll find herself in one hell of a firefight if they fall back to the mill at once.

The noise from the plant cuts out as the machinery powers down. Someone turned it off. The lumber company falls silent, making Victoria's escape even harder. She waits for the lights to cut out. They don't.

Victoria desperately wants to find Ian but isn't going to in this place. There are too many hiding places, and she's too exposed. She darts across the driveway and ducks into a lumber storage structure. Seeing nobody, she creeps around the building and finds a shadowy area to lie low in. A building directly in front of her has light streaming from a pair of side windows. She can hear voices but can't make them out. That could be their command center.

She thinks about conducting an assault, but they must be armed, and she doesn't know the numbers. Victoria can handle one or two. Any more than that, and she could end up being carried out of here in a body bag. It's not worth the risk. The tactical team will take care of them.

Victoria moves forward and crouches alongside the building. A door opens, and a man in body armor, armed with an AR-15, steps out to scan the surroundings. She quietly moves to the rear of the structure, knowing that she'll need to take the scenic route back to the bunker.

There are lines of evergreen trees to the west and south that provide concealment, some cover, and shadows. To the south is another log storage area. From there, she can move between piles along the hundred yards to the bunker. There are no floodlights in that part of the mill, so she has a fighting chance.

She walks slowly, reducing the noise of her steps to the extent possible. She can't see if the guard has changed positions. It's a chance she'll have to take. Victoria passes through the trees to the packed dirt and checks her route from the relative safety of a stack of thick tree trunks. It looks clear.

She makes a break for it, ducking behind every other pile of smaller logs so nobody can track her movement in the low light conditions. She reaches another stack south of a mound used as an earthen ramp. What they use this mountain of compacted dirt for is anyone's guess. Right now, it's providing her needed cover.

She moves along the west side of the mound, putting the three parked loading machines between her and the building with the lights and guard. As she rounds the north side of the ramp, Victoria finds herself shielded by a massive log pile and stops to catch her breath for the last sprint to the bunker. Doubled over with her hands on her knees, she realizes she should have checked the far side of the dirt mound.

Gunfire erupts from the north. The heavy barking of machine guns shatters the night's stillness in a way that even a high-tech lumber manufacturing plant couldn't. It covers much of the sound of the voices behind her moving in from the south.

"Hey! Who are you? Oh, shit!"

The two men realize she's an intruder and scramble to train their AR-15s on her. She raises her gun and fires twice, hitting one man in the body armor and rifle slung across his chest. He raises the weapon and tries to fire it. Nothing happens.

The other man brings his rifle to his shoulder. Victoria does a combat roll to her left. Rounds stitch the logs behind her, and the fire shifts in her direction. She dives forward as shots sail over her. Years of experience have taught her that because of the rifling of a barrel, shooters tend to scatter shots high and right as they continue to fire.

This guy had an armorer modify his AR to fire full auto. Fortunately, he can't control it and just wastes ammunition. He adjusts his fire, but his bolt locks to the rear after his magazine runs dry. He drops the mag and reaches into a pouch to load a new one. He's too slow. Victoria pushes out her Glock, ignoring the second man, who dropped his damaged rifle and is rushing toward her. She fires, hitting the first man in the face. Shooting center of mass would do nothing against the ceramic plate body armor.

She hastily swings her weapon to the right and fires but misses the oncoming assailant. He kicks the Glock out of her hand and quickly readies for a second strike at her midsection. His foot breezes by as he whiffs when she rolls away. Victoria scrambles to her feet and takes up a fighting stance.

"I'm gonna enjoy this, bitch."

"Come and get me, hero."

He swings wildly with his right. It's a powerful punch but incredibly slow. Victoria dodges it and slides to her left, placing a roundhouse kick into the back of his thigh. The blow knocks him off-balance but doesn't knock him down.

Victoria is strong, but not that strong. She can't hit as hard as most men and has to fight smarter, not harder. That's how she beat the giant Sven during the abandoned mill ambush.

The man swings again. This one was faster. Victoria blocks the strike but doesn't see the follow-up in time. His left jab hits her in the temple, causing her vision to explode into stars. He bull-rushes her, using his size to knock her backward into the wood pile. Victoria tries to slide to the left, but he moves his beefy leg to block her escape. Her guard down, she pays for the attempt with a pair of agonizing kidney punches to an area not protected by her body armor.

Fighting through the pain, she blocks two punches aimed at her head and misses with a throat punch of her own. That opens her up for another left that hits her mouth and cuts her lip. The man pushes into her, pinning her off-balance against the logs. She can't win this way.

"Now you're gonna pay!"

There is no such thing as fighting dirty when your life is on the line. This isn't a competition. It's survival. Victoria knows she won't have much force behind this, but it should be enough. She snaps her knee into the man's groin with all the strength she can muster.

The effect is immediate. The man clamps his eyes shut and doubles over. Victoria reaches onto his vest and retrieves his Bowie knife. Reversing her grip on the hilt, she buries the blade into the base of the man's neck. He doesn't even groan as the blade slices his brain stem. His legs buckle, and he's dead before he hits the ground.

Victoria collapses to her knees, fighting to control her breathing as her vision slowly restores. She raises her head, scanning the area. If there were two of them, there could be more. She can't stay here. Still a little woozy and powered by pure adrenaline, she rushes the remaining twenty yards to the relative safety of the bunker.

CHAPTER EIGHTY-SEVEN

IAN DRUCKER

"The Forge" Militia Compound
Liberty, Pennsylvania

Ian's head jerks up. He heard claymore mines detonate when he was in the Army. He knows the sound of them. Even though they were emplaced in the trees a distance away and he's behind the meeting room walls, he knows what happened.

"No, no, no!"

"What's wrong?" the young militiaman says as Ian rushes to a window.

He can't see much from here. The fully illuminated work yard would make the tree line look jet-black even if he could see it. This small window only has line-of-sight to a covered lumber storage several meters away. It was too early. They weren't in range.

"It was too soon. Way too soon. The feds weren't in the kill zone yet."

Realizing how fruitless staring out the window is, Ian rushes back to the radio. "OP One, OP Two, report!"

"OP One here."

"Were any hostiles in range of those mines?"

"Negative. When you turned on the sawmill and the lights, the feds pulled back."

Ian takes personal offense to the insinuation. "I didn't turn them on!"

"This is OP Two. Feds incoming up the slope from the north are holding their positions. The mines didn't do shit to them."

Ian rubs his forehead. Intelligence. They must be waiting for an overhead drone to collect information on positions. They don't know that the minefield activating was a mistake. They must assume there are more and are taking precautions.

"Prepare to defend yourselves. OP Three, Four, report!"

"We left one man behind at Three," a man breathes into the radio. "We're on our way to join our guys to the north."

"Negative. We may have an infiltrator in the Forge. Someone activated the plant. Find whoever it is and put a bullet in his head."

"Roger!"

"Do you want me to join them?" the kid asks, staring out the window at nothing.

"No. You see that door?" Ian asks, pointing at the main meeting hall entrance.

"Yeah."

"Defend it with your life."

Ian goes back to staring at his map. He imagines the military symbol for an infantry unit, a box with lines forming an "x" from corner to corner, holding their position partially up the plateau's slope. He checks the locations of the observation bunkers and the individual foxholes. The militiamen still have interlocking fire.

The bright LEDs in the lumber mill make night vision devices unusable. The FBI likely has air assets like drones and helicopters monitoring the Forge from above. Ian freezes. Helicopters. A team could fast rope right into the middle of this compound, and there would be nothing they could do about it. The thought is unsettling.

"This is OP One. We're under fire!"

Ian keys the radio. "Then return it."

He hears the guttural sound of an M240B machine gun belching lead. He rolls his eyes. That's not the way you fire a machine gun. They should fire short bursts because longer groups rapidly diminish accuracy and blow through ammunition. A fully automatic machine gun should fire rounds in groups of three or four in successive waves of fire until it's time to reload.

That's the problem with this militia. Nobody wanted to put in the training. They're about to find out the folly of their ways when he hears OP Two's machine gun engage even before the cry comes over the radio. The next three minutes will determine if any of them leaves this place alive.

CHAPTER EIGHTY-EIGHT

BRIAN COOPER

Raleigh Convention Center
Raleigh, North Carolina

The people in this room live and die with every result announced on television. It's a rollercoaster ride of highs and lows, especially when the returns don't match expectations. Years of effort have gone into this. Naturally, there is a considerable emotional investment tied up with the verdict.

When it comes time to watch the results, politicians choose whom they want to spend the time with. Some will only be in the presence of their families. Others prefer to have their close friends nearby. Presidential campaigns often add their closest advisors to the watch party. Colin Bradford is no different.

Along with the governor's wife and two children are his running mate and his family, countless friends and supporters, and most of the senior campaign staff. Joel is here, as is Monica Stengel, the chairwoman of the Republican National Committee.

Brian checks the clock on the wall. The polls closed in five states at eleven o'clock: California, Hawaii, Idaho, Oregon, and Washington. The media called them almost immediately, with Standish winning four of them. Alaska is the only state in the union with polls still open. That will fall into the governor's column, even with the uncertainties of ranked-choice voting.

A number of swing states haven't been called. Arizona and Nevada are still toss-ups. Texas not having a winner is a mystery considering that the governor has a seven-point lead. Michigan, Wisconsin, and Ohio should see the media report a probable winner at any moment. As Cubic correctly predicted months ago, and as Brian advised, this race will be decided by Pennsylvania.

When the Keystone State gets called, the race is over. Standish has the most paths to victory, but that doesn't mean she'll win. Brian is confident in his analysis. He could easily run the table with outstanding states and win this thing.

Brian tunes back in to the pundits bantering back and forth at the anchor desk. Governor Bradford has opted to watch one of the network news channels for the past hour. They've changed channels every now and then, but he and the staff have settled on this coverage.

"What are your early thoughts about polling today, Mark?" the anchor asks.

"Honestly, what strikes me is that there haven't been many surprises."

"Well, there is one for me," another guest interjects, pushing her glasses back up on the bridge of her nose. "There haven't been many reports of interference or intimidation around the country."

"Nearly none," Mark chimes in.

"I didn't expect that in a close race," she continues. "I expected a lot of turmoil surrounding mail-in voting that just hasn't materialized anywhere."

Brian throws his hands up in the air. There is a collective moan that ripples through the room. He's heard enough and walks to the back of the room to pour a cup of coffee. He hangs his head and closes his eyes for a moment. The media like to set the narrative. Despite all the evidence to the contrary, a pristine election, especially in Pennsylvania, is what they're going with.

"Are you okay, Brian?" Heidi Bradford asks, coming up alongside him and pulling a Styrofoam cup off the top of the stack.

"Yes, ma'am. I'm fine."

"Don't lie. You have an anguished look on your face."

"Is that your professional opinion?"

"I don't need a psychology degree to see that."

Heidi Bradford is a remarkable woman. Brian didn't know much about her before he joined the campaign. She's a devout Christian, extremely intelligent, and drop-dead gorgeous. Fit and always put together, she looks like she's in her early thirties instead of late forties.

"I'm sorry," Brian utters, unsure what else to say.

"It's not your fault that the press isn't covering the stories they should be."

Brian grimaces. "It's my job to ensure they do."

"Yes, I suppose that's true…and you walked up to the deputy attorney general as he was taking questions and practically challenged him to a duel with pistols at sunrise. What more could you do?"

"I don't know. Something."

She pours a coffee and stares back at the group huddled around the television. "For what it's worth, my husband doesn't think so."

"Mrs. Bradford, with all due respect, this is a race to become president of the United States. Second place is only the first loser. Winners serve four or eight years and join an exclusive club. Their opponents are relegated to the dustbin of history and rarely get second chances. Your husband is a good man. He would be an excellent president. If he loses, the country will never know that."

She laughs. "It's funny to hear you talk that way. He asked me what I thought when you approached him to work on the campaign. I thought he was crazy for considering it."

"Most people did," Brian says.

"Yeah, that's true, but he saw something in you that I didn't. That's a shameful admission for a psychologist, by the way."

"What was that?"

"Passion. Not just for winning. For *him* winning."

Brian presses his lips together. It didn't start that way. He wanted to stick it to Alicia after New Hampshire, plain and simple. He still does. Badly.

"Most people would say that it's because I despise Standish."

Heidi rocks her head from one side to another, weighing the sentence. "I would agree with that, to a point. I think this started as revenge. It became something more."

"I'm not sure it will make a difference."

"You think Pennsylvania is going to Standish?" the governor's wife asks, turning to him.

"I think the media will paint it that way, yeah."

"Brian, I've been watching the vote totals. It's tight. The media won't risk declaring a winner and being wrong. It's another Dewey beats Truman moment."

Brian smiles at Heidi's slightly incorrect account. Thomas Dewey had the presidency locked up heading into Election Day in 1948. Polls and pundits all predicted victory for the gang-busting attorney turned New York governor. Everyone got it wrong, including the unfortunate editors of the *Chicago Tribune*. Harry S. Truman's shocking upset was one of the biggest in U.S. presidential history and was forever memorialized by a photograph of the president-elect holding a copy of the newspaper emblazoned with the headline, "Dewey Defeats Truman."

"I'm willing to bet they do, even if the official result takes weeks."

"What should he do if Standish declares victory?"

"That's not the question you should be asking. He's the candidate. What does he want to do? What will you tell him?"

"He's my husband, Brian. I love him more than anything. I will support whatever decision he makes. If he loses this race after what happened in Pennsylvania, he will need guidance. There is a room full of people who will be eager to chime in with their opinions."

"That's what leaders do, ma'am. They solicit advice from those around them."

"Of course, but yours is the only opinion I want to hear when the time comes. You got us to this point, Brian. This race is competitive because Colin listened to you. Why should he stop now?"

Heidi touches his arm and heads back to the governor. Brian sips his coffee as he focuses on the television. It's not over yet. Arizona was just called for Bradford, causing the room to erupt in cheers and high-fives. The rightward trend in that state continues. That's one step closer. The only question that remains is whether it will be enough.

CHAPTER EIGHTY-NINE

DEPUTY AG CONRAD WILLIAMS

U.S. Department of Justice
Washington, D.C.

Conrad picks up the receiver and slams it back into the cradle. The third attempt was no more successful than the previous two. Is this guy purposely letting the phone ring because he's too cowardly to send him to voicemail? Conrad hits the speaker and redial buttons and listens to the tones, followed by a ring…then two…then three.

"Hello?"

"Agent Murphy?"

"Hello? Who is this?"

Conrad lowers the volume on the speaker. It sounds like the FBI agent is at a rock concert. He glances at his television to see that VH Media just called the election for Standish.

"It's Deputy Attorney General Conrad Williams."

"Who?"

He can almost imagine the agent pressing his phone into one ear and plugging a finger into the other.

"Con-rad Will-iams."

"I can't hear you."

"Get somewhere you can!' Conrad bellows.

"Let me find someplace quieter. Hold on."

The deputy AG taps his fingers impatiently on the desk. He thought it would only take a few seconds to find a closet or side room to duck into. Now he's wondering if the agent traveled to a different state.

"Can you hear me now?"

"Yes, sir."

"Where are you?" Conrad asks, hoping the man has a good explanation.

"The Boston Convention Center. We tracked Tierra Campos and her peers here."

A jolt of electricity shoots up Conrad's spine. "Did you find her or her *Front Burner* co-conspirators?"

"No, sir. There's no sign of them. I have agents checking the entry logs just to be sure."

That is going to take too long. Every available agent needs to be hunting her down, not checking paperwork. If Campos and part of her *Front Burner* team went to Boston, it wasn't to attend a Patriots game. She's there because that's where Alicia Standish is, and there is only one reason he can think of for her to pay the senator a visit. She has Isiah Burgess's files.

"She's there," Conrad concludes, rubbing his forehead. "Did you check the media area? They'll blend in there."

"We did. Nothing. The journalists haven't seen any of them, and given her lack of popularity in those circles, I don't think they'd lie."

"Forget finding her. There are thousands of people in that building. It's like searching for a needle in a stack of needles. Alert the Secret Service."

"Sir?"

"Tell them there's an infiltrator that could be an imminent threat to the soon-to-be president-elect."

"Sir, with all due respect, they're only journalists."

"I shouldn't need to explain this to you, Special Agent Murphy. If Tierra Campos is in league with Victoria Larsen, they could be more than that. We are responsible for ensuring there is no threat to a presidential candidate, and we have intelligence that there could be one."

"Sir, nobody got in this building without being screened."

"You don't know that! I want Campos found. Keep her away from Senator Standish at all costs and alert her detail. Do you understand?"

There's a long pause. Conrad stares at the phone and rubs his chin while awaiting a response. It has been ten seconds, and that's nine seconds longer than it should have been.

"Right away, sir."

The call disconnects. Conrad leans back in his chair. So much for this agent following orders without question. He's beginning to wonder if Agent Murphy is as loyal as the director thinks.

CHAPTER NINETY

TIERRA CAMPOS

Boston Convention & Exhibition Center
Boston, Massachusetts

The awkward conversation with the state troopers in the room was short. While I think they enjoyed making the journalists invading their space uncomfortable, they respect Seth enough to not relentlessly badger us. I don't think he told them why we're here. I'm not sure if he should have or not. I guess we'll find out.

Twenty minutes go by as we watch the election coverage on television. It's nearly one in the morning, and most Americans on the East Coast are in bed, content to find out who won in the morning. There is a trend of not learning who the victor is on Election Day. It has continued.

I'm beginning to think something went wrong. Maybe Seth wasn't able to reach the senator. Maybe she said no. Whatever the reason, I'm about to lose hope when the burly detective returns. Two other men dressed in suits follow him into the room and look around. They nod, and one of them pokes his head out the door. Senator Standish strides into the room.

"Give us the room."

The state police officers recover from their surprise and follow the Secret Service detail out into the corridor. Seth follows them out while Austin remains at my side. The senator waits until the door closes, cocking her head to the side until she hears it click. She holds the note up.

"I should be preparing to give a speech, not dealing with you, Tierra."

"I would congratulate you, ma'am, but declaring any winner in this race is premature."

"You really don't want to see me win, do you?"

I shake my head. "If that were the case, Burgess would have been accepting the nomination at the convention, not you. I could have killed your campaign in its crib."

Standish's campaign was dead in the water. When *Capitol Beat* was broadcasting at Granite State University on the eve of the primary, she confessed that she planned on dropping out of the race on my show. I asked her to hold off, knowing what I had in store for Machiavelli. Isiah's non-confession was headline news that gave her the boost she needed to secure a victory in the state. With Burgess dropping out of the race in embarrassment, she coasted to the nomination.

"Fair enough. What's this about?"

"A conspiracy to hijack your presidency led by your campaign manager, DeAnna Van Herten, Deputy Attorney General Conrad Williams, and at least one other key player."

That sounded ridiculous coming out of my mouth.

"Did you hit your head?"

I offer a knowing smile. "I'm well aware of how that sounds. I'm not here to waste your time, Senator."

"Give us five minutes to explain," Austin pleads as Standish turns toward the door. "Trust me, you need to hear what Tierra has to say."

She checks her watch and scowls. "Okay. I owe you for New Hampshire. You could have reported that I was planning on suspending my campaign and didn't. Five minutes."

I have rehearsed this recap in my head a thousand times. She gets the SparkNotes version as I walk her through the search for Isiah's files and what I believe is happening in Pennsylvania. To her credit, Alicia listens intently. I wasn't sure she'd be willing to hear this if I could even get her to speak to me.

"Andrew Li has been indispensable to my campaign, and I've known Conrad Williams since before I ran for the Senate. VH Media has been an ardent…they've been fair with us. I assume you have evidence to support these outlandish accusations."

"I have the money trail."

"Show me."

"I don't have it here. Given the stakes, we're keeping it someplace safe. Have you ever heard of Actyv Private Equity?"

The senator perks up. "Yes. They made a massive contribution to the DNC's legal fund. Andrew Li secured their support."

I smirk. That's not surprising at all.

"We have convincing evidence that they supported the SOF, Vassyl Strachenko, and Ian Drucker through the Kratos Holding Company. They have since cleared out their office."

"How do you know that?" the senator asks, folding her arms.

"Victoria Larsen paid them a visit."

Standish shakes her head. "Before or after a warrant was issued for her arrest? According to the FBI, she's working with Drucker. And since the two of you are BFFs, I can't help but wonder what your true agenda is."

"That's what they want you and the public to believe. You can't think that it's actually true."

"I have no reason not to. But let's take the large leap to suspend disbelief and assume you're telling me the truth. What do you expect me to do? These are law enforcement matters."

"Don't declare victory tonight," Austin says.

The senator looks at him like he just walked off a flying saucer and asked her to take him to her leader. Her eyes track back to me to see if he's kidding. I remain stone-faced. The president-elect needs to understand how serious this is.

"You've lost your minds."

"No, ma'am," I say. "Pennsylvania is still in doubt because it was engineered that way. We're asking you to tell your supporters that every vote counts and that you're encouraged by the results but are waiting for confirmation before declaring victory."

"What good will that do?"

"It buys us time. When you declare victory, you become the presumptive president-elect, and this cabal will own you. Give us the chance to use our evidence and accumulate more to expose it first."

Disbelief is a powerful thing. It makes people completely blind to alternatives and locks them into a single train of thought. When someone thinks something couldn't possibly happen, they're powerless when it actually does. The problem I'm facing is that we're asking her to take a course of action without proof.

"Tierra, we have a history. You *spoke* at the Republican National Convention. You just snuck into my victory party. Are you really asking me to believe that this isn't personal; that you aren't doing this to save *Front Burner?*"

"Senator, if this were about saving our company, you'd already be reading about this. And, yes, we have a history. I know why you ran for president and the type of leader you want to be. You can't do that with this cabal's hands around your throat. We only ask you not to declare victory for a few days."

I wasn't sure what reaction I would get from the senator. I was hoping she would be conflicted. She isn't. It's something more akin to indignant anger. She believes she won fair and square, and nobody, especially me, will keep her from the prize.

"You're asking me to not claim the victory I rightfully earned. I can't do that. I trust the people around me who got me here, Andrew Li included. Conrad works for Lisa Ehler, and she's a staunch supporter who will continue serving as my attorney general after the inauguration. VH Media is a titan in the industry. DeAnna Van Herten would never jeopardize that. I think this is all in your head, Tierra."

"Ma'am, I implore you—"

FBI agents burst into the room with their weapons drawn. Agent Murphy leads the charge and points his gun directly at me. The Secret Service is right behind them.

"Stand back," one of the agents orders Austin and me. We comply immediately, keeping our hands up and visible.

"Mayflower is secure," an agent says into the microphone in his sleeve. That's not the codename I would have picked for her.

"Ma'am, you need to leave," the other agent insists.

"It looks like you've stepped in it now, Tierra."

"Why do you think that is, Senator?"

"It's time you and I have another chat," Special Agent Murphy says as the senator is escorted to the door by her well-dressed bodyguards.

"One more thing, Senator," I call out, prompting her to stop without turning. "When you learn the truth, reach out to me."

"Ma'am, we need to go. Now!" the Secret Service agent on her left insists. She disappears out the door, leaving Austin and me with the trio of pissed-off FBI agents.

"I'm not going to bother asking how you got those passes, Miss Campos."

"I work for a media outlet, Special Agent Murphy. Are you arresting me this time?"

"No," he says, pulling out a chair, "but we're going to discuss exactly what you think you're doing here."

CHAPTER NINETY-ONE

IAN DRUCKER

"The Forge" Militia Compound
Liberty, Pennsylvania

The defense is a disaster. The activation of the head saw and board cutting equipment slowed the agents' advance, and mines blew long before the assault team was in range. A firefight was the last resort. The remaining militiamen are spraying and praying like Rambo instead of using accurate fire to suppress the tactical teams. This is as good as over.

The assault element will subdue the two heavy machine guns. Once they fall silent, nothing will stop them from breaching the camp's perimeter. Ian hears the bark of one of the 240Bs go silent. They could be reloading, but there is still no fire after thirty seconds. That's one.

"All units retreat to the second defensive line. I say again, all units fall back to the perimeter and form a second defensive line!"

There is a smattering of acknowledgments. Ian doesn't know whether that is from not hearing the radio over the gunfire or men being down. It doesn't matter. He just needs them to buy him time.

A young militiaman barges through the door. Ian has seen him a half-dozen times around the Forge and has watched him operate a forklift during the day. The kid can't be older than eighteen or nineteen and looks scared to death.

"What do you need me to do?"

"I need you to defend this command center until I return. Do not let them take it."

"Where are you going?"

"There are more explosives in the supply shed. We can set them up around the perimeter while we plan to exfiltrate."

"Will that stop them?" The kid looks hopeful.

"If we cause enough casualties, they'll pull back," Ian assures him. "Think about Waco and Ruby Ridge. The government can't stomach losses. Trust me."

"Okay."

Ian heads out the door with his weapon drawn and heads south. The log area has just enough light to allow him to move along the hard-packed dirt without tripping. He can't make out much detail in his surroundings, but he doesn't need to. He's made this trek a hundred times.

There are no explosives left. Even if there were, Ian has no reason to waste his life defending the Forge. He isn't an ideologue or a revolutionary. This bankrupt country and the American way stopped being worth defending decades ago.

Ian ducks behind a pile of logs as a helicopter makes a pass with its spotlight. Men engage it with fire as it nears the perimeter. He can see the tracers from their assault rifles force the chopper to pull back. Good men. He's sure there are drones overhead, but the FBI isn't arming those…yet. He has no doubt that they will someday.

The men are putting up a hell of a fight against highly trained agents, but they're being picked off one by one. There aren't more than eight or nine left now. It's time for him to vanish and enjoy the fruits of his labor. Marx stayed too long and didn't live long enough to regret it. He's not going to make the same mistake.

Ian reaches his bunker and pulls open the steel door, surging inside and turning to close it behind him. Once the door meets the jamb, he uses the steel bar to secure it. That will take the bastards a while to get through.

He is a tunnel away from freedom. From there, he can head south through the woods, find a vehicle, and disappear forever. Ian Drucker will remain the most elusive man on the FBI's most wanted list for all eternity. He smiles as he turns and is greeted by a sight he never imagined.

"Hello, Ian. It's been a long time."

CHAPTER NINETY-TWO

SPECIAL AGENT VICTORIA LARSEN

"The Forge" Militia Compound
Liberty, Pennsylvania

The smile on his face turns to shock. It causes Victoria to grin. After all this time, she has finally caught up to him. He escaped after she had him pinned down in Loughborough. That isn't going to happen this time, and he knows it.

Ian doesn't flinch. He knows any sudden move he makes will be his last. He turns his head to see the open access to the tunnel below the bunker and grins.

"I'm dying to know how you found that tunnel."

"Men talk to pretty girls," Victoria says. "Using militia as hired thugs. I have to admit, that was a smart move, Ian."

"It worked out okay. The Keystone Militia gets to die for their country, or whatever, and I get to accomplish my mission. So, are you going to order me to drop my weapon?"

"I'd prefer you didn't."

"Ah. You want me to point it at you so you can shoot me."

"That's *exactly* what I want."

Ian nods and looks around. "You're a better shot than me on my best day. No, Victoria, you're going to have to take me in. Oh, that's right. Fugitives can't really do that, can they?"

"Name one reason I shouldn't shoot you where you stand."

"I can't name one," he says, grinning. "But you won't."

Ian holds his weapon out with the barrel pointed at the side wall. He slowly takes three steps into the center of the bunker and gently places his gun on top of the map on the table. Then he steps away.

She was hoping he would take his chances. One aggressive move would have spelled his end. Unfortunately, Ian knew that, too.

"You may be a fugitive, but being an agent is in your blood. It's who you are. You won't murder an unarmed man. Even me."

"You were an agent, too, Ian. It's what Takara Nishimoto was. It's what Lance Fuller was. Tell me again why I won't shoot you."

Ian laughs. "Fuller was a jackass. I think part of you is happy he's dead."

"You're right about him being a jackass. But there's a difference between despising someone and wanting him and his family dead. Only a psychopath doesn't realize that."

"What can I say? Vassyl Strachenko really enjoyed his job."

The memories of what happened in Boston come flooding back. The assassin was baiting a trap for her. Not only did he arrange the assassination of Takara, but Ian joined the ambush at Fuller's house. It was bad enough that he was strangled with a garrote, but then Vassyl murdered his wife and children. It was a horrific thing to do.

"Are we really going to let this cliche play out? I'm beginning to feel like I'm in a Bond movie. Or Austin Powers. We're on the clock. What's your play, Vic?"

This isn't how Victoria envisioned this going down. She was convinced Ian would never let himself be taken alive. He wants her dead and is arrogant enough to believe he could make it happen in a confrontation. That's not his game. She didn't give him enough credit, and he outplayed her.

"Here. I'll turn my back to you if it makes it easier. Go ahead, shoot me. Or cuff me, and we can have adjoining prison cells. Either way, Machiavelli and Robespierre still win. You can't change that."

"Watch me."

"I admire your tenacity, Victoria. I always have. Unfortunately, it really is over. You have no idea how hard they'll come for you and Tierra Campos. One way or another, you'll both be dead before Inauguration Day. I only hope Robespierre springs me from prison so I can kill you both myself."

Victoria feels the surge of anger burning her face. Considering the adrenaline, emotional memory of Fuller and Takara, and the threat to her and Tierra's lives, she's struggling to maintain control. He's goading her, and it's working. She desperately wants him to make a move. To give her the excuse she needs....

Ian moves his wrists close together behind his back. "You're not going to shoot me, Victoria, so let's get moving. These militia boys won't last much longer. Just don't make the cuffs too tight. I have delicate wrists."

"Don't worry, Ian, you won't feel a thing."

He turns to face the door, chuckling. Victoria takes aim at the back of his head and fires. The shot goes clear through his skull, blowing blood and brain matter all over the steel door. Ian collapses on the bunker floor, his blood pooling around his head.

Victoria slowly lowers her weapon and moves to the opposite side of the table. Ian's lifeless eyes stare at the wall, frozen forever. She can hear a truck engine fire up in the distance. The volume of gunfire increases. There's no time to debate with herself what she just did.

She closes Ian's laptop and rips out the cables before stopping. She stares at the lone king positioned on the map. She knocks it on its side before heading back down the hatch into the tunnel. Swinging the cover closed, she switches on her flashlight and quickly moves to the other end. When she reaches it, she opens the trap door and peers out. There's nobody here, but probably not for long.

Victoria climbs out and flees up the service road to the truck. She doesn't have time to skirt the wood line. An overhead drone would spot her anyway, and it's a much slower route. With the lumber mill assault ending, they will move the drone to a higher altitude for a better picture of the scene. She needs to get out of this area.

The truck's engine is warm, and it fires up immediately. Victoria spins the truck around one-eighty and floors it, leaving the headlights off while tearing in the opposite way she came. She needs distance between her and any pursuers, and the road back to the gun club is too close. Any vehicle leaving the area around the mill will be stopped and searched. She only hopes that they haven't set up roadblocks.

Windmills rip past her as she screams along the service road. She can hear the tires crunching the gravel as they search for traction. She veers to the right and what she hopes is the other access road out of here, registering the presence of the gate too late to do anything about her velocity. She rams the truck through it, jerking forward as the grille smashes into the barricade.

"Damn it!"

The radiator begins to hiss, and the smell of antifreeze fills the truck's cab. Victoria can't see the gauge but knows the engine temperature is climbing. The vehicle is going to overheat, and the engine will seize up. When that happens, the rest of this escape will be on foot.

Her mind is racing about what to do next when she sees movement on her left. A car pulls out from a side road leading to a pond and partially blocks her path. Victoria never saw it there. She veers to miss it, running off the road and over a small tree. The truck's axle is lifted off the ground by its trunk. She's stuck.

The game is over. Victoria stares at a man climbing out of the unmarked FBI vehicle. He hustles over to the wreck, and she grips her gun. She isn't about to shoot a fellow agent, but he may not realize that. She sticks the gun in his face when he reaches the window.

"Geez, Victoria, is that any way to greet your rescuer?"

"Rigo?" she asks, lowering her weapon as he pulls the driver's door open. "What are you doing here?"

"Helping you. Run now, talk later. We've got to go."

The agents scamper over to his car and climb in. Rigo slams the vehicle into gear and heads south the way she was traveling.

"You ran me off the road!"

"Have you ever heard of brakes? Would you rather me have put on the strobe and tried to pull you over?"

It's a good point. Victoria wouldn't have stopped for anyone. "How did you know where to find me?"

"Your friend Imani contacted me. The Philadelphia Field Office is supporting this operation, and she vectored me into this area. The drone caught your truck leaving the area, and I just waited here until I heard you coming."

"Speaking of drones…."

"We have a short window to get out of here," Rigo says, pulling onto State Route Fourteen and heading through Ralston.

"I'm a fugitive, Rigo. If you get caught, your career is over."

"Yeah, well, your life is over if you get caught. I don't plan on letting either happen."

Victoria nods and stares out the window. The adrenaline is wearing off. They are in a federal vehicle, so they may not garner much suspicion. Then again, it could be the worst thing to be driving in if they are spotted. She's left to wonder if they will make it out of Pennsylvania at all.

CHAPTER NINETY-THREE

TIERRA CAMPOS

Boston Convention & Exhibition Center
Boston, Massachusetts

It's been more than an hour. VM has called the race for Standish despite Pennsylvania being far from decided. A couple of other news organizations joined them, not wanting to be too late to the party. That sent her supporters into a frenzy and turned the convention center into a massive party.

It's not the case here. The questions keep coming, and the answers are always the same: Nothing. I'm not about to say a word to the FBI. I know who Agent Murphy works for, even if he doesn't see the complicity of those issuing the orders. My refusals are starting to turn this awkward situation tenser as his frustration grows.

I start running through all the cliches in my head. "Tension so thick that you need a jackhammer" is the one I'm settling on. Austin hasn't said anything, and neither have the other agents. They are content to stare at each other. It adds to the drama.

"Are you going to answer any of my questions?"

"Am I under arrest?" I ask, cocking my head slightly.

The corner of Agent Murphy's lip curls. He likes the idea. "Is that what it will take to get you to talk?"

"Not really, no. Why are you continuing to ask questions despite my requesting a lawyer? Is there any rule the FBI isn't willing to break these days?"

"Perhaps you should ask Victoria Larsen."

"Maybe I will."

"Do you need a lawyer to answer a couple of simple questions?"

"You tell me."

I can't determine if this dance is a waltz or something more akin to a tango. I was content saying nothing but was afraid Agent Murphy would grill me for hours. Maybe my short responses will deter that.

Not a single question has been lobbed in Austin's direction. He isn't on the FBI's radar...yet. This is about me and me alone. He may eventually get caught in the crossfire, but their sights are solely trained in my direction.

"Miss Campos, I'm tired of playing games with you."

"Good. Am I free to go?"

Agent Murphy looks around the bland room. "I think we'll stay here for a while."

"Why?"

"Because I want to ensure the president-elect is out of the building before you are."

I lean against the back of my chair and show him the palms of my hands. "Do you think I'm a threat to her?"

"In one way or another, yes."

I nod. "Interesting."

"What is?"

"Your conclusion."

"If you think so, prove me wrong."

I clasp my hands and rest them on the table. I make a show of checking out the sterile room. The walls are bare and painted a bland taupe color. There's nothing more than the standard drop ceiling tiles and harsh fluorescent lights above me. This room is unexceptional in every way. The only action is happening outside its doors.

"Well, Miss Campos, your nightmare is happening right out there. The media has called the race, even with Larsen's shenanigans in Pennsylvania. Do you want to listen? I think you should hear what your failure sounds like."

Murphy nods, and one of his agents unmutes the television. Standish has already taken the stage and begun her non-victory victory speech. Just because the media calls a race for a candidate doesn't mean it's official. I'm certain that's the exact argument Governor Bradford will make in North Carolina.

"Governor Bradford has not yet conceded the election," the president-elect says, eliciting a chorus of boos from her supporters. She settles the crowd. "This is a time when we need understanding. There was a great deal of confusion in Pennsylvania, and I'm sure he would like to see that sorted out. We would ask for the same if the roles were reversed. We will wait patiently, certain that the outcome will not change."

There is more applause, and Alicia gestures off-stage.

"To my new campaign manager and chief strategist, Andrew Li, you lead the best campaign team ever assembled. We have crafted a platform that benefits all Americans, and I will be forever grateful for the skill displayed in getting that message to the voters of this great nation.

"You had big shoes to fill. Angela Mays was more than a campaign manager, political operative, and confidante. She was a friend. My parents were ripped out of my life at too young an age. She was as well. Angela, you are as responsible for tonight as Andrew is. You made this happen, and I know you're enjoying watching this from wherever you are. I miss you, Angela. I will make you proud.

"Above all, I will never forget who this victory truly belongs to – all of you. This election has seen the most voters in American history. Lines stretched around schools and churches as some waited three to four hours to perform their civic duty. Americans across this great land mailed in their votes in near-record numbers. Voter participation among the youngest of this nation far exceeded expectations. They understand their voice makes a difference. Your voice made a difference. Now, I must honor you by going to Washington to make a difference.

"This election was a defining moment that will mark the day change came to America! We will remind the cynics and the naysayers why this is the greatest nation on Earth. Thank you, America. God bless you and all these United States."

Alicia Standish's supporters go crazy. There is less enthusiasm in an Ohio State – Michigan football game. I've heard enough. Listening to her acceptance speech is rubbing salt in the wound of our failure. I don't care that she became president. I care that she won't be the one actually running the country.

Agent Murphy makes a slashing motion across his throat. One of his peers walks over to the television and powers it off. He just stares at me, or more accurately, stares through me. As much as I try to remain poised and confident, it's unnerving.

"Miss Campos, I don't know what your agenda is. I can't begin to fathom what your plan with Victoria Larsen is. Just know that I'm going to find out. When I do, our next conversation will be far less pleasant. We raided your hacker friend...Dial Pirate. We will find him. We'll find Agent Larsen. If you don't tell me your plan, one of them certainly will."

"Good luck with that." The glib retort causes Agent Murphy to shake his head, and I lean forward to make the next part clear. "I appreciate the warning, so let me offer one of my own. There is going to be a point where you begin to learn the truth. You'll start questioning everything you've been told and the motives for telling you. Trust that instinct, and then remember this conversation. Remember that I warned you about being misled. Then call me."

He looks at his fellow agent and then at me before gesturing at the door. I don't waste time getting out of there, Austin tailing right on my heels. There is nothing left to do here. I'm not sure what's left for us to do at all.

CHAPTER NINETY-FOUR

BRIAN COOPER

Raleigh Convention Center
Raleigh, North Carolina

The room is a morgue. The staff and the Bradford family stare at the television like mute zombies as Alicia declares a victory she hasn't yet earned. Every word out of her mouth describes utopian promises of unity and transparency that will never be realized. They make for good television, and it's what Americans want to hear. Too bad it isn't reality.

"America is a nation of diverse opinions, varied beliefs, and conflicting ideologies. What we have in common is the glue that binds us: a belief in freedom and individual liberty. We are not as divided as the pundits suggest. America is a nation of optimists, not cynics. We're only made to feel that way.

"The United States measures its elections as red and blue states, but that is not who we are. We are bigger than our differences. America is not just an idea but a nation that has prospered and been a force for liberty throughout the globe. A country that, at its core, believes in government of the people, by the people and for the people."

Brian grimaces. The country believes that. The people running it certainly don't. The new president-elect drones on as Brian is lost in his thoughts. This doesn't feel like it's over. Part of that is denial, but there are still too many variables in the election equation.

"This election was a defining moment that will mark the day change came to America! We will remind the cynics and the naysayers why this is the greatest nation on Earth. Thank you, America. God bless you and all these United States."

The room erupts in thunderous applause. Alicia's husband and adult children make their way on the stage as she's joined by the vice-president-elect and his family. Brian has always found this scene awkward. It's the first time a candidate has to start playing the role of president, and it's painful to watch.

"CNN, MSNBC, the AP, Decision Desk, and the New York Times have joined VH Media in calling the race," the communications director says. "FOX News is still holding out, but their pundits are starting to admit the defeat."

"Wilson Newman hasn't declared a winner on *Front Burner* either, for what that's worth."

"Nobody should be declaring anything," Joel says, throwing his hands in the air. "It's irresponsible! They're crazy to think this is decided after what happened in PA."

"They don't care," Monica Stengel argues. She has a say in where the campaign goes from here. "They got the result they wanted. If the roles were reversed and you had the lead, FOX would have called it, and the rest would be waiting."

"It's not that simple," Brian mutters.

"It really is," Joel argues.

The campaign manager shakes his head. "Stop being partisan for a second and look at it from the media's perspective. They can call the race because they believe nothing will change the result."

"They're wrong. The destruction of the ballot boxes is enough to question the outcome."

"Except those incidents haven't been covered in the news except by conservative outlets," the communications director says. "That means half the country has no idea it happened."

"The media is expecting a concession speech. They will brutalize you if you don't give it to them," Monica concludes.

She should have more fight than she does. That was always Brian's opinion of GOP leadership – they're soft. They don't want to make waves and are too willing to fight the wrong battles instead of the ones that need fighting. Monica isn't a bad person, but her leadership has done nothing to reverse that unfortunate trend.

"We don't work for the media. The people—"

"The people get their opinions from them, Joel," she interjects. "The media sets the narrative, and anything short of a concession will make the governor look like a sore loser trying to steal an election, full stop."

Governor Bradford stops pacing to rub his temples. Brian once told him that the success or failure of a campaign comes down to a few moments. This is one of them. He has a decision to make and can't seem to bring himself to choose his path. It's something he needs to learn. The president of the United States makes hard choices every day.

"You have a ballroom full of people waiting for you to speak," Heidi says, touching his shoulder after realizing he's tortured by the decision. "One way or another, you need to decide."

"Brian, you're the campaign chairman and my closest advisor. Do you think I should concede?"

"Not a chance," Brian says after staring at his hands for a moment. "And, Monica, you're the chair of the Republican Party. You shouldn't want him to, either. Not under these circumstances."

"I don't want him to concede," Monica backtracks. "I don't. But Governor, the party needs to look to the future. We may have lost this round. If you don't graciously accept defeat, you'll be lucky to ever be re-elected as governor, much less hold a national office. This is about the future – your future."

"It's about this nation's future," Brian argues, standing up and addressing the staff assembled in the room. "We aren't crying about unfairness in the media. This isn't hurling excuses about broken voting machines, voter suppression, clandestine ballot counts, or little green men kidnapping voters in swing districts to hide our shortcomings. There were multiple instances of legitimate interference in Pennsylvania. Screw what the ethically bankrupt media has to say. That needs to be sorted out before any concession is made, for the good of our Republic."

"As much as it pains me to say, I'm with Brian on this one, Governor," Joel says. "I think we should fight this all the way to the Supreme Court if we have to."

Governor Bradford closes his eyes briefly before turning to Monica. "Is the party going to help me fight this?"

"You are the party leader. We'll stand behind you, but you need to carefully consider your next steps."

The governor turns to face the television. "I don't know what to say. Monica is right, Brian. I could be jeopardizing my political career, and I'm not ready for that yet. I could always withdraw the concession."

Brian rubs the back of his neck. Bradford is thinking too much about saving his future and not worrying about the nation's fate. He wants to believe that it's the 1980s. That the political process hasn't devolved to where it is today. Optimism is rare for a politician. It's also a weakness. He needs to get out of his head and go with his gut.

"Then you will look like a spineless pansy," Brian says, causing Bradford's head to jerk around. "It's true. You'll look like a coward who couldn't summon the courage to fight the last remaining battle. Your supporters will think they wasted their vote on a garbage candidate who didn't have an interest in winning."

"I'm not a quitter!" the governor shouts. "If Alicia Standish won fair and square, I'll have to live with that. But what happened in Pennsylvania can't be ignored. There are serious questions about the legitimacy of this result, and I will not rest until those issues are resolved."

That's the kind of resolute stance he was waiting for. That's the determination that America needs in a leader. He can't stare into a crystal ball and predict how this will turn out, but he knows what will happen if Bradford goes out with a whimper. It's a political death sentence for him and his party.

"Don't tell me, sir," Brian says, pointing at the television that has cut over to a shot of the governor's supporters waiting for him to take the stage. "Go tell them."

CHAPTER NINETY-FIVE

DEPUTY AG CONRAD WILLIAMS

Outside the J. Edgar Hoover Building
Washington, D.C.

The sun isn't coming up yet, but it won't be long before the first hints of light appear on the eastern horizon. Elections are intoxicating in this city. The day after one typically results in nursing a collective hangover. Conrad isn't, but he wishes he were. Instead, he's having his driver take him home for a couple of hours of sleep. Before that, there's a detour he needs to make.

Conrad has the driver pull up outside the Hoover Building. The director got his message and is waiting for him. The driver exits as Michael Krekstein climbs in the back and closes the door behind him.

"What happened last night, Mike?"

"A tactical team moved in on a lumber company in Liberty, Pennsylvania."

"You could have just gone to Home Depot."

The director is exhausted and scowls at the cheeky comment. "It was a base of operations for a group calling themselves the Keystone Militia. We believe they were responsible for the ballot box bombings, much of the political graffiti, and the truck bomb that was intercepted on the Pennsylvania Turnpike."

"From the look on your face, it didn't go well."

"It was taken by a joint HRT-ATF task force. Six militia members were transported to the hospital suffering from gunshot wounds. Two surrendered and are being interviewed by agents. The remaining twenty were killed. We also found Ian Drucker."

That gets Conrad's immediate attention. "Is he in custody?"

"No, he was drilled in the back of the head with a nine millimeter."

"One of your guys?" Conrad asks.

The director stares out the window. "That hasn't been determined for certain, but I don't think so. It was likely a dispute with another militia member. We're investigating."

"Any casualties on our end?"

"Nothing serious, but...." Krekstein stares down at his hands.

"But what?"

"They set up an impressive defense. They had heavy machine gun emplacements, assault weapons modified to fire full auto, foxholes, and homemade antipersonnel mines daisy-chained around the perimeter. Fortunately, the mines detonated early for some reason."

"Sounds like your men were lucky."

The director nods. "Maybe. It saved a lot of lives. The assault team would have been decimated."

"Any news on Victoria Larsen?"

"The militiamen in custody say there was never a woman at the compound. There is no evidence that she was there. A maintenance vehicle was spotted leaving the wind farm to the south. It's possible she was there and fled, but more likely, it was someone in the militia."

How anyone managed to escape a cordon around that lumber mill is anyone's guess. It's sloppy work when you have sophisticated surveillance drones and a small army at your disposal. That's a problem for another day.

"I want Agent Murphy to focus on finding her."

"What about Campos?"

If *Front Burner* has the Isiah files, there is no putting the genie back in the bottle. They can work to limit damage, but that will be easier when they have their patsy. Much of this can be publicly hung on Victoria Larsen being a rogue agent with Drucker, and everybody knows the relationship those two women formed in the wake of Brockhampton.

"The priority needs to be Larsen. I know she is involved in what has happened in Pennsylvania and was working with Drucker. I want her in custody."

"You know Campos and *Front Burner* went to Boston and met with Alicia Standish."

"I eventually want to know how they got into that convention center. Was Murphy able to determine what she discussed with the president-elect?"

"No. Campos wouldn't talk without a lawyer present."

"What about Alicia Standish? Did she convey any information regarding the conversation?"

Krekstein scoffs. "She was too busy gloating over her victory. We requested a meeting with her, but that line is already long, and she doesn't seem interested in having that discussion."

Conrad frowns. Standish was told what *Front Burner* found in those files. He can't imagine what Isiah was able to uncover, but much of it would be viewed skeptically. Standish and Campos don't have a cozy relationship, and the president-elect will soon learn the truth.

"When is the information on the Pennsylvania raid being released?"

"I'm briefing the president this morning. It will be sometime after that."

"Okay. I'll be back in the office in a few hours. Let me know if you have any new information."

Krekstein nods and climbs out of the town car. The driver returns a few seconds later, and Conrad orders him to continue the journey home. He slides the vehicle off the shoulder and heads out of the city. Conrad stares out the window at the nearly empty streets.

Against all odds, Rasputin's plan was successful. It wasn't executed without a few missteps. Failing to neutralize the two women will come back to haunt them if they aren't dealt with. Campos has Isiah's files. Larsen is still at large and a threat. Those problems need to be solved.

And they will be. Larsen and Campos are proving to be formidable opponents, but they're reaching the final chapters of their story. They are going down. Now that they have reached their goal, every member of the cabal will see to it.

CHAPTER NINETY-SIX

SPECIAL AGENT VICTORIA LARSEN

Interstate 83 Southbound
Shrewsbury, Pennsylvania

Victoria stares out her window at nothing in particular. Interstate travel allows people to traverse the country without seeing anything interesting. The drive to escape Pennsylvania has been long and quiet. The only noise comes from the engine, and the Spanish music turned down low on the radio.

"Is Drucker dead?" Rigo asks after a silence that has spanned almost three hours and the hundred and fifty miles to the Maryland border.

"Yeah."

"Do you want to talk about it?"

"Not really."

Victoria didn't know how she would react to ending Ian Drucker. Killing is never easy, even when it's necessary. He deserved to meet his maker, just like Marx and Vassyl before him. They were not good men, and this world is a better place without them in it. That doesn't make her feel any better. His death may be justice, but it doesn't bring Takara Nishimoto back. It won't breathe life into Lance Fuller and his family. The victory isn't as satisfying as she imagined.

"Was HRT there for the militia or you?"

"I'm not sure that the Bureau draws a distinction anymore. Where are we going?"

"Baltimore."

"What's in Charm City?"

"The safest place I can think of to bring you."

To say that Victoria was surprised to see Rigo in a back woods Pennsylvania town is an understatement. She didn't expect a rescue at all. If one was in the cards, he would have been way down on the list of potential saviors.

"Not that I'm ungrateful for your help, but I thought you were done with all this."

"I was," Rigo admits.

"What changed?"

"Your persistence. That, and I lost it when Williams and Krekstein announced the warrant for your arrest. I realized that nobody is safe if this cabal seizes power."

"Well, thank you for helping."

"Don't thank me, Victoria. If I were half the agent I should have been, we would have taken Drucker down together. I hope you'll forgive me for that someday."

Victoria forces a weak smile. "I already have."

They fall into another long silence until they reach the heart of Baltimore. It's the thirtieth largest city in the U.S. and is ranked one of the worst for violent crime. Of all the places she expected to end up following her escapade at the Forge, this is one of the strangest.

"Don't fugitives usually hide out in rustic mountain cabins?"

"That's what Conrad Williams and Director Krekstein are expecting. They'll order every storage shed in Pennsylvania searched. When in doubt, do the opposite of the obvious."

"You know this area well?"

"You could say that. I grew up in Spanish Town. I spent most of my free time in Patterson Park."

Upper Fells Point neighborhood was the original home of Baltimore's dock workers. Today, the brick rowhouses aligned neatly along tree-lined streets are the heart of Baltimore's growing Latino community. Although most Hispanics in the neighborhood are Mexican, there is a significant Salvadoran, Puerto Rican, and Honduran population.

Rigo pulls up in front of a red brick rowhouse on East Pratt Street. Victoria climbs out of the car and stretches as she looks around. Children are playing in the street under watchful eyes. This is a community that looks after its own. They make their way up the front stairs, and he rings the doorbell.

"You're not worried about cameras?"

He smiles. "Not in this neighborhood."

A man answers the door and flashes a beaming smile. "Rigoberto! *Hijo*! Come in, come in."

The pair enters, and Victoria looks around. It's a nice house. Nothing fancy, but very neat and well-maintained. The elder Benitez takes pride in where he lives.

"You must be Victoria. I've heard all about you. You're more beautiful than my son described."

"Is that so?" Victoria asks, turning to Rigo to add to his embarrassment.

"Thanks for that, Papa."

"*Gracias, Señor Benitez. ¿Puedo hablar con tu hijo solo?*"

Rigo's father beams at the request in his native language to speak with his son alone. Victoria thinks she may have butchered the wording, but he's too polite to correct her.

"Of course. I will get breakfast started," he says before moving into the kitchen.

"I think you may have just made his day with the Spanish."

"Rigo, I can't stay here."

"Why not?"

Victoria stares into the kitchen. "Does your father know that I'm a fugitive?"

"He knows your whole story starting with Brockhampton. He may even know about the *Diablo Ranchero*. I feel bad for you. He's going to have a thousand questions."

"I'm not going to stay here and put your father in danger."

Rigo nods several times and then shrugs. "He'll insist."

"This is serious. You know the people after me play hardball. Do you think they'll draw a line with your father?"

"They have to find you first, Victoria. We've been out of contact. There is no reason to suspect we're working together again. If they decide to keep an eye on me, I come here a lot, and it won't look out of the ordinary. This is the safest place I can think of to put you. The task force will search Pennsylvania motels for you, not Baltimore rowhouses in Spanish Town."

Rigo's father emerges from the kitchen with two mugs of coffee. Victoria takes a sip and savors the brew's strength and flavor. The blend is amazing. She needs to find out where he got these beans.

"That can't be comfortable," he says, pointing at her body armor. Victoria forgot she was still wearing it. "Please."

"Mr. Benitez—"

"Please, call me Guillermo. And before you say you will not stay, this is something that I want to do. This country has done many good things for me. I want to repay that. Besides, what can they do to me? I'm an old man who's lived a good life."

Victoria wants to argue but can't find a polite objection. "Okay, but only for a few days."

"As long as you need, Victoria *hermosa*. I will enjoy the company. *Mi hijo* doesn't seem to find the time to visit as much as he should."

"*Papa....*" Rigo begins to protest before shrugging. "*Es la verdad.* It's true."

The trio takes seats on the living room sofa and chairs. It's apparent to Victoria that Rigo is close to his father. He's right that there isn't a better place for her to hide. She feels safe, at least for the moment. Victoria also knows that the feeling will be fleeting.

CHAPTER NINETY-SEVEN

BRIAN COOPER

Executive Mansion - Asheville
Asheville, North Carolina

The average temperature in North Carolina for early November is fifty-eight degrees. It's chillier than that on top of this mountain since the sun has dipped below the horizon. Brian throws another piece of firewood into the pit and sits back in the Adirondack chair.

The Governor's Western Residence is a relaxing spot. It's reachable only via a winding drive that climbs thirty-two hundred feet to the top of Town Mountain. The house is not a castle or mansion but a comfortable eighteen-acre refuge for the state's chief executive.

Brian slipped out of the meeting in the main living area when the conversation about the next steps became heated. He's an observer now. Not wanting to participate, he retreated to a quiet area of the grounds featuring chairs, a fire pit, and a magnificent view of the Appalachian Mountains.

"I didn't picture you as the outdoorsy type," the governor says, coming up alongside Brian.

The campaign manager begins to stand and is waved back into his chair. "I'm not. It's a little stuffy in there, and I wanted some air. This is a beautiful spot."

"It's one of the perks of being governor," Bradford says, taking a seat. "I love this state. We have mountains, beaches, the best college basketball rivalry, cities, towns, villages, and the best food on the planet."

Brian isn't sure about that last part, but the rest of his sentence was true. "If you love it so much, why did you decide to run for president?"

"I love America just as much, for many of the same reasons. I thought I could make a difference in Washington. That sounds crazy considering what's going on, doesn't it?"

"Nah. Every politician starts off that way."

"And then?"

"The cold, hard hand of reality squeezes the life out of them."

The governor nods. "I want to be different. Do you still think I have a shot?"

"It's a crazy world. Anything can happen."

"But you don't think it will?"

Brian exhales. "No, sir, I don't. Regardless of how Alicia Standish got to two-seventy, she still did. It's hard to ask the courts to overcome that without it appearing that unelected judges are changing the results of an election. It's not Bush-Gore 2000."

The Bush v. Gore case was decided in the Supreme Court on December 12, 2000, by a five to four decision. It reversed an order by the Florida Supreme Court for a selective manual recount of that state's U.S. presidential election ballots, and effectively awarded Florida's twenty-five Electoral College votes to George W. Bush. That gave him one more than the necessary number to win the presidency. It's also the point where Brian thinks American politics went off the rails.

"Is that why you left the meeting?"

"I'm a political strategist, not a legal one."

"Joel is contributing." Brian snickers. "Yeah, I laughed, too. Do you think I should concede the race?"

Brian lowers his eyes. "No."

"Why not? You think it's a lost cause."

"It's not that simple, sir. Tens of millions of Americans pulled a lever or checked a box for you. Millions of them contributed money to your campaign that they probably couldn't spare. You aren't fighting for your political career. You're fighting for them. That's what this has to be about."

Bradford settles into his chair to admire the view as the golden orange rays of the setting sun turn the sky pink behind purple mountains.

"I bet Alicia Standish kicks herself for letting you go."

"I would love to think so. It's good for the ego, but Alicia isn't the type of woman to admit a mistake, let alone live with regret."

"Ouch. Well, hiring you as my campaign manager was the best decision I've ever made. You should know that I agonized over it."

The admission doesn't surprise Brian in the least. "I didn't expect anything less, sir. If our roles were reversed, I don't think I would have hired someone who played for the other team."

"That's one hell of an admission."

Brian shrugs. "It's true. It's also why I get paid to advise candidates instead of throwing my hat in the ring and becoming one."

It takes someone special to run for office. People can argue whether those traits are good or bad. Is a political run an egotistical lust for status and notoriety or a real desire to serve the people? Brian never has an intention of finding that answer.

"You're leaving, aren't you?"

"I'm no good here."

"I still need your counsel. Not to mention the optics of having my campaign chairman bail on me before the fight ends."

"I will stay on as your campaign manager for as long as you need me to. I just can't sit here on my hands."

"What's your plan?"

"I'm going to go up to Washington and move some pieces around the board. I want to talk to the clerks and take the Supreme Court's temperature. The interference in the Pennsylvania election was on a scale never before seen. They will have to weigh in if the secretary of state certifies the result."

"You think this will go to the Supreme Court?"

"Bank on it."

Whether the American public accepts the ruling is another question entirely. The Supreme Court was once lauded as a non-partisan body that rendered thoughtful decisions based on foundational documents and the U.S. Constitution. That perception may have been another casualty of the 2000 election, rightly or wrongly.

"When are you heading out?"

"In the morning."

The governor stands, and Brian rises from his chair. The two men shake hands.

"Thank you for everything, Brian."

"It was my honor, Governor Bradford. I'll keep in touch."

"Are you sure you don't want to join us upstairs?"

"No, sir, I'm going to enjoy this fire and view for a while longer."

The governor takes a deep breath of cool air and steals a final look at the view before retreating toward the house. Brian retakes his seat and stares at the fire. He finds it soothing. Fires are when they are under control. It's the ones that rage and consume everything in their path that people need to worry about. There was never a more perfect metaphor for the American two-party system.

CHAPTER NINETY-EIGHT

TIERRA CAMPOS

Front Burner Washington Office
Washington, D.C.

Two Days After the General Election

I need to be alone. Josh is doting on me at the apartment, and it's starting to drive me insane. I appreciate the concern and his attention, but my failure is something that I need to deal with on my own. So, I take a rideshare to the only place I know I can be by myself.

The *Front Burner* office is dark, just as I expected it to be. I arrive on the desolate floor that has been my workplace for the past few weeks and immediately sense that something is off. I'm on high alert as I walk quietly around the cluster of empty cubicles toward the war room. Then I stop in my tracks.

I closed and locked that door. Only three people have the key, and neither Austin nor Naomi is here. There are no lights on, but I sense a presence. Then I get a whiff of a pungent odor. It's cigarette smoke.

I look back at the elevator and think about calling the police. I reach for my phone and stop. That's ridiculous. Nobody breaks into an office building just to smoke. This is something else, and I need to know what. It could be the FBI paying me another visit. I summon some courage and walk to the war room. When I reach the door, I flip on the light.

A man is seated with his feet up on the conference table. He's not wearing an FBI windbreaker, nor is it a suit. He's not a federal agent. In fact, he looks like a bum. The mysterious man takes a long drag on his cigarette.

"Who are you?"

"It's about time you showed up. I thought I would have to wait here until morning."

I cock my head at the sound of the familiar voice. I just can't place it. Then it dawns on me.

"Dial Pirate?"

He smiles and crushes his smoke in a makeshift ashtray. "We're beyond that now, Tierra Del Fuego. You can call me Bri."

"That would be weird. You know that this is a non-smoking building, right?"

It was a ridiculous thing to say, but the only thing that popped into my mind.

"It's the least of the laws I've broken in my life, believe me."

"How did you get here?"

"You have no security. I was surprised to see this place empty."

"We're a small outfit now and flat broke. Everyone went home to get some sleep. I meant, how did you get to Washington?"

"I crawled."

"No, really."

"I took a bus. The government hasn't figured out how to track bus passengers."

Dial Pirate stands as I walk over and offers me his hand to shake. I ignore it, opting for the hug I promised him not long ago. It takes him a moment to wrap his hands around my back. I get the impression that the younger hacker doesn't see much in the way of female companionship despite being a good-looking guy.

"As promised," I say with a beaming smile. "I'm sorry that you got raided. I can't help but think—"

"It wasn't your fault. You did nothing wrong."

"You stated that definitively."

"Because it's true. Someone gave me up, for sure. I just know it wasn't our communication. The hacker community is trying to figure that out."

"I'm glad you're okay. What are you going to do now?"

"Finish what we started."

"It's too late for that, DP. The election was the deadline, and it's over."

DP presses his lips together and awkwardly wags a finger. "No, the election was the opening bell. I did some reading on the bus. You still need all fifty states to certify the vote and confirm their slate of electors. Then the Electoral College has to meet to cast their ballots. Once they have their say, the Senate has to confirm the result. The fat lady hasn't sung yet."

He's right on the money. That is the process, but it's more of a formality. At least, it was until more recent election cycles.

"We've identified Andrew Li, DeAnna Van Herten, and Conrad Williams, but we don't know who the big kahuna is. Our evidence on them won't be enough to bring them down. Without Isiah's final files, there's nothing more for us to do."

"You mean *these* files?"

"You have them?" I ask, my voice an octave or two higher.

He looks at the thumb drive he's holding and then back at me like I'm a moron.

"I figured since we've already come this far…."

"What do we do with it?" Another stupid question.

"We use your laptop to open it, Tierra."

I pull the laptop out of its carrier and hand it to him. "Don't we need to open that on an air-gapped computer or something?"

I heard that on a television show somewhere along the line. It was probably *The Newsroom*. I don't watch too many shows. The confused look means I just asked the third stupid question in a row. I think I'll just shut up now.

"Do you want to see what's on this or run to Best Buy?"

Dial Pirate opens the lid and powers it on. He stares at the screen before opening settings that I didn't even know existed.

"Damn, this thing is wide open. No wonder the NSA could read your email."

He pulls another thumb drive from his pocket and plugs it into a USB slot. He opens a folder and begins running a series of executable files. I have no idea what they are. For all I know, he could be installing a backdoor into my system.

"What are you doing?"

"Installing some tools of the trade, my dear, installing tools of the trade."

Once he finishes, he swaps the flash drives and goes to the directory. There are four folders. He opens the one named Rasputin and finds five files in it.

"Okay, let's find out who the man behind the curtain is."

He opens the first file. There isn't much in it. Opens the second, third, and fourth. It's all supporting data, like phone records and financial data, but nothing that will help us identify the person behind the codename. I'm starting to lose hope. Isiah mentioned that he hadn't figured out who the cabal's leader was. Maybe he never did.

"Okay, let's see what's behind door number five."

I lean in as he opens the file. We read, and he scrolls the window lower. That's when I see it. The blood drains out of my face. My legs get wobbly, and I sit down next to him. It's unmistakable but far from hard proof. We have a name now, and of all the people who could be involved in this, he's the last person I expected.

"I'm blissfully ignorant about these things. Who is this guy? Do you know him?"

I nod slowly, staring at the screen in utter disbelief.

"Yeah, I know him. Everybody here does."

CHAPTER NINETY-NINE

DEPUTY AG CONRAD WILLIAMS

The Hay-Adams Hotel
Washington, D.C.

The transitional period between presidential administrations is run from a ninety thousand square foot transition headquarters located at 1800 G Street NW. The office building was formerly the headquarters for Y2K activity, although most interns working there were still swaddled babies when that was a thing. It is run by the U.S. General Services Administration and offers use of the facility once a victor in the election has been confirmed.

Despite the media calling the election for Senator Standish, there remains doubt because of what happened in Pennsylvania. If no slate of electors is chosen to represent that state because the result isn't certified, the election will go to the U.S. House of Representatives since neither candidate will reach the two hundred and seventy vote threshold in the Electoral College.

Without access to government facilities, the president-elect is starting the transition from the Hay-Adams Hotel across Lafayette Square from the White House. Conrad is escorted by a campaign staffer past the Secret Service to the Windsor Room. The magnificent space is small and adorned with brass chandeliers, an ornamental fireplace, ornate ceiling details, and silk-covered walls.

Two of his co-conspirators are already waiting there. It's the first time the three of them have been in a room since this plan was hatched. A part of Conrad didn't think they would be successful, despite Rasputin's assurances.

The group stands when the door swings open, and Alicia Standish enters the room. The door is closed behind her, and a Secret Service agent is likely posted on the other side.

"Madam President-Elect. Congratulations on your—"

"Stow it, Conrad. I didn't know you were involved in this, too."

"All three of us are," DeAnna purrs as she retakes her seat. "And you should be more polite. We handed you the presidency. Isn't that what you always wanted?"

Alicia closes her eyes. Conrad knows that she was warned. He probably wouldn't have believed *Front Burner* if he had Alicia's history with them. Still, she must be kicking herself. If she hadn't declared herself the winner, she'd still have a card or two to play despite having a weak hand.

"Tierra Campos was right all along."

"You should have listened to her," Andrew says. "Although, listening to others has never been one of your strong suits."

"We should get down to business," Conrad declares. "There's a lot to cover."

"If you think you can make demands and expect me to go along, save your breath. You're sadly mistaken."

The three conspirators look at each other.

"We tried to be reasonable."

DeAnna stands, and they begin heading for the door.

"Where are you going?" the president-elect demands.

"The press corps is right outside," Conrad says, pointing a thumb over his shoulder at the door.

"We're going to tell them everything," Andrew finishes.

"And VH will cover every word of it. It will be breaking news for a month."

"What do you mean? You're turning yourselves in?"

Andrew smiles. "The American people have a right to know that you paid us to ensure you won the Democratic nomination and the election."

"I did no such thing!"

"Oh, I'm certain that your financial records will say differently, Alicia," Conrad says. She shakes at his use of her first name.

"Who do you think the American public will believe?" DeAnna asks. "A desperate candidate clinging to a narrow win in a state with as much upheaval as Pennsylvania, or the deputy attorney general, a media titan, and your own campaign manager? Let me see...."

"You won't get away with this."

"You're going to ensure that we do," Andrew says.

"What happens from here on out is your choice, Alicia. You play ball, and you're the president. If you don't, you're a disgraced cheater who will set a record for the time it takes to get impeached, assuming you even take office. What would your parents think?"

Conrad hits her below the belt. He knows her too well and can play with her emotions, especially when it concerns her deceased parents.

"What are the demands?"

The three conspirators take seats at the table. Now that the shock has worn off and reality has set in, it's time for them to explain the first moves they want their marionette to make. Strings are only good when you pull them.

"Andrew Li is going to be named your White House chief of staff. That's an easy one. Lisa Ehler is to be thanked for her service, and I will become your new attorney general once you are sworn in."

"No way. I can't do that. I made her a promise."

"Break it," Andrew says, his voice definite and threatening.

"White House chief of staff and attorney general. That puts the two of you in a position to practically run this country."

"Now she's getting it," the media mogul says.

"What do you get out of this, DeAnna?"

"Access. As much as I need, whenever I need it. And you are going to rewrite a digital media law or two."

The president-elect sits down. Conrad can almost feel her internal struggle. She's finding out how little power she has and is desperately looking for a way out of this situation. He smiles, knowing that she won't find one.

"You three couldn't have pulled this off on your own."

"That's insulting," Andrew says, grinning.

"Campos mentioned that there was one more player. Who is it?"

DeAnna checks her Patek Philippe watch. "He should be along shortly. I don't want to ruin the surprise. The look on your face will be priceless. It's the last person you would ever expect."

"You get to be president, Alicia," Conrad says. "None of this changes that. You're just going to take your lead from us."

"Don't worry. We won't have you declaring any wars or anything," her future chief of staff admits. "On most issues, you can do whatever you like. However, when we give you instructions, you'll follow them."

"Or else?"

"Or else you'll be removed from office so fast that you won't have time to pack."

Alicia shakes her head. "This is un-American."

"Are you kidding?" Andrew asks. "This is exactly what this country has turned into. The only difference is instead of being beholden to special interests and big corporations, we own you."

"Call it a realignment," Conrad says. "You're giving government back to the people. At least four of them."

Alicia's face turns bright red. She stands as they enjoy a laugh. "You're bluffing! You can't take me down with wild conspiracy stories. It's hearsay."

DeAnna sighs heavily. "Since when do Americans look for facts, Alicia? Distrust of government is already an epidemic in this country. Do you really want to destroy what little faith there is in it?"

"You'll be destroyed. You already know that," Andrew warns her.

"Which one of you three dreamed this up?"

They smile at each other as the door to the room swings open again. Rasputin strides in and stands directly in front of the president-elect. Alicia's jaw drops, and her eyes balloon into the size of saucers. If there were a picture for "speechless" in the dictionary, this would be it.

"We didn't dream this up," Andrew confesses. "He did."

EPILOGUE

TIERRA CAMPOS

Dupont Circle
Washington, D.C.

Three Days After the General Election

Orange rays from a fading sun glisten on the kings and queens and what remains of the other pieces scattered on the ten or so chessboards in Dupont Circle. Lawyers, writers, and the homeless flock to this area to play game after game for hours at a time. The stench of urine and the unmistakable scent of marijuana permeate the air as street vendors sell water and loose cigarettes nearby.

Dupont Circle is surrounded by pubs and mansions, but chess is the main entertainment here. Tourists and local residents visit the fountain but stay to watch some of the city's best chess players try to outmaneuver each other. Washington is a city where people talk, and games are rarely played in silence. The Bible, politics, and life are among the topics I hear people bantering about while I wait for Brian Cooper to make his way over to my table.

"Thanks for meeting me," I say as he sits in the flimsy plastic chair across from me.

"I wish I could say I had something better to do."

"You're no longer with the Bradford campaign?"

"Officially, I am, but I'm no use in a legal battle. This next phase of the Standish-Bradford war is being fought by lawyers."

I nod. Most of the presidential elections during my lifetime resulted in lawsuits seeking to confirm or undo the result. Americans vote, but courts have the final say about who governs the nation.

"Would you like to play?" I ask, gesturing at the board.

"You play chess?"

"On occasion."

"Who taught you?" Brian asks.

"Josh did. He's always had a fascination with the game. I think it might have something to do with the two hot sisters he watches play on YouTube."

Brian chuckles. "That sounds like a typical guy thing."

I place a pawn in each hand and close my fists around them. He selects my right, and I reveal the white piece. He opens with a move to e4, which I match. With no thought, Brian brings a knight and bishop out, which I counter with two knights.

We banter about what happened in Pennsylvania and how it affected the outcome. It's interesting hearing it from his perspective. The campaigns are closer to events than the average person watching the news, and I get some of the insights I was looking for. Some, but not all.

"The country is tearing itself apart over this."

Brian takes a deep breath. "The two parties have been cheating for so long that a blind man could see it would eventually get out of hand. Lines were crossed. The result is chaos."

"Chaos is exactly what you expected," I say, eyeing him. "In fact, you wanted it. Isn't that right, *Rasputin?*"

Brian locks his gaze on me for a long moment before castling his king and leaning back. It was almost a symbolic move.

"It took you long enough to figure that out."

"You're admitting it?" I say, trying to recover from the shock of those words.

"Sure. Tierra, you're a fantastic journalist and a bright young woman. I knew you would eventually. It probably should have been sooner than now. You had all the pieces to put it together but were too reliant on waiting for Isiah's evidence. If you have an Achilles' heel, it's that you don't stop and think things through."

He gestures at the board. I move a pawn, which he takes with his. I retaliate by moving my knight to d5.

"You act like it's too late for me to stop you."

Brian smiles broadly. "It is too late. Alicia Standish is the president-elect. The courts aren't going to undo that, and neither will you. Everyone wants this election over."

"That's the part I don't understand. You hate Alicia Standish. Or *do* you?"

"No, I absolutely despise her." He shrugs. "Now I own her."

"All because you threw the election."

He scoffs. "Hardly. I did everything I could to keep it competitive. If Brevin Hawkins was still at the helm, Standish would have won by three percent and eighty electoral votes."

"What if Bradford had won?"

He stares at me. "Think it through."

I hate that he's right about me. I move so fast sometimes that I don't stop to think about strategies. My world is about uncovering the truth, not reflecting on where it could lead. As we exchange moves, I run his tactics from before the New Hampshire Primary through my head. It dawns on me when his rook captures my bishop at e6. It was obvious.

"You owned both campaigns. Machiavelli had Standish, and you had Bradford. It was a no-lose proposition."

"Bravo. Fair fights are for suckers, Tierra. The hard part was getting the both of us in place."

"That was the point of New Hampshire. You needed Standish to hire Andrew Li."

He touches his nose and points at me. "Then I had to convince Bradford that I switched sides and had dirt on her. I wasn't sure he would go for it. Brevin Hawkins hated me. Once the governor brought me on board, all we had to do before the election was not get caught making a mess of things. That was easier said than done, believe me."

"And Angela Mays?"

Brian frowns. "Collateral damage. Machiavelli got a little impatient."

"So, he had her murdered?"

"Andrew sicced Drucker on her without telling me. My plans for her didn't involve a casket."

"Aw, is your cabal fraying a little at the edges?"

"That's really not an appropriate term for us. We're more of a loose alliance of power players with a keen interest in the future."

"You went too far, Brian. The Pennsylvania election might not get certified after what you orchestrated there."

"Rest assured, it will."

"Why go through all that if you already own the candidates?"

He sighs. "Think it through, Tierra."

I will rip his head off if he tells me to "think it through" one more time. The smug bastard thinks he has me beat. He's going to find out how wrong he is. Until then, I'll play the game.

"Control. Half the country will think one side or the other won. There will be constant questions about the president's legitimacy."

"It's not enough to infiltrate campaigns. Any fool can do that. It has to be orchestrated to look like a candidate won because of it. That gives me leverage. Alicia Standish has wanted to be president since her mother was killed. It's why I wanted her in the White House. Now that she's heading there, God himself couldn't convince her to give it up. She'll do exactly what we tell her or risk losing the job she covets most."

After losing two pieces, I pull my knight back to defend. That is the most brilliant plan I have ever heard. I couldn't imagine having a mind devious enough to conjure something like that up or the guts to go through with it. Brian Cooper may be a despicable human being, but it's a ploy that the real Machiavelli would have admired.

"I want to know why."

He glances up at me from studying the board. "Why what?"

"Why you kept me close…fed me information. We've known each other since Brockhampton. You knew I would eventually figure this out. Why feed me clues?"

Brian moves his queen to h5. "Check. I have my reasons. Maybe you'll learn them someday."

I bristle at the non-answer. "I could publish all of this."

"Go ahead and do it. You'll watch *Front Burner's* relevancy take the short fall from where it is to zero. We own the media."

"Van Herten only owns one station and has competitors eager to pounce on any story she won't run with," I argue.

Brian shakes his head slightly. I can't tell whether it's disbelief, disappointment, or something else. All I know is that he's too relaxed for a man who just admitted to treason, election interference, and other crimes too numerous to count.

"You're getting emotional, and it's clouding your thinking. Nietzsche owns an empire that sets the narrative. The press is monolithic and staffed with journalists who aren't inquisitive and don't investigate. They're lemmings that follow each other from story to story. You know that better than anyone. How many times were Oliver Jahn's attacks on you parroted in the mainstream media?"

"His supporters almost killed me!"

Brian sighs. "I'm truly sorry that happened. I went to great pains to ensure that you weren't harmed during this journey. Andrew Li has wanted you dead for a while now."

"That's comforting. Did Machiavelli want Victoria dead, too?"

"More than you know," Brian says with a chuckle. "Although that was more of an Ian Drucker thing. Poor bastard. Do you happen to know where Special Agent Batwoman is hiding out these days?"

"Do you think I would be stupid enough to tell you if I did?"

"No, probably not, but it was worth asking." He moves his queen to the eight-line to threaten my king. "Check."

My eyes grow wide. That was a mistake. I take it with my knight and hold the piece in front of his face.

"I'm not going to let you get away with this. There will be a reckoning."

He offers an amused smile. "Threats aren't your strong suit, Tierra. I know you think that, and I know your colleagues at *Front Burner* think that. That's why you're trying to record this conversation so you can report it to the world. I hate to disappoint you, but I took a few precautions. Not a word of this conversation is being recorded. Check if you'd like."

I lower my eyes. I won't give Brian the satisfaction of doing as he suggested. I'll check later, but I already know he's right. He wouldn't bluff about that.

"Don't be too hard on yourself, Miss Campos. The NSA has some neat toys that Americans won't ever know about. Having Robespierre on the team comes in handy. The deputy AG has friends willing to help with everything."

"Clearly," I mumble.

"Here's some friendly advice. Don't batten down the hatches and think you can weather this storm, Tierra. I *am* the storm. You'll be fine so long as you don't forget that." Brian inhales deeply and looks around Dupont Circle. "It's such a beautiful day for early November. I think I'll take a walk."

Brian stands, and I set the queen down next to the board. I never thought he would have expected me to record this. He either suspected what this meeting was about or is incredibly paranoid. Either way, he's two moves ahead of me. Again.

"It's not over," I blurt out.

I'm eager to let him know that his threats don't intimidate me. I didn't mean the chess game, but Brian leans over and moves his other bishop to h6.

"Checkmate. There's one lesson you've failed to learn during your time in Washington, Tierra."

"Oh, yeah? What's that?" I ask through clenched teeth, now even more pissed off.

Brian looks me in the eyes and smirks.

"Games here are won before they're ever played."

ACKNOWLEDGMENTS

When I wrote *Justifiable Deceit*, I had no idea what was in store for Victoria and Tierra. This story arc didn't begin until *Devious Measures*, and it has been a blast writing since. I love these two characters and can't wait to see where they end up when this is over.

All authors like to have their work acknowledged, and I'm blessed to have won countless awards for mine. That's not where my true happiness comes from in writing. I like creating characters and stories that people enjoy. I have gotten a wonderful response from readers about these two amazing women. Keeping you engaged and entertained with their exploits is what brings me joy. Thank you for spending your time with them. I sincerely hope you find them as engaging as I do.

My mother and entire extended family have always been there for me in my writing journey. Thank you for suffering through my rants and enduring my mental gymnastics as I work through creating these stories.

We all admonish each other about judging a book by its cover. Then we go to a bookstore and do precisely that. Great covers get attention, and I have one of the best cover artists in the business. Working with my team is one of the best parts of finishing a novel. Thank you to JD&J Design for yet another catchy cover. They make it very hard to pick a favorite.

Dene October says, "A good editor is someone who cares a little less about the author's needs than the reader's." Well, some care a lot less. I struggled to find an editor I could connect with until Mike Waitz of Sticks and Stones Editing arrived on the scene. Since then, I couldn't imagine working with anyone else. I'm waiting for him to break out the "repeated mistakes" jar and force me to put a dollar in every time he has to correct something I should have learned five novels ago. Crap. He's going to read this. And then he's going to do it.

Moving on…

I waited to thank the most important person in my life to force her to read the whole section. It's not mean…it's good for her. To Michele, the love of my life who encourages me and grounds me, you know you will always have my eternal thanks. And you get sole possession of the television remote while I write. I guess we all win.

ABOUT THE AUTHOR

Mikael Carlson is the award-winning author of the novel *The iCandidate* and the Michael Bennit Series of political dramas. He also has written two other ongoing series: Tierra Campos Thrillers and Watchtower Thrillers. His newest series, America, Inc., is a retelling of the futuristic dystopian Black Swan Saga that serves as a cautionary tale of life in a world following a global economic collapse.

A retired veteran of the Rhode Island Army National Guard and United States Army, he deployed twice in support of military operations during the Global War on Terror. Mikael has served in the field artillery, infantry, and in support of special operations units during his career on active duty at Fort Bragg and in the Army National Guard.

A proud U.S. Army Paratrooper, he conducted over fifty airborne operations following the completion of jump school at Fort Benning in 1998. Since then, he has trained with the militaries of countless foreign nations.

Mikael earned a Master of Arts in American History in 2010 and graduated with a B.S. in International Business from Marist College in 1996.

He was raised in New Milford, Connecticut, and currently lives in nearby Danbury.

Made in United States
North Haven, CT
10 July 2023